ACCLAIM FOR WAYNE JOHNSTON'S

The Navigator of New York

"A historical novel with a resonant significance for the present. . . . The detail in *The Navigator of New York* is exact and gripping. . . . It is good that people write novels like this: bold, fat, story and character-led, filled with traditional novelistic virtues."   —*The Ottawa Citizen*

"Generously stuffed with crisp writing, rich characterizations, and haunting descriptions of the harsh beauty of the Arctic. . . . Johnston is a great novelist in the making."   —*Kirkus Reviews* (starred)

"It is a great pleasure to see Johnston continue to work this fictional territory he has discovered and claimed, with much finer results than the claiming and discovery of physical landmarks by such 'navigators' as Cook and Peary."   —*The Toronto Star*

"Johnston has written yet another historical novel worth faking the flu and staying in bed to read. . . . As Stead emerges a richer character at the end, so, too, will you."   —*Chatelaine*

"The thrill of polar exploration, the beauty and terror of glaciers, and the horror of the long Arctic nights are splendidly evoked. The secrets . . . are slowly revealed, adding intrigue and suspense."

—*Library Journal*

WAYNE JOHNSTON

The Navigator of New York

Wayne Johnston is the author of several novels, including *The Colony of Unrequited Dreams* and *The Divine Ryans*, and the memoir *Baltimore's Mansion*. He was born and raised in Newfoundland and now lives in Toronto.

Also by Wayne Johnston

The Navigator of New York

The Navigator of New York

WAYNE JOHNSTON

ANCHOR BOOKS
A Division of Random House, Inc.
New York

FIRST ANCHOR BOOKS EDITION, SEPTEMBER 2003

The Library of Congress has cataloged the Doubleday edition as follows:
Johnston, Wayne.
The navigator of New York / Wayne Johnston.—1st ed.
p. cm.
ISBN 0-679-97352-1
1. Cook, Frederick Albert, 1865–1940—Fiction. 2. Canadians—New York (State)—
Fiction. 3. Explorers—Fiction. 4. Orphans—Fiction. 5. New York (N.Y.)—Fiction.
6. Arctic Regions—Fiction. 7. North Pole—Fiction. I. Title.
PR9199.3.J599 N38 2002
813'.54—dc21 2002416583

Anchor ISBN: 1-4000-3109-5

Author photograph © Jerry Bauer

www.anchorbooks.com

147028534

To Clio

BOOK ONE

· CHAPTER ONE ·

IN 1881, AUNT DAPHNE SAID, NOT LONG AFTER MY FIRST birthday, my father told the family that he had signed on with the Hopedale Mission, which was run by Moravians to improve the lives of Eskimos in Labrador. His plan, for the next six months, was to travel the coast of Labrador as an outport doctor. He said that no matter what, he would always be an Anglican. But it was his becoming a fool, not a Moravian, that most concerned his family.

In what little time they had before he was due to leave, they, my mother and the Steads, including Edward, tried to talk him out of it. They could not counter his reasons for going, for he gave none. He *would* not counter the reasons they gave for why he should stay, instead meeting their every argument with silence. It would be disgraceful, Mother Stead told him; him off most of the time like the men who worked the boats, except that they at least sent home for the upkeep of their families what little money they didn't spend on booze. This was not how a man born into a family of standing, and married into one, should conduct himself. Sometimes, on the invitation of Mother Stead, a minister would come by and join them in dressing down my father. He endured it all in silence for a while, then excused himself and went upstairs to his study. It was as though he was already gone, already remote from us.

Perhaps the idea to become an explorer occurred to him only after he became an outport doctor. Or he might have met explorers or heard about some while travelling in Labrador. I'm not sure.

At any rate, he had been with the Hopedale Mission just over a year, was at home after his second six-month stint, when he answered an ad he saw in an American newspaper. Applying for the position of ship's doctor on his first polar expedition, he wrote: "I have for several years now been pursuing an occupation that required arduous travel to remote places and long stretches of time away from home." Several years, not one. He said that for would-be expeditionaries, such embellishments were commonplace.

He signed on with his first expedition in 1882. A ship from Boston bound for what he simply called "the North" put in at St. John's to take him on.

First a missionary, now an explorer. And him with a wife and a two-year-old son, and a brother whose lifetime partner he had pledged to be. My aunt's husband, my uncle Edward.

Father Stead had been a doctor, and it was his wish, which they obliged, that his two sons "share a shingle" with him. My father, older by a year, deferred his acceptance at Edinburgh so that he and Uncle Edward could enrol together. The brothers Stead came back the Doctors Stead in 1876. In St. John's, Anglicans went to Anglican doctors, whose numbers swelled to nine after the return home of Edward and my father. On the family shingle were listed one-third of the Anglican doctors in the city. It read, "Dr. A. Stead, Dr. F. Stead and Dr. E. Stead, General Practitioners and Surgeons," as if Stead was not a name, but the initials of some credential they had all earned, some society of physicians to which all of them had been admitted.

Three years after their graduation from Edinburgh, Father Stead died, but the shingle was not altered. Until his death, the two brothers had shared a waiting room, but afterwards my father moved into *his* father's surgery, across the hall. From the door that had borne both brothers' names, my father's was removed. It was necessary to make only one small change to the green-frosted window of grandfather's door: the initial *A* was removed and the initial *F* put in its place. *F* for Francis.

Even without Father Stead, the family practice thrived. When asked who their doctor was, people said "the Steads," as if my father and

Edward did everything in tandem: examinations, diagnoses, treatments. When they arrived at reception, new patients were not asked which of the brothers they wished to see—nor, in most cases, did they arrive with their minds made up. Patients were assigned on an alternating basis. To swear by one of the brothers Stead was to swear by the other.

But with the departure of my grandfather, the Steads were no longer the Steads, and for a while the practice faltered. And no wonder, Edward said, what with one of them having gone off, apparently preferring first the company of Eskimos and Moravians to that of his own kind, and now the profession of nursemaid to a boatload of social misfits to that of doctor. If one of them would do that, what might the other do?

The family itself dropped a notch in the estimation of its peers. It was as if some latent flaw in the Stead character had shown itself at last. My father's patients did not go across the hall to Edward. They went to other doctors. Some of Edward's patients did likewise. He had no choice but to accept new ones from a lower social circle.

My father, in letters home, insisted that he would take up his practice again one day. He promised Edward he would pay him the rent that his premises would have fetched from another doctor, but he was unable to make good on the promise, having forsaken all income.

Rather than find another partner, rather than take down the family shingle and replace it with one that bore a stranger's name, Edward left my father's office, and everything in it, exactly as it was.

That door. The door of the doctor who was never in but which still bore his name. It must have seemed to his patients that Edward was caught up in some unreasonably protracted period of mourning for his absent brother whose effects he could not bear to rearrange, let alone part with. Every day that door, his brother's name, the frosted dark green glass bearing all the letters his did except for one. He could not come or go and not be prompted by that door to think of Francis.

The expedition "to the North" he said, immeasurably improved the map of the world, adding to it three small, unpopulated islands.

Soon, my father's life was measured out in expeditions. When he came back from one, it was weeks before he no longer had to ask what month or what day of the week it was. He would go to his office, turn upside down the stack of newspapers left there for him by Edward and read about what had happened in the world while he was absent from it. He searched out what had been written about the expeditions he had served on, the records they had set. As my father had yet to command an expedition, none of these records was attributed to him. Rarely, these records were some "first" or "farthest." But most of them were records of endurance, feats made necessary by catastrophes, blunders, mishaps. Declaring a record was usually a way of putting the best face on failure. "First to winter north of latitude . . ." was a euphemism for "Polar party stranded for months after ship trapped in ice off Greenland."

He was no sooner up to speed than he was gone again. Once the circumstances were right, once the backing for the next expedition had been raised by its commander and his application accepted, he was off.

He was never able to tell my mother the exact date of his arrivals home, only that his ship would dock sometime in the spring. He made almost random visitations. As my mother recalled those times, he seems to have been not so much present as less absent, known to be at home but rarely seen. She said we spent our dinnertimes in awkward silence. Otherwise, he holed up in his study, preparing, she presumed, for his next expedition, reading, poring over maps and charts. He kept the door of his study closed when he was in there and locked when he was not.

In my father's absence, we rarely had visitors or invited people over, and my mother received few invitations.

Edward and Daphne came to visit, though only, at Edward's insistence, infrequently.

According to Daphne, Edward, rotating his bowler hat by the brim, would sit on the edge of a chair in the front room, looking from the moment he arrived like he was on the verge of leaving. That was Edward, she said. No matter who they were visiting, his hat was always either on his head or in his hands. His back never made contact with a chair. After perhaps fifteen minutes, during which my mother and Edward rarely spoke, they were gone again.

"People feel embarrassed if they say 'husband' or 'father' or 'doctor' or 'son' in front of me," Mother told Daphne. "At least I think they do. I feel embarrassed, so I avoid those words, too, along with about half the others in the dictionary. People don't think of Francis only when I'm around or when Devlin is with me, you see, because there are always stories about him in the papers."

These stories, Daphne reminded her, were not about my father *per se*. They were about the expeditions he took part in. They were picked up from foreign papers by the local ones, which tacked onto them a paragraph about my father.

"Still," she said, "with his name so often in the paper, I'm sure that people talk about him a lot. Dr. Stead the explorer. Even if he came home between expeditions like other explorers, they'd talk about him. But he doesn't, so they talk about him even more. Explorer *and* delinquent husband and father. Which makes it impossible for them to act as if they've never heard of him in front of me. Impossible not to be transparent about it anyway, though I pretend not to notice. So much tactfulness. Everyone so ill at ease, including me. I can stand only so much of it. I don't know…"

"Don't worry about your husband, Amelia," Mother Stead told her once in the evening, when all the Steads were congregated in the front room of her house. "One day, he'll realize how much he misses us. He'll come home, and he'll never go away again."

"It is marriage he is running from," she said another time. "Not you and the boy. Marriage. Responsibility and its confinements." She spoke in the same tone as she did when predicting his return, her voice as flat as though she was reading from a prayer book.

Mother was an only child whose father died when she was eighteen and her mother soon after, leaving her the house that she and I lived in and a considerable sum of money that, despite the absence of any contribution from my father, would have been enough to sustain us both for life if wisely used.

But it was with part of her inheritance that my father set up his practice, and with her money and without consulting her that he bought his way onto his first expedition.

Father Stead had left everything to Edward, even though my father was the older brother, with Mother Stead, as was the custom with widows who had sons, getting nothing, not even the house she lived in.

Edward made me and my mother the conspicuous measure of his generosity and sense of family honour. My mother had only, in front of him and a witness, to make casual mention of something she didn't have and that something would so soon after be delivered to our door it was like an accusation, the suggestion being that haste was necessary to prevent my mother from complaining or speaking badly of him to others. He affected the air of a good, generous-to-a-fault, easily imposed-on man, harried by his spendthrift sister-in-law, the wife of his delinquent brother, whose ultimate intention was to milk him dry.

Going by the surgery, Aunt Daphne would look at Edward's name just below my father's on the shingle. There he was, the shingle seemed to say, the last in the line of succession; the inheritor not just of my father's practice, but of his brother's debts and obligations, all of it trickling down to him like the raindrops on the sign.

My mother and I did not go out often. Our one regular and unavoidable outing was Sunday service, where everyone's lot in life was on conspicuous display. Nothing so invoked my absent father like the sight of my mother and I making our way up the centre aisle to the pew we shared with Edward and Daphne. A widow's widowhood was never more apparent than when she appeared in church without her husband. Likewise our abandonment, my father's delinquency. We would not have been more gawked at if, as we entered, we had been loudly announced as "Amelia and Devlin Stead, forsaken wife and son of the improvident explorer Dr. Stead."

Daphne could tell, from the way we were regarded in church and from things she overheard, that there was the feeling among some people that our isolation was contrived, that the two of us preferred to be left alone, that we were outsiders by nature, wilfully, even haughtily, aloof. When the service was letting out, the men tipped their hats to Mother and the women nodded their acknowledgment and said good day in a way that forbade anything except a like response. One or two said, "How are you today, Mrs. Stead?" then looked at me for the answer. They smiled reassuringly at me when my mother told them she was fine. Otherwise, we were like rocks around which the congregation flowed.

She kept her horse, whose name was Pete, in a small barn behind the house. "I've always taken care of my own horse," she said. It was something she took pride in. The only thing she needed help with was hitching and unhitching Pete from what she called the carriage. It was a cabriolet with a maroon-coloured leather hood that folded back. When no one she knew was around, she would simply stand at the end of her driveway and wait until some man or boy whose assistance she could ask for came walking past.

"I wish now that I had defied Edward and spent more time with her," my aunt once told me.

My mother and I became, as my father and Edward had once been, "the Steads," a legendary pair, driving about in that cabriolet, sheltered by the hood, looking intent, preoccupied, as if hurrying home to resume some entirely unique, unprecedented way of passing time.

She took me shopping with her, and once or twice Daphne went with us. For the first few seconds after we went into a store, all conversation stopped, then resumed at a more subdued level, as if to speak in normal tones in the presence of the Steads would be an intrusion on the privacy that they so famously preferred.

"How are things with you, Mrs. Stead?" the butcher would say, and Mother would barely audibly reply to this relative torrent of conversation that things were well with her. He would wrap her purchases in brown paper, then tie them round and round with string, all the while looking at me and every few minutes winking, as if I shared with him some secret that we must not divulge in front of her.

Mother once overheard the two of us being referred to by women whom we passed in our carriage as "a pair of hermits."

"A pair of hermits," my mother said to Daphne, as if no path that she could make out led from what she had been to what other people thought she was.

There came an expedition after which my father did not come home. From then on, in his letters to my mother and Edward, he kept up the pretence that he was forever being kept from returning by circumstances beyond his control. Delays because of heavy ice off Labrador. Emergencies. Mishaps. Requests to join rescue missions for fellow explorers that in all good conscience he could not refuse. Excuses that he did not even hope to fool us with, that he meant for us to see through and made only for form's sake.

"I am ill," one letter read. "Not grievously so, but it is thought best for my recovery that I refrain from travelling."

In the spring of 1886, in a letter sent just before he went south from Battle Harbour, Labrador, on his way back from an expedition, my father wrote that he was moving to New York. In fact, he was going straight there and, when he found a house, would send for the two of us. He said he had made a "great decision." He planned, as soon as possible, to lead a polar expedition of his own. For so long, he had taken direction from "lesser men," obeyed commands that he knew were "ill-advised," kept silent when he should have spoken up. He said he had spent "as much time in the polar regions as any man alive." (Nothing to write home about, Edward said, even if it was true, which it wasn't.) But as so many of the others had done, he must, for the time being, make New York his port. "New York is to explorers what Paris is to artists," he said.

He must go to New York, where he could choose, from among the many men who went there in the hope of signing on with a polar expedition, the best crew yet assembled. Where he could get to know the great men of industry, the financiers who thought they had everything until they met a man like him, and who, for merely vicarious glory, were willing to underwrite the cost of adventures they dared not embark upon themselves. Great contests were under way, races for the North Pole and the South Pole, and no one who did not live in some great city like New York was considered a serious contender. He claimed that by moving to New York, he would make enough money that he could send some home.

"It is even likely, my dear wife," he wrote, "that one day, these lonely wanderings of mine will make us rich."

New York. That it is the best place from which to set out for the Arctic is not for most people the main attraction of that city.

My father never did send for us. It was the last letter my mother received from him.

I don't know exactly where Aunt Daphne's version of my life leaves off and mine begins, but I often think it might be here:

One day, when I was in the first grade, I came home from school to find the house empty. The barn out back was empty, too, the horse and carriage gone. Assuming my mother was out on some errand, I waited for her to return. I waited until after five, when it was almost dark. Then I walked up Devon Row to Uncle Edward's. He was not home yet from his surgery, which was farther up the street. I asked Aunt Daphne if she had seen my mother.

The next day, the horse and carriage were found on top of Signal Hill. Her death was officially declared to be an accidental drowning. But the story, which some children were only too glad to let me overhear, was that she had climbed down the steep slope that faced the sea, down to a grassy ledge, from which she jumped into a narrow channel of water between the shore and the ice that stretched off to the meeting place of sea and sky.

· CHAPTER TWO ·

FOR TWO YEARS, DURING WHICH WE GOT NO ANSWERS TO THE letters we sent to my father in New York, not even the one telling him about my mother, I lived with Uncle Edward and Aunt Daphne in my mother's house, to which they had moved after a kind of will was discovered. It was a note, what Uncle Edward called "a pithy bequeathal": "I leave everything to Daphne." Mother Stead had died a year before my mother. For that year, Uncle Edward and Aunt Daphne had been the sole occupants of the Stead home. My mother's house was smaller and more suited to a couple with one child. The Stead house had been sold.

The day, in the fall of 1888, when they were officially declared my guardians, the day the court ruled that they would remain so even should my father come back home, Aunt Daphne made a special dinner. She had me wear my best blazer. She dressed as though for some formal occasion. Beneath her wrap, she wore a close-fitting silk dress that might have been new, for I had never seen it before, striped black and green with bands of jet embroidery, complete with drapery and bustle.

Uncle Edward wore a double-breasted frock coat with silk-faced lapels. His hair was slick with pomade, brushed back and parted down the middle.

"So, Devlin," Aunt Daphne said before we took our places at the table, "how are things with you?"

Uncle Edward looked at her with amazement, as if it had not

before occurred to him that when not in his presence, I continued to exist. But Aunt Daphne persisted. She wanted to know how everything was with me: school, sports, choir practice. I told her how things were while Uncle Edward made such a clatter cutting up his food that I had to raise my voice to make myself heard.

When the subject of what was new with me was exhausted, there was silence. The wind was on the rise, and a sudden gust sprayed the window with particles of grit and stone. Uncle Edward stared at the fire behind me as if driven by one element into brooding contemplation of another. I looked at Aunt Daphne, who seemed so vulnerably hopeful in her finery. I imagined her preparing for this evening, choosing her outfit, making sure that everything looked just so, urging a reluctant Uncle Edward to do the same. There was something touching about the absence of all subtlety in her attempt to convey by her costume what she could not convey with words.

It had been a rule of Father Stead's that there be no talking at the dinner table until everyone had finished. This was Uncle Edward's rule as well, though impossible to obey because he ate so slowly. He seemed to go into a trance while eating, eyes staring blankly while he chewed.

"You'd think the two of us were bolters," Aunt Daphne said. "We finish so far ahead of you."

At first, Uncle Edward ignored her, but when provoked several times in this fashion, he said, "You eat too fast."

"We would eat more slowly if you would speak from time to time," she said, to no reaction from Uncle Edward.

The meal was passed in this manner, protracted silences interrupted by remarks from Aunt Daphne and laconic, chastening retorts from Uncle Edward. When he emptied his plate but did not push it away, she got up and refilled it, glancing apologetically at me. When he was finished, he abruptly stood and went into the front room to have his brandy and cigar.

"Can you imagine what it was like when there were just the two of us?" Aunt Daphne said, smiling. She leaned across the table towards me and whispered: "Their plates wiped clean they sit and wait / While at the trough he ruminates." It was as if she believed the specialness of the occasion called for the disclosure of a secret.

By consulting the dictionary, I discovered what was meant by *ruminates*. I repeated the couplet at school, which in itself was harmless, since none of the children really understood it, perhaps because of how ineptly I explained it to them. But the couplet, its author and the couple about whom it was written became known to teachers at the school, and from them, by exactly what means I would never know, it got back to Uncle Edward.

I found on my pillow one night when I went up to bed a note from Uncle Edward, which read: "I am told you go about repeating rhymes about my 'ruminations.' I am sorry that my hospitality does not inspire you to greater things."

Whenever there was mention in the paper of one of the expeditions on which my father served, Aunt Daphne would make some mischievous remark about it to Uncle Edward, not realizing I could hear her.

"I know it is cold in Greenland," she said. "I don't need men to prove it by going there and coming back with frostbite."

"White men study Eskimos," she said. "Do you think the day is coming soon, Edward, when a band of Eskimos sent to study you and me will turn up on the sidewalks of St. John's?"

She spoke of a recent publication that bore my father's name, a dictionary of the language spoken by a small tribe of Eskimos in Greenland. "The Akkuk, they're called," she said. "No longer, Edward, must I remain mute in the company of Akkuks. No more shall dinner parties in St. John's end in an argument about the spelling of some Akkuk word."

"Just what I have always wanted," she said one night, after she read aloud an account of a stranded, recently rescued expedition, "people to say, 'There goes Daphne Stead, whose brother-in-law once kept himself alive for months by eating dogs.'"

After they had gone to bed, Uncle Edward would retaliate by

holding forth to Aunt Daphne about my mother, his voice so loud he must have known it carried to my room.

"Small wonder," he said, "that my brother, after two years of marriage to her, decided that the North Pole was a better bargain."

Aunt Daphne said something in reply, but I couldn't make it out.

"How many women are there, I wonder," he said, "whose company makes the prospect of spending six months of darkness in bone-marrow-chilling cold seem irresistible?"

"Edward," Aunt Daphne said, then went on in a remonstrating tone, clearly telling him to lower his voice, though again I could not hear the words.

"What I say about Francis, I say in jest," she said. "But you—"

"Thank God the boy is only half composed of her," he said. "The other half is Francis. At least there is that. There was much to admire in Francis at one time. Before he wound up with her."

In a scene that might belong to memory, imagination or Aunt Daphne, I am walking down the hallway when my father emerges from his study and, seeing me, stoops down to my height and says something. All I can see is a shape that might be that of any man.

I had more memories of my mother, but they were all very much like the one I had of him. I remembered a featureless, peripheral presence that I knew was her. I remembered being in her company in different rooms of the house. Riding in the cabriolet with her beside me. Walking hand in hand with her along a street that I assumed was Devon Row. But I remembered nothing of what she wore, nothing of what she said or did or what our destinations were. I could not see her face.

I was six when my mother died. It made sense that I retained only that one vague, possibly counterfeit image of my father, given how young I was when he went away. But it seemed I should have had a few memories in which my mother was more than just a presence, someone whose only trait was her relationship to me.

It was as if my memory of my mother was joined to that of my father, as if my mother was being pulled under by my father, who had sunk from sight. I could still see her, but she was at too great a depth to make her out in any detail. One day, just as he had, perhaps *because* he had, she would vanish altogether.

It was strange that two people about whom I remembered little could affect me so profoundly, two people who, it seemed to me, I had never known but yet were constantly with me. Others—Aunt Daphne, Uncle Edward—remembered them, were reminded of them when they looked at me. It was as though they stood on either side of me, visible to everyone but me.

There were a couple of photographs of my father in the house, discreetly, neutrally displayed. One, a small cameo daguerreotype, stood among an assortment of others on the sideboard in the hall, just at the foot of the stairs. The other was the third of four photographs arranged on the wall as you climbed the stairs, only just visible by the light from the lamp outside my bedroom. It was as if they were meant to seem to visitors more like acknowledgments than mementoes, the message being that we would not stoop to repaying his delinquency by denying his existence, but nor did he any longer play much on our minds. It wasn't true, of course. There was never a time when I was not fascinated by those images of my absent father. Hair slicked close to his skull and parted down the middle. A large moustache that scrolled upward on both ends. As with all eyes in daguerreotype portraits, his seemed to be lit from within. I didn't know this was an effect of the photographing process.

In the front room, there was a daguerreotype of my mother, on the back of which was scribbled, in what Aunt Daphne said was my mother's hand, "Amelia, the wicked one." Aunt Daphne said the picture was taken not long after their engagement. She was standing, hands on hips, lips pursed, eyebrows lifted, perhaps in amusement at the very idea that by having this new-fangled gadget called a camera aimed at her, she could be made to lose her poise.

Aunt Daphne took a great deal of pleasure in spoiling me, though Uncle Edward seemed to take none in watching her do so. I think that when he looked at me, he was reminded of his brother, so undeservedly blessed with a child whom he hadn't bothered to see in years.

At Christmas, on my birthday, he sat watching from a distance while Aunt Daphne joined me on the floor as I tore the ribbon and wrapping from my presents. Each time I let out a shout of delight or surprise, she would look at Uncle Edward and smile, and he, unable or unwilling to pretend that he was not merely doing it for her sake, would smile back, the tight-lipped smile that one would give a child whose belief in the possibility of happiness might as well be indulged.

I thought that perhaps this was how men were with children—reserved, disinterested—my father having taken to extremes an attitude typified by Uncle Edward. Uncle Edward seemed generally aloof, sceptical, as if his vocation and his character had blended, and he viewed all things with diagnostic objectivity, forever watching and keeping to himself a horde of observations, his expression hinting at a shrewdness he could not be bothered demonstrating.

Aunt Daphne went with me when I fished for trout in the ponds and streams around which the city had grown up. For bait, I used night crawlers, large earthworms that came up on the grass at night, and that, even with a lantern, were very hard to see, let alone catch. The grass in the yard behind the house was not very high and so was perfect for night crawlers.

"It's time for Spotters and Grabbers," Aunt Daphne would say when it was dark. The spotter held the bucket and the flashlight, and the grabber crept up on the worm and, before it could dart back underground, grabbed it with both hands. I was usually the grabber, but Aunt Daphne would help me if a worm I had hold of was partway underground. She would put down the lantern and the two of us would kneel, hunching over the worm like a pair of surgeons. Using all four hands, we would ease it bit by bit from the ground, she with her face averted in case the worm broke in half. Uncle Edward watched from the kitchen window. When Aunt Daphne waved to him, he would turn away.

"We used to play Spotters and Grabbers, didn't we, Edward?" I heard her say once after I had gone to bed. "We had our own version. It was very different from Dev's, wasn't it?" It sounded like she was standing at the bottom of the stairs. There was no answer. "Well," she said more tenderly, "we still have our games." He made some inaudible reply.

Because of a high hill on the south side of the city called the Brow, you could see the harbour but not the sea from most parts of St. John's. It was easy to pretend that the harbour was a lake, and that nothing lay beyond the Brow but still more lakes and hills. Only from a certain place could you see out through the Narrows, at the mouth of which the sea abruptly changed, churned up by the wind that one foot the other way you couldn't feel, the harbour and the sea in such opposing states of agitation it was hard to believe that both were water.

"It's time you really saw the sea," Aunt Daphne said one day.

She and I drove in my mother's cabriolet, pulled by Pete, to the top of Signal Hill. As we ascended, I looked behind me at the city, which from that height assumed the shape it had on maps. We lived on the edge of civilization. North of St. John's there were settlements with names, but you could not call them towns. St. John's was on the edge of a frontier that had not changed since it was fixed four hundred years ago. I imagined what it looked like from the sea, the last light on the coast as you went north, the last one worth investigating anyway. The forest behind the outlying houses was as dense as the forest in the core. In the woods between neighbourhoods, men set snares for rabbits, hunted birds with rifles within a hundred feet of schoolyards. Not outside the city but at some impossible-to-pinpoint place inside it, civilization left off and wilderness began.

Halfway up the hill, the road reached a plateau on which there were two hospitals, both strictly quarantined, one for diphtheria and fever, and one for smallpox. The road gave them as wide a berth as was permitted by the tolts of rock. I looked up at the blockhouse, from which mercantile flags were hoisted whenever ships making for St. John's came into view. The purpose of the flags was to alert waterfront firms that their ships were coming, giving them time to prepare for docking and unloading.

"I saw the sea for the first time when I was twelve years old," Aunt Daphne said. She described how one day, in defiance of her parents and her teachers, she first went up on Signal Hill. It was not to see the sea, she said. She went with some other girls, whose real goal was to see the gallows, about which they had heard so many stories. But they went off course and wound up on the summit of the hill.

"The open sea," she said. "I had known all along that it was there. But that's like knowing that the pyramids are there."

We crested the hill, and Aunt Daphne brought Pete to a halt. I saw the open Atlantic.

"Well," she said, turning her face sideways, shouting above the roar of the wind that suddenly was everywhere.

"It's so flat," I said.

She smiled. I could think of nothing else to say. Sky. Wind. Light. Air. Cold. Grey. Far. Salt. Smell. Now all these words meant something they had never meant before, and the word *sea* contained them all. The word *sea* spread outward in my mind, flooding all its chambers until, by that one word, every word I knew was changed. I would find, the next day, that from having seen the sea, I was better able to smell and taste it, too, no matter where in the city I was—indoors, outdoors, at home, at school, in my bedroom late at night.

"They don't know we're here," she said. "We know we're here. We know all about them. But they don't know we're here."

"Who?"

People elsewhere, she said; the people we knew about from reading books and magazines; the people on whose lives we modelled ours, like whom we ate and dressed, like whose houses our own were furnished and whose pastimes we pursued.

"England is that way," Aunt Daphne said. "Canada that way. America that way." Then she pointed up the coast. "Labrador," she said. "And Greenland. To the right. Northeast of Labrador."

"Where my father goes," I said.

She smiled and nodded. The smile faded. She looked at me for a long time. I realized that it was to encourage me to talk about my mother that she had brought me here. It was a subject that both of us had been avoiding since she died.

"They found my mother down there," I said, pointing, though we couldn't see the water's edge from where we stood.

"Somewhere down there, yes. If it bothers you to be here, we can go."

"It doesn't bother me," I said. "Was she nice? I don't really remember her."

"She was very nice," Aunt Daphne said.

"Why did she jump in the water?"

"No one really understands such things," she said. "It wasn't anybody's fault. Not even hers."

So she believed that what I had heard at school was true.

She drew me to her and kissed the top of my head.

In the evenings, Daphne read aloud from books. She was not reading to me or Uncle Edward. She did it whether there was someone in the room with her or not, and often after we had gone to bed, her voice faintly eerie as, late into the night, she read to herself in the front room.

Nor, she said, did it have anything to do with being lonely or having no one to talk to, or being unable to bear it after we had gone to bed and the house was silent. It was simply how she preferred to read. Even had she been a social gadfly, she said, she would have read aloud whatever books she still had time to read.

She had got into the habit, she said, from reading aloud to her parents, who found it relaxing to listen to her after dinner.

Whether or not she did it to dispel loneliness, she *sounded* so lonely I could not bear to hear her down there by herself, as though she were conversing with imaginary friends, as though the only life she had aside from me and Uncle Edward was the one she found in books. I could not, when I heard her, help thinking of my mother.

One night, I sat at the top of the stairs until she noticed me.

"Am I keeping you awake?" she said. I shook my head.

"You can read in my room if you want to," I said.

She sat in a high-backed wicker chair beside my bed, beneath the gas lamp on the wall, the only one she left on, so that her image was cast in shadow on the opposing wall, her every feature magnified and sharply drawn. I watched her shadow each time she turned the page, as she paused in her reading, then began again.

She read Jane Austen, Charles Dickens, Fanny Burney, Thackeray, the Brontë sisters. I took little notice, at first, of the titles of the books she read. All that stayed with me from one night to the next were the names of the characters. For a stretch of nights, it would be Camilla, Sedley, Mandelbert. Then Cecilia, Delvile, Mortimer and Monckton. Emma, Harriet and Knightley. Elizabeth, Darcy, Bingley, Lady Catherine. She was often well into a new book before I realized that a different set of characters was recurring.

"That's a new one," I'd say.

Even though it was our understanding that she was not reading to me, that we were merely keeping each other company, it irked her that I was so oblivious to the meaning of what she read.

"Yes, it's a new one," she said. "It's so new that I have only ten pages left."

At some point, I began to follow along as she read, which she discovered when one night I asked her to remind me who some character was who had been offstage for a hundred pages.

Long after I dropped off to sleep, she went on reading. I would sometimes stir myself awake to find that she was reading still, her voice more subdued, her tone introspective, for though I lay there close beside her, there was not even the illusion now that she was reading to anyone but herself. But I stayed awake for as long as I could, propped up on the pillows, almost sitting, with my back against the headboard. To an observer, it would have looked as though she was reading to an invalid, seeing him through the nights of some long convalescence.

I would wake up, sometimes hours after dropping off, when it was very late or even getting light outside. I would see her, asleep in the chair, head to one side, her book still open on her lap. If it was past two when I awoke to find that she was sleeping, I should leave her be, she said, for she could never, after waking from a deep sleep, drop off again. She sometimes spent the entire night in the chair in my room, which Uncle Edward would remark upon disapprovingly at the breakfast table.

· CHAPTER THREE ·

I WENT TO BISHOP FEILD, WHICH ALL THE CHILDREN OF THE
Church of England upper crust attended.

Boys my age, who were either unaware of my father's continued
absence or didn't understand its implications, were eager to talk to me
about him. They envied me my famous father, whose romantic occupation was "explorer" while their fathers were barristers, merchants,
politicians. They would have me point out to them on the classroom
map his present location in the North, and they asked me what adventures he had related in his last letter home. I obliged, making it all up.

"He's right there," I'd say, pointing with my finger at some part of
Labrador or Greenland, or farther north at some landmass or stretch of
frozen sea that had no name, and whose shape and even existence were
entirely conjectural, a fact signified by its being stamped all over with
question marks.

"He's probably around there," I said, "but this is the *arctus incognita*,
so no one really knows." Dr. Francis Stead of the *arctus incognita*. I told
them of near drownings; encounters with polar bears, walruses and
other monsters; blizzards that went on for weeks. There were, in my
stories, many mishaps, all of which necessitated on my father's part an
act of heroism or a heretofore undreamt of feat of surgical skill. I
caught the attention of a boy named Moses Prowdy.

Moses was the son of a judge and the grandson of a sealing skipper in comparison with whom Captain Ahab was the very picture of
benevolence and moderation. "Follow On" had been the skipper's

nickname, for even when his ship was far beyond the point at which even the most reckless of the other skippers turned around and made for home, he ordered his crew to "follow on" in search of seals, his ship often so weighted down with pelts it sank to the gunwales in the ice. Only once had a crew convinced him to lighten his load, which he did by setting thirty-five men adrift in lifeboats.

There was more in Moses of the sealing skipper than the judge, though academically he was one of the school's best students, scoring top marks with an effortless brilliance that went uncomplimented, unremarked upon by the masters, who wordlessly and with faint, ironic smiles returned his papers and examinations to him. They seemed to believe that, Moses being Moses, the knowledge he acquired at the Feild could only be misused.

He had a smooth pink complexion, a small round mouth that always looked as if he had just gobbled a grease-laden piece of meat. He slicked his hair back with pomade, wore a vest, a gold fob watch. He was, at fourteen, more than six feet tall. It was said that his father, whom he towered over and outweighed by fifty pounds, was afraid of him. The masters were not, at least not collectively. It was said that the masters had told Moses to remember that if he tried anything with one of them, he would have to deal with all the others.

He carried about in his pocket cigars that, in full view of the masters, he puffed on reflectively while watching the school and the playground from across the street. For smoking cigars, for coming to school smelling of whisky, for being found in possession of books of "filth," he was frequently caned, barely wincing, as if his hide was made of leather.

"Moses Prowdy," Aunt Daphne said, "has caused me to radically revise my definition of the word *boy*."

But he was also regarded with a certain fondness by the masters, who would look at him and say that it was often the boys who outwardly seemed the most unpromising who inwardly, sometimes unconsciously, were harbouring a vocation for the ministry. Moses would smile and raise his eyebrows.

"You have charisma, Prowdy," said Headmaster Gaines, the principal of Bishop Feild, "which is, literally, the light of the Holy Spirit. You are, like it or not, a leader. It is at your age that boys are least able to resist temptation, most vulnerable to Satan, whom their innocence and promise makes spiteful and envious. It may be that, knowing what you might become, he tempts you even more than he tempts other boys. Satan, if God calls you, cannot prevail. You, if God calls you, cannot resist. Or it may be that, after all, there is nothing in your future but imprisonment. Only time will tell."

Moses fell in beside me one day as I was walking home. He looked down at me and smiled.

"You're Stead, aren't you? The son of the famous explorer Dr. Stead?"

I nodded.

"May I call you Devlin?" he said.

"Of course," I said.

"Of course," he said. "How magnanimous you are to those of us who know what our fathers look like." He smiled, so I smiled back.

"Devlin," he said, putting his arm around me, his merely doing that enough to earn us stares from the other boys. He was so much older than I was, so much bigger. Older, bigger boys did not walk home with younger, smaller ones. And Moses, of all the older, bigger boys, was most conspicuous doing so.

"MOSES," one of his friends shouted, but he pretended not to notice.

Moses, I was about to discover, knew as much about the parents of his schoolmates as most grown-ups did. Truth, half-truth, gossip, rumour—Moses knew it all. He mocked and pestered other boys, too, but seemed to have focused on me, and on my parents, as the most promising, most interesting targets.

"All the ships coming south stop off in St. John's on their way to the mainland. Did you know that, Devlin?"

I shook my head.

"Your father's ships, for instance, stop off in St. John's. One of them was in St. John's last spring. *He* was in St. John's, but he never came to see you, did he? Strange that he would come so close and not even say hello. Or pay a visit to your mother's grave."

When I asked Aunt Daphne if what Moses had said was true, she said that on two occasions in the past two years, expedition vessels on which my father had served as medical officer had made port in St. John's. But she knew of no one who had seen him, not even the reporters who went looking for an interview and were on both occasions told that he was sick.

"You knew he was here?" I said.

"Yes, I knew he was here."

"Why didn't you tell me?"

"Once, I sent a message to the ship," Aunt Daphne said. "He didn't answer it. I don't even know if it got to him. I didn't want to raise your hopes."

"What about my mother? Did any of his ships make port when she was still alive?"

"Yes," she said.

"Did she ever go to see him?"

She shook her head.

"Why not?"

"He knew where you lived," she said. "He would have come to see you if he had wanted to."

"How come he doesn't want to?"

"I don't know. I really don't, Devlin."

Moses again. "Devlin, you were born seven months after your parents were married. Do you know what that means?"

"Yes," I said, hoping that would shut him up, though I had no idea what difference it made when, in relation to my parents' wedding, I was born.

"It means they couldn't wait till they were married. Your mother was a minx and your father was a goat. He only married her because he had to. Because of you. That's why he ran off. Because he couldn't stand his shotgun marriage any more."

What should I do? Run away? How could I defend my parents when I only dimly understood his accusation? My greatest fear was that others would overhear him. Any reaction from me was certain, given his reputation, to attract an audience.

Again I consulted Aunt Daphne.

"My God, I can't believe it," she said. "Fourteen years old. What a fiend, what a devil that Prowdy boy must be."

She explained the significance of my being born seven months after my parents were married.

"I should have told you myself," she said. She said there had been nothing you could call a scandal. My parents were, after all, not the only couple in St. John's to consummate their marriage in advance. When, seven and a half months after their marriage, she gave birth to me, people tactfully pretended to believe that I was premature.

"The day they were married, they loved each other very much," she said. "When you were born, they were still in love and they loved you. I don't know why your father changed; I really don't."

Moses. "Stead wouldn't know his father if he met him on the street." Included now among his audience were the younger boys who had once hung on my every word. "Nor would the great explorer know his son. Stead has no more idea where his father is than do we who read the papers. His father never writes to him or to his aunt and uncle. The great explorer has disowned them."

He walked home with me again. He put his hand on my far shoulder, inclined his head towards me.

"Why do you think it is, young Devlin," he said, lowering his voice, "that your father would rather do it with a squaw than with your mother?" I knew what "it" was, the mechanics of it and its biological purpose at least. "I pity your poor mother," he said. "She was left to a widow's consolation even though her husband was still alive. Do you know what a widow's consolation is? No? You should ask your aunt and uncle, then."

With that, to my great relief, he walked on ahead of me.

But it was the same the next day.

"*Now* do you know what a widow's consolation is?" he asked.

I shook my head.

"They wouldn't tell you? Well, I'm not surprised—"

"I didn't ask them," I said as neutrally as possible.

"A delinquent father, a dead mother and guardians who ignore you. You poor fellow. Well, let me help you, then. A widow's consolation. I must put it in some way that won't upset you. You see, when you were at school, men went by your mother's house. She took them upstairs to her room. They paid her money. The house you live in used to be a whorehouse. Everyone knows about it."

When I reported this latest "revelation" to Aunt Daphne and asked her if it was true, she said that she had had enough.

She had me stay home the next day. After school, she went to see Headmaster Gaines.

When she returned, her cheeks were red with anger.

"Well, that's that," she said. "There'll be no more problems now. Headmaster Gaines said that among many other things, he would cane this Moses Prowdy. 'Moses will leave Devlin alone,' he said. 'You have my word on it.' It took some doing to get him to say it, but he said it."

Headmaster Gaines was right that Moses Prowdy had charisma. It was not long before the other boys, even the ones my age, were urging him to, as they put it, "hold forth on Stead," crowding around him to hear what he would say next about me or my parents.

"Devlin," Moses said, "your mother once asked the bishop for an annulment on the grounds of desertion, but he said no because your father might have come back. An annulment means she wouldn't have been married to your father any more, and if she'd wanted to, she could have married someone else. Desertion means—"

"That's not true," I said, and knowing full well what my reward would be, I kicked him in the shins.

He hopped about briefly on one foot. Too briefly for me to run away.

I went home, nose bloodied and mouth on one side swollen and coloured like a plum. When Aunt Daphne admitted that what Moses had said was true, I asked her why she kept so many secrets from me.

"I was waiting until you were old enough to understand them to tell you all those things," she said. "I never imagined that a boy as much older than you as Moses Prowdy is would attach himself to you the way he has."

She went to Headmaster Gaines again, saying that because Moses was undeterred from disobedience by caning, he should be suspended. In the past, Gaines said, Moses had been suspended, but to little effect. Then, Aunt Daphne said, he should be expelled. To which Gaines replied that while they could expel Prowdy from school, they could not expel him from St. John's. He would have no trouble finding me if he wanted to, and he *would* want to when he heard he'd been expelled because of me. The masters had long ago decided to keep him within the jurisdiction of the school for as long as possible, for everyone's sake, including his. "We have not given up on Prowdy," Headmaster Gaines said. "It is never foolish to be hopeful. Only he will be diminished if he proves us wrong."

I was soon coming home every day with fresh bruises, Moses no longer needing the provocation of a kick in the shins.

"What will we do, Edward?" Aunt Daphne said one night. "That Prowdy boy will never stop, never. It will be at least four years until he graduates."

"I suspect," Uncle Edward said, "that young Devlin could be more resilient if he wanted to. Schoolyard disputes should be settled on the schoolyard."

She talked about sending me to another school. "But they'd eat you alive there, too," she said, "once they found out why you left the Feild. And Moses would still know how to find you."

At dinner, her food went cold on her plate as she sat there, head resting on her hand, tilted sideways, her thumb on her cheek, fingers splayed on her temple and her brow.

By the time I went to bed that night, she had been silent for hours, staring at the fire.

"Follow On Moses, they might as well have called that boy," I heard Aunt Daphne say after they had gone to bed. "He will no more give up on Devlin than his grandfather would have given up on a herd of seals."

"You dote too much on Devlin," I heard Uncle Edward say.

"I can't have that giant of a boy picking on my son."

"Your son? You see? You see how easily you can fool yourself? He is your nephew. He will never be your son. You've been to see Headmaster Gaines twice in one month. You baby him so much he can't defend himself at school. Soon he'll be afraid of cats."

"You and Francis had each other, Edward. Dev has no one."

"I've seen Prowdy. I faced up to boys as big as that and bigger when I was your nephew's age."

"Oh, Edward, don't be ridiculous. Francis was always protecting you from bullies. And none of them was half as big as Prowdy."

"You don't know," he said. "You weren't there. I—"

She laughed, not meanly but fondly, in spite of being in the middle of an argument, because he sounded so earnestly convinced that he was good at something that he was known all over to be hopeless at.

"You sound as though you think I'm a coward, a weakling."

"I'm sorry I laughed. Really I am. I didn't marry you because of how many boys you beat up at Bishop Feild."

"He's not your son, you know. You make yourself look pathetic when you call him that. Pathetic. He is his irresponsible father's son. He is his mad mother's son. There is not a drop of your blood in him, and there never will be. There will never be a drop of your blood or mine in anyone."

I heard Aunt Daphne get out of bed and soon after go downstairs.

"My aunt will make up a rhyme about you," I foolishly said the next time Moses picked on me at school. "Like the one she made up about my uncle."

"I, too, can make up rhymes," Moses said.

Soon, copies of an anonymously written, printed-in-pencil rhyme called "Pilgrim's Prowess" were being passed around among the boys.

"The doctor married Mrs. Stead / And he with her did go to bed. / Alas for her he could not please / Though with his straw he made her sneeze." Anonymously written but assumed to be the work of Moses Prowdy, who on the playground recited it by heart. The masters seized all the copies they could find, caning those boys who did not volunteer theirs, but many escaped detection and made their way into other schools, and from them into the hands of grown-ups, until there were few people in St. John's who hadn't read it or at least been told about it.

After the circulation of that letter, it was, for most of the boys of the Feild, out of the question to associate with me, to be seen doing anything but ignoring me. Even the most unpopular, picked-upon boys kept their distance, not wanting to give their tormentors one more reason to torment them.

Even for Moses, I ceased to be a target. I think I came to be regarded as a kind of mascot of the banished, looked upon almost fondly by the boys as the ultimate excommunicant.

· CHAPTER FOUR ·

IT WAS FIVE YEARS SINCE MY FATHER HAD MOVED TO NEW YORK, and he was still unable to finance an expedition of his own. He signed on once again under someone else. He was one of two medical officers under Lieutenant Robert Peary on the North Greenland expedition. The purpose of this expedition was to discover what I overheard Aunt Daphne say "everyone was just dying to know": was Greenland an island or a continent?

In July 1892, a great fire destroyed much of St. John's, though Devon Row, on the heights of the far east end, was spared. Uncle Edward and the other doctors of the city were pressed into duty at the hospitals. Aunt Daphne volunteered for numerous women's committees and foundations for the relief of those affected by the fire. I was one of many schoolboys enlisted to help cart away what was left of people's houses so that new ones could be built.

All of us were still caught up in the relief effort when, unheard from for fifteen months, Peary's ship, the *Kite*, docked in Philadelphia in September 1892, with Peary declaring his expedition an unqualified success. He told the reporters who swarmed him before he had a chance to disembark that the Greenland ice-cap ended just south of Victoria Inlet, and he claimed that by this discovery, he had proved that Greenland was an island. He also relayed a piece of information that, in the papers, appeared in sidebars—alone of all the expeditionaries, Dr. Francis Stead had not returned.

It was from the local papers, most of which were devoted to

stories about the rebuilding of the city after the fire, that we first learned of my father's disappearance—or rather, that Uncle Edward first learned of it. "DR. STEAD MISSING." "DR. STEAD LEFT BEHIND." "DR. STEAD'S WHEREABOUTS UNKNOWN." These were the headlines of the papers that Uncle Edward found waiting for him on the front porch of his surgery the morning after the *Kite* made port in Philadelphia. Word of my father's disappearance had not reached local newsrooms until late the night before, too late for reporters (who assumed the Steads already knew about it) to contact family members for their reactions. It would not be until days later that Peary would telegraph his condolences to Uncle Edward, who was listed in the ship's log as my father's next of kin. Uncle Edward received no reply to a letter he sent to Peary rebuking him for not informing us through proper channels of my father's disappearance.

I heard of my father's death from Aunt Daphne, who let me sleep until my usual hour before waking me. She was crying, and I knew, before she had a chance to tell me, that something had happened to my father. My father, of whom I had one probably false memory and one photograph, was dead, presumed dead, though all Aunt Daphne could bring herself to say was that the *Kite* had come back without him. Still "up there," my father was. And perhaps he always would be. I had been certain that one day I would meet him, seek him out.

We spent the morning at the kitchen table, on which Aunt Daphne laid out, along with a glass of milk, all the sweets she had on hand: half an apple pie, a piece of pound cake, a heaping mound of shortbread cookies. A gloom made worse by the extravagance, the incongruousness of a table spread with sweets at nine-thirty in the morning, hung heavy in the house. Uncle Edward spent most of the day upstairs, though I caught a glimpse of him from time to time and was surprised by what I saw.

By the sorrow on his face and in his eyes, you would have thought that my father had never left, that Uncle Edward had last seen him just hours ago, that he had lived the life the Steads expected him to live until that very morning, when, on the way to his surgery, he had had some fatal mishap. I had thought it would seem to Uncle Edward that not much was different, that he had expected never to see his brother again and now his expectations were confirmed.

"Your mother kept writing to him long after he moved to New York," Aunt Daphne said. "Long after he stopped writing back. I've been trying to remember him. From before he went away. From when we met. But I can't separate the younger Francis from the older one. I can't picture that young man in my mind and pretend, even for a second, that I don't know what became of him."

"I don't remember him at all," I said, in the foolish belief that it would be a comfort to her that my memory of him was even more wanting than hers.

"I'm sorry, Devvie, for what was done to you," she said.

She looked at me as if she thought she ought to pronounce upon my father's passing in some manner, sum up his life and death for me in a way that would make sense of them. But all she did was take me in her arms.

The local papers, in the pieces they ran about my father's death, made no explicit reference to the estrangement of my parents, only noting without comment that "Dr. Stead was based in Brooklyn," and that his wife had "drowned" some years ago.

Two days after the docking of the *Kite*, there appeared in the papers an official "report," an account of my father's disappearance that was written, at Lieutenant Peary's request, by the expedition's other medical officer, Dr. Frederick Cook, during the voyage from McCormick Bay, Greenland, to Philadelphia. Its purpose was to set out what its author called "the strange case of Dr. Stead," and to pre-empt suggestions that Peary had in any way been negligent.

This "report" by Dr. Cook contained all the official information that would ever be released about my father's disappearance. The crew, as was usual on such expeditions, had signed a legal pledge of silence. Only Peary, who had sold the rights to his story in advance, was allowed to write about, or give interviews about, the expedition, and when he did, in the weeks and months to come, he made no mention of my father.

September 9, 1892
Aboard the S.S. *Kite*

Regarding the manner of the disappearance of my colleague and companion Dr. Stead: On August 18, when we awoke at Redcliffe House, Dr. Stead was missing. His sleeping bag lay unrolled but empty on the floor. A thorough search was conducted. A reward of a rifle and ammunition was offered to the native who found the missing man. Some footprints, as well as the label from a can of corned beef, were found at the foot of a glacier, but nothing more.

It was discovered that Dr. Stead had taken with him or hidden all his journals. Most of his clothing he had concealed in various places throughout the house, for what reason none of us could fathom.

On the fifth day of the search, freezing weather set in, and Captain Pike informed Lieutenant Peary that if we did not leave soon, we might be forced to winter at McCormick Bay for another year.

Just before the *Kite* set sail, Lieutenant Peary wrote and left at Redcliffe House a short note which we feared that Dr. Stead would never read, but which nevertheless informed him that in case he should return, the Eskimos would look after him until the following June, when a whaling ship would put in for him at McCormick Bay.

I cannot arrive at a positive conclusion as to the peculiar, sad and mysterious disappearance of Dr. Stead. He had not seemed to me to be debilitated, mentally or physically, when I saw him last, which was the very night of his departure. Nor had he said anything to anyone about his plans to leave the house.

Though it moves the mystery no closer to being solved, it seems worthwhile to point out that the strange case of Dr. Stead is by no means the strangest in the annals of Arctic exploration. Others have disappeared as surely as if, while sleepwalking, they attempted a crossing of the crevassed glaciers onto which not even the Eskimos will venture after dark.

Whatever is or may have been his fate, I feel satisfied that his commander, his companions and the natives did all in their power to discover his whereabouts.

> Respectfully submitted,
> F. A. Cook, M.D.
> Surgeon and Ethnologist
> North Greenland Expediton
>
> Lt. R. E. Peary
> Commanding

In spite of the publication of Dr. Cook's report and the pledge of silence taken by the crew, it was not long before rumours began to spread. On September 24, a story in *The New York Times* in which no sources were named suggested that a falling-out had taken place between my father and Lieutenant Peary. It was said that from the start of the expedition, my father had "pestered" Peary to let him stay up north so that he could better acquaint himself with the culture and language of the Eskimos. Peary, supposedly convinced that my father's real reason for wanting to stay behind was to achieve a farthest north, and perhaps the pole, refused.

The *Times* wrote: "It is said that Dr. Stead wore American trousers and the scantiest kind of clothing, and that almost every day he would go naked into the water where holes had been cut in the ice. He would protest that he was not cold and did everything in his power to inure himself to the hardships of the climate. He went around with his shoes torn, his bare feet making contact with the frozen ground, much to the amusement of the Eskimos." The story said that at a reception held for him in Philadelphia, Peary had referred to my father as a deserter for whom neither the government nor the backers of the expedition were under any obligation to send out more searching parties. "Lieutenant Peary said that to search further would at any rate be pointless. Though he said he had no right to indulge in surmises, he gave the impression that he believed there was no chance that Dr. Stead was still alive."

The thought that this description of my father's comportment in the Arctic was being read by millions of people throughout the world distressed Aunt Daphne.

"I wouldn't care if it *was* true," she said. "It's not fair of them to speak like that when he can't defend himself. But I don't believe it is true. Obviously I did not know him as well as I once thought I did, but I am sure he would never carry on that way."

She wrote, and convinced Uncle Edward to be the sole signatory to, the following statement, which was sent to all the local papers, as well as to *The New York Times*: "I know my brother. I know that in his right mind, he would not have conducted himself in such a manner. It is obvious that owing to the rigours of the expedition, he suffered an imbalance of temperament that must surely have been apparent to both Dr. Cook and Lieutenant Peary. Why such precautions were not taken as would have prevented him from injuring himself is something that these two gentlemen must answer for, if not in this life, then in the next. My brother's reputation has in no way been diminished by his disappearance, the real manner of which may yet come to light. Nor has his memory, in the eyes of those who truly knew him and from whose thoughts he has never long been absent, been besmirched."

Other stories from America were reprinted in the local papers. When I came home from school one day, I found Aunt Daphne at the kitchen table, her hands all but covering her face as she looked through them at a copy of *The Telegram*, on the front page of which were illustrations of the interior of Redcliffe House, based on descriptions of it provided by members of the crew.

Peary's wife, Josephine (Jo), had been, if not exactly a member, then a guest of the Greenland expedition. She had wintered with Peary and the crew in the grandly named Redcliffe House in McCormick Bay. The whole "house" was smaller than my bedroom. The walls, inside and out, were covered with tar paper and further insulated with red woollen blankets. There were two rooms, one with a bed for the Pearys and one with pallets for the crew, a half-dozen men, my father and Dr. Cook among them. The rooms were divided only by curtains that Jo Peary had made from two silk flags. The Pearys' bedtable was a steamer trunk, and on it stood a bowl and pitcher. Along one wall were crude shelves containing books, the reading of which was their main pastime once the Arctic night began. "On the wall," the story said, "Mrs. Peary hung pictures of her dear ones back home, whom she thought of constantly." In the other room, where my father and the rest of the crew slept, there was a pot-bellied stove, a table and some makeshift chairs, and one bunk with a mattress made of carpet. The men took turns sleeping in the bunk and otherwise lay out on their pallets in a circle around the stove, their heads just inches from it. From this circle, my father had removed himself so quietly that he did not wake the others, his absence going unnoticed by them until hours later. I stared at the illustration as if it was a photograph, at the artist's rendering of the crude wooden floor as if it depicted the very spot where my father had last been seen alive.

There was a photograph of Jo Peary by which I was especially transfixed: Jo standing on the barren rocks of Greenland, dressed as though for a Sunday walk in a belted silk dress and matching waistcoat, and shielding herself from the sun with a large parasol. Her glance was downcast on an Eskimo family, over all of whom, even the parents, she towered like an adult over children. The Eskimos in their furs and skins, and Jo Peary wearing what might have been one of my mother's dresses, so incongruous she might not really have been in the photograph but merely standing in front of one so large that all signs of civilization lay outside the frame.

"She must be a remarkable woman," Aunt Daphne said, though

Uncle Edward would later say that according to a friend of his, she was "the laughing-stock of Philadelphia."

I looked at Jo Peary, eyes demurely downcast as she sheltered from the sun beneath her parasol. The cracked, creased faces of the Eskimos; their long, tangled hair. For the first time, I noticed the baby the woman carried on her back, its eyes peering out just above the brim of the papoose.

There was a story about Peary's family and with it a photograph of his little daughter's room. It was full of souvenirs, polar souvenirs piled on the bed. Toy seals and shells and feathers and pieces from the meteorites that Peary had discovered in the Arctic, and that he called the star stones.

The next day, in a butcher's shop, a man who had seen Aunt Daphne and I come in but must not have known that I could hear him told another man, "He went insane or something. Walked off one night when the other men were sleeping. Never seen again." There was in his tone the suggestion that the odd manner of my father's death was somehow in keeping with the odd manner of my mother's. This, I soon sensed, was the general view: that my father's death was final confirmation of the oddness of Dr. Francis Stead and his wife, Amelia.

Although, from the beginning, the prevailing view was that my father was an irresponsible, wanderlusting man whose desertion of his family was inexcusable, there had always been rumours, vague, sourceless rumours that, as Uncle Edward seemed to think but would not have said in public, it was to escape my mother that my father took up exploration. I remembered what Moses had once asked me: "Why do you think it is, Devlin, that your father would rather do it with a squaw than with your mother?"

Now it was as if it made sense that a man who had not so much chosen exploration as been driven to it would one day be driven mad by it. Or by his wife, by *her*, by *that one* with her odd ways, whom, even when he was in the Arctic, even after she was dead and he had not set eyes on her for years, he could not forget.

What, people seemed to say as they looked at me, will become of this boy who was the issue of two such odd people as his parents?

Just as he was preparing to go to New York to settle my father's affairs, Uncle Edward received a letter from a man who described himself as an "associate of Dr. Stead's" and said that my father had rented an almost unfurnished flat and, in between expeditions, worked for little compensation at a hospital for the indigent in Brooklyn. He died intestate, having at any rate but $140 in a bank and no personal effects besides clothing and books. The money, Aunt Daphne decided, would be kept in trust for me until I was twenty-one. Uncle Edward instructed my father's associate to dispose of the clothing and books in whatever manner he saw fit, since it would cost more to transport them to Newfoundland than they were worth.

A month passed in which nothing new about my father came to light. Uncle Edward said it would be pointless to wait until next June, when the whaler referred to by Dr. Cook in his report would go through the formality of putting in at McCormick Bay. Pointless, he meant, to wait until then to have a funeral service for my father. All the papers agreed with Peary that, given the circumstances, there was no chance that Dr. Stead was alive now, let alone that he would make it until June.

Uncle Edward placed a notice in the papers that would have given to people who did not know my father no clue that he had ever deviated from the path the world expected him to follow all his life, no clue to how he had spent his past ten years or how he had died: "Passed away, August 17, 1892, Dr. Francis Stead, son of Dr. Alfred Stead and Elizabeth Stead, née Hudson, lately of St. John's. Leaving to mourn his son, Devlin; his brother, Dr. Edward Stead; and his sister-in-law, Daphne Stead, née Jesperson. Predeceased by his wife, Amelia, née Jackman."

Beside my mother's, a stone was erected in my father's name in the family plot in the cemetery not far from the house. There was a short, private service presided over by a minister who had long been one of Uncle Edward's patients. Aunt Daphne cried, though less for my father than for me, it seemed, for she kept looking at me and trying to smile. In Uncle Edward's face, there was a shadow of the grief I had seen there the day we learned about my father, but more than that he either would not or could not show.

My father's headstone, token of his unmarked, unknown final resting place. There were other stones in the cemetery for people, most of them men who had died at sea, whose remains were never found.

"Poor soul," Aunt Daphne said, looking at the stone. Poor soul, I thought. The stone, the portraits in the house, the words *poor soul*, the picture of the room he once occupied at Redcliffe House, the accounts of his disappearance in the papers were to me the sum effects on the world of his existence. I tried to think of myself as an effect of his existence but could not.

Aunt Daphne still read aloud in the evenings, sometimes downstairs, sometimes in my room.

I noticed that often, from the strain of reading night after night, her voice grew hoarse. She would drink frequently from a glass of water that she kept beside her chair, sipping after every page.

"Why don't I read to you for a while?" I said one night.

From then on, we took turns reading to each other, handing a book back and forth two or three times a night. Sometimes she had to help me with a word, inclining her head to see which one I was pointing at. I learned the knack of pronouncing words I didn't know the meanings of, and then the knack of guessing their meanings from the words around them.

"Why don't you read to blind people?" Uncle Edward said. "At least then it would make sense to read out loud."

"It's a way for two people to read the same book at the same time," Aunt Daphne said. "Or three people, for that matter."

But as soon as we began to read, he went upstairs to listen to his Victrola.

I liked the tandem journey through a book. It was different from co-witnessing a real event, even if that real event was a performance like the concerts and plays she took me to. Reading aloud to each other was like collaborating on some endlessly evolving secret. By tacit understanding, we never talked about the books we read, as if we did not want to know if or how our impressions of them differed. I liked the idea, even if it was just illusory, that for a while each day, my mind mirrored hers.

"I want you to understand something," she said one evening, after we had finished reading. "Just because something happened to your parents doesn't mean that it will happen to you. You are not the sum of your parents. You are you. Devlin. Do you understand?"

I nodded. I was relieved, grateful to her for having said it, for having guessed not only that I needed reassurance that I would not end up like my parents, but that I lived in such dread of the possibility that I could not bring myself to speak to her about it. That she had sounded, just faintly, as if it were herself as much as me that she was trying to convince didn't matter. She, too, needed reassurance, could not help having doubts, however transient they might be.

· CHAPTER FIVE ·

THE WINTER I TURNED SEVENTEEN, UNCLE EDWARD SUGGESTED TO Aunt Daphne that I go to his surgery for a check-up. He said that he thought I was not looking my usual self, and that, although it was probably nothing, it was best not to take any chances.

I went the next day after school, glancing at the shingle that no longer bore my father's name, nor Father Stead's, only Uncle Edward's. Inside, I glanced at the door across from Uncle Edward's. It remained unchanged. "Dr. Francis Stead." Uncle Edward no longer even pretended to be looking for another partner.

There were several patients ahead of me in his waiting room, but when the patient he was with came out, he called me in.

"Sit down, Devlin," he said, motioning to the chair opposite his at the desk.

"You think there might be something wrong with me?" I said.

He shook his head.

"This is the best place for us to meet," he said. "The safest place." For a few seconds, his elbows on the desk, his fingertips touching so that his fingers formed a cage, he was silent, as though he were deliberating, trying to foresee what my reaction would be to what he was about to say. He sat back in his chair and turned it so that he faced away from me.

"I have had a letter." he said. "A letter from Dr. Frederick Cook, the man whose account of your father's disappearance was published in all the papers. Do you remember?"

I nodded.

"The letter is for you. He did not send it directly to you because he did not want Daphne to see it. I have, at Dr. Cook's suggestion, not read it, but I believe that it contains...no falsehoods. I have decided that I will speak about this matter to no one but you. I believe that once you have read the letter, you too will see the wisdom of discretion."

My heart was pounding. I had never been spoken to like this before by any adult, let alone by Uncle Edward.

"Why does he want me to keep it secret from Aunt Daphne?" I said. "Does she know him—"

"You need not read it at all. You don't have to. I can simply burn it if you like." He looked briefly at the fireplace.

"I'm not promising to be discreet before I read it," I said. Discreet. I had never used the word before, never spoken so formally to anyone. It seemed impossible, under the circumstances, not to imitate the way he spoke.

He shrugged. "Even if you did promise, you could change your mind. I'm simply acting here as a kind of postman for Dr. Cook. A go-between. When you have read the letter, *if* you read it, you can do as you see fit. I think I know what you will do, but of course I could be wrong."

"I could just give it to Aunt Daphne," I said, "and let her read it first."

He shook his head. "I would hate to have you wish too late that you had opted for discretion. I think you should read it in my presence, then give it back to me."

"All right," I said. What harm would it do me or Aunt Daphne if I read the letter?

Why had Dr. Cook waited for three years after my father's death to write to me about him? I assumed that his letter contained news about my father. I could think of no other reason for Dr. Cook to write to me. Perhaps he had things to tell me that he thought I was only now old enough to understand.

Uncle Edward opened the drawer of his desk and removed from

it a small, once white envelope that now was yellow, so flat and thin it looked as if it was empty. It was sealed, but there was nothing written on it but my name. It must have come inside another envelope that was addressed to Uncle Edward.

"I will step out onto the rear landing," Uncle Edward said, rising and walking around his desk, extending the letter to me. "I will come back in ten minutes." He went to a windowless door across the room from the one I came in by, slowly opened it, went outside and just as slowly closed it.

I broke the seal, tore a corner of the envelope, removed and gingerly unfolded the single page, which looked so old that if mishandled it would have crumbled into pieces. The layers were compressed together, as if they had been ironed or had lain for months beneath some flat and heavy object. The handwriting, which appeared on both sides of the paper, was minuscule, barely decipherable, the words extending to the bottom line of the last page, the final words crammed into the right-hand margin, as if their author had exhausted his supply of paper.

My dearest Devlin:

I think constantly of you. Strange words from a man whom you have never met. I feel strange writing them. But from where I am writing—where in the world, where in my life—everything seems strange.

When I wrote your uncle Edward, I should have been well launched on my quest for the South Pole, not in the cabin of a ship that had yet to leave the dock, not in the swelter of Rio de Janeiro. Since I wrote that letter, I have not left the ship more than half a dozen times. Just before we were due to leave last spring, Devlin, a fear I had never known before took hold of me.

I imagine Peary coming back in triumph from the North Pole. Newspapers whose headlines proclaim his accomplishment figure so often in my dreams that I have banned all papers from the ship.

Peary, who has never acknowledged in public that your father and I
saved his life on the North Greenland expedition. His leg was shat-
tered in a storm by the ship's tiller. Had he been attended to by
lesser doctors, he would have died.

Devlin, the most mundane things seem ominous. In part, I
have worked myself into this state through debating whether it
would be fair of me to confide in you.

I find myself on all matters unresolved. I find even the simplest
of decisions impossible to make. I have heard that Peary, in a letter
to his mother that he wrote when he was twenty, said, "I must have
fame. I must." His advantage over me is that he will do anything to
achieve his goal, whereas I . . . I lack the ruthlessness that I fear may
be essential to the task.

Devlin, no one knows what I am going through but you. I dare
not tell others of my doubts. Who would back my expeditions, who
would trust me to command them, if they knew my state of mind?

I have been waking up, drenched in sweat, from nightmares I
cannot remember and during which, the captain of the ship informs
me, I scream incomprehensibly, as though at some intruder in my
room.

Such has been my physical state these past few months that the
captain is certain I have caught malaria. I have told him that I suffer from "transient debilitation" owing to the energies I expended
raising money for this expedition. In three weeks, we are supposed
to leave for Patagonia, from which, in July, we set out for the
Southern Ice. But the captain and the others will not make for
Patagonia until what they call my condition has improved. Nor will
they let another spring go by without either heading for the pole or
turning back. We have been stalled here now for seven months.

I know the cause and therefore, I hope, the cure of my despair.
It is a piece of information that I have been keeping to myself since
just before your father disappeared. What you are about to read will
surprise or even shock you, so prepare yourself before you read on.

I could not imagine what sort of disclosure Dr. Cook was about to make. I felt so light-headed I almost fell from my chair.

Not long before he disappeared on the North Greenland expedition, your father took me aside and told me something that I dismissed at first as the delusion of a man who had for some time, owing to the rigours of Arctic exploration, been acting strangely. But he repeated what I would have called an accusation against his wife except that his tone was so deliberate, so calm. He said that you were not his son.

In the hope of making him see how much the strain of the expedition was affecting him, I asked him what proof he had that he was not the father of the boy whom the rest of the world knew to be his son. He supplied certain details that convinced me his revelation was true. These details convinced me of something else, too, which I kept to myself. I have had few enough liaisons with women in my life to remember all of them. But even if I was a man of the world, I would remember my first time. It came to me, as your father told his story, that the boy he was speaking of could be no one's son but mine.

You have only my word that all of this is not complete invention on my part. Aside from having no reason to invent such a story, I am putting myself at great risk in confiding in you. You hold in your hands a document, in my handwriting, bearing my signature, that if made public could do me and mine great harm. You and your aunt and uncle would likewise suffer, and great harm would be done to the memory of your parents, your mother's especially. My heart has never been so close to breaking as when I heard from your father—that is, from Francis Stead—the manner of your mother's death.

You are, Devlin, too young to understand how rare a thing true love is, how unlikely in this world to happen, and when it does, how unlikely to endure. And once it is lost, how hard to live without. I have tried "writing" to your mother, directing my thoughts to her, as though she was still alive, but I derived no comfort from it. Finally, I realized that it was to you I should be writing.

I write in the full understanding of how this letter will affect you. I cannot myself imagine receiving such news at your age. Only by blood now, the cold blood of biology, are you my son and I your father. How this can change, I am unable to foresee. I cannot, for obvious reasons, publicize the contents of this letter. (Your uncle will speak to you of this at greater length.)

Nevertheless, may I write to you again? In my next letter, I will provide you with such details as will convince you beyond all doubt that my claim is true. I have omitted to do so in this one not to whet your curiosity, but because I could not bear to relate the whole of my story to someone from whom I might never hear again.

In your uncle's presence, after he has finished speaking to you, I want you to write "Yes" or "No" on this envelope and give it to him. He will forward your answer to me. If your answer is yes, I will write to you and you will receive my letters by an arrangement of a sort that I suggested to your uncle. If your answer is no, I will not write to you again.

> *Yours truly,*
> *Dr. F. A. Cook*

> *February 11, 1897*

By the time I finished the letter, my mind was a riot of half-formed thoughts and questions. I jumped with fright when the door off the landing opened and Uncle Edward stepped inside. He looked composed until he saw how *I* looked. I did not realize how badly my hands were trembling, and with them the pages of the letter, until I saw that he was staring at them with a look of sheer dread in his eyes.

"It goes without saying," he said, struggling to control his voice, "that Daphne would disapprove of your corresponding with Dr. Cook. If she were to find out about it, she would contact him and you would never hear from him again. If you agree to receive letters from Dr. Cook, I will burn each one after you have read and copied it by hand, just as you will copy this one. You will stay and watch while the letter burns. We will meet from now on in your father's surgery. Remember, it would be assumed that letters in your handwriting had been written by you, however advanced in style and content they might seem to be for a boy your age, so it would be foolish to show these copies to others, who would think that you were writing letters to yourself."

He motioned to the pen and inkwell on his desk.

"Write your answer," he said.

I went to the desk, wrote "Yes" on the envelope, then handed it to him.

He looked at the word I had written. He sighed, with resignation, relief, regret, it was hard to tell.

"Copy the letter," he said, handing me two blank sheets of paper. "And be quick about it." I copied out the letter as fast as I could, Uncle Edward standing, arms folded, with his back to me, as if to ensure that he did not see a single word.

"I'm finished," I said.

"Put your copy in your jacket pocket," he said. When I had done so, he turned around.

"The original letter," he said. "Fold it first."

I did and held it out to him. He took it. Holding it at arm's length between his thumb and index finger, as if he wanted as little to do with it as possible, he spun it into the fire.

"Uncle Edward—" I said, but he raised his hand. He was as deeply into this subterfuge as he cared to go, his expression seemed to say. Why had he ventured even this far into it? He had seemed very anxious that I should correspond with Dr. Cook. What did he have to gain if I said yes or lose if I said no? No doubt he liked the idea of my going behind Aunt Daphne's back, perhaps foresaw the whole thing driving us apart someday. He was jealous of me, as absurd as that seemed, believed she was fonder of me than she was of him. Perhaps he saw these letters as his one hope of not spending the rest of his life second to me in her affections. But that, surely, could not be why he was acting as Dr. Cook's "postman."

No doubt he thought that with him as go-between, there was less chance that yet another scandal would be put against the name of Stead. That Dr. Cook's letter to me was of a scandalous nature he knew. That was clear from the way he was acting. He knew that Dr. Cook had asked me to write my "answer" on the envelope. But he really seemed not to have read the letter—it was still sealed when he gave it to me, and he had told me in advance that he would burn it when I gave it back to him, as if it was necessary that I see him burn it, be witness to the fact that he had never read it. Uncle Edward went to his desk and sat down, reversing his chair so that it faced the window.

"I don't know when Dr. Cook will write again, or when his letter will arrive. He must wait to hear from me before he sends it. Coming from"—he gestured vaguely at the ceiling—"from God knows where, it may take a very long time. I therefore tell you in advance that you must be patient. I doubt it will get here any sooner than December."

Three months from now.

"This is how you will know that a letter has arrived." When he came down for breakfast in the morning, he said, he would wear, in the pocket of his vest, a red paisley handkerchief, the one that Aunt Daphne disliked so much she would think it was for her sake that he wore it no more than once every few months—which was likely how often a letter would arrive. "Whenever I wear it, it will be your red-letter day," he said, wincing ruefully, as if it was I who had punned at his expense. On that day, he would tell his nurse that he was going to have his lunch across the hall in his brother's surgery, where he could relax in quiet with a book. I was to tell Aunt Daphne that because of choir practice, I would not come home for lunch. Making sure that none of the other boys saw me, I would go to his surgery, walk around to the iron gate by which one entered the secluded back garden, and which he would leave unlocked, and using the door marked "Doctor's

Entrance Only," go slowly and quietly up the stairs to the landing. He would be sitting in a chair on the landing just outside my father's surgery, the patient's entrance to which was permanently bolted from the outside. There would, in other words, be no way I could come and go without him seeing me. I would arrive promptly at 12:30 and, saying not a word to him, go inside, where the letter would be waiting for me in the top drawer of the desk. I was not to turn the lights on in the office. By day, there would be light enough to read and copy out the letter. When I was done, I was to come out to the landing and, without speaking a word, hand him the original. Then both of us would go back inside, where I would watch him burn the letter in the fireplace and then leave. Upon arrival and departure, and throughout my time in my father's surgery, I was not to say a word. If anyone saw me leave by the doctor's door and asked what I was doing, I would say that I had been to see my uncle for a check-up. If it somehow got back to Aunt Daphne that I had been to see him, our story would be that it was to save her needless worry that we had not told her about the check-up.

I did not go back to school after I left the surgery. Nor did I go straight home. I had to prepare myself before I saw Aunt Daphne, before she saw me and started asking what was wrong. She would not relent until I told her something. Fearing that even strangers would notice my distress, I took the shortest route to the woods, followed a path some distance, then left it and sat down against a tree, where no one passing by could see me.

No wonder Dr. Cook could not imagine how his letter would affect me. Now that the original no longer existed, it was easy to imagine that it never had. Or that Dr. Cook had lost his mind, or even that the letter was from someone pretending to be him.

But another one was coming, for I had written "Yes" on the envelope. How, having read the letter, could I have told him not to write to me again? My head was spinning. If the claims made by Dr. Cook were true, my father had gone from being a man whom I could not remember to one whom I had never met.

My father had always been a stranger to me, in life, in death. And now, it seemed, in life again. Now this stranger had a different name and was still alive. Both my fathers were doctors turned explorers. There was little to distinguish one from the other except that one had written me a letter.

I remembered phrases from it, not bothering to consult the copy in my pocket. "The cold blood of biology." "How this can change, I am unable to foresee." "You hold in your hands a document... that if made public could do me and mine great harm." The original document could have done him great harm. My copy, as Uncle Edward had said, could harm no one but me were I to show it to others.

Why had he written to me? If, as he hinted, we could never meet, never appear in public as father and son—if he did not even want me to write him back—why had he written to me? Why did he think that writing to me would restore his courage? He had more or less admitted, in the first few paragraphs, that he had nearly lost his mind.

And my mother. To think that she had allowed, even encouraged, me to think that her absent husband was my father, all the time knowing he was not. Our short life together was not what she had made it seem. Every moment of it had been undercut by irony, by what she knew and I did not, a bit of knowledge that she must have planned to withhold from me forever.

I started back towards home, wondering if I should tell Aunt Daphne. I had not, by the time of my arrival, made up my mind. When I opened the door, she was coming down the hall to meet me, all but running.

"There you are," she said. "My God, you're so late getting home from school I was about to... Edward didn't find anything wrong with you, did he? Devlin, what did he say?"

I would have spoken, said no to prevent her from jumping to the wrong conclusion, but I did not trust my voice.

"Devvie?"

I shook my head and gulped hard to keep from crying.

"Darling, you look... What did Edward say?"

"He said I'm fine," I said quickly. I gulped again.

"But *something's* wrong. What is it?"

I doubted that I could make any explanation sound convincing.

"It's just something I don't want to talk about, that's all. Something Moses Prowdy said."

"You're sure Edward found nothing wrong with you?"

I nodded. "Ask him if you like."

I went upstairs to my room and lay down. Was it possible that *she* knew, that she, too, had misled me all my life? I decided I would hold off from telling her, at least until the next letter came.

I thought of how it would be. Entering my father's office by the door reserved for him. Opening the desk drawer. Reading the letter. Making my copy. Watching Uncle Edward burn the original.

The day after my talk with my uncle, I half expected him to come downstairs for breakfast with a red handkerchief in his vest pocket. He wore a blue one instead, and a green one the day after that.

It was hard to think about anything else knowing that a letter was on its way to me from Dr. Cook. Pointless to expect a letter any sooner than three months from now, Uncle Edward had said. Every morning for three months, I looked to see what colour handkerchief he wore, revelling in the day when he would come downstairs with the red one protruding from his pocket.

When the three months was up, three months to the day from when Uncle Edward had called me to his office, his handkerchief was grey. What, I asked myself, were the chances that my uncle's estimate of when the letter would arrive would be exact? It meant nothing that the letter had not come.

How eagerly, from then on, I waited to see what he'd be wearing when he came downstairs. It was hard to hide my disappointment when there was either no handkerchief or one that wasn't red. I ate my eggs and toast and gulped my tea with consolatory gusto. How strange it seemed that my mood depended on the colour of my uncle's handkerchief.

I went through the same thing every morning for the *next* three months. Finally, I began to wonder if something was wrong. Perhaps my uncle had changed his mind about acting as "postman" for Dr. Cook. Surely, if he had, he would break our agreement never to speak about the letters and not leave me wondering forever what was wrong. Or perhaps Dr. Cook had changed *his* mind, decided that he could not trust Uncle Edward after all, or that he would make no further revelations to me, a mere boy.

I considered pretending I was sick so I could go to see Uncle Edward at his office, but I thought better of it. Around the house, he was careful that we were never alone together. In the company of Aunt Daphne, he looked at me and spoke to me as he always had.

I remembered a paragraph from Dr. Cook's official "report" on my father's death: "Though it moves the mystery no closer to being solved, it seems worthwhile to point out that the strange case of Dr. Stead is by no means the strangest in the annals of Arctic exploration. Others have disappeared as surely as if, while sleepwalking, they attempted a crossing of the crevassed glaciers onto which not even the Eskimos will venture after dark." This man from whom I was waiting to receive a letter about my father might easily be dead.

As I lay in my warm bed, as I watched Aunt Daphne pile up heaping helpings on my dinner plate, I wondered where at that moment Dr. Cook was, wondered about his safety as I never had about my father's.

· CHAPTER SIX ·

NEARLY SIX MONTHS AFTER OUR MEETING, BY WHICH TIME I HAD
almost given up hope of hearing from Dr. Cook, Uncle Edward came
downstairs for breakfast wearing the red paisley handkerchief. How
conspicuous it seemed. It seemed impossible that Aunt Daphne would
not guess why he was wearing it. As hard as it had been to hide my
succession of disappointments, hiding my elation now was all but
impossible. I was sure that my face matched the colour of the handkerchief, at which I could not stop staring. My heart was pounding.
Uncle Edward was his usual impassive self. Not even I who knew what
he must be thinking, how anxious he must be that I do or say nothing
to make his wife suspicious, could detect in his face anything unusual.
How would I make it through a morning of school?

Somehow I did, and at lunchtime I went to Devon Row, crossed
the street, stopped. A hansom cab went by, but there were no pedestrians. I went around to the back, opened the gate, let myself in
through the door marked "Doctor's Entrance Only," closed it quietly
behind me, then tiptoed up the stairs.

Uncle Edward was sitting in a chair on the landing, far enough
from the window that he could not be seen from the outside. He was
no longer wearing the red handkerchief. (But he was wearing it later,
when he came home from work.) On the upper of his crossed legs was
a book from which he glanced just long enough to put a finger to his
lips. With a shooing motion of his hand, he indicated that I should not
stop but go straight into the office.

The rear door of it was wide open, left that way by him, no doubt, so that his nurse and his patients across the hall would not hear me. I pictured him sitting there on the landing the past few minutes, dreading my audible arrival. I went inside. I had been there once or twice before, but never by myself. I could hear murmuring from across the hall. A shadow fell across the frosted glass of my father's door. A man putting on his hat. On the desk, there was nothing but a blotter and the pen my father had used to write prescriptions and referral letters, attached to the metal holder in which it stood by a gleaming silver chain. And his beach-rock paperweight, which rested on the far right corner of the blotter. The only wall-hanging was his Edinburgh diploma. There was an empty bookcase with glass doors, a dark brown leather sofa whose armrests were scrolled with studs of brass.

The top drawer of the desk was open. Another precaution. It was as if Uncle Edward was sitting there in the gloom with his finger to his lips. Looking up at me from the otherwise empty drawer of the desk was an envelope that bore my name. DEVLIN. Only that. No doubt mailed like the first one, I thought, inside another envelope addressed to Uncle Edward. It bore no postmark, no return address. It was slit open. I took from inside it a note that read: "Just a rehearsal. No letter yet." I replaced it in the envelope.

Bitter with disappointment, I went back out to the landing. Uncle Edward extended his hand. I gave him the envelope. We went back inside. He struck a match, held it to the envelope, which he stood flame down in the grate of the fireplace so that in seconds there was nothing left but a wisp of glowing ash. Eyes fixed on it, he motioned with his hand for me to leave. I walked down the stairs slowly, as per his instructions.

Only a few days later, he wore the red handkerchief again. I suspected another gratuitous rehearsal.

Again he was in the chair on the landing, with what looked like the same book as before on his lap. I went straight into my father's surgery.

Again Uncle Edward had opened the envelope, slit it so cleanly he might have used a scalpel. But it looked to me as if he had not removed the letter from inside. He had opened it as a precaution, to reduce the rustle and ripping of paper. I eased a sealed letter from the envelope, broke the seal, which was made of red wax and bore the imprint of a sailing ship. There was not just a single page as before, but several, tightly folded. I eased them open and began to read.

My dearest Devlin:

When Francis Stead took me aside on the North Greenland expedition, he said that twelve years before, in 1880, his wife had attended a party thrown for the graduates of the College of Physicians and Surgeons at Columbia University. He correctly named the man and woman at whose house the party was held. Your mother told Francis Stead that at this party, she had got drunk and been taken advantage of by someone about whom she remembered nothing, not even his face or name. She could remember nothing of the party, she said, but the first half-hour. Her next memory was of waking up just before dawn, alone, in one of the many bedrooms of a strange house. As a result of this encounter, she was pregnant.

Your mother, when we met, had told me neither the first nor the last name of her fiancé, so I had, up to the point where Francis began his story, no idea what my fellow medical officer and I had in common.

He was in mid-story when I realized who he was, who I was, that the supposedly nameless, faceless man she had met at that party was me. "Amelia." Not even when he first said her name did I suspect a thing, though of course I noted the coincidence. Bit by excruciating bit, I learned the truth. I had fathered a boy whose name was Devlin Stead, and who was being raised by his aunt and uncle. I could barely keep from crying when Francis told me that his wife was dead, when it hit me that the woman whom he said had accidentally drowned was my Amelia.

I am the cause of all of it, I thought as he kept on talking, all that has taken place without my knowledge. His abandonment of you and her, the ruination of his life, the awful state of mind he was in. Even, in a way, the death of my Amelia, who, had she never met me, would have been led by the dictates of chance away from the accident that took her life. And later I would blame myself for the death of Francis Stead.

It took a great deal of effort to keep my composure. I sat there listening, one of the characters in his tale, but acting as though I was waiting to hear what would happen next. Had a third man been present, I'm sure he would have noticed the effect Francis Stead's story had on me. But Francis was too absorbed in the telling of his story to notice.

"I was not with her before we married," Francis said to me. He looked at me to be sure I knew what he meant by "with her." I nodded.

He said that your mother implored him to keep her secret, which there were two ways of doing. He and your mother chose the more honourable one: they told their families that she was pregnant by him. Their wedding soon after followed.

"Nor was I with her after our marriage," Francis Stead said as he walked away from me.

A few nights later, he disappeared from Redcliffe House. Most of what I wrote in the report that appeared in the papers is true, as is what was written later in The New York Times. *Francis Stead, long before he confided in me, did have a falling-out with Peary and did ask for permission to remain up north after the rest of us had left for home. His interest in the Eskimos exceeded even my own, which is considerable.*

Peary forbade him to stay behind, and they did not speak for months. Although I do not wish to imply that Peary was in part to blame for Francis Stead's death—I myself, as I have said, must bear the blame—I can tell you that I will never again be a member of an expedition led by Peary. I will have no more to do with the man and so will say no more about him.

What follows is the full story of what happened in Manhattan eighteen years ago.

Your mother had a cousin named Lily in Manhattan. Her mother and Lily's had been close sisters. Now Amelia's mother was dead and Lily's a widow who had remarried.

They had decided by correspondence that although they had never met, Lily would be the maid of honour at Amelia's wedding, which would take place in St. John's. To Amelia, it was a way of honouring her mother's memory, to name as her maid of honour the daughter of the woman her mother had been closest to.

Lily invited your mother to spend a few weeks in New York with her so that they could get to know each other before the wedding. She in turn would spend the few weeks immediately before the wedding in St. John's. It would be a chance for your mother to spend time away from Newfoundland, which she had never done and, life being what it was, might never do if she waited until after she was married.

The two of them attended a graduation party for Columbia medical students.

There was a great deal of drinking done by the young men and women. Among the latter was your mother who, like the other young women, was not so used to drinking as the men were. Perhaps she had never had more than a glass or two before.

I was not a guest at the party. I was just sixteen years old. I had a weekday job as an office boy, and on the weekends, I did whatever odd jobs I could find. The couple, both doctors, the man a professor of medicine at Columbia, the woman a homeopath, hired four boys about my age to help out at the party, a notorious annual event that no serving girl, no matter how needful of work, would have had anything to do with. We fixed and served drinks, served food, cleaned up discarded plates and glasses to make way for others.

Even in being hired as a servant for this party, I was above my station. The other three boys were the sons of doctors, semi-guests for whom helping out at the party was a rite of passage to Columbia.

The real-estate agency for which I collected rent was owned by the couple who threw the party but managed by someone else. The couple made one of their rare visits to the office at a time when I happened to be there. They engaged me in conversation. When I told them that my deceased father had been a doctor, they became very interested in me. The woman, one of the few women doctors of any kind in the country, wanted to know where my father had "gone to school." All I knew was that it had been somewhere in Germany— Hamburg, I thought.

I remember the expression on the woman's face when I said "Hamburg." It was not unkind or condescending, but knowing. She knew my family story in an instant. My parents were immigrants from Germany, where my father had been not a doctor but a "doctor." Dr. Koch. He had somehow gained enough knowledge of medicine that the people of the small town where he came from, and where he "practised," called him Doctor. His patients, having no money, paid him with what they grew or raised on their farms. The same was true of the people of the small town in New York State to which he immigrated, and where, despite being a doctor, he died of a disease, pneumonia, to which the New World poor were prone, leaving us to eke out an existence like any immigrant family. (Like you, Devlin, I grew up without a father.) My family moved from Port Jervis to New York. I pitched in with my three brothers to help support the family when I was old enough to work. I saw that this woman saw all this, and perhaps she detected in my face some measure of humiliation or resentment. At any rate, she invited me to be a servant at their party. I eagerly accepted.

Although I had told no one, I wanted to be a doctor because my father had been one. How serving sandwiches and drinks to medical students and professors would bring me closer to that goal I didn't know, but I sensed it would. I told my mother on Saturday morning that, as I often did, I was going over to Manhattan to see if someone would hire me to do chores at Fulton Market. Instead, after killing time in Manhattan, I went at five o'clock to the address they had given me.

The eldest of us four boys was drunk before the party was an hour old. When they saw that no one seemed to notice, the other boys sipped from every drink they made before they served it.

I had never been at such an event before. The house was so crowded that the guests had to keep their drinks up in the air to keep their glasses from being crushed.

I assumed it was a typical New York party. There was enough food there to feed my family of six for a year. Everywhere there were sandwiches that had been nibbled and then put aside; the same with helpings of smoked salmon, chunks of watermelon, wedges of grape-fruit. There were such things as pâté, caviar, aspic, which I had never seen before, did not know the names of or how they should be served. These nameless dishes, too, went uneaten, were barely picked at. I thought the food had to have something wrong with it. I would not have eaten a morsel anyway, though I was starving, for the other three boys showed no interest in the food, and being naïve enough not to realize that my clothes gave me away, I wanted those boys to think I was just like them.

This was not my world. I had for hours been moving about in a world that, before that day, I had got only glimpses of. I had walked along the city streets at night, taking home from work short-cuts that wound through neighbourhoods like this one. I had looked in through the large windows from across the street, the best vantage point from which to see into such houses, since it was impossible from the near sidewalk to see anything above the level of the windowsills but chandeliers. In the brightly lit rooms of these houses, I had seen briefly, not daring to stop and stare for long, groups of men and women in what I now know was evening dress sitting down to dinner, waited on by maids and butlers who, for all the attention that was paid them, might as well have been invisible. I had seen young families, a man and a woman watching from their chairs as their children ran about. My family, the six of us, lived in

two rooms in a section of Brooklyn known as Williamsburg. We
were a stone's throw from the East River and forever in the shadow
of what we called the sugar towers, a sugar refinery whose days were
longer than my mother's, and from which the noise of men and
machines and the sickly smell of liquid sugar issued ceaselessly.

Now, this day, I was in one of these very houses, had spoken to
people who lived in others like it, had served liquor and carried trays
of food such as I had never seen before.

They kept on drinking, the other three boys, not even bothering
to hide what they were doing, for after a while the party guests
began to serve themselves.

There were a pair of fiddlers in one room, playing reels that
Lily, announcing your mother's "Irish" heritage, insisted Amelia
dance to. She had done quite a lot of step-dancing as a child
and was soon alone in the middle of the room while the others
clapped along.

It was early summer, much warmer in New York than she was
used to. She removed her jacket. She was wearing a plain bodice
with a row of buttons down the front, a flounced skirt with drapes,
stockings and buttoned boots. The skirt came barely to her knees, so
it was good for dancing.

Whenever she declared that she was thirsty I was called for, and
there was much amusement as, with the guests urging me to work
faster, I fixed her a drink and brought it to her. If not for the dancing, I think she would have been sick.

The point came when she could dance no longer. As soon as she
stopped, she fainted, or began to. I caught her. There was a great outburst of applause and cheers, which was so loud that they revived
her somewhat and I managed with Lily's help to get her to her feet,
though she kept saying that the room was spinning.

Lily said it might be best if they went home, but your mother
was adamant that both she and Lily would stay. She said that if
she could lie down for a short time, she would be all right. Lily,
whom I could tell was reluctant to leave such a lively party, agreed

that a lie-down might be just the thing. There would be no harm in it if your mother fell asleep. We led her to the stairs, at the foot of which she stopped and said that she could go the rest of the way herself. She went up the stairs quite briskly, God knows how, and Lily turned back to the party.

I followed her up the stairs. On the landing, she made for a door and either tripped on something or fainted again. She fell forward and instinctively threw out her arms to break her fall.

"Are you all right, miss?" I said.

She turned her head and looked up at me. She had the most remarkably large, round eyes, blue though her hair was black.

"I hope you haven't hurt yourself," I said. "I think there is altogether too much drinking being done. You are not used to it. Not like the others seem to be. The last two drinks I gave you were water, and you didn't seem to notice."

"What's your name?" she said, and I detected what I thought was an English accent. I assumed that any accent I had never heard before was English.

"Fred," I said. It seemed absurdly short, too abrupt to be a name, an impression she confirmed when she said, "I am Amelia." Six syllables, four of them her name. I am Amelia. I could not have said, "I am Frederick," without sounding ridiculous, but she sounded as if Amelia was not just her name but what she was.

I crouched down on one knee, one foot on the floor. Our eyes were level and inches apart. "Where do you live?" she said.

"Brooklyn," I said. "Where do you live?"

"Newfoundland," she said. "But I've been telling people I'm from Ireland just so I don't have to explain where Newfoundland is."

"Ships on their way from England and on their way up north stop off in Newfoundland," I said. "I've never been there. I've never been anywhere except Brooklyn and Manhattan."

"Who would need to go anywhere else if they lived here?" she said.

I saw that she was looking at my clothes.

"Each thing belongs to someone different," I said. "My brother;" I pointed at my trousers. "My uncle;" I pointed at my vest. Not even my shoes were mine, I said, explaining that they had belonged to my father, who had died some years ago.

"You are a very kind young man," she said. When she smiled at me, I looked away for a moment, then met her eyes again.

"You should go home," I said. "I'll get your friend."

"Cousin," she said. "Cousin and dear friend. But I'm all right."

"You're a good dancer," I said.

"It's been years since I danced like that. When I was a girl. It's funny, dancing by yourself. I'd never do it back home in St. John's, now that I'm grown up. I don't know why they taught us if they wanted us to stop once we grew up."

"You're getting married soon," I said, looking at her engagement ring.

"Yes," she said, also looking at the ring. "Eighteen and engaged to be married. He's a doctor." She fell silent.

"Do you like New York?"

"It's so much bigger than St. John's. But yes, I do like it. I wonder what sort of person I'd be if I had lived here all my life."

"My mother's never come across the river to Manhattan," I said. "She says she doesn't like the look of it from Brooklyn."

She laughed.

"Someday," I told her, "you're going to be very happy." She looked at me, wondering, I think, if her unhappiness was as obvious to everyone as it was to me. She smiled, as if to assure me that she was not universally regarded as unhappy. A young man born into poverty feeling sympathy for her. Any other such man she would have resented perhaps, dismissed his sympathy as presumptuous. But she said later that she could see that I did not begrudge the privileges conferred on the people at that party by accidents of birth. She said she believed that to inquire into the natures of other people

was the main pleasure of my life. Which in part was true.

"It's just that I feel a little out of place," she said, but she looked as though she were pondering some deeper discontent.

"Playing marbles, are we?" a voice behind us said. It was Lily, at last come to see how your mother was doing.

"She just tripped," I said.

Lily and I helped your mother to her feet.

"I'll take it from here," Lily said, and led her off to a room down the hallway. I went back downstairs.

She said she thought of me often the next day, how I seemed to know how coming to New York had made her feel, knew the doubts she had about her fiancé, the many times she thought about escaping, walking away from her life, losing Lily in the crowd, losing herself in the limitless swarms of Manhattan rather than returning to Newfoundland.

She asked Lily to arrange for us to meet again. Lily knew right from the start that your mother was taken with me. She, too, knew that your mother was unhappy. It was obvious that your mother had told her so, perhaps in a letter. It might have been for this reason that Lily invited her to New York. I think Lily saw me not as a marriage prospect, a replacement fiancé, but as the first of many steps your mother needed to take to extricate herself from her situation back home.

With Lily's help, we met almost every day for the duration of your mother's stay in Manhattan. The three of us went to pleasure palaces—amusement parks, we call them now—panoramas, museums, vaudeville shows at Tammany Hall, art galleries, theatres. We walked about in Long Acre Square, a neighbourhood built by a rich family called the Astors. They call it Times Square now. It has become famous for its high-class "houses," which are known as silk-hat brothels.

Lily was our chaperone, our alibi, our disguise. So that your mother and I could link ours, we all three linked arms, Lily and your mother on either side of me as we strolled down Broadway, *looking at the stores. To observers, we hoped, Lily would appear to be "with" your mother as much as I did, and Lily as much with me as your mother did. Lily walked with us, hardly saying a word as your mother and I talked, sometimes trailing slightly behind when she sensed that we would like some time alone.*

Your mother and I sat on benches in the parks while Lily idled up and down in front of us beneath her parasol.

We went to the largest of the pushcart markets, the one on the Lower East Side. The city has changed much since your mother was there, but even then the Lower East Side seemed to her so dense with people and with buildings that she found herself gasping for breath, clinging to Lily or me as we walked unmindfully along.

There were markets everywhere, in most parts of the city, sudden swarms of people in the distance that always made your mother think an accident had happened or a fight was taking place—the usual reasons, she said, for which crowds gathered outdoors in St. John's.

I told her that more than half a million people lived on the island of Manhattan. More than two million people live there now. That New York seems to me like nothing next to this one.

To think, she said, that on an island thirteen miles long and two miles wide, not all of which was inhabited, there were five times as many people as lived in all of Newfoundland. She was overwhelmed by the density and clamour.

The Brooklyn Bridge was not quite finished, but you could see it from almost everywhere in Brooklyn or Manhattan, arching off into space at such an angle that from one side of it you couldn't see the other. It was being built from both sides and would be joined in the middle. As the middle span was not in place, each half seemed suspended in mid-air, as if the span that joined the arches had collapsed. It was such a spectacle, she said, seemed so perfect as it was, that she forgot it would soon have a practical purpose.

There were so many vessels in the river you could barely see the water. We crossed from shore to shore on ferries just to feel the cooling East River breeze.

Lily and I took her to see Trinity Church, then the highest structure in Manhattan, a towering Gothic Revival at Broadway and Wall Street.

We took cable cars and elevated trains throughout Manhattan. The latter were very popular because, the joke went, the only way to avoid the red-hot cinders, oil and coal ash that rained down from the steam-powered el was to ride the wretched thing. Cinders burnt holes in the awnings that stretched out above the sidewalks, landed on horses and pedestrians, the latter examining their hats for damage and choking on the dust as the train rattled overhead. Everyone cursed the el except its passengers. It was great fun. Most of the lines are electrified now, not as much of a nuisance as before.

Manhattan filled your mother with all sorts of conflicting feelings: on the one hand a craving for privacy and space, on the other a yearning to feel at home as Lily did, as she thought I did.

It made her miss her fiancé, she said, and it made her wish that they had never met. (Neither she nor Lily ever spoke the first or last name of Francis Stead.) One moment, she wanted to leave for home as soon as possible, and the next, she could not imagine ever living in St. John's again.

She had always suspected that, in the greater world, families like hers were "insignificant" or "unimportant." But these words, she now saw, were inadequate. She was witnessing the collective pursuit of something for which its pursuers had no name, for which no one knew the grand design, though everyone acted as if there was one. Newfoundland's complete obliteration would not have made one person in this city pause, she said. If Newfoundland were to vanish from the earth, it would not slow down the progress of the Brooklyn Bridge.

"Some of the men building the bridge are from Newfoundland," I said.

"The replaceable ones," she said. "The ones who are interchangeable with all the other men who have come from far away to build that bridge."

She said that Lily's "crowd" seemed limitless. At a succession of dinners and parties, she had not seen the same face twice. She wondered what Lily's impression of St. John's would be. For the first time in her life, she felt insecure, inadequate in social situations.

She told a woman that she was from Newfoundland. "Oh, yes," the woman said. "I've heard of it, I think. Where did you learn English?"

There were times, she said, when it occurred to her how easy it would be here to escape. She would look at the Manhattan span of the great bridge arching off into the sky like some monument to opportunity, and it would occur to her that if she wanted to, she could simply disappear. Unlike in St. John's, it would take no effort. She could simply walk away. She pictured herself boarding a ferry and sitting alone as it made its way across the Hudson River to New Jersey. That was as far as her imagination took her. Where she was headed, what her plans were, how she would support herself, she stopped short of considering. All she wanted was to escape.

Escape. Escape from what? I asked her. She merely shrugged.

The three of us took a hansom cab one evening along Madison Avenue, which was a residential street for the well-off but not quite rich, and then we turned off into Central Park. The windows were open, the canvas top was rolled back. Your mother said she had not looked up at the night sky since coming to New York. It was clear, but the stars were not as bright as in the sky above St. John's.

"They say that at night, from the high point of the Brooklyn Bridge, Manhattan looks like the sky," she said. "Constellations of lights with nothing but darkness in between them. Don't you think that's wonderful?"

I told her I thought it was. Central Park at night. A wilderness within the city, enclosed by the city. It no longer seems quite so wild as it once did. That descent into the park conferred upon those who made it some sort of exemption from inhibition. It was like bathing at the seashore or being at the seashore after dark. This, it seemed, was the purpose of the park: to allow the furtive expression of things that people of a certain class must otherwise pretend do not exist. The clopping of horses' hoofs. The murmured conversations that would stop as you went past, then resume again. The unlit parts of the path between one gas lamp and the next. The grass a silver sheen of dew down where it was cooler. The smell of the water through the trees. You could faintly hear the treetop breeze, though on the ground the air was still. Things were said there that could not be said elsewhere, desires admitted to, secret fears and hopes acknowledged. You were never unaware that you were hemmed in by the unseen city. The knowledge that none of this would last was necessary to the effect. It cast over everything an elusive, wistful, enjoyable sadness. To leave the park, to go back up into the city, was like waking from a dream. No one ever spoke of the dream, and most of it was soon forgotten.

Poor discreet and patient Lily, pretending that we were not whispering, that my arm was not around your mother's waist, that she was unaffected by the park, that she alone was able to resist its spell.

"They say that by 1900, every inch of Manhattan will be so lit up the stars will be invisible," your mother said. By 1900. Not long from now. She had every reason to think that she would live to see if this was true. It is not. You can still, in Manhattan, see the stars.

She told me, as we sat the next day in Madison Square Park and Lily, as if by prearrangement, walked farther from us than usual, that she was engaged to a man she did not love and did not wish to marry.

At first, I did not know what to say.

"He is very kind," she said. "He comes from a good family, as do I, though my parents are deceased. We are said to be a 'good match.' Many good matches make good marriages. But this one will not. I should have declined his proposal. Now it seems to be too late."

"It is not too late," I said. "You are not yet married. You should not make yourself unhappy just because of how it would look if you changed your mind. Perhaps you are not cut out for

marriage. Or is it that you think marriage to some other man
would make you happy?"

She looked at me.

"I have met the man who would make me happy," she said.

"I believe you have," I said.

On her second-last day in New York, knowing that she would
be expected to spend the last day with Lily's family, we met one
final time, without Lily's help or knowledge.

We intended only to have one afternoon completely to ourselves, to say what, in the company or near proximity of Lily, we
dared not say. But we found that even without Lily, we could not
speak as intimately as we wished to, not in public. She said she felt
as though she was in St. John's and everyone was watching us. I
said that, as large and crowded as Manhattan was, I had sometimes
encountered acquaintances by accident while walking in the street.

We agreed that we should find somewhere private where we
could talk. When I told her that I knew of a cheap but respectable
hotel on lower Broadway, she nodded and looked briefly at me in a
way that I knew I would never forget. How beautiful she was. "I
love you," I whispered.

We took separate cabs there, arrived separately and rented separate rooms. We would not have been allowed to register together
without proof that we were married—nor, even had we been
allowed, could we have endured the awkwardness and embarrassment of doing so. For a young woman to register alone was
embarrassment enough.

I registered first, then read a paper in the lobby until she
arrived. She held her key so that I could see the number, then went
upstairs. Fifteen minutes later, I joined her in her room.

Alone, secretly alone at last. Soon to part, soon to be a thousand miles apart, but together now. For hours, together in that room
into which sounds drifted from the outside world, from the oblivious
swarm of people passing on the street below. It did not seem possible
to me, as we lay there in each other's arms, that anyone else had

ever been in love. For a short while she slept, her forehead against my cheek, her warm breath on my neck.

It occurs to me now that I knew, I must have known, that she was risking more than I was. I was risking losing her. She was risking everything.

Over and over, we said we loved each other. I asked her if she would marry me, and she said yes. I told her that when she returned to Manhattan, I would give her an engagement ring.

I told her that she had to formally break off her engagement with her fiancé before we met again and make a public announcement of it in the papers, saying that the decision to end the engagement was wholly hers and not motivated by anything said or done by her fiancé, whose conduct, throughout the term of their acquaintanceship, had been above reproach. She would move to Manhattan and live with Lily, and we would then begin a courtship that would lead, without unseemly haste, to our engagement and eventual marriage. Until her prior engagement had been severed, we would say nothing to Lily—nor, though your mother said she was certain of her support no matter what the circumstances, would we ever tell her about our afternoon together.

If we proceeded cautiously, there would be no scandal, I told her, only at worst some short-lived rumours as to how and when we met relative to the end of her first engagement.

She said it would be best if I did not write to her.

We parted. She went back home.

I received letters from her, through Lily, sometimes two or three a day, unopened. Lily knew which letters addressed to her were for her and which for me because mine bore an X beside her name.

The letters from your mother contained no news, only expressions of anticipation and impatience with herself for not having yet worked up the nerve to do what she knew had to be done. After one in which she wrote, "I will tell him very soon," they stopped coming.

I never heard from her again.

*After three weeks, Lily came to me to pass on, she said, a mes-
sage from Amelia, who wanted me to know that she and her fiancé
would soon be married.*

*For a long time, I was so fretful I could neither eat nor sleep.
She had changed her mind. She had fallen in love not with me, but
with Manhattan, with the fantasy of leaving Newfoundland, with
her dreams of nebulous escape—escape not just from a marriage to a
man she did not love, but from everything she was disenchanted
with. Or perhaps she really did love her fiancé. I found that thought
especially intolerable.*

*I know now, of course, that she did what she thought was best
for everyone. I have known it since Francis Stead confided in me.
She married the man who loved her, but whom she did not love.
Spared me from scandal because she loved me, from having to choose
between her and the good reputation that I had made clear to her I
was determined I would have one day.*

*The hosts of the party at which I met your mother took it
upon themselves to better me. I became their protégé. They treated
me as I am sure they would not have if they knew my secret. They
invited me to help out at their annual party every year until I
myself became a medical student. I dared not decline their invitations for fear that it would make them lose interest in me.*

*At every party, I invented some excuse to go upstairs so that I
could see the hallway where I met the woman with the strange
accent who had said, "I am Amelia."*

*The couple helped me earn my way through college, loaning me
money first for a printing business and then to expand a small
milk-and-cream company that I ran with my brothers. In 1887, they
helped get me accepted to the College of Physicians and Surgeons at
Columbia, convincing the college deans that as the son of a "physician," I should have my matriculation fee reduced. The balance of it,
they paid.*

*I am friendly with them to this day, though when my family
moved to another part of the city, making a commute to Columbia*

impossible for me, I transferred to the New York University medical school and did not see my patrons as often as before.

I do not go to their annual parties, which they still hold at their house. I am rarely in the city when these parties are held, but even when I am, I stay away, for the house contains too many memories for me, memories that have been unpleasant ones since the day Francis Stead confided in me.

Devlin, I am, however indirectly, to blame for the deaths of both your mother and Francis Stead. She was so dazzled, so over-whelmed by New York that her better judgment was overthrown. I have no such excuse. When Francis told me of your mother's death, I felt such shame, such guilt as I had never felt before—which, only days later, was compounded when he disappeared. For years, I have lived with the burden of this secret, trying to convince myself that I was not to blame, that however shamefully I acted when I took advantage of your mother, I could not possibly have foreseen the con-sequences.

For years, I have tried without success not to think of you, the boy who was parentless because of me, the third and only surviving victim of my recklessness. The son of the woman who, though I knew her for but three weeks, I am still in love with. Recently, after my torment reached its height with such effects as I described to you in my first letter, I realized that I had to make myself known to this boy whom I alone knew to be my son. That and nothing else would do. That, it seemed to me, would be a first step towards redressing the harm I have done. A part of her lives on in you. I am done with pretending to myself that you do not exist.

Francis Stead put forward sufficient proof to convince me that what he said was true, but you, being unfamiliar with the people and the places he named, may still have your doubts. I believe that, upon reflection, you will realize there exists no motive that would cause me to mislead you on this matter.

To confess is to ask forgiveness, but it would be presumptuous of me to ask for yours so soon. Instead, I ask only that you renew your promise of discretion, if you still think any request of mine to be worth honouring, and your permission to write to you again. (As before, write "Yes" or "No" on the envelope.)

I am not yet ready to meet you, but I hope that by the time I am, I will, in your judgment, have earned the right to do so, and that by then, you will find the idea of such a meeting as appealing as I do. I wait in hope for your reply.

Yours truly,
Dr. Frederick Cook

March 14, 1898

P.S. I must ask that you not write to me. For reasons I cannot now explain, it will be better for both of us if you do not.

How many boys had ever been spoken to about their mothers as he, by way of proving that he was my father, had spoken to me about mine? Was ever a person given so detailed an account of the circumstances of his own conception? By anyone, let alone his father? How easily the most intimate details seemed to flow from the mind and the pen of Dr. Cook. All this he was relating to the son who had issued from his one encounter with my mother. I doubted that most men would have been anywhere near that forthcoming, even in a letter to a friend. Far from being offended, I was greatly flattered.

I wrote "Yes" on the envelope, then copied out the letter on blank pages that I withdrew from the pocket of my jacket, writing furiously, for I feared that sooner or later Uncle Edward would grow impatient, come inside and burn the original whether or not my copy was complete.

I copied Dr. Cook's letter word for word, punctuation mark for punctuation mark. I as good as had the real thing with me when I left. I had no intention of showing it to anyone. I did not doubt my own ability to keep a secret or to keep a mere few pages hidden from the world. (I put this letter, as I had done with the first one and would do with all the others that came after it, inside a bedpost in my room, the top of which, as I had discovered by accident when I was eight, unscrewed quite easily. I scrolled the letters, one inside the other, knowing they would last longer this way than if I folded them.)

I went out to the landing, handed the original and the envelope to Uncle Edward, who, receiving them silently, did not look up from his book as he rose from his chair. I followed him inside. I stood silently at the fireplace while he performed again the solemn ritual of burning the letter. He struck a match and lit the envelope, which he placed flame down in the grate between two bars. We watched it.

When it was burnt, he nodded almost imperceptibly. I left, descended the stairs slowly, closed the outer door behind me and hurried to the garden gate.

The letter left me with no doubt that Dr. Cook was my father. I thought he put far more blame on himself than he deserved. The line of causation was clear, that of culpability much less so. But I supposed that when it came to such things as guilt and shame, rationality and logic mattered no more to Dr. Cook than they did to me. For I realized now that I had believed what Moses Prowdy had only hinted at: that it had been because of me, an accidental, unhoped-for child, that my parents married, that my father deserted my mother, and that my mother, and then my father, died.

How strange it was reading about my mother, being made to see her from someone else's point of view, that of a man who knew her when she was in no way defined by her relationship to me. The young woman in the letter was not the young woman in the photograph on which "Amelia, the wicked one" was written. She was posing in that photograph.

Poor Francis Stead. Even though she was pregnant by another man, he married her. Why? Because he loved her? Because she "implored him to keep her secret"? But once they were married, things must have changed.

I was glad that the man who disappeared on the North

Greenland expedition was not my father, not only because it restored my father to life, but because I was relieved to know that I was not the son of a man who had given in to desolation, a man whose death was a morbid enigma that those he left behind would never solve but would have hanging over them forever. I was still the son of just such a woman, but I, at least, was free of *him*. For me, the enigma of him was solved.

As for my mother, for five years she had harboured her shameful secret, keeping it from everyone, especially me, me the evidence of it, the ever-present reminder of it. All those years wondering if her husband would reveal their secret to someone else. Which in the end he did.

I would tell Aunt Daphne nothing, or else she would write to Dr. Cook, and that would almost certainly mean never hearing from Dr. Cook again. I felt guilty about deceiving her, but I told myself that by keeping silent, I would spare her feelings. She would not rest knowing there existed this Dr. Cook by whom she and Uncle Edward might be supplanted as my parents. I could not imagine telling her about an affair my mother had had when she was engaged, an affair of which I was the issue; could not imagine Aunt Daphne hearing from my lips that my mother had conceived me with a man she hardly knew, and that I bore to the man whom the world knew as my father no relation whatsoever. No, for my own sake and for hers, I would not tell her.

"Did my mother ever take a trip away from Newfoundland?" I could not resist asking Aunt Daphne one night at dinner when Uncle Edward was working late. I searched her face but saw nothing.

"Once," she said. "She went to New York. She had a cousin there named—what?—Lily, I think. Your second cousin. She invited her. Your mother was getting married soon. Lily told her she should see the world, a bit of it anyway, before she settled down."

"Did she say what New York was like?" I said.

"Oh, she said it was exciting. Lots of people." I searched her face again. Still nothing. It was something that hadn't crossed her mind in years.

My mother had gone to Francis Stead and told him she was

pregnant. I could not imagine what sort of exchange must have taken place between them.

Being a doctor, he could, if she was willing to go along with it, have chosen what Dr. Cook, by implication, called the less honourable option. I wondered if they had talked about it, the simple procedure that would have cut me off in pre-existence. "Nor was I with her *after* we were married." What a lonely marriage it must have been for both of them.

In my room at night, by the light of a candle, I read the letter over many times. How unlike any man I knew was Dr. Cook. He had written me a letter asking me for my forgiveness, my absolution. He seemed to think his sanity, his very life, depended on it. How much I would never have known if not for that letter, which, for all I knew about its author, might have fallen from the sky.

Another letter came.

My dearest Devlin:

I cannot tell you how happy you have made me. Your "Yes" has renewed my spirits and my courage. I did not, until hearing from your uncle Edward, quite believe that you were real.

My first marriage was to Libby Forbes, who died after giving birth to a child who lived but a few hours. A double sorrow from which, for a time, it seemed I would not recover. Anna Forbes, my fiancée, is Libby's sister. Anna, when I last saw her in New York, was ill, in part from fretting about what might happen to me on this voyage. All this is by way of saying that as yet I have no children except for you.

I am happy, Devlin. Or at least, for the first time in ages, I believe in the possibility of happiness. How differently you see the world, knowing, as I never really have done until now, that there exists in it a child of your creation, a person half composed of you.

In two days, we set out for Patagonia. Tomorrow I will write

*and send to you another letter. By the time you read it, I will have
arrived in Patagonia. My soul is on the move again. The world, for
so long stalled, has lurched into motion.*

*I am headed, once again, for the Old Ice. Those of us who have
been there cannot even tell each other how we feel about it. But I
know of no one who, having been there once, has not wished to go
again, no one who, by the mere sight of it, was not profoundly
changed.*

*An opaque, impenetrable wall divides those who have travelled
in the polar regions from those who have not. The first have seen
not only the best but also the worst of human nature. That polar
exploration brings out the "best" in men you will have often heard
it said. That it brings out the worst, never, unless in my letters to
you I have hinted at it. I daresay you believe that you understand
what, in the context of exploration, is meant by those two words,
best and worst. You do not, however, and nothing I could write
would make you understand. I have seen and done things that
make it impossible for me ever again to take seriously the great
game known as society. I should add that not taking a game seriously often makes one quite adept at playing it. Such is the case
with both me and Peary. The motives, the supposedly secret longings
of the non-explorer seem as transparent to me as those of children. I
am no longer misled or confused by language. The eyes, the face, the
colour of a man's complexion and the carriage of his body are as
revealing to me of his real self, whether I meet him on a Brooklyn
street, on the Old Ice or in some port in Patagonia. I once had my
ear bent for hours by a man whose measure I took in a few seconds
by the simple sound of his voice, a sound independent of, and usually at odds with, the meaning of the words he spoke. This is one of
the reasons I have asked that you not write back to me. By writing,
you would, without intending to, either cause me to see you as
someone you are not or, more likely, try to create what was so obviously a posture that it would dispose me against you. You may
think you have caught me at a double standard, may wonder why, if*

I am so distrustful, even disdainful, of language as to forbid you to write to me, I am writing to you. It has for obvious reasons been impossible for us to meet, but even if it had been possible, it would have been unwise. You are on the other side of the wall I spoke of earlier. I have been lobbing messages to you in the only language that you understand by the only means available to us.

Goodbye for now.
Yours truly,
Dr. F. A. Cook

August 3, 1898

CHAPTER SEVEN

THE LONELINESS AND TEDIUM OF THE MISFIT LIFE I HAD BEEN living was dispelled by the letters. They were my life outside the classroom and the house. Everything else—church; the outings to concerts, plays and picnics that Aunt Daphne was forever arranging for me in the vain hope that through them I would make some friends; even the readings with Aunt Daphne—were little more than distractions that made bearable the intervals between one letter and another, or the intervals between bouts of solitude, when I was content just to think about them. They were also ways of disguising, camouflaging, my obsession with the letters. Only when I was reading or re-reading them, or wondering when the next one would arrive and what it would contain, did I feel like I was going about the true business of my life. Perhaps, if not for the letters, I would have found, would have been forced to find, some way of fitting in.

But far from feeling that I was missing something, I believed that the life of the most popular boy at Bishop Feild did not come close to matching mine. In which boy's life was there such excitement as I felt when I climbed the stairs to "my father's" surgery, knowing that inside it there lay waiting for me a letter from the man who was secretly my father? It was the stuff of boy's adventure books. But to me, and only to me, Uncle Edward's strange contribution notwithstanding, was it real. Each time I slowly climbed the stairs, there was the inscrutably accommodating Uncle Edward, on whom Dr. Cook relied, on whom I relied, a mute sentinel requiring from me no tribute but discretion.

(Always the handkerchief was gone, and always it was back when he got home.)

Walking along the street, I would, just for the illicit fun of it, mutter to myself, "I am the son of Dr. Cook. I am the son of Dr. Cook. I am not the son of Dr. Francis Stead. Dr. Cook is my father, and Dr. Francis Stead is not." I made a game of it. How close dared I get to someone approaching me on foot, or someone I was catching up to, before I stopped chanting my secret out loud? Some people heard me—heard my voice, that is, heard the weird rhythm of it—but they could not make out the words. I didn't care that this behaviour earned me a reputation for talking to myself and prompted observations that I was clearly headed where my parents had gone.

In a way, the letters were almost as profound an intervention in my boyhood as physical confinement would have been.

I felt as though I was in them, contained by them, more set apart from everyone and everything around me than I had ever been. The world of the letters became my preferred one, and it made my own world seem less real, less substantial. I saw the danger in this, the danger of remaining so long in the letter world that the door to it would close behind me, trapping me inside. I imagined this happening, the better to revel in my power to prevent it, for I was certain that I could.

Indeed, a time came when I was no longer able to will myself away from his world. Walking to school, sitting in the classroom, I was there with Francis Stead and Dr. Cook on the North Greenland expedition when Francis Stead told him the story that, except for the ending, Dr. Cook already knew. I was side by side with Dr. Cook when, at age sixteen, he helped my mother up the stairs of that house in Manhattan in 1880. I walked home from the party with my mother, back to her cousin's house, and watched her as she lay on the bed, unable to sleep, though her eyes were closed. What Dr. Cook left out, I imagined in detail, fashioned lengthy stories out of single sentences. I sweltered with him in his quarters on the ship in South America when he awoke from nightmares, screaming. I watched him while he wrote to me, watched his face and sometimes his pen as it moved across the page, forming the words that, from having read them so many times, I knew by heart. I watched him write my name. DEVLIN. Six letters.

I went from reading him to hearing him. Phrases from his letters came unbidden to my mind, the voice that I invented for him declaiming at such volume while I sat in the front room that it seemed impossible that Aunt Daphne had not heard it or that I had not said the words out loud.

Once, in my room at night, I stared at the bedpost that contained the letters, all of them scrolled one inside the other. How easy it would be to burn them as Uncle Edward had burned the originals, tell Uncle Edward I had had enough; what a relief, in one way, it would be to never again have to wait in suspense at the breakfast table to see if Uncle Edward's handkerchief was red. The whole thing would be over.

But there was nothing in my life more precious to me than those letters. I could not imagine living without the expectation that another one was coming, without the thrill of being unable to foresee what path my life and Dr. Cook's would take.

I unscrewed the bedpost, unscrolled the letters, holding them open with two hands as I had seen done with navigation maps. "Dr. Cook is my father," I said. "He met my mother in New York in 1880." It gave me some relief to say the words out loud, right there in that house in which Francis Stead and my mother had once lived and Uncle Edward and Aunt Daphne now lay sleeping.

The one drawback for me, where the letters were concerned, and therefore the one advantage to Uncle Edward, was Aunt Daphne.

The letters subverted so much of what she believed was true.

I could think of nothing while in Aunt Daphne's company but that my whole life rested on a premise that I knew to be untrue, but that she still believed. *Francis Stead was not my father.*

My father had not been my father, and my mother, every moment that we spent together, had pretended that he was. I imagined her, pictured her sitting in the front room at night, reading or staring into the fire. There she sat, impassively keeping her secret to herself, dissembling with such self-incriminating ease. But this was not fair. It was not so that she could regard me as a fool that she had misled me. Nor to make Francis Stead one that she had married him.

Uncle Edward was not my uncle. I was in no way connected to the Steads by blood. Not even Uncle Edward knew this. It seemed he did not want to know why Dr. Cook was writing to me. So much wanted not to know that he made sure I witnessed the burning of each letter, which, when passed from his hand to mine, had been sealed. It was as if, in the event that our arrangement was discovered, I could testify to Aunt Daphne, to whomever, that he had not read the letters. Uncle Edward was assisting Dr. Cook in a subterfuge for reasons that he would not divulge. Uncle Edward and I were conspiring against Aunt Daphne, but not one word about this conspiracy ever passed between us. Duplicity was everywhere. I doubted that anyone was what he seemed to be. *I* was not what I seemed to be. I could not for a second forget what I was hiding, or who I was hiding it from.

"You don't seem to look forward to our readings or lose yourself in them like you used to," Aunt Daphne said. "I hope it's not because you think you're too grown up. Not because you think you're too old to be read to by your aunt." I assured her this was not the case. "I've been choosing all the books," she said. "Why don't you choose them for a while?"

I chose, borrowed from the library, books I knew she would like, all the while thinking what it would be like to divide between us my entire cache of letters and read them to each other.

I imagined Uncle Edward panicking, his carefully cultivated equanimity gone for good when he realized that what he was hearing from downstairs, from her lips and mine, were the forbidden words of Dr. Cook. I thought of how much, under other circumstances, she would have enjoyed having such letters read to her, and reading them to me. The person who could best appreciate what they meant to me was the last person who could know of their existence.

I could not help feeling that the balance of my allegiance had shifted from her to him, from my aunt to my uncle. He and I shared a secret that we kept from her. That this secret only increased the enmity between us did not matter.

As Uncle Edward was excluded, even if by choice, from the readings, Aunt Daphne was excluded from the letters, and not only from their contents, but from knowledge of their very existence. What were a few pages of some novel written fifty years ago to what was in those letters, whatever it might be, Uncle Edward's expression sometimes seemed to say. We shared knowledge and an arrangement for its conveyance from him to me that allied us more profoundly than she and I could ever be allied by reading to each other from Jane Austen or Fanny Burney.

She and I could read to each other as long and loudly as we liked, his expression seemed to say as, when we began to read, he went upstairs. He knew it for the sham it was, and me for the hypocrite I was. He didn't dare go so far as to make a face, or even smile at me, lest she detect it or he provoke me. But he so rarely looked at me that these looks could have had no other meaning but the one I gave them.

I *felt* like a hypocrite, especially when I read to her. I could not stand the sound of my voice, the sound of me compounding my betrayal of her with every word. I read tonelessly, for to read with feeling, with sincerity, made the whole thing seem like a joke at her expense, the words undercut with an irony that she was blind to and I shared with the absent but eavesdropping Uncle Edward. When she read, I felt chastened. It was as if, during the readings, there were now three of us: the two who read and the one who neither read nor listened, but sat there in subversive silence.

I half hoped that she would find us out. I imagined her saying something like: "Why is it that Edward always wears his red handkerchief on the day you have choir practice?" And then me confessing everything.

"What's wrong Devvie?" Aunt Daphne asked me one day in the study. "You haven't been yourself lately."

"I've changed for the better," I felt like saying. The "self" I hadn't been lately I didn't want to be. Why did she assume, from my having changed, that something was wrong? Because she knew of nothing to attribute the change to. But couldn't she see that I was happier, livelier?

"You seem so listless all the time," she said. "You look so tired, so pale."

What she saw was just the opposite of what I felt, but I looked in a mirror and was startled to find that she was right. What *I* saw was the opposite of what I felt. How could my inner and outer selves be so at odds?

"Maybe it's just adolescence," Aunt Daphne said.

I realized that I was exhausted. I had been drugged on euphoria for months, narcotized to the point of almost total self-absorption, literally feverish with an excitement that had started with Dr. Cook's first letter and had not abated since. It got so that to appraise myself in a mirror was more than I could bear.

"The boy has 'it,' too; just you wait," I heard a woman behind me say one Sunday as we were leaving church. Her tone suggested that people had been saying this or something like it for years. If Aunt Daphne and Uncle Edward overheard the remark, they gave no sign.

I wondered if this state that I had worked myself into was the first manifestation of "it." It didn't matter that I could point to a cause for feeling and looking as I did. In my mother's life, too, there had been such causes.

But the notion of my having "it" was based on *both* of my parents having had "it." And I knew that there was nothing in me of Francis Stead. And nothing of "it" in Dr. Cook. There was no reason to think that for keeping the same secret my mother had kept, I would pay the same price. It was not my secret nearly so much as it was hers. It was more for her and Dr. Cook that I was keeping it than for myself. And the burden of doing so was nothing like the one she had borne. I told myself it was absurd to think that because Aunt Daphne had said, "You haven't been yourself lately," she had detected in me what she thought might be the first signs of the morbid turn my mother took when she was in her late twenties. I watched her to see if she was watching me, to see if I could tell by her expression whether she was wondering if, as other people thought, "it" was in my blood. I saw nothing in her face, however, but the usual quiet confidence that no real harm would come to anyone while they were in her care.

She sent me to Uncle Edward for "another" check-up. "Just to be on the safe side," she said.

This time he actually gave me a check-up, examined me, poked and prodded, asked me questions. Not until just before I left did he refer even obliquely to the letters.

"Be careful how you act," he said. "You act like you think you're invisible. Be careful how you look. I hope your recent behaviour is not a prelude to something worse. A breakdown of some kind. You understand that I have not been involved in all of this, don't you?"

"Yes, of course I do," I said.

"And that nothing exists that could prove otherwise?"

"Yes."

If, as he said, there was no way that anyone could implicate him in anything, why was Uncle Edward so afraid? The likeliest result of my telling someone about Dr. Cook, or showing *my* copies of his letters that bore, in *my* handwriting, *his* signature, was that I would be laughed at, or worse. Writing letters to himself in which he pretended he was someone else, in which he spoke in the voice of a man he had never met but imagined was his real father—was this not just the sort of thing that Devlin Stead would do? Not even Aunt Daphne would believe my story. Dr. Cook himself, though *I* believed him, could not prove he was my father.

It struck me, quite suddenly, why Uncle Edward had arranged things as he had. Not to provide himself with an alibi, should I go to Aunt Daphne and tell her about the letters. He didn't *need* an alibi. It wasn't Aunt Daphne whom he needed to convince that he hadn't read the letters. It was Dr. Cook.

By passing the letters on to me without having read them, the seal on them unbroken, by burning them in front of me the instant I returned them to him, he had not been taking precautions—he had been following instructions. Dr. Cook had told him not to read the letters and had somehow convinced him to comply.

There was only one explanation: Uncle Edward was acting as "postman" for Dr. Cook and me against his will. How did Dr. Cook *know* that Uncle Edward did not read the letters? I was the only one who knew that, and Dr. Cook had expressly asked me not to write to him.

Perhaps I was wrong. There was no telling why Uncle Edward had arranged things as he had. But I was perversely flattered by the notion that Dr. Cook might have gone to such lengths as blackmail to communicate with me. And I felt a little more certain of where I stood with Uncle Edward.

· CHAPTER EIGHT ·

My dearest Devlin:

This is the last letter you will receive from me until I return. We are travelling by sled. The last members of our support group turn back tomorrow, bringing with them from each of us letters for our loved ones. Previously, I have, at this point of an expedition, felt a certain gloom come over me, there being no one to whom I could say "good-bye for now" except my siblings (with whom I have never been very close). I must confess that even with you and Anna to write to, I feel some measure of gloom. One always feels it on the eve of undertaking in earnest such a feat as for the chosen few of us begins tomorrow.

    The expedition, once it does begin, is certain to fail. My goal, which I have not disclosed to the backers of the expedition or the crew, is that we will learn enough this time that the failure of the next expedition will be slightly less than certain. That is how the poles will be achieved, by a succession of enlightening, educative failures. But that is not what people want to hear. It is not what the backers want to hear. The backers. This is my second time as commander of an expedition and already I am sick of them. Rich men and women pay me for naming something I discover after them, some island, cape or bay, which on maps now bears their name. The more money someone gives me, the more prominent is the landmark I name for him. Millionaires pay me to take their sons with me on my expeditions so that I can mould them into men.

I have been named co-commander of this expedition to the South Pole. What a waste of time it seems, to be trying for the South Pole, to be headed for the Antarctic instead of the Arctic, where I have been so many times before and which I know so much more about. It is the North Pole I want—"the top of the world, not the bottom," as Peary once put it.

But I must try to focus my mind. I can learn much from this expedition that I can put to use in the Arctic. The North Pole will be reached. It will not take forever. I believe it will happen before I am too old for leading expeditions. And I believe no man alive is more likely to get there first than me.

When there is light enough, I read The Rubáiyát of Omar Khayyám, my copy of which is held together with surgeon's plaster. The Rubáiyát. Not exactly an antidote to Antarctic gloom! "In the fires of spring, your winter garment of repentance fling!" I speak that line over and over in my head. What it means in the context of the poem no longer matters. How I long, as I trudge across the ice, weighted down by my winter garments of repentance, to fling them off and feel warmth from a source outside my body.

At night, there is something about the air, the water, the ice, the land that fixes my attention and makes it impossible for me to sleep. To see the night sky, I have taken to lying on the ice some distance from our tents in my sleeping bag. At first, my teeth chatter, every muscle in my body quivers. I want the heat to leave my body faster and thereby faster warm the air inside the bag. I close the bag until all that remains open is a kind of blow-hole, a slit through which I can breathe and see the stars. Others watching from their tents say that in the moonlight, they can see my breath spouting up at intervals. They think me strange and wonder how it is that I can stand the cold why it is that, although I have to myself the largest sleeping quarters, I come out here every night like a child on a camping trip. They would not tolerate my oddness if I was not in

*charge. There is no wind, no sound but that of the snow that
crunches loudly underneath me when I move. I am glad I cannot
sleep, much prefer this silence to the clamour of my dreams.*

*My dearest Devlin, such is the nature of polar exploration that
I have no idea when you will hear from me again. I hope that you
will think of me and in your prayers remember me. I bid you goodbye for now.*

> *Yours truly,*
> *Dr. F. A. Cook*

> *April 17, 1898*

Moses Prowdy had told me, and Aunt Daphne had confirmed,
that my father's ships had sometimes made port in St. John's, my father
declining to contact us despite his close proximity. I wondered if Dr.
Cook had been in St. John's since the North Greenland expedition,
since finding out that he was my father. By checking back issues of
newspapers in the library, I was able to determine that he had not
been, that he had not gone north since the Greenland expedition.
Perhaps for reasons having to do with more than just the whims of
"the backers." Once he turned his attentions back to the North Pole,
his ships might stop off in St. John's. Would he want to see me, arrange
some sort of meeting? Or would he avoid me as my father had done?
I was old enough now to seek him out should a ship of his make port.
A chance for us to meet, though he had said nothing about it in his
letters. Since he did not want anyone to know that he was writing to
me, he would not want a public encounter with me. But I vowed that
if he ever stopped off at St. John's, I would find a way to introduce
myself to him, or at the very least set eyes on him without giving anything away.

I decided to find out as much as I could about Dr. Cook, to piece
together a version of his life from the books he wrote and the magazines and newspapers that carried accounts of his expeditions. But it

was impossible to do so. As he had been forbidden to write or give interviews about expeditions that were led by other men, there was not much to read about him from his early days of exploration.

He had published, as per his agreement with expedition commanders like Lt. Robert Peary, articles only in scholarly journals that paid him nothing and were read by no one but the handful of doctors who believed the cause of medicine could be advanced through polar exploration. These included "The Most Northern Tribe on Earth," *New York Medical Examiner*, 1893; "Peculiar Customs regarding Disease, Death and Grief of the Most Northern Eskimo," *To-Day*, June 1894; "Gynecology and Obstetrics among the Eskimos," *The Brooklyn Medical Journal*, 1894; "Some Physical Effects of Arctic Cold, Darkness and Light," *The Journal of the American Medical Association*, 1897. "The Aurora Borealis as Observed from the *Kite*" was a clinical, twelve-page description of the northern lights. I read all these, unable to understand most of them, searching for the rare, brief anecdotes and impressions he allowed himself. But nothing of the Dr. Cook of his letters to me could be found.

· CHAPTER NINE ·

THE *BELGICA* WAS SIX MONTHS OVERDUE. I HAD BEEN FRETFUL LONG before I had reason to be, and now I had good reason. There was speculation in the papers that she had ventured too far south and, before she could make it back, the ice had closed in behind her. Unless her wooden hull could withstand the compression of the ice, she would be crushed and all aboard her lost. Doom-dreams woke me in the middle of the night. I read again Dr. Cook's report on the inscrutable disappearance of Francis Stead on the North Greenland expedition. Francis Stead, whose body had never been recovered and must even now be wedged in the fissure of some glacier, looking not much different than it did the night he fell. I read, over and over, Dr. Cook's letters to me. If not for having my copies of his letters to look at, I might have stopped believing he had ever written to me. It sometimes felt as if all that stood between him and obliteration was me. As if, as long as I kept him in mind—read his letters, tried to summon up an image of him as, at this or that moment, he might really be—he at least had a chance of making his way back from that other world to this one. But if I was not vigilant, if I let long spells of time go by without paying him the slightest thought, he would be lost.

I did not know, could not have endured knowing, what the waiting would be like. I took from the library and read Richard Hakluyt's *Principal Navigations* in which explorers were referred to as "navigators"; I read Dr. Elisha Kent Kane's book *Arctic Explorations*. It was an account of life on board a ship that was frozen in for months in the

Arctic at Smith Sound. A ship that returned long after it was written off as lost. I looked for other such books, tales of ships long thought to be sunk and men long thought to be dead returning to the world. I stumbled upon one about the men of the Greely expedition, ship-wrecked at Cape Sabine, who were rumoured to have eaten their own dead to keep from starving. Though Greely denied the rumours, it was now commonly believed that they were true. I read about the Franklin expedition, which was lost without a trace and had itself become the quest of other doomed expeditions.

Surely Dr. Cook and I had not found each other after so long only for him to disappear so soon. Every morning, I waited eagerly for Uncle Edward to come downstairs, hoping to see the red handkerchief protruding from his pocket, unable to help hoping, though I knew it was pointless, knew it would be in the papers, not in a letter from him, that I would first hear of Dr. Cook's return.

I wondered what Uncle Edward was thinking, wondered if he, too, was scanning the papers for news of the Antarctic expedition. If he knew how long the *Belgica* was overdue. Perhaps what I was dreading he was hoping for: that the world would never hear from Dr. Cook again.

In time, the *Belgica* was so long overdue that it was assumed by even the most optimistic that some misfortune had befallen her.

I all but resigned myself to Dr. Cook's having perished in his bid for the South Pole. There were fewer stories, fewer updates in the papers stating when the ship was supposed to have returned and made port in Patagonia.

Then one morning, thumbing through the first of the papers after Uncle Edward was done with it, I saw the headline: "*BELGICA* RETURNS SAFELY." And a subheadline: "All Crew Survives But One." All but one. I scanned the story for the name of Dr. Cook, and unable to find it, I read more slowly. After having spent thirteen months trapped in the southern ice, the Belgica had turned up at Punta Arenas on March 28, 1899. The member of the crew who had died was a Lt. Emile Danco. No mention was made of Dr. Cook.

I was now less concerned for his safety than I had been when the ship was missing, but I was still uncertain, still unwilling to tempt fate by presuming he was safe. The first stories about returning expeditions were often inaccurate.

Finally, a month after the first press reports, Uncle Edward came downstairs for breakfast sporting the now somewhat faded red handkerchief. A letter had arrived for me from Dr. Cook.

I might have had the last one from him only the day before, to look at Uncle Edward. I saw nothing in his face, neither disappointment nor relief, nor any indication that this day was in any way remarkable. Uncle Edward had as good as come downstairs proclaiming, "Dr. Cook is alive and well," yet he did not so much as glance at me. I looked at the handkerchief, looked and looked at it, afraid to look away in case, when I looked back, it would be gone. I was for a moment certain I would cry, but the urge to do so was succeeded by a wave of elation that made me let loose with a laugh that Uncle Edward pretended not to notice.

"What's so funny, Devvie?" Aunt Daphne said.

"Nothing," I said, and obviously tickled to see me in such good spirits, she did not pursue the matter.

My dearest Devlin:

You have grown to near manhood since I wrote you last. No doubt you have read much about my expedition in the papers. I hope you did not fret too much for my safety; on the other hand, I would hate to think that over the course of my long silence, you lost interest in my fate. I fear it may be impossible to rejoin a world that has for so long been reconciled to my extinction.

We accomplished nothing really except a farthest south. We may or may not have set foot on the Antarctic continent. No one seems to know or care.

I would have written to you sooner except that, in Montevideo, I found waiting for me a letter informing me that my beloved Anna had, during my absence, passed away. I am told that for a while after my departure for the pole, she seemed to be recovering, but once the press reports began, with the speculations that the Belgica *and all its crew were lost, she suffered a relapse and slowly succumbed to an illness that was more sinister than the specialists who examined her before I left New York had led me to believe. I have been fighting the double demons of guilt and sorrow since hearing the sad news of her passing.*

I will write you again when these afflictions do not press so heavily upon my heart.

Yours truly,
Dr. F. A. Cook

April 15, 1899

"My beloved Anna." He had mentioned his fiancée in previous letters, but I had not thought of her, this kindred soul who, a thousand miles away, had been suffering the same ordeal as I was and had died unaware of my existence. How well I could picture the course of her decline.

Before I heard from him again, he published an account of the *Belgica* expedition in the *New York Herald*. I read it with great interest, but the photographs he published in a series of articles in *Century* magazine affected me even more. Each month, I borrowed *Century* from the public library and smuggled it into the house beneath my coat. I wasn't sure what Uncle Edward and Aunt Daphne would do if they saw me with it. I doubted that Uncle Edward would take it from me, but I didn't want my reading of it to be prefaced by anything he said.

Dr. Cook dedicated the articles to the memory of Francis Stead, the "resourceful, patient, kind and reflective Dr. Stead, to whose courage and ingenuity the surviving members of the North Greenland expedition, myself included, owe their lives." He said that had Francis

Stead lived, he would one day have taken his place among the great explorers of the world, "although I can think of no man to whom self-glorification mattered less, no explorer whose motives were more pure than Dr. Stead's. He laboured in the service of mankind, his goal the furtherance of human knowledge. For him, as for all explorers worthy of the name, exploration was not a contest but a calling."

I fastened on this description of Francis Stead's character. No one, not even Dr. Cook in his letters to me, not even my mother or Uncle Edward in his excoriations, had ever described him at such length. The dedication and description were no doubt inspired in part by guilt, and were perhaps written in the knowledge, or with the possibility in mind, that I would read them.

The *Century* articles were less interesting than the photographs. They were written in the tone of adventure stories. "Dr. Cook confronts perils of the Arctic and survives!" read the subheadline to one story, whose headline read, "STRANDED." The articles were nothing like his letters, and it occurred to me that the former might have been ghost-written.

In a future letter to me, Dr. Cook would say this of the photographs:

"How often I told myself that if we did not survive, the photographs I took would be our legacy. I remember thinking, What a pity if by the time they are found, they are spoiled, or are spoiled by some well-intended fool before they make it home. I wrote a letter for whomever might have happened on the ship after we were gone, instructing him on the importance of the photographs and their proper care. My main concern, of course, was for the welfare of the crew, but I could do little more for them than they could do for me. I stayed on deck or on the ice all day exposing plates. One hundred of them. With the poison we had planned to use to kill animals for specimens, I made prussic acid, which passed for a fixing agent when my hypo ran out. Needless to say, I had the darkroom to myself. To think that, out there in the Antarctic, my life was never more at risk than when I was at my photographs!"

According to the credits, all the photographs had been taken by Dr. Cook. Polar bears, penguins. One of the ice-bound *Belgica* looking almost haloed in the moonlight, its masts, spars, rigging, furled sails and lifeboats rimed with frost. Three crew members, two of whom, according to the caption, "hailed from Newfoundland," looking cheerful despite their thirteen-month confinement in the ice. There was one photograph of the burial in a trench of ice of Lt. Emile Danco, who, in spite of Dr. Cook's ministrations, had died from pneumonia.

By far the most interesting of the photographs were those of Dr. Cook—that is, those he had taken of himself. I had seen photographs of him before in newspapers, but none like these.

There were six photographs, each titled "Dr. Cook, self-portrait." It seemed somehow apt that he should have no one to take his picture but himself. To me, it was the measure of his solitude, the loneliness of the life he led. Who better to photograph a man who, having gone for so long without friendship, had written as he had to a sixteen-year-old he had never met?

He always photographed himself in profile, always from the right, never, except in one case, looking at the camera, seeming not to know that it was there as he stared off at some point outside the frame. This illusion was subverted by the caption, "self-portrait," and by the high quality of the photograph, evidence of the effort he had put into it, into making himself seem disdainful of the camera. The amount of contrivance that had gone into making the photograph seem uncontrived.

I tried to imagine him out there in the Antarctic, setting up his camera on its tripod, looking to an observer as if he was preparing to photograph whatever the lens was pointed at, then coming out from beneath the blanket to assume his position in front of the camera, composing his expression, clicking the button on the shutter release that was attached by a cord to the camera. He could not have been satisfied with just one try. He could not have been sure that in one try, or even in ten, he would get a photograph that he liked or would survive the journey home. Click after click of the button, puff after puff of smoke, slide after slide of magnesium igniting, the polar white for an instant becoming whiter with an incandescence that in the photographs was reflected in his eyes. Dr. Cook, posing for hours, engrossed in self-commemoration in the middle of the Antarctic, watched from afar by his subordinates, who, while he was thus engaged, went about some tedious tasks he had assigned them. Self-portrait. Another way of saying that in every one of these pictures, in his right hand, which is always out of frame, he holds the shutter release.

I could manage no suspension of disbelief when I looked at those photographs, could not help seeing the out-of-frame camera or the shutter release in his unseen hand.

"Self-portrait, 1898." Glass-plate negative, the method used in studio portraits—a studio being the only place other explorers would have their portraits taken, for in a portrait one is meant to look one's polished best. Like Peary, who in his portraits always looked so forthright, so earnest, so unashamed of wanting to create a good impression. But not Dr. Cook. In one photograph he faced away from the camera, almost at a right angle, turned just enough towards it that both eyes were in the picture, the far one hardly more than a glint of light on the bridge of his nose, the near one partially obscured by a lock of hair he could not have bothered brushing back. He looked as though no one would see the photographs but him, as if the camera was a means of self-examination, as if his intention was to produce a picture of himself that he could study in detachment, pore over to see what this individual could tell him of his species.

None of the photographs showed enough of his surroundings to give a sense of context. Some snow on a rock behind him, over his shoulder a glimpse of what only someone who knew the circumstances of the photograph would recognize as cloud or ice. One photo of him indoors, in profile to a bare wall. Another, captioned "Cook the photographer, by Dr. Cook," must have been a photograph of his reflection in a mirror, taken so close to the mirror you could not see any of its border, Dr. Stead holding in his hands a large box camera and smiling: a photograph of a man staring into his own eyes. A clever trick. And perhaps, therefore, that smile.

The only hint to the uninformed of what was taking place when these photographs were snapped was his dishevelment: his long hair, uneven beard, sunken eyes, gaunt complexion; the frayed edges of his coat and shirt. He looked resigned to the fact that by the time the world saw these images of him, he would be no more.

I scrutinized Dr. Cook's face in the photographs, searching for ways that he resembled me. I stood in front of a mirror that hung on the wall of my bedroom and compared my face to the face in one of the photographs from *Century,* which I had pasted on the glass (and which I took down afterwards so that no one else would see it). I looked at my reflected face. I looked at Dr. Cook's face. I felt foolish. The mirror was no help. I had fancied that, using it, I would be able to see both of our images at once, but the only way to see Dr. Cook's was to look away from mine and vice versa. I had never examined my face in this manner before, assessing every feature, staring into my own eyes. I felt self-conscious and at a disadvantage to Dr. Cook in his time-stopped, static world, his face composed, frozen, while mine changed from one moment to the next. It was not until I placed a recent photograph of myself beside the photographs of him that I was able to make a proper comparison, though still I did not find what I was hoping for. We did not look completely unalike, but nor was there an unmistakable resemblance.

I took from my bureau drawer a photograph of Francis Stead that I had cut from the newspaper, the photograph that had run with the story of his disappearance. I placed the three photographs side by side on my dresser. I looked as much like Francis Stead as I did like Dr. Cook. Or rather, I bore no particular resemblance to either. I placed a photograph of my mother ("Amelia, the wicked one") in between those of my father and Dr. Cook, and the one of me directly below hers. My mother with Dr. Stead on one side and Dr. Cook on the other. (I did not, it seemed to me, even resemble my mother. I hoped this meant that in other, less superficial ways, we were also unalike.)

Judging by how old she looked, the photograph must have been taken just before or just after her trip to New York, on one side or the other of her meeting with Dr. Cook.

I tried to imagine a blending of my mother's features with those of Dr. Cook, but I could not. They were of opposite physical types, she delicate and small-boned to the point of near translucency, while he was generally large-featured. His hair was straight but thick, his forehead high. He had full lips, sharp cheekbones and a nose that looked thinner in profile than it did from the front. He had let his hair grow long on the expedition, though it looked as if he had washed and brushed it frequently. His beard was unkempt, but affectedly so, as if he was cultivating a certain look, as if he did not trust being an explorer to make him look like one.

Perhaps, when I was older, I would look more like Dr. Cook, I thought, until I realized that no one who did not have eyes like his could ever really look like him.

Though he almost never looked at the camera, the first thing I noticed in all the photographs were his eyes. Whether he was at the centre of the photograph or just within the frame—if his face made up the entire photograph or just a fraction of it—my eyes went instantly to his and would have, I was certain, even if I had never heard of him before. However much my face changed as I matured, I would never have eyes like his. It was partly because of their shape: the whites were so large that the asymmetric lids did not reach the irises, either above or below, so the irises were wholly visible. But there was something else about them, an impression they conveyed for which I could find no words.

· CHAPTER TEN ·

My dearest Devlin:

In my second letter to you, I spoke of redressing the harm I have done. What, if these letters are the first step on the path to atonement, is to be the second step?

I decided, during my long confinement in the Antarctic, that I owe you nothing less than to be your father. I also decided that a public acknowledgment of my patrimony would be folly for both of us, not only for the reasons I set forth in my first letter, but because it would deprive me of my most valued possession, and therefore would prevent me from giving or leaving it to you.

I am an explorer. Before all else—doctor, brother, husband (should it be God's will that I become one)—but excepting father, I am an explorer. What greater thing, therefore, can I offer than to make you one? What greater thing can I offer you but my vocation?

When you are old enough, and strong enough, will you go with me on my expeditions? It would mean a great deal to me, more than you can possibly imagine, if one day you said yes.

As I wrote to you before, I have often taken the sons of rich men with me on my journeys to the Arctic. They think that by sailing to the North with Dr. Cook, they make their passage into manhood. At the same time, I am under instruction from their fee-paying fathers to satisfy their every need and make sure they endure just enough hardship to convince them that they are having an "adventure." A trip north with me has been the graduation present of many a student from Harvard and Yale.

I mention these young men only to allay any concerns you may have about your lack of experience in Arctic travel. I am quite adept at taking young men to the Arctic and bringing them back home alive and well again. With the Arctic, as with all things, there has to be a first time. Even to those of us who know it best, it was once unknown.

It must seem strange to you, my extending this invitation, in light of what happened to Francis Stead and the part in it that, however inadvertently, I played.

I must confess that it is not only by way of discharging my debt to you, not only so that, as father and son, we might assay a common goal, that I am making this request. Nor am I unaware of how presumptuous it is of me to ask that you commit to such an under-taking with a man whose hand you have yet to shake, whose face in the real light of existence you have yet to see, who has forbidden you to write to him.

If you were to join me on my expeditions, I would make you my protégé. And if, under any circumstances, it becomes apparent that I will never realize my life's ambition, you, my son, if by then you felt I had prepared you well enough, could take up my quest.

I have felt more oppressively than ever lately, in the wake of the Antarctic expedition, what the Eskimos call piblocto, *the weight of the world, pressing down upon me. The strain of standing alone beneath that weight, supporting it without even the hope of being relieved of it at some point in the future now seems more than I can bear. Often, during the long wait in the Antarctic for a deliverance that for all I knew might never come, I thought of you, took solace in knowing that even if I died, I would leave behind a son who might himself have sons and daughters. I thought of my first wife, Libby, and our unnamed baby girl, and of how, when Francis Stead told me that the boy whom all the world thought was his was really mine, it seemed that both of my lost children had been restored to me.*

Not even if he had sons old enough to play the part could Robert Peary see the point of protégés. The only success that will please Peary is his own. But I, too, it seems, am trapped. No one but you can free me from the isolation of ambition. Nor would renouncing my ambition free me, even if I could renounce it, for I believe that I was called to my vocation as priests and ministers are called to theirs. I believe that, as I once wrote of Francis Stead, I labour not only for myself, but in the service of mankind.

It may seem to you that there are any number of young men who would be willing to pledge themselves to me—men in their twenties who, unlike you, are now old enough to go with me on my expeditions; men I could now be tutoring instead of waiting for you to come of age, thus increasing the likelihood that I or someone of my tutelage will gain the prize. But none of them is my son.

You are only eighteen years old. It may be that you are too young to understand the implications of saying yes or no. For yourself and for me. It would not be fair to exact from you a promise that years from now you might regret but would hold yourself to anyway because you gave your word.

You could say no and think that your doing so was the cause of some misfortune I might suffer in the years to come, some mishap in the Arctic that, if not for my preoccupying doubt, would not have happened.

So let me be clear about what it is that I am asking of you. First, any feelings of guilt on your part would be unwarranted. You should not accept my invitation out of fear of what will happen to me if you do not. I have described my condition only so that you could better understand my nature, not to extort from you the answer that would please me most.

I am sure that your aunt and uncle, for obvious reasons, would not want you to take up exploration. Weighed against the consideration of whatever distress you might cause them are things for which I and no man I have ever met can find the words.

One either feels in one's heart and in one's soul a desire for the *sort of life I lead or one does not. It is my hope that you do. If you do, if, as I suspect, the lure of the Old Ice runs as surely in your blood as it does in mine, no litany of the hazards you would face would deter you. If am wrong and you do not feel as I do, then such a litany would likewise be unnecessary.*

But you are young. And therefore, the only answer that I will not accept, at least not now, is yes. You may tell me no, or you may tell me perhaps, but you may not tell me yes. (Write your answer on this envelope and leave it for your uncle Edward as you did with the other letters I sent you.) If your answer is perhaps, then we will leave it so until you are old enough to fully understand what saying yes or no might mean. If your answer is no, I will understand and will make no further efforts to convince you. But I will go on writing to you.

If, by the time you are old enough to travel in the Arctic, I have not reached the pole, I will take you with me and teach you everything I know, things that fewer than half a dozen men alive could teach you.

And if, at some point, I am forced to renounce exploration, I would not be sorry if you attained the pole instead of me.

If, with my help, you reach the pole first, I will have ensured that no man who does not deserve it wins the prize.

> *Dr. Frederick Cook*
> *April 19, 1900*

He had forbidden me to tell him yes? "YES," I wished I could have written in large letters on the envelope. What would he do if I wrote "Yes"? Would it please him or make him wonder if I was so excitable that he could not count on me to be discreet? I wrote "Maybe," wishing more fervently than I ever had before that I could write to him directly and tell him that any time he said the word, I would follow his instructions, whatever they might be. Next week, next month.

I felt no apprehension at the prospect of exploration. On the contrary, it was life as I would live it unless I went exploring that I dreaded, a life like Uncle Edward's. To become a man who could take no joy in being married to such a woman as Aunt Daphne, that was what I dreaded.

Exploration. How appealing, in spite of all its dangers and its desolation, in spite of Francis Stead, it seemed to me. There *was* a lesson to be learned from the life of Francis Stead. It was not because of the rigours of life in the Arctic that he had walked out across the glacier that night. It was the rigours of the life he could not put behind him that made him do it. From the life and death of my mother, too, there was something, if not to be learned, then at least to be remembered: it was not because her husband took up exploration that she died.

To Dr. Cook and all others who wrote about it, no greater life could be imagined than that of an explorer. I was certain that the hardships and risks involved in it would not deter me. I would much rather have been on board the *Belgica* for thirteen months with him than home here fretting for the safety of a man I'd never met.

It didn't matter that nothing in my life so far had prepared me for polar exploration, that I had yet to set foot on a boat or fire a gun or sleep outdoors. It didn't matter that I had never seen a dog sled, let alone a team of dogs. Expeditionaries relied on their crews, their ships' captains, their manservants, their native guides to perform the thankless task of keeping them safe so they could make their bids for glory.

How different was my upbringing from Dr. Cook's, of whom I was half composed; he was a city man, as most explorers were, who, relatively speaking, came late to exploration. As Dr. Cook had learned from men like Peary, I would learn from Dr. Cook. "Even to those of us who know it best, it was once unknown."

The wisdom, the reflectiveness, his sceptical but sympathetic view of life as it was lived in cities, the desire to accomplish something he would be remembered for and thereby set himself apart from the common run of men, but only if that something was truly worthwhile—all these qualities, I felt certain, he had acquired or refined since he took up exploration. "Whoever reaches the pole first will do so in the name of humankind, cause a worldwide enlivenment of spirit, wonder, awe and fellowship," he had written in a magazine article. I had believed it when I read it, but not like I believed it now.

"Will you go with me on my expeditions?" The instant I read those words, it seemed to me that I had been waiting for that invitation all my life, hoping for it. As Dr. Cook on the ice-trapped ship had awaited his deliverance, not knowing when or if it would ever come, so had I been waiting. I believed that I had as much cause as anyone to be sceptical of civilization. At the same time, I did not wish to renounce it altogether.

Civilization. Except by becoming an explorer or by doing what my mother had, one could not escape from it. Exploration was certainly the only escape that did not involve surrender or retreat. Men who simply ran away and spent their lives in service to a succession of masters accomplished nothing.

He had said nothing to me of how our association would come about, what we would tell others of how we came to *be* associates, what reasons he would give the public for conferring upon me, a stranger, an honour that many young men of his acquaintance would have eagerly accepted.

Most important, he had said nothing to me of *when* he would send for me, of how, without ever having met me, he would deem me "old enough and strong enough" for exploration. I was still drifting like the *Belgica* in the pack ice, still waiting for my deliverance, which though it seemed assured now, might not seem so six months or a year from now.

· CHAPTER ELEVEN ·

IN ONE OF HIS LETTERS TO ME, DR. COOK WROTE THAT FRANCIS Stead had told him that as a boy, he liked to go up on Signal Hill in the spring to "see the ice." I knew of nowhere else to see it from, but I had not gone up there since I went with Aunt Daphne when I was a boy, because I did not want to be reminded of my mother's fate.

"The ice" was pack ice drifting south from Labrador and bringing with it icebergs from the sea-level glaciers of Greenland. Its southward drift past the east coast of Newfoundland in spring was as regular as the changing of the leaves in fall.

I had "seen" it before, glimpsed it through the Narrows from some height on the north side of the city, seen it in the harbour after it had been forced in through the Narrows by a storm, filth-ridden after bobbing there among the soot and bilge for weeks. These, I thought, these all-but-black bobbing chunks of matter, were what people meant when they talked about "the ice."

For weeks after reading of Francis Stead's sojourns to see the ice, I watched the horizon, knowing the ice was coming, waiting for a change in the line where the sea met the sky. Finally, one morning, I saw it from the window off the landing, saw what might have been the teeth of a jagged, uneven saw blade. The leading edge was still fifty or sixty miles away.

It was another two weeks before I made the ascent, sharing the road one Sunday afternoon with other pedestrians and people in carriages, other pilgrims, as Uncle Edward called anyone who thought the ice "worth gaping at."

When the ice was in this close, there was not much shipping. Today, no flag flew from the signal pole. A stream of smoke made almost horizontal by the wind poured from the chimney of the blockhouse.

Even had I been with someone else when I got my first look at the ice, I could not have spoken. Not even the sight of the sea had brought home to me the existence of "elsewhere" or stirred in me the urge to travel as the ice did. The ocean disappeared as if the ice extended all the way to England. Pack ice, slob ice, raftered ice—all of it was crammed and smashed together. I went up there often between that day and early summer, and the only indication that there was water underneath the ice was the change in the location of the icebergs, whose southward drift was imperceptible except at intervals of days or weeks.

This ice was nothing like the inshore ice, the "young ice," which was clean, thin, flat, almost transparent. This Old Ice *looked* old, a jagged scree of pieces many feet thick, as if a vast field of wreckage from some world-altering catastrophe was floating by. It was hard to believe that all that caused what lay before me was the start of spring, the warming of the air and the water by a few degrees, the lengthening of days.

Hard to the coast from which the snow was long gone, where the grass was bright green and the trees were thickening with buds and even leaves, was pressed this other world, where abruptly, it was winter—where everything was so white that on clear days the ice shone like a second sun. It was hard, in that ice-field, to distinguish one shape of ice from another. Even the icebergs were hard to make out, except the ones so far from land that they stood out like clouds against the sky. From the scree of ice, a berg so large its underside must have been ploughing the seabed ahead of it like snow reared up, vast, incongruous. This was not winter as I knew it but some absolute of winter. The snow of which this ice was made had not fallen from the sky but was ancient and prevailed like stone. It was as though all of Greenland had broken up. It was hard to believe that the whole thing would be repeated the following year, that there was any ice left where this ice had come from.

I went up on the hill to see the ice as often as I could. I felt as though I was standing on the brink of the new life I was soon to begin with Dr. Cook. I imagined myself down there on the ice, side by side with Dr. Cook on the runners of a sled pulled by a team of dogs. I could think of no greater thing than to be an explorer, the epitome of my most cherished belief, which was that a man's fate was not determined by the past.

But word was soon going round that I was paying some sort of obsessive tribute to my mother, whose body had been found at the edge of just such ice as I was looking at, a mere few hundred feet below. It was said, I overheard it said, that I was keeping some sort of delusional vigil for her and for my father.

I was looked upon as the son of parents whose sheer oddness had brought about their deaths, a boy who had inherited that oddness and was probably doomed by it to a fate much like theirs.

"Right there where he is standing now, that's where they found the horse and carriage," one man who stood right beside me told another one day. It was as if he believed that because he was not speaking to me, I could not hear him. "She started down the hill right there. He stands there every day, just staring." The two men seemed to believe I was oblivious to scrutiny, that the riddle of Amelia and Francis Stead could be solved by a close examination of my face.

I came downstairs one night when I heard my aunt and uncle talking. I stopped outside the front room, assuming that they had heard me, and that Aunt Daphne would soon ask me what I wanted. But they went on talking.

"Taking after his parents, people are saying," Uncle Edward said.

"Oh, they've been saying that for years," Aunt Daphne said.

"He goes up on the hill and stands for hours every afternoon looking at the ice. Other people go up there once a year. With him, it's every day. No matter how cold it is, no matter how hard the wind is blowing, there he is, as still as a statue, looking out across the ice. Obsessed, they're saying. With where his mother . . . fell in. They say he has told people that his father is not really dead, that someday the ice will bring him safely home, that he will walk ashore from it and everything will be the way it was before he left."

"Whoever said that made it up," Aunt Daphne said. "He never speaks to anyone about his parents. Not even me. It's perfectly normal for him to think more about his parents than he used to. It will pass. He's only now really beginning to understand what happened to them. Or to realize that he may never understand it."

How guilty it made me feel to hear so much sympathy and understanding in her voice. I wondered how Uncle Edward felt, having to feign ignorance of what he knew, being unable to tell her that her sympathy and understanding were misplaced, that I was undeserving of them. And he knew only that it was Dr. Cook's letters that had set me to keeping vigil on the hill. He did not know what was in the letters, and not knowing was working on his mind. Not knowing the contents of the letters, he had no way of predicting what I might do, what Dr. Cook might do.

His state of preoccupation rivalled mine. Yet he couldn't resist telling her about the gossip, even at the risk of making her pay closer attention to me, which I was sure she would.

One night, after I went to bed, I noticed that the moon was full and saw a faint glow from the ice between the Narrows. I remembered the photograph of the *Belgica*, the ship moonlit, haloed and white with frost. Dr. Cook had often spoken, in his letters, of the endless Arctic night. I had so far seen the ice only by day, only as, in the Arctic, it looked for half the year. I had yet to see how it looked during the other half, the half that took the greater toll on expeditionaries, especially their minds. I went to my stash of letters and searched through them for the one in which Dr. Cook had written about what he called "night never-ending."

"Imagine," Dr. Cook wrote. "The sun goes down, and though

you know it will not rise again for ninety days, you cannot help hoping each 'morning' that it will." His putting *morning* in quotation marks made the hair stand up on the nape of my neck. Three months without mornings. Three months during which morning exists nowhere but on your pocket watch and in your mind. "Temporal disorientation is not uncommon," wrote Dr. Cook. "For a few days, there is zodiacal light, the blue corolla that traces the horizon after sunset and before sunrise. And after that, the most you can hope for by way of light is what I call illumoonation. If there happens not to be a moon, you are left with the feeble light of stars. And should there be an overcast, not even that..."

Another section of the letter: "You have not really heard the ice until you hear it late at night. There is no room for the ice to expand, but expand it must and so it seems that the whole mass of it begins to stir. I once heard what I would have sworn was the weary tramp of footsteps, the slow going-round of wooden wheels and the clopping hoofs of horses. I had been reading *War and Peace* and so was 'hearing,' out on the ice, the French plodding west across the frozen mass of Russia after their defeat outside of Moscow. There is no end to the tricks the ice plays on the ears at night...."

I realized that I did not have to wait to see and hear such things as he described in this letter.

The next night, a Friday, Aunt Daphne and Uncle Edward went to a charity ball, a benefit for the still-ongoing rebuilding of the parts of the city that in the fire of 1892 had been destroyed. They told me they would not be home until late.

There would be no one else on the hill at such an hour at this time of year. And I could easily be back home before Uncle Edward and Aunt Daphne. I prayed, looking out the window as I waited for them to leave, that the sky that now was clear would stay that way.

After they had left, I waited until twilight. Up north, in summer, this was how it looked at the twin times of least light, at the nadirs of the morning and the midnight suns.

In the pantry, on the bottom shelf, there were two oil lanterns that had not been used in years, lanterns Francis Stead had hung on his hansom cab when he went out making house calls after dark. I filled one of them with seal oil, the oil of last resort, which Aunt Daphne kept for emergencies in metal cans in the shed behind the house. I quickly skirted the city streets just after dark and, the lantern lighting my way, followed the narrow road up Signal Hill.

The sky was cloudless, the moon almost full. All that remained of the wind that all day had been blowing from the west was a faint breeze.

I stood on the hill, looking down at the blue-white ice. The ice. A world in which everything was made of the same substance. I tried to imagine a world of wood. A world of rock. A world of salt. A world of coal. The closest thing to it was the desert, but the desert did not have this infinite variety of shapes. Like a great city in the early stages of construction. Or the late ones of disintegration.

It was an eerily beautiful sight. Would it still seem so halfway through "night never-ending"? For a man whose mind was in such a torment as Francis Stead's had been, to be part of a small band of expeditionaries with nothing but *that* as far as you could see in all directions might be unbearable. To be, to believe yourself to be, the one thing in the universe not made of ice. I could not help thinking of Francis Stead out there alone in his last moments, wandering about on the ice, oblivious, dazed, caught up in the panic that for men lost in the darkness and the wilderness meant the end was near. He had risen from his pallet on the floor of Redcliffe House and, without waking anyone— Dr. Cook, his fellows in their sleeping bags, the Pearys in their room behind the drapes, the dogs outside, the Eskimos whose cluster of igloos you could see from Redcliffe House—had walked off onto the glacier.

I told myself that I should stop thinking about Francis Stead and think instead of Dr. Cook and all the other men, and of Mrs. Peary, who had *not* walked away from Redcliffe House.

Facing away from the lighthouses at Fort Amherst and Cape Spear, on the far side of the Narrows, I listened. I heard a drawn-out creaking, then a snap, as if a tree had been slowly bent until it broke. A series of booms from somewhere down the coast as a fault line formed. What might have been a massive sheet of glass smashing into pieces, then a scattering of small explosions as shards of ice at intervals fell back to earth. So many sounds it seemed there should have been some corresponding lights, but there were none. Only the ice, the strange blue-white cast of it. Illumoonation. The lighthouse beacons flashed and the ice was for an instant super-illuminated, as though it had been photographed.

"There is no end to the tricks the ice plays on the ears at night." I doubted that any listener had ever been more receptive to such tricks than I was. It was as though a mass of animals that by day hid themselves among the caves and warrens of the ice were moving about, rearranging things to suit themselves or tending the ice in some seemingly random but necessary fashion, compelled to do so by an instinct they were helpless to resist.

I held up my lantern and swung it like a censer, back and forth, as people did on stormy nights to signal ships at sea.

I remembered more of Dr. Cook's letter: "The city-dweller imagines the polar night to be a misery, but the unbroken darkness has its charms. The pleasure of feeling on one's face a draught of warmth when one goes indoors. The sight, from outside the ship, of the lights within. The sight, from outside an igloo, of the light within, which makes the dome of ice translucent, opalescent. The moonlight silver on the seas of ice, the clarity of stars. There is a naked fierceness in the scenes, a wildness in the storms, a sublimity of silence in the night that one appreciates despite the gloom. The attractions of the polar night are not to be written in the language of a people who live in a land of sunshine and flowers. In the polar night, one occupies a world where animal sentiments take over and those of the timid human are forgotten."

I could still see the moon when it began to snow, so I assumed that a sea-effect flurry was passing. There were more and more sounds from below, as if the ice creatures, able to see the end of their labours, were making one last concerted push. From all directions came the sounds of eruption and collapse, of creaking, as if beams of ice were being hoisted up or, top-heavy, were snapping off and landing with crashes that gave rise to new effects.

I swung the lantern, raised it higher and swung it in a wider arc.

The wire slipped from my hand and the lantern fell, the flame in it still burning until it hit the rocky slope below. I heard the glass break, saw a small spurt of flame, a patch of rock uplit for an instant, and then it was dark again and silent, except for the droning clatter of the ice.

I looked up and could not see the moon. Snow was falling heavily now, straight down because there was no wind. It, too, was invisible, but I could feel it on my upturned face. I could see nothing, not the lights of the city or those of the two quarantined hospitals halfway down the hill.

I would never find my way back down safely without a lantern. Perhaps not even with one. If I wandered too far left, I would step straight off the cliff, too far right and I would wind up in the woods. Or on one of the ponds, where what was left of the ice would not bear my weight. Even if by chance I kept to the trail, the slope was so steep and rocky that to stumble and pitch forward to either side might prove fatal.

I shouted "Help" as loud as I could, thinking that I might be heard by someone in the fishing village called the Battery, which lay in the western lee of the hill. But there was no reply.

It was cold already and would get much colder, too cold to spend the night without some shelter. I thought of the blockhouse from which the signal flags were raised. I knew it was off to my right, though I could not make it out.

Remembering that there was a small fence around the blockhouse that extended to the ridge, I got down on my hands and knees and felt my way along the ridge with my left hand. After a few minutes, I nudged the fence with my right shoulder, felt my way along the fence to the gate, which I opened, and then stood up. I knew that I was within a few feet of the blockhouse, but still I could not see it. I walked slowly forward with my arms raised until my hands brought up against what turned out to be the door.

With a stone that I pried loose from the ground, I broke the lock on the door and went inside. Feeling my way around in the dark, I found a still-warm woodstove and, beside it, a small supply of kindling, but no real firewood. I threw the kindling in the stove, from which there was soon light enough to see. On a table against the near wall, there were lanterns, some candles and a box of matches. I considered lighting one of the lanterns and attempting a descent, but thought better of it. I lit a candle. The fire in the stove would not last long. There was a day-bed, a bunk where, on their breaks, the men who ran the blockhouse must have taken naps. I sat down on the bunk with my back against the wall. In the middle of the floor was a ladder that led up to a trapdoor in the ceiling. I presumed the men climbed up there to hoist the merchant flags. In the far wall there were slit-like windows from which they must have scanned the sea for ships.

I told myself that I was not lost, just temporarily stranded, knowing exactly how long I would have to wait, certain that what I was waiting for would come. I was not even in such straits as I would be in daily on my first trip up north with Dr. Cook. I recalled with pride that I had not panicked when the lantern fell from my hand. I hoped that one day I could relate this feat of self-preservation to Dr. Cook.

What to tell Uncle Edward and Aunt Daphne the next day, that was all I had to worry about. But what *could* I tell them except the truth?

I slid farther down on the bunk until my head was on the pillows. It was cold, so I crawled beneath the blankets. What would Aunt Daphne think, what would she do, when she got home and saw that I was gone?

I fell asleep and had no dreams. Perversely, my body did not wake me until later than it did at home. When I awoke, the fire in the stove was out. But there was light at the window in the wall that faced the sea, and not the faint light of dawn, but that of morning.

I got up and looked out the window. The sky was overcast. The ice, like the foothills of some mountain range, stood out in stark relief against the sky. I guessed, from how fresh it looked on the ground, that the snow had only recently stopped.

Just as I turned around, the door of the blockhouse swung open. A portly, long-bearded man in coveralls looked at me, then at the unmade bunk.

"You're the boy they're looking for," he said. "The Stead boy. Tried to run away, did ya?"

I shook my head and told him about losing the lantern.

"Why'd you come up here in the first place?"

To see the ice, I almost said. To listen to the ice. I thought better of it. I shrugged. He did likewise.

"Well, I s'pose I'll have to take you home," he said.

He did so by a circuitous route through the streets of St. John's, presumably so that as many people as possible would see that it was him who had found me, had found "the Stead boy," so that he could tell his story to as many people as possible with the living proof of its veracity right there by his side.

I sat beside him on the buckboard of his wagon. I would have bolted from it, except I knew that I would be pursued and it would serve only to enlarge my reputation.

"Who's that with you, Charlie?" an old woman asked.

"The Stead boy. Found him in the blockhouse. There all night, he was."

"In the blockhouse. What was he doing in the blockhouse all night?"

"Wouldn't say," Charlie said.

"Is he all right?"

"Seems to be. As all right as he ever was."

"That's a sin for you."

"Are you all right, Devlin?" a man in a bowler hat like Uncle Edward's asked, saying my name as if he knew me, though I did not know him. I presumed he had heard of the search. I nodded.

A man riding horseback drew up beside us.

"Is that him?" he said.

"That's him," Charlie said.

"I'll go on ahead to Dr. Stead's," the rider said and went off at a gallop.

Word of where I was found, and that I had been missing all night, spread quickly after that.

"In the blockhouse. All night long. Went up there after dark," one woman told another, as if discretion would be wasted on me.

"What were you doing all night in the blockhouse, Stead?" a boy I went to school with asked. I ignored him.

"That's Devlin Stead," a small boy said, as if he had heard of me many times but had never seen me before.

In our neighbourhood, the door of every house was open. People were standing outside, arms folded, talking, shaking their heads and saying, "Poor thing," "Poor soul." Already aware that I'd been found, they stopped talking when they saw me, looked at me as if I had not so much been found as captured.

On either side of the front door, the lamps were still lit. Had been all night long, no doubt.

I opened the door.

"DEVLIN?"

Uncle Edward.

I said nothing, and perhaps because of that, he did not come out to meet me. When I turned the corner from the vestibule, I saw him sitting in the armchair that faced the door, his face just visible by the light of what was left of the fire in the grate. I felt as if, by not answering when he spoke my name, I had confessed to something.

"Where have you been?" he said.

"Up on the hill," I said.

"I was out half the night in the carriage, searching the streets for you. Every time I came back without you, she sent me out again."

"I'm sorry," I said.

"Up on the hill."

"Yes."

"There have been men out looking for you since the sun came up. Daphne, too. She asked me to stay here in case you came back. She said she couldn't stand to just sit here and wait any longer. I'm not even sure if she knows yet that you've been found."

"I was in the blockhouse," I said, explaining to him as I had to Charlie about the lantern and having to break the lock on the block-house door.

"'The Stead boy is lost.' That's what they've been saying. All over town. 'The Stead boy is lost.' They meant more than gone astray, of course, though they'd never say so in front of me or Daphne. 'The Stead boy.' It makes you sound like some sort of freak. It makes any-one whose name is Stead sound like one. They wouldn't have been surprised to hear that someone found you in the harbour. Nor would I. All night long Daphne kept saying you might be with some girl or you might have got drunk. I felt like telling her that those were rea-sons for which *normal* boys went missing. But I pretended that both were possibilities. I knew it would turn out to be something like this. Brought home after a night in the blockhouse. Brought home on the buckboard of a wagon at seven-thirty on a Saturday morning. Brought home from Signal Hill about the same time they brought your mother home from there. That's what our neighbours must be thinking."

"Don't talk about my mother," I said.

How easy it would have been to shock him into silence, to ask him why he was so afraid of Dr. Cook or tell him what was in the letters.

"Why did you go up there?" he said.

"To see the ice," I said. "To listen to the ice."

"To see it in the dark. To listen to it. To listen to ice," he said. "Your mother was twenty-five before she started doing things like that."

"I told you not to talk about my mother."

"Keep your voice down."

"Why are you helping Dr. Cook and me?" I said.

"I'm not helping anyone," he said. "Now go upstairs. If I get started on you, God knows what I'll be saying by the time Daphne gets here."

When Aunt Daphne came home and was told by Uncle Edward of my return, she ran upstairs and into my room, where I was lying down. She fell to her knees beside the bed, crying, kissing and hugging me all at once.

"Oh, Devvie," she said. "Thank God. Thank God. Where were you, sweetheart? Are you all right? Where have you been all night? I was so worried. I thought all kinds of things."

I told her about the blockhouse, about going to the hill to hear the ice. She put her hand on my forehead as if nothing but a fever could account for such a story.

"You weren't thinking of...you weren't thinking of doing any harm to yourself or anything like that, were you?" she said.

I couldn't believe she had said it. I rolled over onto my side so that she wouldn't see how hard I was trying not to cry.

"I'm me, remember?" I said. "Remember what you said? I'm Devlin. I'm not the sum of my parents. Why did you tell me that if you don't believe it? Why did you pretend? Did you think I'd feel worse if I *knew* I wasn't normal?"

"But why did you go up there, Devvie, at night all by yourself? If you had told me you wanted to do that, I would have gone with you."

"To keep me from harming myself?"

"To keep you company. And yes, to help you if you had an accident."

"You didn't ask me if I was thinking of having an accident. Doing harm to myself, that's what you said."

"Well, what would *you* think if *I* was gone all night?"

"I'd worry. I'd look for you. But I wouldn't think what you thought. No matter what other people thought of you. Or what your parents were famous for."

I had thought, as I lay on the bed waiting for her to return, that she would accept my explanation. I would say that I went up on the hill to listen to the ice and to see it in the moonlight, and had by accident lost my lantern and been forced to take shelter in the blockhouse. And she, and only she, would see nothing sinister in this, unlike those people to whom my every action was an omen.

"I should never have taken you up there when I did," she said. "When you were still so young. Do you remember? I said, 'It's time you saw the sea,' and we went up there and we talked about your mother. You told me how your mother's horse waited there all night for her, how he was still there in the morning, waiting, when they found him. You never went up there again until this spring."

She was *blaming* herself. She had to have thought something was wrong with me or else there'd be nothing to blame herself for. For how long had she felt this way? For how long had she held out before she admitted to herself that what people like Uncle Edward said was true, that she had been fooling herself?

"I worry so much about you, Devvie. I didn't know what to think. Imagine me coming home to find the house empty. Imagine the hours passing and me knowing that it's cold enough outside for you to freeze to death. I tried to think of where you could possibly be. You wouldn't believe the things I hoped. I hoped that you had spent the night with some prostitute. I hoped that you had got drunk and fallen asleep somewhere indoors. If I didn't trust you, I would never have left you alone in the house in the first place. You have to admit that what you did was dangerous."

Even allowing that she knew nothing of what had happened to make me so caught up in Signal Hill, my having done a dangerous thing should not have led her to think what she had, to ask what she had. Would she have asked it of any boy, any young man who had done what I did?

"Never mind," I said. "I won't go up there again. I'll stay away from danger. I'll resist the urge to harm myself, to do what my parents did."

"Devlin, I love you," she said. "I love you so much. You believe that, don't you? I've never told you so before. I should have."

I knew that she loved me. I knew that I had been, just now, last night and often in the past, unfair to her. But I also knew that she no longer trusted me, that she had not really trusted me for quite some time. She was wondering already what came after danger, what came after recklessness, what came after dead-of-night excursions to the top of Signal Hill. She would leave me alone in the house again, just to convince me that she trusted me, and all the while she was out, she would wonder if I would be there when she got back. She foresaw, without resentment or any expectation of reward, a lifetime of protecting me, from others, from myself.

I went up the hill one last time, in the afternoon, ignoring the other ice pilgrims, who gaped at me as if I was about to run straight down the hill into the water.

Weeks before, I had noticed that the northern horizon was straight again, no longer jagged. The end of the ice was coming. So far up the coast I couldn't see it, there was open water. The end, the back edge of the ice. And I meant to see it, no matter what people thought or said.

From the top of the hill, the edge of the ice was even with my vantage point. I was at the juncture of four worlds, land, ice, sea and sky, each a perfect exclusion of the other.

Half the sea was solid ice and half was open water. Abruptly, in a line that extended all the way to the meeting point of sea and sky, the sea left off and the ice began.

· CHAPTER TWELVE ·

"I'M GOING TO NEW YORK TO MEET DR. COOK," I SAID.

We were in Francis Stead's surgery, Uncle Edward having told his nurse that he was going there to have his lunch, just as he did on our red-letter days. I had asked him to meet me there. It was early August. I had read in the newspapers that Dr. Cook had been unable to prepare an expedition, and so would spend the year in Brooklyn and, if all went well, leave next year for a try at the North Pole. I hoped that this time next year, he and I would be setting out for the pole together.

I had not asked Dr. Cook's permission to visit him, I told Uncle Edward, or even informed him I was coming. I was planning simply to show up unannounced.

It was time to go where the letters were coming from, time to stop dreaming about that place and make it real, and to leave behind in fact the world that, in almost every other way, I had left behind already.

"You don't have to say anything to him about the letters," I said. "When I get there, he'll stop sending them. If any arrive after I leave, you can send them on to me."

"For God's sake," he said, glancing at the door. He could not argue with me here. Or anywhere, he must have realized. He must surely have foreseen, when Dr. Cook first wrote to him, when he first called me to his surgery, that something more would come of our "arrangement" than an endless succession of letters. Of course he had. He had foreseen to the point of dread some such culmination as he was faced with now. But not knowing what form it would take, he had not been able to prepare for it. I could see that he was terrified.

He had done everything he could to forestall whatever it was that, on the whim of Dr. Cook, might happen. There was nothing, there never had been anything, that he wanted more than for those letters to stop coming, and for our arrangement to be concluded. But now that it seemed to be concluding, he was terrified.

Of what? I could not ask him, could not antagonize him now, just when I was on the verge of a departure that for all I knew he might, out of sheer spite, prevent. He did not know of Dr. Cook's claim to be my father. I was sure of that. How he had been able to resist reading the letters I had no idea, nor did I have any as to why, in the first place, he had complied with Dr. Cook's requests. Again, blackmail was all that I could think of. But what was it that Dr. Cook knew that Uncle Edward was afraid of?

"I'll make a bargain with you," he said, his voice breaking on *bargain*. I waited. "If you don't tell Daphne you're leaving, I won't tell your correspondent of your plans. Agreed? You can surprise him, or whatever it is you want to do. Just don't tell Daphne you're leaving."

"You won't tell him I'm coming?" I said.

"I won't tell him anything."

Would he send to me in New York, at the address I would give him once I found a place to live, any further letters he received?

"I'll have to think about that," he said. "The best way of doing it, I mean. The safest way. For both of us. Remember: not a word to Daphne."

I was right to have blurted out my decision to Uncle Edward. I could not stand the thought of my one-sided correspondence with Dr. Cook dragging on for still more years. Nothing but living in the same city as him made any sense now that I knew I would be his protégé "someday."

I had become worried that, despite his invitation, he would have been satisfied to go on writing to me forever. It would not satisfy me. I would tire of the letters if they ceased to be a prelude to something more. If I left it up to him, I might still be receiving them when I was thirty.

It seemed strange to think that I would at long last meet him. I thought he would probably let me go with him at least part of the way on his next expedition, whatever misgivings he might have about my age. I had pledged to one day be his protégé in Arctic exploration. I could see no reason why that day should not come soon. I had graduated from school in June. I was almost twenty.

When I got to New York, I would seek him out and, when he was alone, surprise him. As quickly as possible after telling him who I was, I would assure him that my purpose in coming to New York was not to unmask him as my father or to cause him any embarrassment in public.

I wanted to surprise Dr. Cook as he, in his first letter, had surprised me.

I did not want to think it all through too clearly, for fear of encountering obstacles that would make me lose my nerve. I wanted only to get away, to go to New York, to Brooklyn, to the corner of Bushwick and Willoughby, where he lived and practised, to introduce myself to him. What would happen after that I didn't know. I felt that like Dr. Cook, I was in a race—that if he made it to the pole, or if Peary or someone else beat him to it, I might never hear from him again.

How could he, how could we, contrive a reason to associate with one another except on the most casual basis? In society, there would be no place for us. Only outside it, apart from it—only as fellow explorers—could we be anything like father and son.

Following Uncle Edward once again into my father's surgery, I was reminded of the first time I had gone to see him there. He had motioned for me to sit down, then made a cage of his fingers and looked at me through it.

It was apparent that since our last meeting, he had regained his equanimity. He had had time to think, to make plans. I prayed he had not found a way out of our agreement.

"New York," he said.

New York. For my mother, even for Francis Stead, it had been a synonym for calamity, dashed hopes, the end of youth.

"I've been reading about it," I said. "Everyone who goes there says it will soon be the greatest city in the world. Some people think it is already."

He smiled.

"What was it your father said in that letter? 'Brooklyn is to explorers what Paris is to artists.'"

I nodded, though Francis Stead had said "New York," not "Brooklyn."

"Do you think that for your father, leaving home, leaving you and your mother behind, was some great sacrifice in the service of some cause?"

I remembered Dr. Cook's dedication in those *Century* articles. "He laboured in the service of mankind." It sounded as though Uncle Edward had read them, too.

"Something he would rather not have done, but had to do for the greater good? The greater good of what?"

"I don't know," I said.

He smiled. He dropped his hands flat on his desk so suddenly that it startled me.

"Well. As to the first of your requests, I will not tell your correspondent that you are coming. As to your second request, I am going to destroy any letters that arrive in your absence, because neither I nor your correspondent wants you to have originals."

I shrugged.

"You have grown up without the guidance of a father, or even a father figure—the latter office I would gladly have performed, but you made it clear from the start that you did not want me to."

He paused and it seemed for a while that he was finished. I thought of telling him that my father had been writing me for years. He swivelled his chair until he almost faced the window.

"Have you ever tried to imagine my side of it? A grown man

running secret errands for his nephew. I have felt like a messenger boy, delivering to the leading man scripts that I was not allowed to read."

"You could have read them if you wanted to," I said.

"Pawing through the post at my surgery each morning, looking for a letter, an envelope of the right kind and colour. Hiding it in my desk. Wearing that stupid red handkerchief. Climbing to your father's surgery, putting the envelope in the drawer, sitting in that chair, waiting for you to arrive, keeping guard outside while you read your precious letter. Burning the letter."

In truth, I had not tried to imagine his side of it.

"The story of how I found the courage to approach you in the first place must remain untold. I risked a great deal more than you can guess by acting as a go-between for you and your correspondent. I noticed the change that came over you not long after those letters began to arrive. I am not unable to appreciate the yearning for adventure, though I believe it irresponsible to indulge it to the point where it becomes one's main profession. However, you are very much your father's son and will, I am sure, do what you want to do, regardless of how it might affect others."

My face burned with shame. He was right.

"It has occurred to me that you are going to New York not just to see your correspondent, but to someday join him on his expeditions. It has further occurred to me that he is fool enough to take you on. If Daphne knew of your plans, she would never have another minute's peace. Did you know that she wants you to article in law so that you will never have to leave St. John's? She has already made inquiries."

She had said nothing to me about this. She had already begun the business of protecting me from me.

"Have you thought about how you're going to leave without Daphne's knowledge?" he said.

I shook my head. I had put off thinking about it. About what it would do to her.

"You see, she would never let you go to New York by yourself. She would try to talk you out of going, and when that didn't work, she would insist on going with you. She'll never let you out of her sight if she can help it."

There was no question of my arriving in New York and meeting Dr. Cook with Aunt Daphne either by my side or showing up soon after. It might so unsettle him that he would have nothing more to do with me.

Uncle Edward leaned towards me across the desk.

"The best thing you can do for her and for yourself," he said, almost whispering, "is simply disappear. Tell her nothing. Leave a note, but do not tell her where you've gone or why."

The best thing for him, most of all, though he would not say it.

"She'll find out where I went eventually," I said. "And why. My name might be in the papers someday." I had pictured this already. A photograph of me in the local papers, and in the New York papers. "Among the expeditionaries is Devlin Stead, the son of Dr. Francis Stead, who served with Dr. Cook..."

"You will be older then. Perhaps much older. Daphne will be less inclined to interfere, and you better able to resist her. And she'll have got used to your absence by then."

"But if I just up and leave—"

"She'll worry. But not as much as she would if she knew of your decision to follow in your father's footsteps. Let's not forget where those footsteps led or what they left behind. She may adjust to your absence more quickly than you think. There was a time when she had no trouble getting by without you. Such a time may come again. Two-thirds of the threesome disappeared, and we got along without them. We have grown quite used to disappearances. That, with you gone, my brother's whole family will have disappeared may one day seem to her quite natural."

No doubt he thought, or was hoping, that nothing much would come of my meeting Dr. Cook, and that, finally free to forget my childhood, I would, in the immigrant tradition, start all over in America, where it would be easy to believe that my past in Newfoundland had never been.

I never want to see you again, he might as well have said. "My brother's family." He had never thought of me as part of his. I had been merely a guest, and now my stay was over. Soon his arrangement with Dr. Cook would end, those letters would stop coming and his torment, whatever it proceeded from, would be removed. Go, go and don't come back. Ever. Don't write. Allow us to forget that you exist. I had no affection for him, but I could not help feeling the sting of his contempt for me.

"I will buy you a second-class ticket to New York," he said, "and give you as much money as there is in the trust account that Daphne established for you with the money your father left behind. I cannot, for obvious reasons, withdraw money from that account, nor can you without approaching Daphne. I will top up the amount to two hundred dollars. That should set you nicely on your way."

It sounded so much like a bribe, so much like Judas money, that I felt like declining it. But I could not afford to. The question of *how* I would get to New York had been much on my mind.

"If you want to keep your destination secret from Daphne, you will have to keep it secret from everyone. You cannot be seen boarding a passenger ship that all of St. John's knows is going to New York. I will arrange something and get back to you about it."

We met again, days later, and he told me that he had arranged passage for me on a schooner bound for Halifax, where I could catch a passenger ship from England that, not having stopped off at St. John's, would have on it no one who knew me. I would board the schooner not from the waterfront, where I was certain to be seen, but outside the Narrows, sometime after dark, probably very early in the morning, when it was least likely there would be witnesses to the temporary deviation of the schooner's course.

"They will anchor and send a rowboat in to get you," he said. "It's summer. A few hours outdoors at night will do you no harm. This time."

"What about my trunk?" I said.

"You will take no more with you than you can fit in this," he said, handing me a doctor's bag that Francis Stead had once used, and that still bore his initials, *F* below one clasp, *S* below the other.

"You may, when you get to New York, want to use a different name," he said. "See what your correspondent thinks."

Leave her a note. A mere note to the woman who loved me as if I was her son.

Dear Aunt Daphne:

It is not because of anything you said or did that I am leaving. I am going away, but not forever. To where, I cannot tell you. For how long, I do not know. I know now that there is nothing wrong with me. I will make my own fate. If you can bring yourself to believe that, you will not fret too much for me or doubt that we will meet again. "I leave everything to Daphne," my mother said. She knew you could do what she could not. You made me happy. I wish I could have done the same for you. I hope that when we meet again, I will be a more worthy object of your affection. You will always be the object of mine.

All my love,
Devlin

It was so much less than she deserved that I wondered if it might be better to leave no note at all. But anything I wrote would be so much less than she deserved. What would she think when she read it? Despite my assurances, that she was to blame, that I was leaving because she had asked me if I had thought about doing myself harm. That it *was* to do myself harm, to do myself harm in some place where she would never know about it, that I was leaving. If the former, she would be partly right. If the latter, she had even less faith in me than I'd imagined. I vowed that I would somehow, as soon as possible, in some way that would not jeopardize my relationship with Dr. Cook, put her mind to rest.

Holding a lantern in one hand and the doctor's bag that was once Francis Stead's in the other, I made my way down the steep path towards the sea. I had been walking downhill for ten minutes when the slope inclined upward again. I was almost literally following in my mother's footsteps. She would not have taken quite the same route, however, having descended this hill in mid-spring, when there might still have been snow on the ground and the path was hard to find. Nor did anyone know if she had waited until after dark to make her way downhill to the water. I tried not to think about her. I wondered if Uncle Edward had intended this perverse congruity, mother and son "leaving" by the same route. Perhaps there really was no other place that a schooner could wait at anchor unseen from the harbour. I knew of none.

"The Stead boy is gone." It would be all over town by the next morning. Gone for good this time. Left a note in which he did little more than bid his poor aunt goodbye. Aunt Daphne, thinking it might not be too late to catch me, would insist on some sort of search, an investigation. Uncle Edward would go along with it, do everything he could to help, then console her when it turned up nothing.

I topped the second hill and saw the lights of the schooner three hundred feet from shore. I waved my lantern. One of the lights on the schooner swayed back and forth. I descended the hill and saw, just up the rocky shore, another light, that of the rowboat, I presumed.

There was no beach. The land fell off abruptly on my right and the going was treacherous. As I neared the light, I spotted a dry creek bed and followed it until I was just above the rowboat, which was bobbing on the water, kept in place by an anchor and a massive man, who with both hands was clinging to a knob of rock. "Good thing it's not rough," he said. The boat was still at least ten feet below where I was standing.

"How do I get in?" I said.

"You turn down that lantern, then hand it to me along with that bag. And then you jump."

"I'll keep the bag," I said. It contained, along with my personal effects, the portrait photograph of my mother and the collected correspondence of Dr. Cook, the tightly rolled scrolls of paper that for years had been hidden in my bedpost.

"Suit yourself," he said. I reached the lantern down to him. When he removed one hand to take it, the bobbing of the boat increased. He put the lantern as far behind him as he could without losing his grip on the rock.

"All right," he said. "Jump."

I hesitated. I thought of my mother again. They had found her about as far from shore as the boat was now. Even at this time of year, that water would be frigid. The jolting cold, a sudden intake of breath, a great gasp before my head went under. If I was found in the very place where she had been found, how eerily but suitably congruent that would seem.

I felt a spurt of panic. If I was found washed up against the very rocks my mother had leapt from fifteen years ago, who would doubt that I had died by my own hand? I told myself that I was being absurd. Uncle Edward was surely incapable of doing such a thing, and surely not *that* desperate to remove me from his life.

I jumped. As he caught me, the man somehow kept his balance in the lurching boat, his hands beneath my armpits, all but enclosing them, it felt like, his thumbs all but touching his fingers. Even as he held me in mid-air, I wondered if he was about to lower me over the side and hold me under. How easily he could have done it and not left a mark on me. He put me down slowly, sat me down so that I faced him. He sat, pulled up the anchor, put the oars in the oarlocks. With the first stroke, the boat rose on the water. Soon we were skimming along as if we were being towed by a steamship.

I could see him clearly now by the light of the lantern. He was wearing a tattered watchcap, through which showed tufts of thick red hair. As unlikely an associate of Uncle Edward's as could be imagined.

Uncle Edward. Aunt Daphne.

I might be leaving her alone with him for life.

BOOK TWO

· CHAPTER THIRTEEN ·

My dearest Devlin:

*How dearly I cherish my beloved Brooklyn each day when I look
across the river at Manhattan. Or when I am required to make a
crossing of the Brooklyn Bridge.*

*In every field—science, commerce, engineering, transportation,
communications—inventors file for patents every day. It seems that
every resident of Manhattan is a specialist in something, a master of
some task vital to everyone that he alone can perform.*

*The tendency of almost everything is "up." There is no room
left in the sought-after parts of Manhattan for new building sites,
so they are tearing down the old buildings, in some cases less
than ten years old, and building higher ones. Last year, when a
building of twenty storeys was completed, the papers said that no
higher building could be made. Now higher ones are being built,
and even higher ones being talked about—thirty-, forty-storey
buildings that will make the greatest of cathedrals seem like a
parish church.*

*The streets are crammed with traffic, so other "streets" have
been built above them, the el trains that block out what little sun
would otherwise find its way down to the streets. The rivers are
jammed with ferries, so bridges must be built above the rivers, and
bridges built on bridges.*

One walks along a city street as though at the bottom of a

canyon. Except that in the canyons of Manhattan, there is not soli-
tude and silence but the pandemonium of Milton's hell.

The elevated trains were built with no one in mind but the
people who would ride them. It is nothing less than perilous to walk
beneath them when every thrust of their engines and every applica-
tion of their brakes sends showering down on the people below a
multitude of red-hot cinders, sparks and coal and a choking storm
of soot.

Occasionally, I travel to the northern part of Manhattan to
attend to some charity cases. There you can see what the whole
island looked like not so long ago. It is a collection of barely con-
nected shanty towns in which live people who have never seen
Manhattan, whose only proof of its existence is the glow from the
lights of its buildings, which at night illuminates the southern sky. It
is an eerie thing, even for me, to look south from these shanty towns
and see that glow, to stand on the ever-thinning wedge of the past
and see the present / future in the distance. Not many people have
seen, as I have, both segments of Manhattan, the one growing and
the other shrinking, soon to disappear.

Manhattan is like some enormous diorama that illustrates the
changes that have taken place in technology in the past one hundred
years. If in the shanty towns they are ignorant of the city, those in
the city are even more ignorant of them. What lies beyond the
northernmost edge of the city most neither know nor care.

I do not talk to them, the shanties, as they are called, of the
great metropolis that daily lurches farther north, though they have
heard of it. I think that soon they will be able to hear the thunder-
ous advance of its construction. If I were to tell them that just a few
miles away, buildings seem to go up as fast as they come down, that
speed is everything, that it is as if fortifications are being erected in
advance of some invasion force, they would think me mad.

Workers swarm like ants on construction sites. They walk,
without harnesses or safety ropes, with as much confidence in their
balance as cats, on the beams of the iron skeletons on which the

walls of the monoliths are draped as tents are draped on poles, hundreds of feet above the ground.

I once stood in one of these buildings, safely inside one that was finished while across the street another one was being built. I was close enough to the men on the iron beams to see the expressions on their faces. Above, below and all about them there was only space. How incongruous they looked, as if they had not climbed to this height, but had had the earth fall away beneath them, leaving them by sheer chance on these iron beams, horizontal spans that seemed to have no vertical attachments, no anchors, but merely, and who could say for how much longer, hung suspended in mid-air.

If every man now at work on these buildings in New York fell from his place, the next day these construction sites would look the same, so massive is the force of workers now available. I have heard it said that the Lower East Side of Manhattan is the most densely inhabited portion of the earth.

I have read that a "train" of ships, a fleet in single file with less than a few hours' sailing between one ship and the next, stretches every day from America to Europe, every ship filled to capacity, especially in steerage, with what might be just one of the many raw materials this city, this nation, needs to build itself. Passenger ships loaded like barges with their cargo.

The papers say that more than ten thousand immigrants are admitted to America through Ellis Island every day, and that about one-quarter of them settle down forever in Manhattan. It is no longer the Irish and the Germans who make up the largest groups, but the Jews of eastern Europe. Three thousand new strangers in the city every day—strangers not just to Manhattan, but to America, to the English language, to all customs and traditions but the ones of their fellow countrymen.

Three thousand. It seems inconceivable until one sees them wandering bewildered and dumbfounded in the streets, pushing trunks and chests and carts that contain everything they own, the rest of their possessions having been forsaken forever in a homeland they will never see again.

Most of them, upon disembarking from the ferries at the Hudson piers, will never leave the island of Manhattan, not even to cross the river on a ferry or to ride in the most primitive of horse-drawn vehicles across the great arch of the Brooklyn Bridge. They will have that view of Manhattan only once, will see it nearly whole only once.

I doubt that most of them realize this as they jostle at the rails to see our great, green, torch-bearing lady; to see the buildings they have read about in letters they received from relatives who have already moved here, letters embellished to convince the Old Worlders to come, so lonesome and homesick are the New Worlders in Manhattan.

But it is impossible, Devlin, once having seen it, to walk away from it and live as if it isn't there.

They see it, the newcomers, from afar, the frieze of stone that from that distance is Manhattan—great, massive, a joyous sight after two weeks of confinement on the ships. From that prospect, it does not overwhelm, or if it does, they revel in it, for to be over-whelmed is what they want. Nothing less will convince them that the decision they have made and cannot unmake is the right one.

It seems to them that the city will always look that way. But then they enter into it and soon forget that the handful of saplings that mark the boundaries of their existence are part of a great forest that one day long ago they saw the shape of from a distance.

There is something about it all that both exhilarates and fright-ens me. I am frightened not, I think, by the larger implications of the pace of all this growth, which are still difficult to read, so much as at the possibility of being myself unable to keep up with it, of being left behind. I do not give in to this fear; I fight it, resist it, though to do so takes great effort.

It may surprise you that I would say this, given how eager I seem to be to leave all of civilization behind. But it is impossible to look upon it and not feel as though one is being left behind, not feel forsaken. And this is what seems to animate everyone—not just the people who, with their hands, are making the city, but also the people who are paying them to make it, and paying its architects and engineers.

No one wants to be left behind, but as to what the destination is, no one ever seems to give a thought. The papers speak of the thrill of "new beginnings" as an explanation for the frenzy that one feels here night and day. But all of it feels to me not so much like a new beginning as a last chance.

For what? Who knows. That is what I see in people's eyes. One feels that if this frenzy was to increase by just one notch, this race to get ahead would become a race to get away, this pursuit would become a great retreat. What it is that we pursue or might one day flee in panic from, other than nebulous "progress," I cannot say. And yet I, too, am barely able to resist it, despite having no clue what "it" is.

I am myself caught up in a race whose real goal sometimes seems as inscrutable as that of the men who make the buildings.

Explorers set out in noble terms the importance to mankind of reaching the North and South poles as swiftly as possible. But most of them do not labour in the service of mankind.

I believe that I am one of the few who does. I look at the builders of the city as they run about, and I see not myself, but men like Peary.

Each man thinks there must be a goal, or why would everyone be running? So he runs too. Each man thinks the man beside him is the one who knows where he is headed, and who therefore must be followed.

I cannot, each man thinks to himself, I must not, I will not be left behind.

Yours truly,
Dr. F. A. Cook

May 11, 1900

I read Dr. Cook's letter several times over on the voyage from Halifax. The last I had received from him, it had reached me in June and had convinced me to put off no longer the flight from home that I had for so long been contemplating.

I regarded myself not as an immigrant to America, but as a native of the New World, Dr. Cook and I simply having been born in different parts of it. I fancied that at the sight of the strange spectacle he described, the arrival of the immigrants from eastern and southern Europe, I would feel as he had. But I knew I was mistaken when, from the porthole of my berth in second class, I first saw the featureless mass of North America.

We had been two nights at sea. That it was the continent, I did not realize until I had been staring at it for some time. At first I took it to be a small island, a disruption in the horizon so faint that it dissolved, reappearing only after I closed my eyes and opened them again. Soon it seemed that there were several small islands, then that they cohered into a single, larger one. It went on like this for some time, small islands slowly taking shape and then cohering, until it seemed there lay strung out in front of us a broken barrier that we would have to navigate to reach the continent.

Although nothing on the map as I remembered it corresponded with them, it still did not occur to me that these swelling and cohering shapes were our destination, for I did not feel that I had been long enough at sea to have come within sight of a place that had for so long seemed so far away.

The "islands" had assumed two massive shapes with a narrow channel in between before I could accept that even this last passageway would close by increments, and that what I was looking at, what seemed to be rearing up for the first time from beneath the sea, was North America. It was as if I had been for so long and so exclusively an islander that I clung to that mirage of shape-shifting islands until the illusion was so blatant that I had to let it go.

I had never, until this voyage, been far enough from Newfoundland to see it as an island. I had never really thought of it as one, had not really believed that if you followed the coast, you would come back to where you started.

I knew from how long it had taken for land to disappear after we departed from Halifax that we were still hours away from land now. We were not heading straight for the continent but travelling southwest, land on my right, and on my left, though I could not see it, endless open water.

I told myself that this featureless "land" would never resolve itself into shapes and lines and colours as long as I kept looking at it. I lay down on my bunk and, in spite of my excitement, dozed fitfully, half dreaming, half remembering, with images from the past few days passing haphazardly before my mind.

I recalled the strange finality of watching a porter wheel on board someone else's steamer trunk in Halifax while I had nothing with me but a doctor's bag.

I dreamed about the letters on the hull of the British steamship, which I was for some reason unable to decipher, though I knew they spelled out some word in English.

The passengers in steerage I had neither seen nor heard, though I knew them to be directly below the floor of my berth.

A steward whose English accent inspired in me a deference that I tried in vain to hide had shown me how to close the hatch on my porthole window so that I could keep my berth dark and sleep in until my accustomed hour. He then so discreetly paused for a tip that he was gone before I realized what I should have done. I rang for him again, asked directions to the dining room that he had pointed out to me the first time, then thrust a coin at him so soon after he was done that in taking it he flinched as though he thought I meant to strike him.

I walked through the dining room in search of an empty table, declining when an older couple invited me to join them, muttering that it seemed "my friend" was elsewhere.

I had got out of bed one night convinced that someone had woken me by knocking on my door. I stood in the darkness and heard nothing but the dull drone of the ship.

I had a dream in which I tried to contact Dr. Cook by telephone. I had never used a telephone before. Over and over I spoke into the mouthpiece, but there was no reply.

I came fully awake again. It sounded as though the ship was being hastily evacuated. From above and outside in the corridor came the sound of running footsteps and children shouting. From below came the first sounds I had heard from steerage, muffled cries of what sounded like alarm or even panic. Looking out the porthole, I got an oblique glimpse of what I thought was Manhattan but later learned was Staten Island.

I left my berth and joined a stream of others heading for the decks of second class. I did not realize until I was on deck and the sea breeze met my face how hot it was. The ship still contained the cool air of the mid-Atlantic, but up there it was stifling.

I went to the rail, where everyone was staring at the Statue of Liberty, of which people the world over had seen so many pictures that she was already a cliché, massive and heraldic though she was. The polyglot din of the passengers below in steerage fell to a hush. Some people stared back at the statue long after we had passed it, but most looked forward to the primary marvel of Manhattan.

I had seen photographs of Manhattan taken from this vantage point, the ramparts of the Battery looming like a vision in the mist, as if even greater wonders lay in the land beyond them. But the photographs had left me unprepared for this.

Here I must try to remember how the city looked, the impression it made on me before I knew the names of its buildings or had walked the streets that ran between them, before I knew from experience rather than from books that this solid frieze was merely an illusion of perspective, before I knew which pier the ship was headed for, before I knew it had a number, not a name. Things for which I had no name I did not see, or else I saw them all as one thing called Manhattan.

It looked not like many structures, but like one whose towers rose up from a single block of stone. I found myself trying to find the heart of it, the first structure to which the others had been joined. The strangest thing was that this city that I knew from Dr. Cook's letter to be in a ceaseless state of growth and transformation looked so old, the buildings as ancient, as permanent, as the faces of the cliffs along the Hudson, which I had seen in books and magazines.

It was absurd to think that this, *this* should be anyone's first experience of "elsewhere." I was reminded of something I had once seen from the top of Signal Hill, a cluster of massive icebergs rearing up from out of nowhere like some city on an otherwise flat and empty plain.

It was my first sight of something artificially stupendous. There were not, to my knowledge, any other Newfoundlanders on board. It occurred to me that even including children, I was probably the least travelled person on the ship. Even those passengers who had spent all their lives in remote villages had, on some stage of the journey that was soon to end, seen some of the old cities of Europe, with their great towers, palaces, bridges and cathedrals, or the ruins of even older cities, the pillars of colossal temples. Even if they did not realize it, the city they were gaping at had its beginning in the ones they left behind.

Whereas I, I now realized, was of neither the Old World nor the New, but from a place so discrete, so singular that it required a periodic consultation of history books and maps to dispel the notion that human life there had begun independently of human life elsewhere. This in spirit was the city of these new arrivals, but in no way was it mine, not yet, and I could not help doubting that it would ever be.

It seemed to me that I was enlisting in history, their history, one phase of which they had left behind to start another. I had made a jump onto the deck of their ship as it was going by. I was a stowaway, more rootless than that portion of those in steerage who had made the crossing unaccompanied by family or friends.

But that would change, I told myself, for this was the world of the letters I was looking at, the one in which they were written, the one that they described. This, at last, was the world of Dr. Cook. And the place where I began.

For an instant, all the rest—my past, my mother, Francis Stead, Aunt Daphne, Uncle Edward, the house I grew up in, the city of St. John's—seemed like the fast-fading remnants of a dream that I was waking from.

But then this feeling gave way to its opposite, and it was this New World that seemed unreal, remote. I felt that the instant I tried to take hold of it, or made to enter into it, the city would recede from me as all things did when you sought after them in dreams.

I envied the immigrants their lack of choices, these people whose decision to come here could never be reversed, for whom doubts and second thoughts and homesickness were so pointless they could revel in them, knowing that nothing would ever come of them. For them, at the first sight of the New World, it was certain that the old one was gone for good, that never again would they see it or the people they had left behind. It was so awful, yet so simple. It had an absoluteness about it that I longed for.

But my home was so much closer, at least in space, than theirs that I could not divest myself of one world by choosing the other. I could think of no way of choosing irrevocably, of ridding myself of all uncertainty and doubt.

How wrong I had been to think that I would survey my fellow immigrants with the same strange mixture of compassion and aloofness as Dr. Cook had.

The notion of my ever having received a letter from Dr. Cook, let alone my being his son, seemed suddenly illusory. The Dr. Cook who had grown up across the river from this city, who had grown up watching *it* grow up, who had ventured into it so often he as good as lived there, who sometimes sounded as if he had become so used to it that his life had come to seem pedestrian and nothing short of polar exploration could enliven it—this Dr. Cook had felt compelled to seek *me* out, to ask for *my* help, to plead with *me* to share his life?

I was filled with a sickening doubt. What if the idea that I was his son was a fiction that for him served some inscrutable purpose? It was not long after Francis Stead made New York his port that he blundered to his death. There was no telling how a man might be affected who had spent his whole life here.

I crossed over to the other side of the ship, where only a few people who must many times have seen the Statue of Liberty and the skyline of Manhattan stood leaning on the rails, staring vacantly across the way at Brooklyn, an air of irony about them as they chatted, now and then smiling at each other when a shout of excitement went up on the other side.

Brooklyn was itself an impressive sight. Had its cross-river rival been any city in America instead of the borough of Manhattan, it would have been Brooklyn that the passengers were gawking at. Along the shore, beyond the cluster of schooner masts that looked like a forest from whose trees all the branches and the bark had been removed, was a line of warehouses, arranged as haphazardly as the cars of two trains that had met head-on. Above the warehouses and the attenuated smokestacks of an endless sprawl of factories, on a rise of land that I could tell already was more steep than any to be found on the island of Manhattan, was a city that appeared to be laid out on a grid of parishes, each steeple staking claim to a part of Brooklyn. The steeples of churches and cathedrals rose everywhere above the houses and the trees and the buildings that in comparison with their fellows on the other side were small, though far larger than any I had seen before that day.

Once we cleared Governors Island, I could see the Brooklyn Bridge. It seemed, because of two cities' worth of smoke and haze, to be hanging in the air without support. Dr. Cook lived at the corner of Bushwick and Willoughby, in a neighbourhood called Bushwick. But where this was in relation to the Brooklyn tower of the bridge, how far from it and in which direction, I had no idea.

I cursed the provinciality and introspective turn of mind that had made me hole up in my berth on the voyage from Halifax as if to be in the company of non-Newfoundlanders or strangers of any kind was either beneath me or beyond me. Whether it was pride or shame that held me back I could not say. But vowing that I had not come to New

York to spend my time wondering what I was doing there, I went down to my berth for my belongings.

I collected the doctor's bag that bore Francis Stead's initials and contained Dr. Cook's letters. I thought of them as my letters of introduction to Dr. Cook, even though they were written by him and copied in my hand.

I had planned, in preparation for transporting them, to combine all the letters in as few as half a dozen scrolls, but this had proved impossible, first because there were simply too many pages, and second because it was years since I had read some of the letters, years since they were last unscrolled, and I dared not disturb them for fear that they would fall apart.

My valise, therefore, as I went back up on deck, contained about three dozen scrolls, some tied with string, some with ribbon as if they were diplomas. To keep them from being crushed by the other articles, I had placed the scrolls on top, so it seemed that they were all the bag contained. It occurred to me what an odd sight the scrolls would make to anyone who looked inside the bag. They might have been some strange form of contraband, something that passengers were explicitly forbidden to take on board the ship. But I had no reason to think that anyone would look inside the bag. The men on the schooner that took me from St. John's to Halifax had told me that first- and second-class passengers who showed no outward signs of being ill were allowed to disembark with only a cursory inspection.

The ship docked starboard to the pier, which jutted out three hundred feet from the waterfront. When it became clear that it would be some time before our disembarkment got under way, I walked along the rail of the ship until I encountered a wire-mesh barrier.

I was now on the port side, where a drama that seemed to be of no interest to anyone on starboard or onshore was taking place. Looking out around the barrier, I saw that steerage passengers were disembarking over several gangplanks onto ferries that bore the name of Ellis Island. Some passengers, who seemed to think that they were being turned away from America, tried to resist, sobbing and protesting as they were dragged along by implacable officials who, I guessed, were well used to such behaviour.

I knew that you could be refused admittance to America at Ellis Island if you showed signs of mental instability, an *X* scrawled in chalk on your shoulder or your back. My mother, had she travelled to America in steerage, might not have been admitted.

"No outward signs of being ill." The mentally ill were easiest to spot. I wondered if, to the trained eye, to an expert in such things, I showed any "outward signs" of the illness that so many were convinced was in my blood. I did not feel ill, but then my mother had not seemed so to those who knew her either.

I could just imagine with what haste a man from steerage clutching to his chest a bag of paper scrolls would be deported, especially if some official went so far as to read the letters. I could not think of any explanation that would save me, not even the far-from-simple truth. Least of all the far-from-simple truth. The redhead on the schooner had told me that I should say, if asked, that my possessions had been sent on ahead of me in a steamer trunk. "Don't tell them you have nothing but that little bag," he had said.

Suddenly fearful of discovery, I felt wash over me a sense of the oddness of my mission. For a second I regarded myself as others would if they knew not only the contents of my bag, but the purpose of my trip. And in that second, it must be said, what an odd young man I seemed to myself to be.

I went back to starboard. The stewards asked us to form a line beginning about ten feet from the stairs that had been lowered from the ship. I was well back in the line and could not see the head of it, but I could hear that before each person disembarked, a man spoke so briefly he might have been extending to them some sort of official welcome.

It looked as if the entire city had turned out to meet the ship. At the front of the crowd was what I would have called a cordon of policemen had they in any way been acting in consort. They seemed randomly spaced at the head of the crowd, here a threesome of them, then a gap of a hundred feet where none was stationed. Some stood with their backs to the ship, but only so that they could chat with people at the head of the crowd; others stood with their backs to the crowd, hands in their trouser pockets, trying not to look as if they had no idea why they had been posted there.

Now and then, to the apparent amusement of the cops, little begrimed boys broke through the line of grown-ups at the front and ran straight at passengers who were just setting foot on land. They grabbed the handles of their bags and suitcases as if they meant to steal them. Some passengers gave up their bags without resistance and, as the fierce-faced boys disappeared into the crowd, ambled after them with an air of unconcern. Others held firm to theirs, and the boys, after a short, comical struggle, gave up and ran back into the crowd again.

When I saw that beyond the crush of people lay an army of conveyance vehicles and horses, I realized that the boys were freelance porters. I saw them climb up on hacks, hansom cabs and carriages. Standing beside the drivers, who in their tall black hats sat so motionless they might have been asleep, they waved to the people they had pressed into being customers, holding their bags aloft so they would know which vehicle was theirs. Once the customers and bags were aboard, the boys accepted payment from the drivers and ran back towards the ship again.

One man relinquished his bag to a boy who was running flat out, holding it about a foot from his body to make it easier for the boy, who came up from behind him to close both hands upon it. There was a smattering of applause, as much for the man as for the boy, it seemed to me, for the exchange had taken place as smoothly as if they had been practising for years. It might have been anything from a custom peculiar to this pier to one common throughout the harbours of America. It was neither forbidden nor encouraged by the cops, just wryly observed. There must have been a point at which they would have intervened, however, or why else were they there?

Everyone whose bags were not toted by a porter in uniform was expected to fend for himself when set upon by those little boys. People, even newcomers, would somehow sort themselves out and need not be interfered with by officials, the assumption seemed to be. I would have been more disposed to appreciate how entertainingly anarchic a spectacle it was had I not been about to make my descent into the luggage rats myself.

I decided I had no choice but to hold my bag with both arms against my chest just as I had pictured some poor immigrant doing, thereby giving himself no hope of passing inspection.

I would hold the bag in one hand until I made it past the man at the head of the line, who, as I heard someone in front of me say, was a doctor, though he was not even wearing a token stethoscope.

"Where are you from, young man?" he said when my turn came. He was bald, his face beet red and sweating. He was impeccably dressed and without a doubt well on his way on that early afternoon to being drunk.

"St. John's, Newfoundland," I said, but he had already shifted his gaze to the person behind me, as if my ability to speak English was proof enough that I carried no contagion.

Holding my bag high and with both hands, I descended the stairs. Once on the ground, I veered away from a boy who came running at me as if he meant to knock me down, and was by him distracted long enough that I did not see the boy who came at me from the side and jumped half his height into the air to grab the handles of my bag with both hands. When he landed, he almost yanked the bag from my hands. I improved my grip.

"I can carry it myself," I said. The boy, as if he had either not heard or not understood a word I said, looked not at me but at the bag, his face contorted with exertion, cheeks puffed, eyes squinted almost shut. I could not believe his strength. Exerting equal force, we began to go around in a circle, four feet scuffing on the cobblestones as though we were playing some sort of game. "You'll break the bag," I said, but still the bag was all he stared at. I glanced at the police, half hoping for, half dreading their intervention, wondering what would happen if the bag burst and the odd-looking scrolls spilled out.

Finally, afraid that if the struggle went on much longer the cops would intervene, I relented, releasing the handles so suddenly that the boy went flying backwards and lost his balance, skidding on his backside on the cobblestones but holding the bag clear of the ground.

He was still skidding as he turned and gained his feet. He ran off through the crowd towards the carriages, ran at full speed as the bag was all but weightless. I ran after him, trying to keep sight of him through the crowd, terrified that I might mistake some other boy for him and never see the scrolls again. I brushed up against scores of people and was glad that, on the advice of the redhead, I had moved my money from my wallet to the pockets of my slacks. Leg pockets were harder to pick, he said, and assured me that in New York, pickpockets were everywhere. "Two hundred in cash," he said, shaking his head as he watched me transfer it from my wallet to my pocket. I had seen American money before but had never held it in my hand. "Put some in each pocket," he said, "and once you're squared away, put it in a bank or you won't have it very long."

I saw the boy jump onto the sideboard of a hansom cab. I grabbed my bag from him just as he held out his hand to receive the penny the driver was extending to him between thumb and forefinger. The driver, a beefy fellow with an ill-fitting bowler and a square moustache, closed his fist around the coin and looked at me.

"Do you want a cab or not, sir?" he said in what I took to be an Irish accent. I looked at the boy, whose eyes were glued on the driver's fist, which held the penny he had earned but might not get, still as oblivious to me as when we had struggled for the bag.

"Yes," I said, though I had planned, unladen as I was, to walk, exactly where I wasn't sure. The driver dropped the penny. The boy was already in mid-stride when the penny hit his hand. He bolted back into the crowd towards the ship. I asked the driver to take me to some moderately priced hotel.

That night, I lay above the blankets in my sweltering room. I had opened both windows but could not sleep because of the noise, which even at that hour showed no sign of dying down.

How could the air, in a city so close to a river and the sea, be so still, I wondered. I longed for a breeze as the thirsty in the desert long for water. The curtains hung motionless. It had never been as warm indoors in St. John's as it was outdoors in Manhattan at that moment.

When I closed my eyes, I saw the face of the boy who had fought me for the bag, and whom I doubted I would ever see again, though I was sure I would recognize him if a year from now I passed him in the street. A child as old as the city itself, he might have been; a Manhattan artifact on whom my existence had in no way registered. I wondered if he had been able to speak English.

I felt vaguely, obscurely, disappointed by what had seemed certain, this time yesterday, to be one of the great days of my life. What had I expected? Some feeling of momentousness, I supposed, at my first sight of the city in which I was conceived; perhaps even a sense of homecoming, of returning to the place where I began. It had often struck me, when I looked at photographs or postcards of Manhattan, that I was looking at the place of my conception. I suppose I had thought that what I felt when I saw these images of Manhattan I would feel with a thousand times the force when I saw the place for real. But it had not been so on the ship, nor as I drove in the hansom cab through the teeming streets, and I was not sure why.

All I could think was that this was the city where Francis Stead had gone to live when he could no longer stand to come back home and be reminded by the sight of me that he was not my father. It was not Brooklyn, not the city where my real father lived between one expedition and the next. But not even the sight of that city had moved me as I thought it would.

I wondered if each time he looked across the river at Manhattan, Dr. Cook was reminded of me, of the day he crossed over on the ferry and at that party met my mother. Of all the lofty thoughts that might come to mind as, from Brooklyn, one watched the sunlight sink lower on the buildings of Manhattan, could Dr. Cook's have been "There, over there, is where my son was conceived"? Did he think of that day each time he crossed the Brooklyn Bridge into Manhattan?

I thought of Aunt Daphne and realized instantly that it was guilt that was smothering the exhilaration I ought to have been feeling— guilt at having deserted her the way I had, even more abruptly than Francis Stead had deserted my mother and me. This was my fourth night away from home, counting the night I left. I doubted she had slept for more than minutes at a time since finding the note I had left for her in the middle of my bed. She was alone again in that house with Uncle Edward, as she had not been for almost fourteen years. "Can you imagine what it was like when there were just the two of us?" she had joked when she told me the rhyme "Their plates wiped clean they sit and wait / While at the trough he ruminates."

Her plate wiped clean *she* sits and waits. She had never said it out loud until she said it to me, I suspected.

Here I was in Manhattan and all I could think about was Newfoundland.

The next morning I vowed to make myself known to Dr. Cook that very day. The bellhop had told me when I checked in that I could take the el train across the Brooklyn Bridge.

I got out of bed and was headed for the bathroom when I saw an envelope on the floor just inches from the door. A message of some kind from the hotel, I presumed.

I picked it up. It was sealed, with nothing written on it, not even my name. I opened it and withdrew a single folded sheet of paper. Even before I unfolded it and saw the handwriting, I knew that Dr. Cook had somehow found me first.

My dearest Devlin:

Welcome to New York! I have known for some time that you were coming. My new wife, Marie, will be out all day. I have dispatched the servants on various pretexts and errands that I hope will keep them occupied all afternoon. If you come to my house at two-thirty, we will have a few hours alone before Marie gets back. I will

explain everything when we meet. I have thought of an arrange-
ment that I believe will work.

There was no closing salutation or signature.

Uncle Edward, despite his promise, had to have told him I was coming. Dr. Cook, or someone acting on his behalf, had to have been there when my ship arrived and followed me to this hotel.

How long had the envelope been lying there? All night? Slipped soundlessly under the door while I was lying on the blankets, too hot to sleep? Or since sometime after sun up?

I felt both cheated and relieved. Cheated out of my chance to, however discreetly, surprise him, drop from out of nowhere into his life as he had dropped into mine. Relieved because I had, as yet, been able to think of no way of discreetly surprising him. I had dreaded making myself known to him so clumsily that he would form an unfavourable first impression of me, or that I would so startle him that he would be loathe to see me again.

It was not two years since the death of Anna Forbes. He had not mentioned in his letters that he was engaged again to be married. He had not mentioned Marie at all. I wondered why.

"I have thought of an arrangement that I believe will work." Another arrangement of his devising. What would it be this time? More letters, only now he would allow me to reply? I had not come to New York merely to write to him.

Two-thirty. It was now eight o'clock. According to the bellhop, I could make it to Bushwick and Willoughby in ninety minutes, even less depending on the time of day I travelled. I could still surprise him, show up early when the servants, who might not know that I was coming, were still there. But *he* might not be there. Or he might be in his surgery, available only to those who had appointments. Or he might be somewhere else.

I could simply ignore his note and send him one asking him to meet me somewhere. But given that he had gone to such great lengths to contact me before I contacted him, I doubted that he would relent and do things my way. I might, if I sent him a note, wait in vain for a second one from him.

I left the hotel and went to a cheap restaurant across the street for breakfast. On the wall beside my table was a poster advertising the "soon-to-be-completed subway," the tunnels for which were now being dug. The poster showed illustrations of the inside of the subway cars. They looked like furnished tombs and the stations like the shafts of horizontal mines.

As I ate, I read a morning paper that was full of predictions, inventions and rumours of inventions. The imminent triumph of the "horseless carriage," the obsolecsence of horse-drawn vehicles. The day when every street of Manhattan would lead to a bridge and the ferry-filled East River would be reserved for pleasure boats. The filing of patents, one for a central cooling mechanism that would counter the heat of summer the way radiation did the cold of winter. I dearly hoped for its success. The subway would make most surface transit superfluous. One day soon, work would begin on the subway to Brooklyn. Trains would run on tracks laid in tunnels that were dug so deep beneath the riverbed that not a drop of water would make it through.

Between the restaurant and the el train station, I saw hundreds of signs advertising jobs. Most of them read: "If you can read this, the job is yours." I could easily get a job if I had to.

I climbed a covered, winding staircase with landings every half-dozen steps on which older people rested, out of breath. There was a waiting room, but it was empty, everyone having proceeded outside to the covered platform, for the train was coming.

The el wound its way among buildings whose tops I could not see no matter how low I slumped down in my seat. The el. It seemed ironically named. It could not have been much more than forty feet above the ground.

From the el train I could see the Brooklyn Bridge, which we were due to reach in fifteen minutes. Traffic of all kinds on the bridge was ceaseless in both directions, as if the two boroughs were exchanging populations.

The train began to go upgrade, and soon the first cables of the bridge reared up outside the window, though land was still beneath us, the distant river barely visible at this angle through the struts and web of cables.

The valise, which now contained nothing but the portrait of my mother and Dr. Cook's letters, including the one I found that morning, was on my lap. I had removed the rest of my scant belongings and left them in my room, unable to bring myself to leave the letters, let them out of my possession, or to think of a foolproof hiding place.

Again I was struck by the oddness of my mission. For a second, as though from some omniscient's point of view, I saw myself: a young man just arrived from Newfoundland, bound for Brooklyn from Manhattan, riding the el train across the Brooklyn Bridge, propping on his lap a leather valise in which lay scrolled the letters of a Dr. Cook, who claimed to be his father—letters written not in the hand of Dr. Cook, but in that of the person to whom they were addressed, the young man himself, as if he were mad and the whole thing a concoction of which the climax, not the resolution but the dissolution, was fast approaching.

I was glad I had the portrait and the letters, glad I would not have to confront Dr. Cook empty-handed. They seemed like credentials of some kind. They made up a partial autobiography of Dr. Cook, an autobiography addressed to me. I imagined opening the bag, holding it out so he could see the heap of scrolls inside. And the picture of my mother.

It was probable that he did not have a picture of her. How accurately, after all this time, did he recall her face? I would take out the photograph and show it to him, give it to him, tell him he could keep it. I had thought of the moment many times since I left St. John's. What more appropriate gift could I give him on the occasion of meeting him than a picture of my mother?

Countless levels of conveyance spanned the river to join the downtowns of Brooklyn and Manhattan. I knew that we were travelling beneath a wooden walkway, though I could not see it from the train, and that beneath us ran cable cars and streetcars, and below or beside them horse-drawn vehicles and motor cars, the latter spooking the horses with whom they contended for space.

Farther below, steamers, ferries, barges drawn by tugboats, expensive sloops and smaller vessels made their way across the river. Below the water and, inconceivably, below the riverbed would someday run the subway.

Dr. Cook had crossed that stretch of water to Manhattan in a ferry one afternoon more than twenty years ago. Because of that, one of his thousands of childhood journeys to Manhattan, I was now going the other way, across the river on the bridge to Brooklyn to see him face to face at last.

I tried to imagine him setting out that day for Manhattan: a boy too lightly dressed for a ferry crossing of the river so soon after winter, teeth chattering, shivering, hugging himself for warmth; a boy who has been working in Brooklyn with his brothers since the sun came up, and whose day, had it ended when theirs did, would still have been too long. He has been hired to "help out" at a party in Manhattan, and what that means he has no idea. All he has is an address that he will walk to if he can find it from the dock. He has made up some story for his mother, who would not approve of his earning money in this fashion, or of his going to Manhattan for any reason by himself.

He looks up as the ferry moves into the shadow of the uncompleted bridge. The shadow bridge, because of the angle of the sun, is bigger than the real one, and in the shadow, it is even colder. The boy looks at the shadow shape, in which everything is magnified to twice its size, then back up at the bridge again.

His mother, who has come to dread the completion of the bridge, says it will mean the end of Brooklyn as they know it.

They have been building this bridge since before he was born. His world has always been one in which "the bridge" was being built. It seems in the nature of bridges to be not quite finished. Though it looks to him like the bridge *is* finished. The last piece of the span will soon be put in place. The braided steel-and-iron cables thicker than a man's body hang taut from the towers and the columns overhead.

The boy, whose glance includes that part of the bridge from which his son will look down at the water twenty years from now, feels no premonition, not of what is to happen in twenty years, nor of what is to happen in two hours. They are just docking at the pier when, up on the bridge, a series of electric arc lights come on all at once. Their light never flickers, not like the light from lamps that run on gas or kerosene. Flameless, unflickering, unnatural light.

Their coming on has for months been a signal to the people of both cities that the day is nearly over. They stay lit long after dark, for the push to complete the bridge is on.

They are still lit when he goes back to Brooklyn after midnight. By then, the licensed ferries have stopped, but he catches a ride for three times the legal fare from a man who runs an after-hours tug across the river, a tug that arrives and leaves at no appointed time. When the number of stranded has grown to the point where he deems a crossing to be worth his while, the tug driver collects his fares and sets out for the other shore. Until then, the boy waits on board, shivering, his mind blank with wonder as he stares down the river at the still-blazing arc lights on the bridge . . .

I roused myself from this revery. A lattice of shadow cast by the cables of the bridge lay over everything. It was coming on to noon, and the sun was beating down so fiercely that passengers closed their eyes as if in prayer and fanned themselves.

At the apex of the bridge, all I could see was a blinding sheen of sunlight from the water. And then the Brooklyn tower of the bridge came into view. I remembered Dr. Cook writing that the great arch had seemed to him like a sculpture, nearing the completion of which someone had by accident discovered that it could also be a bridge.

In each of the towers, there were two semi-ovals, pointed Gothic arches like massive church windows from which the glass had been removed. Rounded Roman arches had been proposed, but they were rejected in favour of the Gothic to appease the clergy, who were affronted by the cathedral-dwarfing bridge.

One arch admitted through the tower traffic that was headed east, the other traffic that was headed west.

Heading east, it was not until we passed through the tower that I felt I had left Manhattan and was truly on the bridge. It would not be until I passed through the semi-oval of the Brooklyn tower that I felt I was in Brooklyn. Between the towers, I felt a welcome sense of placelessness, a respite from the city. There was, suddenly, so much space.

I felt as if I was drawing my first breath since stepping off the ship the day before. As if the train had just passed a sign directing them to do so, the passengers opened their windows and there gushed across the car a cooling stream of air to which they turned their faces, eyes closed. The women put aside their fans, the men removed their hats. Clearly this was a local luxury born of bridges, this immersion in the breeze that came down the river from the ocean but was only at this altitude so free of smoke, so cool and so refreshing. The people looked the way that people in St. John's did when they turned their faces to the sun on the first warm day of spring.

Also admitted to the train when the windows went down were the sounds of the outside world, the clatter of the wheels and the humming of the span beneath them, the eerie buzzing of the cables. No sooner had we passed through the Brooklyn tower than the windows were raised again.

Below, and stretching along the shore on both sides as far as I could see, were the warehouses that from the ship had seemed to form a solid wall along the waterfront. Docks, dry docks, grain elevators, freight terminals, the sugar refineries in the shadow of which Dr. Cook had spent his childhood. It looked as if everything needed to sustain all five boroughs of New York was shipped through Brooklyn.

The streets of this part of Brooklyn were wider than those of Manhattan, as were the sidewalks, so both were less congested. There were far more motor cars than in Manhattan, though they were still greatly outnumbered by horse-drawn vehicles. A gleaming barouche with its hood raised to shield its owners from the sun went by, drawn by two horses as well groomed as the driver, who was standing at the reins as if to signal the priority of his vehicle over all the rest.

There was a station stop at Myrtle Avenue. There I asked one of the passengers who disembarked with me how to get to Bushwick and Willoughby. "You should have stayed on," he said. "There's a stop there, too." He indicated the way.

I walked along Bushwick, through block after block of stolid, free-standing mansions made of brick. With their unremarkable façades, they looked more like fortresses than dwellings.

Dr. Cook's was no exception. It was three storeys high, with a five-storey turret in the middle. There were gabled windows on the upper storey, and on the lower storeys recessed windows with Roman arches. It was enclosed by a fence of iron spikes, though there was no front yard. I could, by extending my arm through the rails, have touched the house. The front door opened almost directly onto the sidewalk. Nothing intervened but a rise of concrete steps. The entrance was recessed with a layered arch of black marble that ended in two inlaid white marble pillars that flanked the door. Nowhere did the name of Dr. Cook appear, nor anything to suggest that the premises were those of a physician, let alone that they contained a surgery. Only upon looking closely did I see that the door was monogrammed just above the mail slot. In small silver letters, the initials *F.A.C.*

I considered knocking but could imagine no outcome from doing so that would not embarrass both of us. There was no telling who else might be inside. Friends. Associates. Patients. I could not identify myself to him in front of others. Just standing there, I risked being seen by him or someone else from the windows. Or he might come out or appear in the doorway to bid someone goodbye.

I took my watch from my pocket. Half past twelve. I had made the trip in half the time the bellhop had predicted. I walked around the neighbourhood for an hour, moving from one place to another, seeking shade, of which there was little. There was no park, no stores I could take shelter in, just an endless succession of mansions.

I stood, across the street from the house and one block down, in the semi-shade of some overhanging leaves, holding my valise in front of me, hands crossed, as if the valise somehow made it more reasonable that I should stand there motionless for so long.

Through a swarm of hacks, coaches, hansom cabs and motor cars, I watched the house. One after another, servants left by a door near the back.

By two-thirty I was dizzy from the heat, my clothing drenched in perspiration. But I could not bear to go back to Manhattan for the night without first meeting him, the day's momentousness uncon-summated, so that when next I crossed from Manhattan to Brooklyn, whenever that might be, I would feel foolish and the whole thing would be spoiled.

I crossed the street. The front door was at the base of the massive middle turret. Barely able to see the knocker, I lifted and dropped it several times. The door was opened by someone who walked back-wards with it, so it seemed that it had opened by itself.

"Please come in," a man said, so loudly and formally I assumed he was a servant, one who had somehow avoided being sent away or had come back early, one whom Dr. Cook could trust with any secret.

I stepped inside. Coming from the daylight into this windowless vestibule, I could barely see. As I turned to face the doorman, he turned to face the door, on which he placed both hands, one on the handle, the other palm-flat on the wood, so that he eased it shut without a sound.

He faced round and leaned back against the door, rested his head against it as if he had just ejected someone he was glad to be rid of. I could not make out his face, but I knew the profile from the many photographs I had seen.

"Devlin," he said.

"Yes," I said, wishing I could have answered my name with his. But "Dr. Cook" was no reply to "Devlin." And it was far too soon to call him what I hoped I could someday.

"You know where I'm staying," I said, not intending it to sound like an accusation. Nor did he seem to take it as one. Rather, he waved at me and smiled as if I had paid him a compliment that he did not deserve. I could see him clearly now. He did not look much different than he had in his *Belgica* photographs. He was clean-shaven, but his hair was long and brushed back behind his ears. He was just as spare, his face as gaunt and full of hollows, as in the photographs. The only differences were that he was clean-shaven and well dressed in a white shirt with bands, a black vest and a pair of light black slacks.

He came forward suddenly and put his arms around me, the crook of his chin and throat hard against my neck as he hugged me to him. He was so strong, his hug so fervent, that I all but fell against him, arms limp, holding the leather valise, which crumpled audibly between us. Just as I let it go to reciprocate the hug, he released me and the bag fell to the floor. So, too, very nearly, did I.

"Are you feeling ill?" he said.

"It's very hot outside," I said. "I guess I'm not used to it."

"You're overdressed for it," he said. "You're soaking wet. Come in and I'll get you a cold drink. There are some things I have to tell you before we can really talk." With what I suspected seemed like peculiar haste, I snatched up the bag, then followed him from the vestibule down a hallway hung with a succession of oval mirrors to an enormous drawing room.

He directed me to one end of a sofa.

"I'll be right back with a nice cool drink," he said. The ceiling was so high that when he finished speaking, there was a prolonged "ping" of vibration in the air. I was vaguely aware of the room. Gilded ceiling. A rug from wall to wall. Black statuettes. Enormous vases with enormous handles. Ferns, fronds that might or might not have been real. A marble-topped writing table that bore a single prop-like book.

He soon returned with a large tumbler of crushed ice and orange juice. I was sitting with the valise on my lap, holding the handle with both hands. I removed one hand from the bag, took the glass and, momentarily unselfconscious, gulped greedily from it.

"That's the trick," he said as if I was ingesting in good humour some foul-tasting medicine that he'd prescribed. I drank until there was nothing left but ice.

"More?" he said, smiling.

I shook my head, certain I would burp if I attempted speech.

He drew up an armchair at right angles to the sofa and sat down.

"It's so good to see you, Devlin. At long last to see you. I had no idea what you looked like. I have no photographs of you." Yet he had recognized me when I debarked from the ship. There must have been no mistaking me, no one else who that furtive-looking, solitary young man could have been but Devlin Stead.

"Usually," he said, "as you write to someone, you have an image of him in your mind. I found myself, as I wrote, thinking of your mother. I should be ashamed to say so, but I'm not. Even before I knew you were my son, I would often recall her face, which I remembered more vividly than any other." Now, I realized, was not the time to present him with the photograph.

"It was hard for me, too," I said. "Being written to. Reading your letters. Not being able to write you back."

He nodded. *For reasons I cannot now explain.* I told myself it was foolish to expect that all my questions would be answered at our first meeting.

"Did you and Uncle Edward correspond a lot?" I said. He pursed his lips as if to say, "That depends on what you mean by a lot."

"Your uncle and I wrote each other only as often as we had to, I suppose." *Your uncle.* And Uncle Edward had called him "your correspondent." Each, as far as the other was concerned, had no name.

"I'm surprised that Uncle Edward went along with it," I said. "With any of it."

"To tell you the truth," he said, "I was somewhat surprised myself. But luckily for us, he did. I will tell you all about it when we have time."

I nodded as if I had expected him to speak those very words.

"Also luckily for us," Dr. Cook said, reaching out and removing my hat, the better to see my face, "you're not my spitting image, though someone who had reason to look for a resemblance between us would have no trouble finding it."

I was immensely pleased to hear it, and wondered why, when I had compared our photographs, I had been unable to detect this resemblance. He had done so without benefit of an image of himself to compare to me. I supposed he had so often photographed himself that he was able to objectively imagine his appearance, which I could not do. My image in the mirror or in photographs always surprised me. I looked at him, trying to see in his face what he had seen in mine.

I imagined how it must have been for my mother, watching me change, as if she had no idea who my father was, no idea from whom I had inherited the half of me that wasn't hers, no idea whose features those were that began to show themselves as I grew older—features that she, like Dr. Cook but unlike me, was able to detect. I imagined her scrutinizing my face, my complexion, my eyes, my mouth, trying to discern in that blending of two natures which features were his. There he was, this stranger, this man she had known for but three weeks, staring out at her from her son's face. Why was I blind to what was so obvious to Dr. Cook?

"This is really quite a marvellous house," I said. Reared up on the spoils of exploration, I presumed, thinking that, in his letters, he had exaggerated his need for "backers." But the smile he had been wearing since my arrival vanished.

"Yes, a marvellous house. A wastefully lavish one, I'm afraid. I tell Marie the house is so large that each room has a different climate. The house built by beer and bought by Mrs. Cook, they call it. Many houses on Bushwick were built by beer, and are still lived in by beer. Beer barons, that is. German brewers. As you know my parents were born in Germany, but my father was a doctor, not a beer baron. This house is also known in the neighbourhood as the house with eighty windows, though in fact it has eighty-four. It was designed and built by Theobald Englehardt for a man named Claus Lipsius, who is remembered as having 'built' it because his money paid for it. I terrify Marie by claiming to have seen his ghost, whom I call the elusive Lipsius. This place is so large that a ghost could haunt it undetected for centuries. I believe that I am looked upon by some as a kept husband, though perhaps it is only because I sometimes feel kept that I suspect others of regarding me that way. Most of Marie's money is in this house. She is nowhere near so rich that she can entirely fund my expeditions. But with her money, I have been able to forsake my white horse and one-lunger for a four-cylinder Franklin. I make my rounds in it. I feel like a boy whose mother has bought for him a toy that no one else's mother could afford. I turn the corners of streets on two wheels. I have also, with Marie's money, bought a roentgen-ray machine. Very few doctors have them, and it is at least of use to someone other than me. I feel, unfairly to myself perhaps, that I have caused the Forbes family much grief. But they, the two remaining daughters and their mother, have told me that they are happy for Marie and me. I had thought that happiness through marriage—that marriage itself—was not for me, until I met Marie. It is for her a second marriage as well, her first having ended with the death of her husband, Willis Hunt, a homeopathic doctor of some renown who left Marie a wealthy woman.

"A fellow physician, upon hearing of my marriage, wrote that he lamented the world's loss of me 'as one of her most enthusiastic, able and determined explorers.' He added, 'But there is no doubt that you have chosen the happier lot.' You'd think that by announcing my marriage, I had announced the end of my career. Has Peary's having a wife and children slowed him down or disqualified him from the ranks? I fear that my friend's remarks arise in part from Marie's inherited wealth. I am looked upon as gentrified. Nothing could be more untrue. Marie insisted, when I asked for her hand, that I continue on with exploration, and she has even hinted at a Jo Peary–like willingness to be my companion in exploration, so far as circumstances will permit."

He stopped speaking and, as if to say that he was sorry for having got carried away, looked at me and smiled.

He leaned his forearms on his thighs, clasped his hands.

"You really should be enrolled in some course of study," he said. "What profession have you chosen?"

"I haven't made up my mind yet. 'All the remaining challenges of exploration will be met in the next ten years,' you said in *Century*. If I enrol in something now, there might be nothing left to accomplish by the time I graduate."

"That's possible. But it's partly to loosen the purse-strings of the backers that explorers speak the way I did. It's also possible that I'm wrong, that ten years from now all those challenges will still be there. Unmet. Never to be met, perhaps. And you will have no paying profession. No status in society."

"The universities and colleges will still be there," I said.

He smiled, nodded his head, then moved it even closer to mine, as if, were he to say them too loudly, the words would still be in the air when his wife returned.

"I have told Marie about you, that you are the son of a former friend and colleague of mine, now deceased, Dr. Francis Stead, who, as she remembers, met such a tragic end on the North Greenland expedition. I told her that we met by chance in Manhattan, and that you wish to spend some time in New York, to gain some experience of real life, before completing your education. I said that you were just off the boat, looked quite hopelessly out of your element, and that if someone did not soon take you under his wing, there was no telling what might happen to you. I suggested to Marie that, what with my practice on the one hand and my exploration on the other it might not be a bad idea if I hired someone, possibly you, as my assistant. I also suggested that given the size of this house and the necessity of having my assistant near at hand, it would make sense if you lived here. She agreed with me."

I must have looked as incredulous as I felt, for he laughed softly. My doubts about him vanished. I felt guilty for ever having had them, and for resenting him for pre-empting my surprise arrival, which I now saw would have been imprudent no matter what sort of "arrangement" I devised. Clearly, the making of arrangements should be left to him. I looked at the valise. The letters no longer had about them the whiff of fiction. He had meant every word he wrote to me.

He was, at that very moment, doing what he had said that he would do "someday." I had come to think of it as some nebulous, forever-in-the-future day because of my impatience. Despite my not having waited for him to formally extend his invitation, despite my having set out to surprise him by showing up from out of nowhere in New York, he was offering to bring me into his life, had already prepared a place in it for me.

"Well?" he said. "Would you *like* to be my assistant and live here with us in this house?"

What he proposed was so appealing to me, so exactly what I wanted, that it had not occurred to me that it *was* a proposition, that he could imagine anything from me but grateful compliance.

"Yes," I managed to say. "I would like that very much."

Again he laughed. I might have been a child whose response to a gift was so exactly what he imagined it would be that he could not help being amused.

"Marie assumes that your aunt and uncle know where you are. You should say nothing to make her think otherwise. In fact, it might be best if you don't speak about your aunt and uncle unless she does, which she probably won't. Marie has told the servants about you. I will introduce you to people, and you will introduce yourself to anyone you meet, as the son of a former colleague of mine who is now employed as my assistant and, for our mutual convenience, staying at my house. As for you and I, we will talk openly only when we are certain, as we are now, that we cannot be overheard. You must be careful not to leave lying about any written material of a private nature."

I nodded, though I felt like telling him that he needn't worry, that I was well practised at the art of deception at close quarters, at withholding from one member of the household I belonged to information that I shared with another.

I saw that my new situation would be eerily congruent with the one I'd left. It was as if I had exchanged Uncle Edward and Aunt Daphne for Dr. Cook and his wife, Marie. Again conspiring with the husband of the house against the wife, maintaining the same pretence as before; again forbidden to talk about it with the husband unless invited to by him. Again a guest in someone else's house. Adopted for the second time, this time by my father.

But I vowed that I would feel no guilt at deceiving Mrs. Cook. It was as much for other people as for ourselves that Dr. Cook and I had to be discreet. Who would benefit by knowing what we knew? Who would not be hurt by it?

"I have been thinking of what you should call me when we are alone. And I have been able to think of nothing but 'Dr. Cook.' If you were to call me anything else, you might inadvertently do so when we were *not* alone. Do you see what I mean? Such a slip would give nothing away, of course, but it might cause both of us some awkwardness."

I nodded.

"We will tell Marie that it appears that your steamer trunk was stolen out of storage at the pier. Such things happen all the time." He knew that the valise was all the luggage I had. I guessed that the manner of my leaving St. John's had been dictated by him to Uncle Edward, right down to the last detail of how much luggage I should take.

Not even while alluding to my non-existent trunk did he look at my valise. He had yet to look at it as far as I could tell. All the while he spoke, I had sat there with the bag on my lap, wishing that I had been able to think of somewhere safe to put it, wishing that I had not brought it into the house, teeming as it was with all that I had just pledged to keep concealed and not be careless with.

He had not offered in the vestibule to take it from me. Perhaps he knew by how I held it that I would not have wanted to part with it. He might even, from that, have guessed its contents. If so, he had perfectly disguised any uneasiness he felt about it.

I was suddenly aware of how I looked, what an odd pose I had struck and maintained since I sat down. I saw myself dimly reflected in the window of a cabinet that held a display of silver plates. Shoulders hunched, knees primly together, feet flat on the floor, holding the bag on my lap with both hands as women hold their purses.

The oddball I had been I would be no longer, I vowed. I was

starting over. No one in New York knew anything about "the Stead boy," who in any case did not exist except in the minds of people I might never see again. In New York, people would have cause to think of me only as Dr. Cook's assistant. "I will introduce you...you will introduce yourself to anyone you meet..." I had no idea how to socialize, what the rules and norms of interaction were. I foresaw, though not clearly, a series of catastrophes, followed by a quick retreat and a reappraisal of my possibilities by Dr. Cook.

I put the valise on the sofa beside me, right beside me, within easy grasping distance should any of the people who were absent from the house suddenly return. I put my hands palms down on my thighs, where, clammy as they were, they adhered to my trousers.

"Someday, Devlin," Dr. Cook said, "you're going to be very happy." He had, I remembered from his second letter, said that very thing to my mother the day they met. I looked at him, wondering if my unhappiness was *that* obvious to him. I hoped that he knew next to nothing about "the Stead boy." He smiled reassuringly. I felt a great rush of emotion I could not name, and my eyes welled up with tears.

"I am placing all my trust in you," he said. "I am entrusting everything to you. All I have and hope to have. Everything I am and hope to be."

Dr. Cook introduced me to Marie when she came home as "the young man I've been telling you about." Nothing about him suggested that anything more momentous was taking place than the meeting of his wife and his new assistant, the son of a deceased colleague and friend.

She had a small, pretty face but was otherwise a good deal on the heavy side. Clinging to her hand, with the fingers of her free hand in her mouth, was a little girl, perhaps three years old, whom she introduced to me as Ruth, the only child of her first marriage. I saw in Mrs. Cook's eyes a protracted fatigue, as well as a general wariness, as if she were forever having to fend off impositions, this young man in front of her clearly being one that she had been unable to fend off. She was very polite with me, pointedly so, no doubt to make it clear that though I was joining the household, I was doing so merely as an employee.

"You've had a long journey, Mr. Stead," she said. "You must be very tired."

"A little," I said. Can *she* see the resemblance? I wondered. Not that it mattered. Even if she thought that in some ways, her husband and I looked alike, she would think nothing of it.

"You're all that my husband has talked about since yesterday. 'Dr. Stead's son will soon be here.' He must have said it twenty times. I understand that he and your father were good friends. Explorers come back from expeditions either the closest of friends or arch-enemies for life. And some, of course, do *not* come back, a fact of which I know you are painfully aware. I am sorry about your father. I hope you do not catch the polar fever from my husband. There is adventure enough, exploration enough, to be done, if explore one must, in Prospect Park."

This was hardly evidence of a "Jo Peary–like willingness" to be his companion in exploration, but I resisted the urge to look at Dr. Cook. *Happiness through marriage.*

"My further advice to you is to stay on this side of the river and have nothing more to do with Manhattan than you have to. But I suspect that instead of my advice, you will follow the example of my husband. Well, I'm sure you will prove an invaluable assistant to him. I hope you enjoy your stay in Brooklyn." She spoke these last two sentences as if she doubted that our paths would ever cross again. She turned abruptly and walked off down the hall.

Dr. Cook told me my room was in an unoccupied wing of the house that was so remote he referred to it as the Dakota, an entire block of rooms on the west side that were never used. It was, as he put it, "simply there." The house minus the Dakota was referred to as the Cooks'.

He told me he had named the Dakota after an apartment building constructed in 1884 on the Upper West Side, at that time so remote a location that the name had seemed appropriate—which it still did. "The city hasn't really pushed that far west yet," he said.

The Dakota. It sounded like not one structure but many. Or rather, like a territory on which a number of dwellings had been built and were being maintained in pristine condition in anticipation of a wave of people who might never come. A ghost town in reverse, never lived in but forever ready to be occupied.

"You are to be its first resident," said Dr. Cook, "and the only resident for now, although I visit it sometimes. It really is quite absurdly huge."

"I hope my being here has not upset Mrs. Cook," I said.

"She is tired," Dr. Cook said. "Anaemic. Otherwise she would be happy to have you stay in the Cooks'. The prospect of getting worse and being pent up indoors by illness has her on edge."

My room was enormous, the ceiling as high as in the main part of the house, the furnishings as lavish. Because of the height of the ceiling and two large revolving fans, the room was cool. I had my own bathroom, my own icebox, which had been fitted with a new block of ice that morning and stocked with soft drinks and fruit. The servants, Dr. Cook said, would keep it stocked and maintain it for me. My only tasks would be the ones he assigned me.

"It's so much," I said. "This is so generous of you and Mrs. Cook."

"It's your salary," he said. "Of course I will pay you something on top of your expenses, but you should think of all this as your salary."

He asked me if I had left anything at my hotel. "A change of clothes and some toiletries," I said.

"I'll have them sent for," he said. "You move in as of this moment." Still he did not so much as look at the valise, which I had put down on the bed. "You will not be having dinner with us most nights, I'm afraid. At least not for a while."

He said that his study and his surgery were at opposite ends of the house, roughly equidistant from the Dakota. A small room just down the hallway from his study would be my office. Exactly what I would do in this office, exactly what being his assistant would entail, he said he would tell me once I was settled in.

He left me to explore the rest of the Dakota. The house, he said, had been designed to accommodate an extended family, but the Lipsians, though they extended, wound up in various residences, and so the Dakota was never used, not even by them.

In the whole house, there had been at least two, and in some cases three, of everything when they moved in—two or three dining rooms, drawing rooms, living rooms, libraries, etc. Some of these rooms they had converted to other purposes, but the Dakota had remained untouched.

In the otherwise dormant Dakota, a few rooms had been revived for me: the bedroom, the bathroom closest to it and the relatively small and cozy library, a room that shared all its walls with other rooms, and thus had no windows. I would take my meals in there at the reading table, Dr. Cook said, the thought of my doing so at a dining-room table whose remaining thirty-nine chairs would be empty being unbearable to him. By pushing a button on the wall outside the dining room, I could summon someone from the kitchen anytime between seven in the morning and eight at night.

I walked through the rooms several times, the last time after dark, switching on lights as I went. Not for a long time had these rooms been lit, I suspected—except by someone checking to see that the lights still worked—though they were cleaned twice weekly. There were not even cobwebs in the corners of the ceilings. The gilded ceilings, panelled walls, and floors and parts of floors that were not covered with rugs gleamed as if the Dakota had been abandoned, the sheets thrown over the furniture, just the day before. All the major pieces of furniture were covered with white sheets. Some of the covered pieces looked like faceless statues, with the faint suggestion of bodies beneath folds and layers of marble garments. It was generally possible, by the shape of a sheet, to guess what lay beneath it.

I had expected that aside from my revived rooms, the rooms in the Dakota would be unfurnished, mere enclosures of empty space, nothing but wainscoted walls and hardwood floors. But if not for the sheets, there would have been little except for the pristine fireplaces and the complete lack of any odours to indicate that no one lived there. There were rugs, tassel-tied draperies, expansive tapestries; peaking beneath the sheets, I saw paintings, man-sized vases, gleaming tables, upholstered chairs and sofas, ottomans, glass lamps, fully stocked china cabinets, hutches of crystalware and silverware. The Cooks could have taken up residence in the Dakota without any sacrifice of comfort, without having to move anything except for toiletries and clothing. Everything the Cooks' had the Dakota had.

It had been designed to accommodate not just one-half of an extended family, but scores of invited guests as well; designed for parties, receptions, seasonal gatherings, annual gatherings of the sort that I presumed took place in the Cooks' while its alternate lay empty.

It had about it an air that reminded me of Francis Stead's surgery, as if it was being maintained for someone whose return was doubtful or no longer possible, no longer believed in by anyone, or as if the doctor and his wife had had in mind for it some purpose, their abandonment of which they could not bear to acknowledge. I could not help asking, as I went from room to room, "What is it *for?*"

In the Dakota alone, a large family could have lived in spacious luxury. It was just as well that everything was covered in sheets. In no way would it have been possible for me to "live" in more than a fraction of it. I would have felt absurd sitting alone in one of those cavernous rooms night after night, reading or listening to music on the gramophone.

Hanging from the ceiling of the drawing room was a chandelier so massive that when it started up, I could hear it hum to life and for a second feel the floor vibrate beneath my feet. It was a great bowl from which depended what looked to me like a vast symmetry of icicles, each one lit from within and casting its reflection on the others, the whole thing a teeming concavity of light, an inverted igloo.

And one part of the otherwise dormant, enormous drawing room had some time ago been revived for Dr. Cook. This was the part he had alluded to when he said that he visited the Dakota sometimes: his "spot," he called it, the place he came when he needed absolute solitude in which to think. It was the far edge of the room, a little semi-circle of unsheeted furniture near the fire. He liked to go there at night and sit by himself on the sofa or in the armchair. Even with me in the Dakota, he would go on doing so, he said, so I ought not to be alarmed if I heard something in the drawing room or saw that the doors were closed and a light was on inside. He said that he wished not to be interrupted when the doors were closed, but that I should take their being open as an invitation to join him.

My main task, said Dr. Cook, would be to "cull the mail." He received, as I soon discovered, an enormous amount of correspondence every day, and he found it a nuisance separating the small portion of it that was worth reading from the much larger portion that was not. Among the latter was an avalanche of correspondence from inventors imploring him to use, and thereby publicize and prove the effectiveness of, some new invention of theirs on his next expedition.

"Invention is the national pastime," said Dr. Cook. He was asked to experiment with outerwear made from some material that was "thermally superior to fur and completely waterproof." Snow goggles that doubled as binoculars. A "foldable, feather-light auger that will cut through ice better than augers made of steel." A sled that was lighter, stronger and faster because its blades were made from some "friction-less alloy." Longer-lasting candles. A miniature stove that required "no fuel but water." A "skin-restorer that can undo the ravages of frostbite." Eye-drops "guaranteed to prevent and cure snow-blindness." Frostbite-proof moccasins. "A never-tiring breed of dog that will put at a disadvantage all who insist on using huskies and the like."

My job was to reply to all these pitches, politely decline them on his behalf, explaining that "Dr. Cook prefers to use equipment of his own design."

"Nothing galls people like having their letters to the famous go unacknowledged," he said.

All letters to him were to be acknowledged, except "crank" letters, of which I should dispose.

There were many letters from people recommending themselves

as members of his next expedition—hunters, photographers, journalists, novelists, businessmen, physicians—or offering to pay him to take them or their sons to the Arctic. I was to write them, telling them that he was no longer for hire as an Arctic guide and now took with him on his expeditions only people he had travelled with before.

He was no longer for hire, he forthrightly told me, because of his wife's money, which it would be pointless of him to refuse just to prove to the bloody-minded that he had not married for money.

He gave me a list of "legitimate explorers," men from all over the world, but mostly from America, Canada, Scandinavia and Europe. All correspondence from these men I was to forward to him unopened. Many of the names—Peary, Amundsen, Dedrick, Cagni, Astrup, Bartlett, Wellman—were familiar to me.

I would, once I knew the city well enough, deliver messages and packages from him to people all over Brooklyn and Manhattan.

His study was cluttered with a decade's worth of polar relics. Sextants and globes. Bird feathers. Snowshoes. Patagonian mementoes. A dictionary of a Patagonian tribe known as the Yahgans. Flinthead spears. Mounted on the wall was a small wooden sled. Even its runners were made of wood. "Ash," said Dr. Cook. "It weighs thirteen pounds. It carried five hundred. Nearly forty pounds for every pound it weighs. I designed it myself."

His desk was layered in maps, each of which traced out a different route from southern Greenland to the pole. He pored over these, making notes in his journals, consulting old journals and the writings of other explorers.

I could not see the walls for photographs, some of which were self-portraits of the sort that had run in *Century*. Beneath one, etched on a piece of wood enclosed in glass, was the unattributed phrase "A very young man who has the silent and unassuming manner of an older one." An epithet, as if the man in the photograph was dead.

"Some of these relics belonged to Francis Stead," he said. "They're from the North Greenland expedition. Peary entrusted them to me. I contacted your uncle about them, but he said they were mine to do with as I wished. He had no intention, he said, of cluttering his house with—what did he call them?—'the bric-a-brac of savages.'"

Francis Stead's relics did not include any photographs of him. There were knives and needles made of bone. A walrus tusk. Mittens made from caribou hide. A reindeer-skin sleeping bag.

Framed in wood and glass was a menu of what had been served for Christmas dinner at Redcliffe House in 1892. Salmon. Rabbit Pie. Venison. Plum Pudding. It was intricately illustrated and featured a caricature of Dr. Cook, showing him long-haired, hands on hips, appraising the body of a naked Eskimo woman. The tailpiece was a potion bottle on which was drawn a fiendish-looking skull and crossbones.

"Francis Stead drew that," said Dr. Cook. "He made one for each of us. Each one was a parody. He even did one of himself, though I forget what it was."

Dr. Cook appraising a naked woman. Surely he was not blind to the accidental irony, yet here was this picture on his wall.

Things that had once belonged to Francis Stead were everywhere. How, I felt like asking him, could he bear to look at them, be reminded by them of Francis Stead and my mother every time he looked up from his desk? Was it a form of penance, a never-ending making of amends?

One afternoon, I asked him if there were any polar expeditions now under way that he thought might be successful. He told me that Peary was up north, supposedly trying for the pole, but in fact prolonging an already failed expedition that in the eighteen months since it was put ashore in Greenland had made no progress because of injuries and bad weather. Peary was now stranded, he said, though his exact location was unknown.

I was surprised that, knowing Peary was trying, with however little chance of success, for the pole, Dr. Cook could be so sanguine, so complacent about it. Meanwhile, here *he* was in Brooklyn, merely making plans for future expeditions for which he had yet to raise the money—nebulous expeditions for which no dates had yet been set.

"Aren't you worried that he'll reach the pole?" I said.

"You don't understand," he said. "It's not that, by now, Peary's chances of success are small. They are non-existent. They were from the start. He and his crew are stranded somewhere. The expedition was eighteen months old when they were last heard from, and that was months ago. They were still on the southernmost coast of Greenland, but were planning to head north when the snow returned. By the time it does, the expedition will be more than two years old. By then, Peary's only real ambition will be to make it back alive. How long it will be before he *admits* defeat is the only question. There was word before he left that this was to be his last try. He is forty-five years old, will be at least forty-six before he gets back, *if* he gets back. These are not surmises. These are certainties. There will be no surprise headlines in the paper. Only the gullible are still waiting for word from Peary that he has reached the pole. Peary knows it. Every explorer in the world knows it. Some members of the Peary Arctic Club know it and are trying desperately to keep it from the press—and from the other members, the ones who skip the meetings of the PAC but put up all the money. I will not say this publicly, of course. I do not want to give a bad impression of a fellow explorer to people who, one or two years from now, will, I hope, be backing *my* attempt to reach the pole."

He told me not to concern myself about Peary, sneering as he spoke the name, and reminded me that the success of any expedition depended on how well one prepared for it. "Better to make one good try for the pole," he said, "than to make five from which nothing more will come than new material for lectures."

Peary, he said, had been to Greenland several times since 1892, and each time he brought back with him something to impress the members of the club and draw attention away from his having failed yet again to reach the pole. He had brought back three meteorites, which he called star stones, and lent them to the American Museum of Natural History, whose president, Morris Jesup, was also the president of the Peary Arctic Club. He also brought back with him six Eskimos, four of whom, while under his care, perished of tuberculosis.

Dr. Cook waved one hand as if to dismiss all thoughts of Peary from both our minds.

CHAPTER FOURTEEN

HE WAS KNOWN TO EVERYONE IN BROOKLYN. I WENT OUT walking with him on Bushwick one Saturday afternoon. He carried his jacket on his left arm and in his right hand held his hat, lifting the latter in greeting to the doorman of a small hotel, who tipped his own hat in reply.

He raised his hat again, this time to a jeweller who stood in the doorway of his shop and then, when Dr. Cook had passed, went back inside, as if he had come out expressly to greet him.

He spoke briefly to people in the waiting rooms of the el trains on the Myrtle Line—people, I realized, who recognized him, but whom he did not know.

People were drawn to him by more than just his fame. He seemed to find no one uninteresting, no one less than fascinating, which flattered people, and which he managed to convey by listening intently while others spoke. He was not outgoing, but he projected such absolute self-assurance that when he smiled at people in that forthright way of his, they looked as if they had won the approval of a man who was uncommonly perceptive. It was as if each person's life, each person's job, was difficult or rewarding in some way that only he and they were able to appreciate.

In Brooklyn, when we were not walking or travelling by train, we drove about in the Franklin, which was greeted by the people of Bushwick like a one-vehicle parade, everyone waving as we passed, teasing him good-naturedly about his "horseless carriage," which by chance bore the name of a famously doomed Arctic expedition. Most of the teasing was about the unlikelihood of the Franklin taking him to the North Pole and back.

"You should have kept the Eskimos," one man shouted from his horse as we sped by.

I was surprised when Dr. Cook explained that this was a reference to the dozen Eskimos he had brought back to Brooklyn with him from Labrador one year, housing them in two large tents that he set up in his own backyard. "I treated them better than Peary treated his," he said, as if he had noticed my surprise. He said they had lived as much like Eskimos as it was possible to do in Brooklyn, all the while being gaped at by the locals through knotholes in the fence. In the winter, on the weekends, he and they drove about Bushwick on sleds drawn by teams of dogs, the huskies barking wildly as hundreds of astonished Brooklynites tried to keep up with the sleds on foot. He had complied with the Eskimos' request to be returned to Labrador when, in spite of all his ministrations, one of their number died.

"I am famous in Brooklyn," Dr. Cook said, "yet all but unknown in Manhattan."

He said it was too much bother to take the Franklin into Manhattan, where the streets were so narrow and congested that cars and horses came too near each other for the horses' liking.

The first time we made the crossing of the bridge together, I saw a horseless carriage send a dozen horses rearing up on their hind legs, spilling drivers, passengers and goods from their vehicles, their scissoring forelegs menacing pedestrians, who screamed at the driver of the car to "get a horse."

Several times a week, we took the el train across the Brooklyn Bridge into Manhattan. If our destination was a part of the borough where the el trains did not run, we took his horse and carriage. He much preferred this to hiring cabs, he said, because cab drivers were notorious eavesdroppers and gossips.

He said it was so that I could see and get to know Manhattan that we made these excursions. And it did seem sometimes that I was being tutored in the layout and makeup of the city, which he said I would need to know as well as I knew St. John's in order to do my job properly.

"The avenues run vertically from north to south, the streets horizontally from east to west. The avenues are longer and farther apart from each other than the streets, which are more numerous. The streets are numbered, the avenues, in some cases, named *and* numbered..." But long after he stopped speaking, he went on driving, driving for hours as if he was scouring the city in search of something he had lost. It seemed that I was only there to keep him company.

We drove at a never-less-than-frenetic pace from east to west, west to east, all the while going north block by block, generally skirting the edge of Central Park unless we could use one of its roads as a shortcut. I wondered if it had been his habit before my arrival to spend his spare time like this. Perhaps, in spite of his urging me to be patient, it was a symptom of explorer's restlessness. He was at home, not on an expedition as he would have liked, so he could not sit still.

Once, when I went by the study prior to yet another evening excursion, Mrs. Cook, wrapped, though it was still September, in a bundle of sweaters and blankets, was just leaving. Though I had been living in her house for weeks, I had yet to meet her for a second time. Dr. Cook referred to her only occasionally, usually to pass on her regrets that her "condition" prevented her from spending time with me.

I said hello and she muttered some reply, sounding exasperated with me, as if she thought it was at my instigation that her husband was neglecting her so much.

I had yet to address him as "Dr. Cook" when we were alone. I could not bring myself to do it, though I saw the sense of not addressing him as "Father." To call him "Dr. Cook," for us to maintain that pretence in private, did not seem right to me. I called him "you," which was awkward, especially as he used my name so frequently. He said it differently when we were alone than when we were not, though it was hard to put that difference into words.

He spoke of Manhattan as if it had been built not for the people who lived there, but for those who came to visit. We might have been making our way through a vast museum called Manhattan, in which all the peoples and cultures of the world were on display—a live exhibit showing all levels and sub-levels of society; the latest advancements in technology; all known occupations, modes of dress, forms of art and entertainment; all known languages. I half expected him to point out two men in a carriage, one middle-aged, one young, two representative visitors from Brooklyn, the older of whom would be pointing directly back at us.

I put it down at first to Brooklynite defensiveness, the aloof, dismissive pose that all residents of the supposedly lesser of the cross-river rivals seemed to feel the need to affect while in Manhattan. But there was more to it than that. Scepticism. Ambivalence. It was as though he was assessing the city for some purpose he was not sure it could serve. Chronically unsure. At the end of each journey, as we returned to Brooklyn by way of the bridge, he fell silent and took on a look of wistful dissatisfaction.

We went to vaudeville shows, and though he would smile at the onstage antics, he spent as much time observing the audience as he did the performers, wearing the same evaluative look no matter where his attention lay.

Late one afternoon, he came by the library, where I was reading *Moby Dick*, which he had recommended to me as a book that might help me understand the "nature of his quest."

"I have to get out of this house," he said, scratching the back of one hand, his fingernails rasping on his skin.

We took his hansom across the bridge. We went to the Lower East Side, to Hester Street, which was home to throngs of Jews and the site of pushcart markets that even at this time of the afternoon were so crowded I could not tell the vendors from the customers. A mass of dark-haired, dark-eyed, dark-bearded men in felt hats and heavy overcoats broke ranks to let us through, their eyes blank, as if they did not so much see as sense the obstacles in front of them.

"They are all Jews," Dr. Cook said. "But they are not all from the same country. They speak different languages. That is why they must learn English."

"Schleppers," he said, pointing as though at a species of tree that did not grow in Newfoundland. Men, women and children toting heaps of unfinished garments from one sweatshop to another struggled by, bent double by their loads. It seemed that everything was being rebuilt in the aftermath of some disaster, people working at this pace for what they knew would be a finite length of time. "But it never ends," said Dr. Cook. A woman wearing a shawl tied in a bow beneath her chin staggered by beneath a massive mound of men's garters bound up with string. Another carried above her head a huge wooden box that Dr. Cook assured me was empty and would be used for kindling.

Only a few blocks away began Little Italy, Mulberry Bend. There were Italians now from Broadway to the Bowery, said Dr. Cook.

Above Fifty-ninth, on both the east and west sides, lived the Irish, and with them, he told me, most of the Newfoundlanders who had forsaken their massive, empty island for this crammed and tiny one. I told him I would rather not tour the Irish neighbourhoods, for fear of being recognized by someone from St. John's. He nodded as if he knew exactly what I meant, knew what Aunt Daphne would do if she found out where I was.

We took the long way round to San Juan Hill, to Amsterdam Avenue between Sixtieth and Sixty-fourth streets, to Seventh Avenue near the future site of Pennsylvania Station. In these areas lived the city's small black population. Conveyanceville, Dr. Cook called it, because all the employed black men conveyed either people or goods throughout the city. They were draymen, hackmen, teamsters, porters, packers, messengers.

He pointed out to me groups of children he said were "street arabs." Born in tenements from which they had been crowded out when their parents could not pay the rent, they now lived on the streets. They looked as if they had just emerged from coal mines, their faces and clothing were so filthy.

He said he had thought of childhood as a stage of life when everyone was disposed to hopefulness no matter what their circumstances, until he set eyes on these boys and girls. "I would look at them and think of you," he said.

They were not children, he said. They could not remain children in this city and survive. So it was as if some whole new stage of life had been invented for them, by them. Only by night did they look like children, when they lay down in the doorways and the stairwells, three or four of them huddled so closely together, so entwined, you could not tell whose feet were whose, whose arms and legs were whose. Sometimes all you saw were bundles of coats and caps and shoes.

"But I should warn you," he said. "You will encounter them as you go about your job. They will see that you are new here, and if they sense that you feel sorry for them, they will take advantage of you. They smell pity the way dogs smell fear. They will tell you that their mother or father or sister needs help, that no one but you has been kind enough to listen to them. Once they have convinced you of how much they value kindness and how exceptional you are, they will lead you down a side street, where the hoodlums they work for will be waiting for you."

We went to the Upper East Side, drove from Murray Hill at Thirty-fourth Street to Ninety-first Street, past mansions that made Mrs. Cook's look like a guest house. Even close up, they looked more like hotels or banks than homes, sprawling over entire city blocks. They had no yardage, front or back or on the sides.

"There is no room in this part of Manhattan for yards," he said. "Not if you want to have houses the size of these. But they have other houses, in the country or at the seashore, as large or larger than these, surrounded by acres of land."

He pointed out the Vanderbilt residence at Fifth Avenue and Fifty-second Street, the Astor residence at Fifth Avenue and Sixty-fifth Street, the Carnegies' at Fifth and Ninety-first.

We toured the Upper West Side, drove along Riverside Drive, where the newest mansions were, some of them still under constuction, draped in canvas hung on scaffolding as if they were soon to be unveiled.

We went to the apartment building after which he had named the west side of his house, the Dakota Apartments at Central Park West and Seventy-second Street. Eight storeys high, with gabled columns topped by minarets like those of Ellis Island on its front façade and a sixth-floor railing on which were propped Zeuses and griffins made of marble, it was, he said, his favourite building in Manhattan.

"They say that looking north from the upper storeys, you can still see the fires of the shanty camps at night. See how it looms up out of nowhere, with nothing but the sky behind it? It is perfectly square, eleven rows of windows on each side. See. They haven't even paved the streets here yet, seventeen years since the cornerstone was laid. The people who live here want them left unpaved. It discourages visitors, developers. Rich people rent here, those who make their money in the arts, publishers of books and music. Theodor Steinway used to live here. That was in the 1880s, when it was the last western outpost of the city. From its north-facing windows, all you could see then were trees and farms and shanty towns. They say that men shot small game from those upper windows. Imagine it: hunting without having to step out-doors or even go downstairs. When the shooting stopped, the shanties would come out of the woods and gather up the game, rabbits, foxes, and cook them over open fires."

He said that the men who had lived on the lower floors rode the elevators with their rifles to the roof gardens. Elevators were new then, to ride one a novelty in itself. I could just see those men pouring like a posse from the elevators, rushing to the rail to get the best spots. I imagined people watching the Dakota from a distance, hearing the sounds of rifle shots, seeing the puffs of smoke from the upper storey, from the battlements, as if its residents were nightly required to defend this fortress from invaders.

It really did rear up from out of nowhere like a castle, as though it were all that remained of a city of which it once had been the centrepiece, a city razed to the ground, the land it once stood on now being claimed back by the wilderness. It was like a bulwark against the northern horde. I thought of the tenants on the roof and at the windows of the floor below, sniping at the shanties as they readied to invade.

There was nothing homiletic in his tone of voice, though it seemed clear from *what* he said that to him the Dakota was a monumental point of demarcation between the old and the new, the wilderness and the city, the poor and the rich.

On the Uppers, as Dr. Cook called the most northerly settled parts of the island, lived the backers, the very men, the "hundred millionaires" of the Peary Arctic Club, who had backed Peary's most recent bid to reach the pole, a bid they thought might still succeed. What would they think, he wondered, if they knew that all they were paying for was a pointlessly protracted, face-saving sojourn in Greenland?

"There are many kinds of wealth, just as there are many kinds of poverty," said Dr. Cook. "The people in these houses, who are so looked down upon by the few aristocrats in England who have heard of them, do not associate with the beer barons of Bushwick, nor do the beer barons associate with the physicians, nor the physicians with the homeopaths. I tell Marie that it is because our ghost, the elusive Lipsius, is such a snob that he never shows himself. Some of our neighbours do not approve of the woman to whom the Lipsius family sold its house. They resent the presence among them of a widow whose first husband made his money selling quack remedies to hypochondriacs. They approve of explorers, but not so much that they boast about having one next door."

He spoke as if these were the objective observations of a sociologist, in no way revealing of his own biases or character.

I saw, I had to see, the city through his eyes, for my own could make no sense of it. It was too far beyond anything I had ever seen before, too expansive, too diverse in both its plenitude and scarcity, extravagance and deprivation, to register on my perception as anything but chaos.

He agreed that it was stupefying, but there was also, he said, something naively futuristic about it, a sense of faddishness, as if all these so-called advancements might one day be abandoned, and those who had fallen for them, invested in them, would be laughed at. As if the city might be going through a phase that people in the future would recall with fond amusement. History might record turn-of-the-century Manhattan as no more than an exemplar of the excesses to which gullibility could lead.

He said he saw it in the faces of the people we passed, and felt it, just barely, beneath all the optimism and excitement. He believed that each time they heard of some new invention, some new and better way of doing things, the people of this city felt a little foolish. Or rather, some of the people felt this way, those whom one might call the marks of this society.

"Do you know who the marks are?" he said.

"No," I said.

Not the rich, he said; not the entrepreneurs, nor the inventors, nor the poor, who built the city with their hands, nor the destitute.

"Then who?" I said.

"You and me," he said. "The middle mass of men." That portion of society on whom, on whose gullibility and guilelessness, all of the above relied for their survival. We were the ones the new city was intended to impress. Did I think it was intended to impress the street arabs or the unseen occupants of tenements that were home to more people than every settlement in Newfoundland except St. John's? Did I think I would ever live to see a man like Jacob Astor gaping at the Brooklyn Bridge? No, the city was intended to captivate us, the ones who, it was hoped, would partake of things we played no part in making, things that, although we could afford them, were beyond our understanding and control.

"Yes, people like me," he said. "At least, people of my station before I fell in love with someone who happened to be rich."

I had only the faintest notion of what he meant, and none at all of why he was getting so worked up.

He pointed out men wearing Homburg hats, men with walking sticks who watched as steam shovels lurched about in excavation sites, gawked in befuddlement at the demolition of a building twice their age of whose imminent demise they appeared to have known nothing until this very moment. This middle class of men, Dr. Cook said, was an invention more profound than all the others put together.

We followed the eastern edge of Central Park, went west for a few blocks, then south until once again the streets were jammed with people and conveyances.

"The noise seems to be part of what drives the city," he said. "As does the lack of light and space and air. Perhaps it has been determined that for New York to grow at its present pace, exactly these conditions must prevail."

Most streetcar lines and el trains were electrified. Overhead there were so many wires it was as though a loosely woven fragment had been draped above the city. "But at least," he said, "soot and cinders do not rain down from above as they did when Amelia was here."

At this mention of my mother, I asked him if the house where he had met her was still standing.

"Almost nothing from twenty years ago is still standing," he said.

After a long interval of silence, he added, "I believe it is still there. It's been more than fifteen years since I went by it. I haven't even seen it from the outside since the last time I waitered there. The doctors who once owned it moved out long ago. I've gone out of my way to avoid them *and* their house. I don't know who lives there now."

"Will you take me there?" I said.

"If you would like to see it, you will have to go alone. I will tell you where it is, but I could not bear to go with you."

"I just want to see it," I said. "I don't want to go inside. I don't see why you can't go with me."

"I don't know why you want me to."

"It will seem less like a secret then, our being related. I know it has to be one, but not between us. It's like your wanting me to call you Dr. Cook even when there's no one else around."

"Going by that house would stir up painful memories for me. Shameful ones."

"Then you must have those memories when you look at me."

"It's not the same, Devlin."

"It feels the same to me. Your not wanting to go makes *me* feel ashamed."

"The more we talk about this in private, the harder it will be to pretend in front of other people."

"Francis Stead and my mother didn't die because of you. All that happened because of you was *me*."

"I'm sorry. I can't go with you. I will give you the address; you can go there in a cab and meet me—"

"No," I said. "I'm tired of sneaking about all the time. If, someday, you change your mind, we'll go together."

He said nothing.

On we drove. After a while, I noticed that we were headed for the bridge. The streets were nowhere near as crowded as before. The sky above Brooklyn was no longer blue. The light was fading fast.

"Not everything I wrote to you in my letters is true," he said, staring straight ahead, as expressionless as if I were a paying passenger.

I felt a spurt of panic. What was I about to hear? Anything seemed possible, here in this city where being unable to speak English would not have made me feel more out of place than I felt already. What a fool I was to think I could simply enlist in a history that wasn't mine. His history, this city's, this country's—none of them was mine.

"What do you mean?" I said, expecting him to reveal nothing less than that, after all, he was not my father; that all my worst fears were justified; that the notion that I was his son was a fiction that for him served some inscrutable purpose that, now that I had stepped out of my life and into his, he was about to own up to to be rid of me. I was not who I thought I was, not his son but Francis Stead's after all, back to being Francis Stead's. I broke into a sweat and felt so weak he had to take my arm to keep me from pitching from the cab.

"I cannot tell you here," he said, half shouting, half whispering. "I thought that driving about the city would divert me from the urge to tell you. Perhaps I should have gone out driving by myself."

I have no proof, I told myself. He has no proof. No proof is possible. I took the word of a man I had never met. Who is he, after all? What, besides what *he* has told me, do I know about him? I had been unable to resist those letters because I *wanted* to believe they were true. How circumscribed the world had seemed, how predictable the future, before the first one came.

"Dr. Cook—"

"We will meet in the Dakota, and I will tell you there."

CHAPTER FIFTEEN

WE MET IN THE DRAWING ROOM AFTER HE WENT TO THE COOKS'
to tell his wife that he and I had business to discuss. The largest room
in the Dakota, it was the one in which we could sit farthest from the
doors and walls, keeping to a minimum the chance that the sound of
our voices might carry through them.

The room, the never-lived-in room that even with us in it still
seemed unoccupied, served only to increase my sense of not belong-
ing, of having made some terrible, irreversible mistake. Going back to
Newfoundland would not reverse it. Nothing would. I had started
down a path that I could not bear to double back from, a path that
even if only in my mind I would follow to the end. Back home—
knowing that what I had been looking forward to for years would
never happen, that the person I thought I was had never been—I
might well end up like my mother. And Francis Stead. Francis Stead's
son after all. Only in dreams had I ever felt such dread.

"Are you my father?" I whispered.

"Of course," he said, looking startled, then nervously about. "Of
course I am. I didn't mean to make you think otherwise. I would
never mislead you about that. It is something else entirely. Please,
Devlin, you must not feel that you have anything to fear from me."

I did not want him to see how relieved I was, how terrified I had
been. It might have made him doubt my emotional stability. Even
once reassured, I doubted it myself. I realized that I had let myself

become dangerously dependent on him, on his approval, on meeting his expectations and on his meeting mine, on the notion that we shared some tandem destiny. No one person should be so relied upon, let alone one whose nature was so elusive.

We sat on either side of the fire, the reflection of which flickered in the mirror above the mantlepiece and on the ornate gilded ceiling. He insisted on a fire, though it was warm outside, telling me that at night this room was always cold. We turned on no lights, though even in the darkness I could see the chandelier. Unlit but faintly luminous, the chains invisible that attached it to the ceiling, it seemed to hang suspended in the air.

We did not face the fire. He sat on a sofa from which he could see both doors. I did not share the sofa with him but drew up a chair beside it.

"Tell me," he said. "What do you think you will do after I am gone? After those who would be most hurt by the truth are gone."

"Some of them are gone already," I said. "My mother. Francis Stead."

"Are you concerned with how people will remember them? Remember me, my wife, my other children? Do you care how people will remember you?"

"I will never tell anyone you are my father," I said. "No one else will ever know. *You* must not believe that you have anything to fear from *me*. You are my father." My father. Father. At last I had said it. And he had winced at the word, at my having broken my pledge never to call him anything but Dr. Cook. Would he never do as much for me and say I was his son? He had often used the words *father* and *son* in his letters.

"I believe you," he said. "If people were other than they are, no one would have cause to fear the truth. But people, if they knew *this* truth, would never understand it.

"I have weighed telling you against not telling you, vacillating back and forth. I have, since your arrival, been favouring the former. I hope I have chosen correctly.

Francis Stead at one time loved your mother very much. More, perhaps, than I ever did."

"He might have loved her," I said. "But he must have hated me."

"I knew him for the length of the North Greenland expedition. Eighteen months. Has anyone told you about him, what he was like?"

"No one ever spoke about him unless they had to," I said.

"I will tell you first about Francis Stead. He had no idea what motivated people, good or bad; no idea how others saw him. He did not think of himself as having a transparent nature. He assumed that he was as inscrutable to others as they were to him.

"He was always telling me things about himself that he thought I never would have guessed. He would make these self-disclosures in such earnestness, almost gravely, as if it were a relief to him that finally someone else knew of this shortcoming that for years had been his shameful secret.

"'I'm not very good at conversation,'" he said once, as if I had never seen him attempt conversation.

"I could never bring myself to tell him that the things he was forever confessing to were common knowledge. I am making him sound almost child-like, which in a way he was. But there was another side to him. If he saw or suspected that people were having fun at his expense, he got very angry, not at them, but at himself for having done or said something—he usually had no idea what it was—to make himself look foolish.

"People laughed at him, but it was usually good-natured laughter. His 'story' was partly known. We had heard that he had left his wife and child to take up exploration, and that in his absence, his wife had died, though the circumstances of her death were not known. We all assumed she had died from some illness. I had no idea then who this wife and child were, who he was. Amelia had only ever called him 'my fiancé.' Lily had never spoken of him.

"He was well liked among explorers, the only people, he said, who could understand why he had sacrificed so much. But explorers laughed at him, too—at his grandiose ambitions, his ever-changing goals, which he talked about as if he had accomplished them already. One day it was the North Pole. The next day the South Pole. The next day the summit of the highest mountain in the world.

"He might have prospered had he known his place, had he understood that he was not cut out for greatness. But to hear him talk, great men *already* included him in their number. People could not help laughing at him.

"'Why am I so often laughed at?' he said on the North Greenland expedition.

"'You're not,' I said.

"'Damn it,' he said. 'I'm just so . . . why can't I . . .' He would never finish such sentences, just go about kicking things, to everyone's further amusement.

"He told me he felt that he was the 'mascot' of the expedition. He might have become the mascot by random choice for all the sense it made to him.

"It was clear, from the start of the expedition, that Peary had hired him so he could bully him about. Francis, who believed Peary to be his friend, indulged his every whim.

"During the early stages of the expedition, I felt sorry for him because of the way Peary treated him, having him perform the most menial tasks. It was as if Peary wanted to see if there was *anything* that Francis would not stoop to doing. Francis, a doctor, disposed of waste, swept the floor of Peary's quarters, filled in when the cook was sick. It was said, among the crew and the paying passengers of the *Kite*, that there were not two doctors and one manservant on board, but two manservants and one doctor.

"But Francis gradually changed. By the time of the land march back to southern Greenland, and especially by the time we returned to McCormick Bay, he was openly defiant of Peary. He stared at Peary while Peary was preoccupied with other things. He looked as though he meant to confront him for treating him so poorly, though Peary was by this time ignoring Francis as much as he could. Sometimes, I would look up to see Francis staring at *me*, wearing the same expression as when he stared at Peary. What he had against me—except that, from the start, Peary had preferred my medical advice to his—I had no idea.

"Francis became more and more of a nuisance to Peary. The pieces that appeared about him in the papers after his death were largely true. He sometimes left the ship or Redcliffe House dressed as though for a walk in Prospect Park. More than once, he shed all his clothing and went swimming in the frigid water, claiming he was insensitive to its effects. He let his hair grow long and kept himself clean-shaven in imitation of the Eskimos.

"He told Peary he would not be returning with the rest of the expedition come the spring but would stay behind to live with the Eskimos, whose ways he preferred. Peary was furious, even though Francis was clearly no threat to reach the pole or even a farthest north.

"The rest of us told Peary that Francis was either 'going Native,' as many explorers have done, or else suffering from what the Eskimos call *piblocto*, a form of Arctic madness that would pass. I told Peary that it was best to indulge Francis until he was himself again, but Peary denounced his every utterance and action, which only made Francis worse.

"When the polar night set in, it became his habit to go outside alone to a tolt of rock. He would sit on the side that faced away from Redcliffe House, in the lee of the wind and out of sight. There was a kind of bench in it, a ledge that he sat on, though it was only a foot off the ground, so he had to extend his legs straight out to keep from squatting. I went out there once or twice myself when he was elsewhere. On the rock and the snow in front of it there were cigar butts and little mounds of half-burnt pipe tobacco.

"It was easy to picture him there in the darkness, bundled in furs, puffing on his pipes and his cigars, brooding on the terms of his existence, dreaming of the day when he would be acknowledged as a great explorer. Perhaps he believed that because he understood the effects that prolonged darkness could have on the mind and body, he was immune to them.

"We all, to some degree, shunned the company of others. The long night made morbid introspection irresistible. But he was fooled by the gloom into thinking that to socialize would be a waste of precious energy. Each day, as he left the house, he told us he was going outside to pursue his own strategy for survival. Everything we did he regarded as a symptom, evidence of some delusion that might be contagious.

"Soon he was finding fault with everything I prescribed for the other members of the expedition. In their debilitated states, they didn't know which of us they should listen to. He said that Peary was getting too much exercise, and that it was best that Mrs. Peary get none at all (the best for women being always opposite to what was best for men). He said that Verhoeff was reading too much. Gibson was getting too much sleep, Henson not enough. We should eat cooked canned meat, not raw fresh meat. A day later, though no one but me seemed to notice, he was saying just the opposite, or had shuffled his criticisms so that now it was Henson's regimen of sleep and Mrs. Peary's reading habits that he found fault with.

"I had to overrule him constantly. The others, who when healthy would not have taken him seriously, were filled with doubt and dread because of this disagreement between the two medical officers. They argued as much with me as they did with him—even Peary, who when I warned him against adding more canned meat to his diet told me that Dr. Stead had said that by increasing his intake of canned meat, he would improve his circulation.

"I would have suspected Francis of trying to sabotage the expedition with bad medical advice except that he was so nearly deranged, so agitated, that I doubted he was capable of devising any sort of plan and sticking to it, even one as pointlessly sinister as that.

"Every morning our rounds would end in an argument, the two of us shouting at each other in front of our disconcerted patients until at last he would storm off, leaving Redcliffe House and not returning for hours. I had to keep the most credulous or most debilitated of the crew from going outside with him.

"When asked for advice upon his return, he would reply that he was sure that Dr. Cook's was just as good, or that people who would not listen to him in the morning ought not to seek advice from him at night.

"It must have been at his bench that he did his journal writing, for no one ever saw him write a word. He carried his journals with him everywhere he went, half a dozen swollen volumes with ragged edges and on top of them a fresh one whose pages were still blank. I imagined him scribbling away by moonlight with a fist-clenched pencil while he puffed on his cigars. All I ever saw him do in Redcliffe House was *read* his journals, looking as absorbed in them as if they had been written by someone else.

"When it was three months since we had seen the sun, his state of mind was such that I doubted he would recover. The weather by then was so bad that even he did not venture out of doors. Redcliffe House was recessed on three sides into a hill, built in a cave-like excavation so that only the front of it was exposed.

"There was a series of blizzards that lasted for weeks. It seemed impossible that the exposed wall would hold up against the wind. It buckled back and forth like a bed sheet. The door, though it had several layers, each one as thick as the entrance to a dungeon, rattled as though some giant were trying to force his way inside.

"Verhoeff curled up in the corner farthest from the door, covered his face with his hands, cringing and whimpering as though someone were beating him. The Pearys stayed in their 'room' behind the curtain. Gibson sat at the table with his hands over his ears, unable to stand the shrieking of the wind. I tried to read, but I could not help looking at the wall to see if it was giving way.

"Francis tacitly abdicated as medical officer, no longer dispensing criticisms or advice. He became so deeply despondent that he spoke to no one, not even me, not even when directly addressed, which seemed a welcome change at first. But the others were soon unsettled by the sight of him sitting against the wall all day long with his lower body in his sleeping bag, as motionless as a catatonic.

"He showed no signs of noticing when, thinking some physical malady might be at the root of his condition, I examined him. But he was, if anything, healthier than some of the others, who were convinced that one morning they would wake up to find him dead.

"The weather was still bad when the sun returned, but he came out of his trance-like state almost instantly when Verhoeff pointed out the light at the edges of the boarded windows. I thought his recovery suspiciously abrupt, but the improvement in all of us was dramatic at this sign of the sun's return. We spoke of nothing but the coming of spring, the prospect of being picked up by the ship and taken home.

"One day, when the ship was nearly due and he and I were returning across the scree, having examined two of the Eskimos who were ill, he asked me if he might confide in me. I said yes, and he led me to the tolt of rock.

"He sat down and patted the bench to indicate that I should join him. I did so. I thought he had taken me aside to apologize. In the past few weeks, he had resumed his duties as medical officer and had seemed almost sheepishly disinclined to talk about the past few months.

"It is not unusual, at the end of an expedition, for people to explain themselves to their commander or whichever member of the crew has held up best. The latter is usually the medical officer, if only because he alone, no matter what the circumstances, has a task he can perform, there being no better antidote to fear and gloom than purposeful work.

"They meet with you in private, in part to find out what account of their behaviour will be offered to the world when they return, or even to influence that account, and in part to be reassured that they did not act cowardly or shamefully.

"I decided I would give Francis a good dressing-down first and then advise him, with as much delicacy as possible, not to apply for membership on future expeditions.

"Surveying the distant glacier, he sighed and settled his body into the rock again as though he were shifting his weight in a favourite chair, as if all he planned to do was watch the sunset and all he wanted me for was companionship. But then he leaned forward, drew in his legs and crossed his feet.

"He told me that he had a wife and boy back home whom he had abandoned because the boy was not really his son. He said that his wife had told him she had been taken advantage of while drunk, but that he did not believe her. He said he had recently found out who the father was, but he did not say how.

"During their engagement, he said, she had told him she was pregnant. There were fewer than twenty doctors in St. John's, including several to whom she was related. She knew of none on whose discretion she could count.

"And so she told him, in his surgery, after hours. She told him that because of having had so much to drink, she remembered nothing that had happened at a recent party from half an hour after getting there to just moments before she left. She said that she knew she had been with someone, but that she had no idea who it was.

"His reaction was not what she had expected. She had thought he would assume that she had wilfully betrayed him. But he believed her, he said. She was not responsible for what had happened, and together they would deal with it.

"Without uttering a word against the man who, when she was too drunk to help herself, had pressed himself upon her, he told her that he would examine her to make sure her suspicions were correct. She told him this was not necessary, but he insisted.

"'There, there,' he kept saying throughout the examination, unaware of how much was already lost.

"To determine if she was pregnant by another man, he examined the woman he had never more than kissed, whose body he had never seen or even touched before.

"'This changes nothing, not really,' he told her. 'It will be as if we adopted a child. We will tell those who need to know that I have made you pregnant. Let them react however they wish. We love each other. That is all that matters.'

"He went on and on, unaware, he told me, that it might be himself he was trying to convince. This Francis Stead who would hold no grudge, who would cope and love his wife no matter what, was as much of a fiction as the Francis Stead who would be the first to reach the pole.

"He said he should have talked her into considering a second option, should have reminded her that because he was a doctor, they were in the position of keeping her pregnancy a secret forever. No one but the two of them need ever know.

"But they did not speak of this second option. He convinced himself that they would marry and remain married, no matter what.

"'It was for the child's sake that she married me,' he said. 'I know that now. And for the child's sake that she tried to make our marriage work.'

"Her family, what was left of it, aunts and uncles, and his family, the Steads, were told. The Steads received the news exactly as he said he knew they would. That he had made her pregnant, his family had no trouble believing. But they did not for a moment have the slightest doubt about who was to blame.

"They allowed it to become an open secret that she was pregnant. The wedding date was changed at such short notice that many who were invited could not come. His sister-in-law, whom he and his fiancée hardly knew, was the maid of honour.

"Francis said he could not help feeling that their real secret was common knowledge, that all of St. John's knew the baby she carried was not his.

"For a young woman to become pregnant by her fiancé was no great shame. The rumours that she had done so would not have bothered him if they had been true.

"For a while after the boy was born, it had seemed possible to Francis that the three of them could be a family. But he could not forget that the boy was another man's son, not his. No one knew this but him and his wife. He said he did not even tell his brother. But still he could not rid himself of the feeling that the whole world knew. It seemed to him that, all along, people had laughed at him because they sensed that he would land himself in some such fix as this, and that they were laughing even harder now because his very determination to prove them wrong, to do what was right, had borne out their prediction.

"He told me he felt foolish for not seeing that when it met its first real test, what he called his 'innocence' would crumble. He did not know, as the days went by, which pained him more, he said—the sight of the baby or the sight of his wife. He felt things he had never felt before: resentment, malice, hatred. These, until now, had been mere words.

"He avoided both of them as much as he could, having his dinner sent up to his study, where, he told his wife, he was reading for some case that was proving difficult to diagnose. In the morning, he would claim to have fallen asleep while working.

"This 'case' went undiagnosed for months. Once, she joked that the disease he was trying to diagnose was obviously contagious, for surely the first person who had contracted it was dead by now. He looked at her as if to say that only the person who had wronged him as she had could joke about such things.

"She, he now told her, had betrayed him with another man, fooled him into marriage and into thinking he was capable of raising another man's child as if it was his. She had what she wanted, and that was her child, so what was the point of pretending she cared for him?

"He said nothing else to her for months other than what their sharing the same house required him to say.

"He did not, would not, after that first outburst, get angry with her.

"No matter what she said—and she said many things to convince him that she loved him, and that their marriage could still work—he would not answer, or even show any sign that he had heard her, other than to simply leave the room with the air of one who had become accustomed to such unprovoked attacks.

"Then finally he did speak to her, told her that this could not go on, as if it had been at *her* insistence that it *had* been going on.

"'I have been thinking for some time now,' he said, 'that I should change my life.' Then he turned about and went up to his study.

"He had decided that he would leave her and the boy. But he could not bring himself to simply disappear, to go to some other country and begin again. He poured over the atlas. Considered England, Scotland, Ireland, Australia, South Africa. But he could not picture himself alone in one of these countries, inventing for himself some less humiliating past, one that would make people feel sorry for him or admire him. These were just fantasies.

"Another possibility occurred to him. In the weeks that followed, he spoke politely to her and even looked at her and the baby with what she mistook for fondness from time to time.

"One night, after the baby had gone to sleep and she was reading in the front room, he came downstairs from his study, stood facing the fire and began to speak.

"'I think it would be best if I went up north,' he said.

"Having no idea what he meant by this, she waited.

"'The Hopedale Mission in Labrador is badly in need of doctors,' he said. 'I have volunteered to join and have been accepted. It is for only six months. And perhaps for another six months after that. It will give me time to think. I have often wondered what it's like up there.'

"'The way she looked told me two things,' he said. 'That she was in love with someone else, and that she had never been in love with me.

"'And where was this other man?' Francis wondered. 'Whose baby she could not stand to be away from for a second? Did he know about the child? Had he turned his back on her, in spite of which she loved him anyway?'

"Francis did not bother asking her these questions. He knew that at this point, she would not relent. It was too late for her to tell the truth. He could not bear to speak to her, to look at her or at the boy, whose father, it seemed to him, might be anyone.

"So he became a missionary, then an explorer. He told me he did not want to be forgotten or to have people think badly of him. Better they think he had forsaken the vocation of marriage for the more romantic one of exploration; that only with reluctance had he left his wife and son, having discovered, alas too late for them, that he was meant for greater things.

"He joined the Hopedale Mission for a year. When he came back home and told her he was giving up his practice in favour of polar exploration, she gave up on him.

"But he did not give up on her. She and the man whose name he did not know were all he thought about, he said."

Dr. Cook turned away from the fire and looked at me.

"It was at this point in his story that he told me that he knew about me and Peary and his wife. As suddenly as that. Up to that point, I had been feeling uncomfortable, but only because of what seemed to me to be a mere coincidence. While engaged to him, his wife had become pregnant by another man. I had made an engaged woman pregnant. It unsettled me to hear him talk about his situation, but nothing more. And then suddenly he said: 'I know about you and Peary and my wife.'

"He knew that the man his wife had betrayed him with was me. He knew what I had done. Had known it, perhaps, since before the expedition left New York, unless Peary had told him more recently.

"What he meant by his reference to Peary, what he need not have bothered recounting, since he had finally sprung his surprise on me, was that he knew that at the party in Manhattan where I met your mother, I also, in a manner of speaking, met Robert Peary. But Francis related this part of the story to me, the part I knew far better than he did, in the same tone he had used so far, as if, though I was now a character in his story, I had no idea what would happen next."

"What did Peary have to do with you and my mother?" I asked Dr. Cook.

"He had just joined the U.S. Navy at the rank of lieutenant," he said, "because of his training as a civil engineer. He was alone and in full uniform at the party, which, as I told you in my letters, was thrown in honour of the graduates of the Columbia medical school. Peary's mother was acquainted with the woman of the house. It seems that out of politeness to his mother's friend, Peary accepted an invitation to the party.

"He looked quite smart in his uniform, what with his height and build and that striking combination of red hair and blue eyes. But he seemed very ill at ease, as if he hated being conspicuous, took no pleasure in the effect of his appearance on others, on women especially. The only person there who looked more ill at ease than Peary did was me. One of four prospective medical students who were acting as waiters and bartenders at the party, I felt hopelessly out of place.

"There was some sort of near altercation at the party between Peary and one of the graduating doctors. It seems that Peary had recently, and abruptly, broken off an engagement with a young woman whom he was said to have treated shabbily. Either the young doctor said something about this matter or Peary misconstrued something he overheard. Peary shouted something at the young man, who at first looked mystified and then became quite belligerent, having to be separated from Peary by his friends.

"Peary moved off to the bar, where I was serving drinks. He stood there in silence for several minutes while I served the other guests, until I realized that he was regarding me with an undisguised look of scorn.

"'They say that you plan to be a doctor one day,' he said when our eyes met. He spoke with a slight lisp of which he has since rid himself. I could see that he was painfully self-conscious of it. I told him that, yes, I planned to become a doctor. He laughed as if he had never seen a more hopeless candidate for medicine, as if he was imagining just how inept a doctor I would be, I who, with my hands that would not stop shaking, was spilling drinks and ice and breaking glasses.

"I fancied he knew that I was more or less being sponsored to medical school by the hosts of the party, who had taken pity on me. I could think of nothing to say. His jaws clamped shut loudly when he stopped laughing, his back teeth clicking together. I believe he was about to address me again in the same manner when a young woman who was standing some feet from Peary, waiting to be served, intervened. Craning her neck around the people between her and Peary, she spoke up loudly.

"'I am surprised to see you laughing, Lieutenant Peary,' she said.

"'I cannot imagine why,' Peary said, looking startled, his voice raised to match hers. 'Especially as, to my knowledge, we have never met.'

"In the near vicinity, all conversation stopped. All eyes were on this brash young woman.

"'Perhaps you are laughing,' she said, 'because you are happier now that it is once again just you and your mother. They say that your mother is very happy to have her Bertie back.'

"Peary laughed again—even more unconvincingly than before—his jaws again clamping shut audibly when he was finished, as if his mouth were some mechanical device whose operation he had yet to master.

"'You are drunk, miss,' he said. 'That, I believe, is obvious to everyone.'

"'May Kilby says you never laugh,' the woman said. 'In fact, she says you smile only when you think that not to do so would be rude.'

"It was clear that this Miss Kilby was the woman to whom Peary had been engaged. The remark was met with an uproar of laughter because it seemed to sum Peary up so perfectly. Everyone looked at Peary as if to measure him against this estimation of him by the woman to whom he had been engaged, and which had just been repeated in public by this other woman, who seemed to be unaccompanied.

"The laughter grew louder. Peary, red-faced, strode off through the guests to a room to which news of his embarrassment had not yet spread.

"The woman who spoke up for me, the woman who embarrassed him, was your mother. Her first cousin, Lily, had told her about Peary and May Kilby.

"I did not see Peary again until, having helped your mother up the stairs hours later, when it really was obvious that she had had too much to drink, he happened upon us as I was crouching on one knee beside her after she had stumbled and fallen.

"'If only those who found your little joke so amusing could see you now,' said Peary.

"'She has had only a *little* too much to drink, sir,' I said. 'That's all.'

"Peary shook his head as though in disbelief. 'She, a stranger, berates me for my treatment of my fiancée. And here she lies on the floor with an engagement ring on her finger and a milkboy from Brooklyn in her arms.'

"Someone must have told him that with my brothers I ran a small milk business. Peary was himself born on a modest farm in Maine, though he has never liked to be reminded of it. He looked down at both of us and smiled. He walked past us down the hallway.

"We saw Peary on one other occasion before your mother left Manhattan. Your mother and I, with Lily between us, were strolling through Central Park when we saw him walking towards us arm in arm with a woman whom I took to be his mother. Your mother and I exchanged a smile, the kind people exchange when they know they are thinking exactly the same thing. Here was the woman whom May Kilby's friend had said was so glad to 'have her Bertie back.' How apt her pet name for her son seemed as they came towards us, the two of them solemn-faced, as if it was a Peary family characteristic to smile only when not to do so would seem rude. Peary stared hard at us, as if he had both recognized us and seen and guessed the meaning of the smile we exchanged. I thought he looked almost shocked to see me in your mother's company. His suggestive remark about having found her in the arms of a milkboy from Brooklyn must have been just an insult in which he could not conceive of there being any truth.

"Peary averted his eyes, and no one spoke as he and his mother went by.

"It was years after this, Francis Stead said, that he moved from St. John's to Brooklyn, where he met and, inasmuch as it was possible for anyone to do so, befriended Peary. Peary did not know of the connection between Francis Stead and the woman who had mocked him at the party years ago. At some point, Francis told Peary that he had a wife and son back home in St. John's. He told him that the child was not his, and that he did not know whose it was, though he believed that the father lived somewhere in New York. He repeated to Peary Amelia's story of having been taken advantage of while drunk, but he said that he did not believe it. When he told Peary his wife's first name and maiden name, Peary recognized it. This woman, speaking in defence of me, had mocked him, slighted him, and Peary never forgot or forgave such things. He likewise remembered my name, the name of the boy whose abject wretchedness he saw as having been the cause of his embarrassment. He remembered us both, remembered seeing us in Central Park and the smile that passed between us when we saw him with his mother. He told Francis what he knew.

"'My dear Stead,' Peary concluded, 'there is no mystery here. The father of the boy your wife is passing off to all the world as your son is Dr. Frederick Cook. It is an open secret, Stead, what happened between Cook and your wife after they met at that drunken party in Manhattan. There are *many* who know that that boy back home is not your son. Even in St. John's there are some who know it. Some who know that you are not his father. These people have been laughing at you behind your back for years. I tell you this as a friend who cannot stand to see you made a fool of any longer. I cannot prove what I have told you of Dr. Cook, of course, and I shall deny having told you any of this story should you repeat a word of it.'

"'Perhaps now,' Francis said to me, 'you understand why Peary treats me as he does. Otherwise friendless when I met him, I worshipped Peary. In public, though he did not reveal my secret, he would make fun of me, make jokes at my expense—ribald jokes that had a private meaning for him and me—order me about, have me run errands for him and for others. I became known as Peary's whipping boy, and I took it all without complaint.'"

Dr. Cook looked at me. "Why, you may wonder, did Peary, having told Francis about me, appoint both of us to his expedition? In Peary's estimation, Francis was an ineffectual cuckold who would never find the nerve to exact revenge on anyone who did him wrong. As for me, when I applied for the position of medical officer on the North Greenland expedition—having set aside my own distaste for Peary in order to gain some experience in polar exploration under a man I knew I could learn much from—and Peary accepted my application, I assumed that he, too, had put aside, for the good of the expedition, whatever animosity he still harboured against me. We did not mention our first meeting. I think Peary thought that to put Francis and me together on the same expedition would be amusing. That it would be amusing to watch Francis trying to summon up the courage to confront me. He might have believed that, at most, Francis would publicly accuse me of having fathered a child by his wife, and thereby humiliate me and possibly ruin my reputation. I'm sure he did not think Francis would act in any way that would jeopardize the expedition. Peary has never been a good judge of character.

"But the Francis Stead who let himself be abused by Peary was not the same man who related his story to me on that bench of rock. Upon revealing that he knew me to be the man with whom his wife had betrayed him, he looked at me with undisguised contempt. I tried to keep my composure.

"'I did meet your wife, Dr. Stead,' I said. 'But ours was but a casual acquaintanceship. I was better acquainted with her cousin Lily.'

"'Cook,' he said, 'I joined this expedition with the intention of killing you. Many times I have had the opportunity, not only to do it, but to do it without detection. Being fellow medical officers, we have often been out of sight of the others, as we are now, sometimes in places where one missed step would mean the end. All I need have done was push you into some crevasse, then report to the others that there had been an accident. But I have been unable to bring myself to do it. My wife, some years after I left her, took her life. She is gone. I hold you responsible for that. Yet for some reason, I cannot bring myself to kill you. It seems, after all, that it was merely to do this that I signed on with the expedition: to take you aside and tell you everything. I no longer have any doubts that you are the father of my wife's son. I know for certain now. And it would seem that knowing is enough.'"

"You must remember, Devlin, that I had just heard for the first time that Amelia was dead, and heard for the first time the manner of her death. Perhaps the pain he saw in my eyes was his revenge.

"His voice was very calm, very deliberate. I should have known that he had but one thing left to do.

"Hearing from him that at one time his intention had been to kill me set me trembling. His assurance that he had changed his mind was not of much comfort to me. That he would talk so openly about such things was an indication of how quickly he could change his mind again. I didn't know what I should do, didn't know exactly how far away the others were.

"He seemed not to have a weapon on his person, but in each of our doctor's kits there were a set of scalpels. He saw me look at the kits, which lay side by side on the ground between us, two burlap bundles tied with rope.

"'Don't worry,' he said, smiling as if he had been dwelling for years on such things as now occupied my mind. 'If you promise to keep my secret, I will promise to keep yours.' He took my silence as agreement. And that, indeed, was what it was.

"He left the tolt of rock and went back to Redcliffe House. That night, he walked away from the house and was never seen again.

"It was because of my supposed closeness with Francis Stead that Peary had me write that report that appeared in the papers.

"When I got back to Brooklyn, I contacted the registry of births and deaths in St. John's. They confirmed for me that Amelia Stead had died, though the cause of death was officially listed as accidental drowning."

Dr. Cook sighed as though his story was finished. But surely it could not be. Surely something more than this had been on his mind since my arrival in Brooklyn. It was a different version of events than he had set forth in his letters. But surely this was not what he had been referring to hours ago, when, his voice quavering with dread, he said that he had withheld things from me, things he could not bear to disclose except in private.

"I don't understand," I said. "You need not have been afraid—"

"I received one letter more from your mother after she returned to Newfoundland from New York than I admitted to," he said.

He reached into the pocket of his vest and withdrew a yellowed piece of paper, unfolded it and, hands suddenly trembling, extended it to me. It read:

My dearest:

I am with child, but my fiancé is not its father. Of these two things, I can assure you. All else seems uncertain, except my love for you. If you still wish to marry me, you have but to say so and I will meet you in New York. As I must have an answer from you soon, send me a telegram saying simply yes or no and sign it "Lily." If you say no, or if I do not hear from you within a week, I will not write to you again. Nor could I bear it if, at some time in the future, you wrote to me. Please do not feel that you have anything to fear from me. I will speak your name to no one.

All my love,
Amelia

When I looked up from reading the letter, I saw that he had covered his face with his hands.

"So it was not her who ended it," I said. "It was you."

"Yes," he said. "'I will speak your name to no one.' I knew that she meant it, that she would keep her word no matter what. That my reputation, or my hopes to one day have one at least, would remain secure. She was willing to forsake almost everything so that she and I, and you, could be together. But I was not. And it did not take me a week to make up my mind. I did not even have the courage to send her a telegram containing that one word. *No.* I did not even tell her no, Devlin. I simply moved on as if we had never met, leaving her with no choice but to do the same. You cannot know how ashamed I am of what I did. How I regret it.

"I convinced myself that no good would come to anyone if I said yes, that my treachery was justified. What sort of life, I asked myself, will the two of us and our child have if I say yes, if I lose my reputation and she loses hers, if she marries a man without prospects, if our child is raised in poverty and shame? I had ambitions, you see. I had told her about them, about growing up poor in Brooklyn, across the river from Manhattan, in tantalizing proximity to it. Yet I might as well have been a million miles from it, so unlikely had it seemed that there would ever be a place in it for me. As a young man, I was determined to make such a place for myself, to succeed on a grand scale at something, anything, just so long as I rose to a higher station in life than most men. I told myself that her fiancé would break off their engagement, that the pregnancy would be kept secret and the baby delivered and raised elsewhere, given up to someone else, with both mother and father standing a reasonable chance of happiness.

"All this driving around that we've been doing—I've been remembering your mother, the endless drives we took with Lily just so we could be together. I've been taking you to all the places I took her. Most of them look nothing now like they did back then, but still they remind me of her, as you do. I've half been expecting to see her on some street or coming towards me in another cab with my younger self beside her.

"I've *felt* her everywhere since you arrived. It's never been like this before, not even when I spent time in Manhattan just after I received her letter, brooding, feeling sorry for myself in spite of what I'd done.

"Amelia. Her name is on my lips halfway across the bridge, and after that . . . it might as well be *written* everywhere, I hear it so often in my mind.

"This is what I gave her up for, I've been telling myself. So as not to lose my chance at this. So as not to be excluded from this, which now seems like nothing next to her."

I could not believe what I had heard.

"When Libby Forbes died in childbirth," he said, "and our baby girl soon after, I thought this was a judgment on all of us for my betrayal of your mother and her child. Libby and the baby died, but I was spared. Amelia and Francis died, but I was spared. My fiancée, Libby's sister, Anna, died, but I was spared. Over and over, I was spared, allowed to survive. It seemed that my punishment was to bring misfortune down upon the ones I loved while being spared from it myself.

"I think that when your mother wrote me that last letter, she knew she would never hear from me again. It reads like a pardon for what I was about to do.

"I could not bring myself in my letters to tell you that I had betrayed her, or that I was, even more directly than I had let on, the cause of her death and the death of Francis Stead. I feared that if I told you, you would not want to hear from me again. It was my plan never to tell you. But now that we have met...I can see her in your eyes, Devlin. It is almost as if she has been returned to me as she was when we first met, when she was just your age and I was even younger.

"As for not wanting you to write me back, I had several reasons. I had left your mother's letter unanswered. It seemed only fitting that mine be left that way as well. But also, I could not bear to think of you formulating replies to letters that were misleading.

"Devlin, you are the son of the only woman I have ever really loved. Marie I feel much affection for and did not marry for her money, but it is your mother's face, her lovely, young woman's face, that comes back to me in dreams. I would not blame you if you went back to Newfoundland, if you moved on and forgot me the way I did your mother."

The fire had burned down and I could barely make him out.

I could not speak. I felt almost as wrenched from my former life as I had when I read his first letter. He and my mother were not who or what I thought they were.

This man whose baby she could not stand to be away from for a second. My mother had loved me that much. Yet she had abandoned me.

"My mother's death," I said, "was officially declared an accident. But Francis Stead was right. It is widely believed in St. John's that she took her life." I realized, too late, that it sounded like an accusation, as good as saying, "She took her life because of you."

"I think it might be best for you to go," I said. "It is very late."

He rose from the sofa.

"I will keep my mother's letter," I said. "For now. I will return it to you soon."

"Goodnight," he said and made his way in silence to the near door, which he did not close behind him.

I sat there for some time after the fading of his footsteps. I thought of the scrolled letters, saw them now in a different, tainted light. I recalled a phrase from his second letter: "I believe that, upon reflection, you will realize that there exists no motive that would cause me to mislead you on this matter."

I left the drawing room and went back to my bedroom. I lay down and tried to sleep.

Though it seemed strange, I felt elated. Also disappointed and betrayed. But elated, most of all. For it seemed to me that the toll his story had taken on him was the measure of his feeling for me. How fearful he was that I would turn away from him. He had seemed, until now, so remote, as if he might be having second thoughts about his promise to include me in his life. Now he was a new, in some ways lesser, Dr. Cook. The ideal, flawless man of the letters and the past few weeks did not exist. No such men existed anywhere. But tonight he had poured out to me his most shameful secrets. And now he was lying awake in bed wondering what I would do.

I would stay.

I still believed in him, still trusted him.

Despite that, however, I compared the handwriting in my mother's letter to that of the handwriting on the back of the portrait photograph of her. In particular, I compared the two signatures, the "Amelia" on the letter and the "Amelia" on the back of her photograph, where she had written "Amelia, the wicked one." They were, as far as I could tell, exactly the same. The paper the letter was written on was creased with age. There was no doubt that my mother had written the letter twenty years ago.

I looked in the mirror on the wall beside my bed. "I can see her in your eyes," he'd said. But as yet I could see no one in my eyes.

I went by the study the next day after he came back from his rounds. It would be even harder now to call him Dr. Cook.

"I want to assure my aunt that I am well," I said, "without revealing to her where I am." It was more of a demand than a statement. But implicit in it was the answer he was hoping for.

"That can easily be arranged," he said. It was the first time he had not looked me in the eye while speaking to me. He looked elated, relieved, abashed, scolded. I think that at that moment, I could have got his consent to almost anything.

"How can it be done?" I said, though I knew how.

"I think I could impose upon your uncle one last time. Send him an unmarked envelope from you. Have him tell her it was pressed upon him in the street by a man he did not know."

"All right," I said.

I imagined Uncle Edward's reaction at the sight of another envelope from Dr. Cook, who had assured him there would be no more. And then his reaction when he saw what the envelope contained. And there would be not just this one last imposition. I owed it to Aunt Daphne to keep assuring her that I was safe.

Dear Aunt Daphne:

This is to let you know that I am well, and that you need not be afraid for me. I want for nothing except your company, which I greatly miss but must do without for now. I hope that these past few weeks have not been too difficult for you, and that you think no less of me for what I've done. One day, I will tell you why I went away, though there are some things that I must leave forever unexplained.

I hope this brief letter finds you and Uncle Edward in good health.

Love,

Devlin

This was the letter I gave to Dr. Cook. Also, I gave back to him the letter from my mother.

"We have begun, Devlin," he said as he took the letters from me. "There are no obstacles between us now."

In the winter, I began to venture out into Brooklyn and Manhattan on my own, delivering messages for Dr. Cook, bringing others back to him. What I was really doing, he assured me, was meeting the people I needed to know.

I went on using Francis Stead's valise. I found a hiding place for the letters: the desk in the library, to which I alone had a key.

Most of my errands took me to Manhattan. I felt as though I were seeing the city with my own eyes for the first time. I saw hope in every face, the faces of the rich and the faces of the poor. In the papers it said that the rich were getting richer and the poor less poor every day. "Why pity a woman, or even a child, schlepping garments through the streets," one paper asked, "when only a year ago these same people were caught up in wars, famine and disease?" The paper said that the lightless, unventilated, suffocating tenements would soon, by an order of the city, be renovated or replaced with better ones.

The city, once it had been reined in, once this irresistible torrent of energy had run its course, would make allowances for everyone, even the street arabs, who, it now seemed to me, were quite cheerfully anarchic, mocking everything they saw so entertainingly that people stopped to listen to them.

I no longer saw, on the Lower East Side, the blank gazes I had seen before. I saw intent, purposeful faces, immigrants pursuing whatever dream they had chosen to pursue from among the millions on display.

I could not bring myself to resent the rich their houses or the other great structures of the city—the buildings, bridges, museums, train stations, monuments and statues that, with their money, had been raised up from the ground. It was impossible to rail against such things when the very sight of them filled you with such wonder. I felt sorry for the poor but did not hold their poverty against the rich.

· CHAPTER SIXTEEN ·

"I BELIEVE," DR. COOK TOLD ME, "THAT ROBERT PEARY WOULD number me among his friends. That I do not number him among mine, I think he knows but does not care. To Peary, friendship is a rank that he bestows on others. The question of reciprocation is, to him, irrelevant.

"I have never told you so before, but I am a member of the Peary Arctic Club. Think of that, Devlin. I am a member of a club whose sole reason for existence is to further Peary's quest to reach the pole."

He said that he had been invited to be a member and, for the sake of appearances, could not decline. He hoped that his own quest to reach the pole would one day become the club's sole reason for existence, and therefore he had to remain on good terms with its members.

"I could not endure membership in the club if Peary lived in New York instead of Philadelphia—that is, if Peary was present at the meetings of the club. Thankfully, he is almost never there when we meet. I skip as many meetings as I can, short of making my record of attendance so unseemly that for me to resign would be less harmful to my reputation. When I do attend, I rarely contribute unless called upon."

It was to the members of the Peary Arctic Club, most of whom were the "backers" Dr. Cook had so often spoken of in his letters, that I delivered messages, returning their replies and other correspondence to Dr. Cook.

He told me that I should say nothing to anyone of his ambitions, or mine. It was thought that he had no designs on the North Pole, that his goals were the South Pole and the climbing of Mt. McKinley, in Alaska, the highest peak on the continent. "The North Pole is the one true prize," he said, a greater challenge than the South, which was a fixed point on an ice-covered continent. To reach the South Pole, you did not have to contend with an ever-shifting surface, with ocean currents, with ice that moved one way while you moved the other, so that you had to walk twenty miles to travel ten, a portion of that ten being undone while you slept or were delayed by weather.

"I do not want them to think," he said, "that I am some sort of spy or saboteur among the members of the club. I am merely waiting for the club to realize what I have known for years: that Peary's day is done; that the mantle must now pass to the man, the American, most capable of completing the quest that Peary has started. They may come to this realization when Peary returns from his present expedition, which his physical state doomed to failure from the start. Peary is the most 'backed' of all the explorers on earth. That, in spite of this, he has still not reached the pole has made some people doubt that anyone can reach it. I will have to assuage these doubts and, at the same time, gently lead the club members to the conclusion that Peary is no longer their best bet. All this will have to be done without unduly offending Peary and his most loyal supporters. It will take a very delicate touch.

"It is no secret that there was antipathy between Francis Stead and Commander Peary on the North Greenland expedition. There were even rumours that Peary was in some way responsible for the doctor's disappearance. He was much criticized in some quarters for his apparent indifference to the fate of Dr. Stead.

"That you are now working for a member of the Peary Arctic Club may surprise some of the other members. They must not think that you bear a grudge against Peary, or that my hiring you hints at some animosity against him on my part. You must seem supportive of Peary and entirely convinced of the inevitability of his success. This will allay any concern they may have that your presence will stir up the controversy surrounding the North Greenland expedition or be an embarrassing reminder of it.

"Make no attempt to conceal who you are—whose son you supposedly are, that is. It would only make things worse for you. People would find out eventually, so tell them straight out. The backers won't feel awkward about it if you show them that you don't."

It would only make things worse for you. He foresaw how difficult it would be for me to go on being Devlin Stead. "The Stead boy" was to me a fiction, but to others, he was very much alive. And this would always be the case.

I hated having to introduce myself as the son of Francis Stead to the members of the club. The son of a man remembered as a fool, a hapless explorer who had been disloyal to Peary and had killed himself. Most of them knew my "story," all but the part about my happening to meet Dr. Cook by chance outside a Broadway beer garden one afternoon last August. They knew Dr. Stead's story and that of his wife. Words like *desertion* and *suicide* hung in the air, unspoken.

"So you're the boy," one man said. The boy the ill-fated Steads were known to have left behind in Newfoundland.

Most of the backers moved on quickly from Dr. Stead to Dr. Cook, for which I was grateful. I always met them in their "business rooms," which were just off to the right as you entered their enormous houses. Of those houses, those business rooms were all I saw, all that I expected I would ever see.

"So you just up and came to Manhattan from Newfoundland?" one man said, nodding approvngly.

These men, it seemed to me, didn't care that I was Francis Stead's son, didn't think my being his son predisposed me to anything. I had come to the city where the past was beside the point, where there *was* no past, where *everyone* came to begin again, not only me. Most of them liked it that I had bypassed college, though they insisted on college for their own sons. I was told many times how fortunate I was to be a young man in Manhattan at the start of what was certain to be the greatest century in history.

I wished I could tell them the simple truth: that it was as my real father's delegate that I was here. I wanted them to know that it was not because he felt sorry for me or out of a sense of obligation to a fallen colleague that Dr. Cook had hired me or invited me into his home.

"It is especially important that you make a good impression on Herbert Bridgman," Dr. Cook said. Bridgman was the secretary of the Peary Arctic Club, a very powerful man, though neither high-born nor wealthy. He was powerful because the backers trusted him to make decisions on their behalf. The club members trusted him to tell them when Peary was asking for more money than he absolutely needed. They trusted him to tell them what amendment of Peary's plans would increase his chances of success. They then proposed that amendment to Peary as if they had thought of it themselves. But Bridgman was also Peary's pitch man. Peary needed Bridgman to convince the backers that his expeditions were worth investing in. Everything necessary to them but not including the expeditions themselves Bridgman organized on behalf of Peary—the raising of funds, publicity, lecture tours, the recruitment of crew members, the purchasing of all supplies (including an ice-breaking vessel should a new one be needed, as it almost always was). Bridgman also negotiated agreements between Peary and the club members as to how the spoils of each expedition would be shared—things like minerals, furs, narwhal and walrus tusks, relics, exhibits (including live Eskimos and animals like polar bears). Bridgman, in short, was trusted by both sides. Everything he did for Peary, Dr. Cook hoped he would one day do for him.

"We are good friends. I have known him since he was the business manager of the *Brooklyn Standard Union*. I believe he knows that I see myself as Peary's successor, though of course we have not spoken openly about it. I am certain that once Peary is no longer a contender for the pole, I can convince Bridgman that no American is more qualified to succeed him than I am."

I guessed that Bridgman was fifty. He was bald, his scalp as smooth, as unblemished, as if it had not grown hair since he was twenty. He had, as if for compensation, a florid moustache that, directly beneath his nose, had begun to grey. His eyes, even had he not been bald, would have been his most prominent feature, but his baldness drew attention to them, made them seem even smaller than they were and his stare of appraisal that much more difficult to meet.

"You must have been quite young when your father took up exploration," he said.

"Yes sir, I was," I said. "I don't really remember him."

"I remember him very well," Bridgman said, but he gave no sign that he intended to elaborate. How, his eyes seemed to ask, do you feel about what he did to you and your mother? What are you doing with that doctor's bag that bears his initials? As if I was as deluded about my father as he had been about himself. Did I have no better sense than to see him as some sort of hero whose life was worth emulating?

"So you're working with Dr. Cook," Bridgman said.

"I'm working *for* him, yes sir," I said.

I could see his mind working. Does this boy think that by consorting with explorers, he will come to some understanding of his father? Establish some sort of connection with him?

More than under anyone else's gaze, I felt, under Bridgman's, like an apologist for Francis Stead, his delegate, his representative.

BOOK THREE

· CHAPTER SEVENTEEN ·

DR. COOK CALLED ME TO THE DAKOTA DRAWING ROOM ONE DAY to tell me that he had been asked by the Peary Arctic Club to lead a "relief expedition" for Peary. It was by then almost thirty months since Peary had set off from Philadelphia with two other Americans—and more than a year since I had arrived in New York.

"The club tells me, 'Peary is lost somewhere in the Arctic. We need the benefit of your judgment,' an admission that Peary himself would never make and, if he is found alive, will rebuke his backers for making, even if my intervention saves his life. I feel that as a fellow explorer, I cannot refuse their request. As you know, I have been north only once since the expedition on which Francis Stead was lost. The prospect of going again appeals to me."

Dr. Cook said that aside from the unwritten code among explorers that obliged him to do all he was able to bring about Peary's rescue, two other considerations inclined him to accede to the Arctic club's request. One was that Peary was unaware that, in his absence, his mother and his infant daughter had passed away.

The other consideration was that Jo Peary and her daughter, Marie, were also missing in the North, unheard from since departing Godhavn, Greenland, on August 24 of last year. Mrs. Peary had left Maine with her surviving child when she received a letter from Peary that was meant to reassure her that he was healthy, but had just the opposite effect. She told the Peary Arctic Club that she was going to "fetch" her husband back. It was uncertain if she and her daughter

223

were now with Peary. Mrs. Peary had planned to go as far north as safety and comfort would allow; if by then she had still not found Peary, she would stay put and wait for his return.

"Therefore I must break the vow I made to have no more to do with Peary," Dr. Cook said.

"When will you leave?" I said.

"Very soon. As this expedition will be a short one and will take place in the summer, I was able to convince Bridgman to let you come along with me. I assume that you would like to." He smiled at me, then laughed when he saw how pleased I was by this surprise. Before I had time to stammer out an acceptance of his invitation, he began to tell me what needed to be done before we left.

"Suppose you don't come back?" I overheard Mrs. Cook say to her husband one morning when she went to see him in his office.

The question kept running through my mind.

But I looked forward to the coming expedition with far more excitement than dread. Death, to me, was my mother's death, and Francis Stead's. My own did not really seem possible. Was I a fool to be subjecting myself to the certain suffering of a polar expedition, even one that it was expected we would return from before winter set in? I did not feel like one. I felt fortunate, as though I had been chosen at random to receive some honour I did not deserve.

Dr. Cook and I took the Intercolonial Railroad to North Sydney, Nova Scotia, where we boarded the *Erik*. Already on board were several young men whose fathers were members of the Peary Arctic Club. Paying guests whose fees covered roughly half the cost of the expedition, most of them would be dropped off in Labrador and southern Greenland, where they would spend their time trophy hunting until the ship returned. They had their own compartment, a bunkhouse whose cramped dimensions they complained about incessantly, especially when they learned that I, who was younger than most of them and had no social standing, would be sharing Dr. Cook's less Spartan quarters.

Dr. Cook put an end to their complaining by telling them "my story." Soon, all of them believed that this would be my one and only visit to the Arctic, a visit I was undertaking to satisfy a lifelong yearning to set eyes on the land where my father disappeared and from which his body had never been recovered. Now the other young men regarded me with a mixture of sympathy and awe. They kept their distance from me, as if they wanted neither to intrude upon my pilgrimage nor to allow my presumably solemn mood to dampen theirs.

Dr. Cook and I shared the captain's cabin at the aft of the ship, a grandly named, sparsely furnished, low-ceilinged room not much larger than the pantry at 670 Bushwick. A bunk was built for me along the wall opposite the one to which Dr. Cook's bed was attached. The bunk was like a large dresser drawer whose sides would keep me from spilling out onto the floor in rough weather. Everything in the cabin was tied or bolted down. An oak desk and a chair without arms were bolted to the floor. You had to squeeze into the chair, which was permanently drawn up to what for someone had been an ideal distance from the desk but was for Dr. Cook a touch too far, so that he had to sit on the edge of the chair as he wrote or read.

Dr. Cook had brought along hundreds of books, which he crammed into what little shelf space there was in the cabin; all the shelves had detachable wooden bars across them to keep the books from falling out. "You will have a lot of spare time," he said. "More than most people ever have. It will give you a chance to read these books. No one who hasn't read them can claim to be educated." He had read them all, he said, and was working his way through them for a second time, more slowly. If not for these books, he said, he might not have survived the thirteen months he spent aboard the ice-trapped *Belgica* as it drifted back and forth across the Antarctic Ocean. I scanned the spines of the books: Herodotus, Thucydides, Plato, Aristotle, St. Augustine, Pascal, Hobbes, Sterne, Fielding, Melville, Darwin, Tolstoy. At college, Dr. Cook had studied only medicine and other sciences. He was otherwise self-educated, having figured out for himself which books were worth his time, and having made his way through them without guidance of any kind.

The *Erik* was an enormous black sealing ship from Newfoundland, recently salvaged from a wreck, whose hull was now reinforced with squares of oak planking fourteen inches thick. It was hoped it would hold up against whatever ice we would encounter. The chunky ship, with its distinctive, overlarge sealer's bowsprit jutting out a third of the ship's length from the nose, looked like a teapot with a straight, elongated spout.

Attached to her aft masts, a hundred feet above the deck, and a good thirty feet above the height of most crow's-nests, were two barrels in which would be stationed "ice spotters" who would have to scan the sea ahead of us through billowing black smoke from the stack in front of them.

We left North Sydney on July 14, crossed the Gulf of St. Lawrence, followed the northwest coast of Newfoundland to the Straits of Belle Isle. On July 21, we rounded Cape Ray Light, on the south coast of Labrador, and, after putting some of the hunters ashore, set out for Greenland's Cape Farewell, across the ice-strewn Sea of Labrador.

On the south coast of Greenland, we put in at Godhavn, where the rest of the hunters went ashore and the Danish governor told Dr. Cook he had no news of Peary. Some Eskimos there said that Peary and his ship, the *Windward*, were lost, but Mrs. Peary and her little girl were safe at Upernavik.

To reach Upernavik, we had to cross the Umanak Fiord. As there was almost no chance that we would encounter ice of any thickness in the fiord, the ice pilots came down from their masts. At my request, Dr. Cook convinced Captain Blakeney to let us climb up and stand in the barrels. Only because the water was so calm would he allow it, he said, though my impression was that he would have taken any request of Dr. Cook's as an order. A Canadian, he had been hired on short notice, having spent the past ten years painting houses, a vocation he discovered when he was fired from the navy.

Dr. Cook and I ascended the mast ladders together, Dr. Cook

waiting for me when I lagged behind. On his instructions, I stared at the rungs and at my hands to keep from getting dizzy. Even though there was no wind, the ship rolled some from side to side on a tidal swell that on deck I had barely noticed—rolled more and more, it seemed, the higher up we went, the cross spars creaking from the weight of the furled sails, my mast swaying like the tree it once was until it seemed certain it would snap off beneath my feet and fall with me still climbing it, still riding on the rungs.

"Is your mast moving?" I shouted across to Dr. Cook, who was twenty feet away from me, though he might as well have been a mile away for all the good he could do me if I got into trouble.

He smiled reassuringly at me through the web of rigging. "Don't look down until we're in the barrels," he said. "I'll climb into mine first to show you how it's done."

We had to climb above the barrels and lower ourselves down into them, for they had no gate or door. I watched as Dr. Cook did it with an agility that I hoped was not essential to the task. He shinnied around the mast, so that for a short while there was nothing under him to impede his fall but vines of rope. Then, with the rungs now on the far side of the mast, he climbed down into the barrel with such ease that I realized he must have done it many times before.

"Your turn," he said. The hardest part was switching sides. I did not shinny around the mast as he had, but kept my left hand and foot on the ends of the rungs as I felt around the mast with my right hand and foot. If not for having long legs, I would have had to do it Dr. Cook's way or climb back down the ladder in defeat. My right foot found the rung first, then my right hand.

"You're almost there," Dr. Cook said. "Let go on the left." I did, and was soon clinging with both hands to one side of the rung and, more ominously, standing with both feet, with all my weight, on one side of it. I quickly shifted my hand and foot to the other side and climbed down into the barrel, where my legs gave way beneath me and I found myself sitting down, panting for breath, heart pounding as I looked up at the sky.

"Devlin," Dr. Cook shouted. "Devlin, are you all right?"

"Yes," I shouted, then I realized how absurd I must seem to him, shouting unseen from inside the barrel. I struggled to my feet. He would have seen first one hand then the other grip the edge of the barrel, then the slow emergence of my head as I peered out above the edge to find that I was standing with my back to him. I turned around, expecting to see on his face some mix of sympathy and consternation, but was relieved to see there instead a grin of fond amusement. "It's easier my way," he said, and we both burst out laughing.

The barrel came up to my chest. I leaned my arms on the edge of it and looked sideways, down the inland length of the fiord. It ended in an illusory vanishing point, a black blur where opposing cliffs that were fifty miles apart seemed to converge like railway tracks. There was a faint, cooling breeze. The sun shone dimly through a gauze of high white cloud.

I could see far inland—beyond the hills on which nothing grew but grass that in June had pushed up through the snow and would do so again in September when the snow returned, beyond a summer-softened glacier whose leading edge had crumbled into icebergs months ago—all the way to where the ice had brought up for good ten thousand years ago.

Dr. Cook pointed. "McCormick Bay is about six hundred miles northwest of here." The site of Redcliffe House.

There was almost no chance, he had told me before we left, that Peary had made it even that far north. Nor, in that case, was it likely that *we* would.

"Do you think they can hear us down there?" I said. We both looked down at the few crew members who were on the deck.

Dr. Cook shook his head. "Our voices carry whichever way we're facing," he said, which at the moment was straight ahead. I nodded.

He looked almost continuously at me as I regarded the landscape, glancing away briefly to note the cause of my stupefaction, then back at me again, so anxious was he to see the effect on me of every wonder we encountered, every fiord, vista, glacier and iceberg. Whenever

I looked at him, he laughed, then surveyed the view with a fond expression, as if mine had helped him to remember how he had felt when he first saw such things.

"Someday we will get there together," he said, looking at the northern horizon as though imagining someplace beyond it—the pole, the ultimate Arctic, where the essence of everything that lay about us now would be revealed. I could not conceive of a place in comparison with which the one he had brought me to would seem deficient.

"We will get there first," he said. I had never heard such fervour, such longing, not even in the voices of preachers when they spoke of heaven. It was as if only those who got "there" first would see it as it really was. By our having been there, it would, for all who might come after us, be transformed.

We saw the calving of a rare late-summer iceberg, a calving caused not by melting, but by the freezing that was already taking place at night. During the summer melting, water ran into fissures and, upon freezing, expanded. Over and over this happened, the fissures growing wider each night, other fissures forming from the first ones, forking out like lightning through the ice. It sounded as though explosives deep within the ice were detonating at intervals, with each blast, though muffled, followed by a general agitation, a faint vibration in the air and in the ground that loosened rocks and slabs of stone on the steeper cliffs like minor avalanches, most of which petered out before they reached the water, though sometimes we heard a single, satisfying "fump," as if a rock had landed edgewise without a splash.

These fissures, Dr. Cook said, would result in icebergs next spring, or the one after that, or a spring ten years from now, when the depending weight of ice was such that whatever was holding it in place would break at last.

"We may see one or two break loose," said Dr. Cook. They would be too small, he said, to make it as far south as St. John's like the spring icebergs. But they would be bigger than any icebergs I had ever seen before.

I was surprised that the surface of the glacier, the walls of the fissures and crevasses, were so discoloured, grey-brown mixed in with white and green. I had expected ice as pristine as that which drifted past Newfoundland each spring. The ice I spoke of, Dr. Cook said, was so white because its outer layers had melted while it was drifting towards Newfoundland. Here, the ice bore on its surface sand that was blown onto it by summer storms, silt left behind by streams that flowed across it from the coastal mountains. Not to mention guano from a dozen kinds of birds, each of whose flocks numbered in the tens of thousands.

Simple exposure to the air, along with cycles of melting and freezing, caused chemical changes similar to rusting, he said. It was really only on the coast that the old ice looked like this. Farther inland, farther north, where nothing ever melted and the mountains that rose up from the ice were covered in snow and devoid of topsoil, the ice was almost perfect. But the only truly perfect ice was the ice of the polar seas.

The sub-surface ice explosions continued night after night, the sound channelled into echoes by the fiord. It might have been an exchange of artillery fire between two distant armies that preferred to fight at night. The explosions sent ripples across the water, just large enough to make the ship bob at anchor, the waves lapping against the hull as if a slight breeze was blowing.

As the nights grew colder, the explosions became more frequent, the artillery bombardment more intense, as if the armies were headed our way, one retreating, one advancing. A decrease in the frequency of the explosions, Dr. Cook said, would mean that less melting was taking place by day; that summer was nearly over and it was time for us to leave, unless we planned to winter here with Peary.

As if the retreating army had decided it would make a final stand, there came from within the glacier one night a constant volley of explosions. In the morning, Dr. Cook pointed out a massive section of ice that he believed was ready to give way.

Captain Blakeney kept the *Erik* far from where it was even remotely possible that any ice would fall, this degree of caution being necessary because the berg, if it was big enough, would displace enough water to send out a series of waves that might damage or even swamp the ship.

It sounded as if massive trees were being slowly bent until they broke, a forest of them creaking, splintering, snapping. The snapping increased to Gatling-gun speed, geysers of ice chips erupting one after the other along a jagged line that traced out the shape of what would be one side of the iceberg. Huge chunks of ice rained down from the top, churning the water white. The staccato of snapping sped up until it became a single sound. There was a deafening severance of old ice from old ice. Then came a creaking screech, as if all that had broken so far were the branches of the tree, but now the very trunk itself had begun to give. I thought it would go on like this, breaking massively but gradually, with an excruciating reluctance. But then the whole thing plunged suddenly, silently, as if it had been hanging by a single cable that had just been cut. It seemed for an instant that it had not so much fallen as been erased from the bottom up; that there would be no splash, no sound. And then all the water that had been displaced rose up at once, as though something the size of the iceberg had been pushed up from the ocean floor to take its place. There was nothing to be heard or seen but water—water roaring, frothing up so high and wide it seemed certain that nothing so inert as ice would appear when it died down. Its height and shape persisted, fountain-like, for seconds. Then the first uprush of water fell and caused a smaller one, which had just begun when the iceberg surfaced, its great mass rolling, the water around it churning as though silent engines were propelling it from far below.

It was still rolling, yet to assume its surface shape, when we saw the series of ice-clogged waves bearing down upon the ship. They broke against the hull, which seemed to rear up beneath them like a horse. Each wave rammed the hull as if we had hit another ship head on. It was as though we were travelling against the current of a river thick with silt the size of boulders. The chunks of ice thudded against the hull with the frequency of hailstones.

When the waves subsided, the iceberg rolled again, teetering, bobbing, its rusted side showing as if it might come to rest that way. But then it performed a slow back flip and the rust went under until the iceberg's white underbelly showed. It stopped bobbing and at the same time rode higher on the water, as though eager to show, after all that thrashing and somersaulting, that it had the knack of floating now. A minute before, the *Erik* had had the water to itself, but it was now sharing it with this massive, unmanned vessel, buoyed up by what might have been its reflection, its submerged portion, which glowed murkily at such a depth I was certain it had run aground.

A great cheer went up from the passengers and crew when the iceberg settled on its final form. The surface berg was just higher than the main mast and so about a hundred feet above the water, which meant the sub-surface berg drew at least eight hundred feet.

But like all late icebergs, it would be short-lived. In the sunlight, it would melt. It would spring a thousand leaks. Fresh water would run down its sides in torrents as water from the sea was doing now. It would drift as treacherous, as deceptive, as an almost sunken ship of which nothing but an unmanned wheelhouse showed above the water. As its shape shifted, so would its centre of balance, until it rolled again and some long-submerged part of it took its turn above the water.

The ship undamaged, we made our way around the berg, then started up the ice-free fiord.

No one at Upernavik knew anything about Peary.

We steamed farther north to Cape York, where we arrived at midnight on the first of August. Captain Blakeney blew the ship's whistle three times. In no time, kayaks were putting out from shore. Many Eskimos came on board, among them three who had served as guides on the North Greenland expedition and had worked with Francis Stead. Dr. Cook introduced me to them as the son of Dr. Stead. As if they thought my purpose for coming along was to rescue my father, they told me with as much regret as if he had departed from them only yesterday that they had no idea where he was. They looked at me as if to gauge my disappointment, my grief. The oldest of them, Sipsu, spoke rapidly but softly to Dr. Cook as if he was relaying to him a message from someone else. He had told Dr. Cook that Peary was either at Etah or at Inglefield Gulf. Dr. Cook accepted their offer to accompany us to Etah and had their kayaks pulled on board.

The first thing we saw as we turned from the fiord into the narrows at Etah was the Eskimo village on the hill above the beach, a cluster of tupiks, which looked much like the wigwams I had seen in books. "The Eskimos stay here during the summer," Dr. Cook said. "There are walrus grounds just up the coast." People whom I mistakenly assumed were all Eskimos came running down the hill. Among them, I would soon discover, were most of the crew of the *Windward*.

Etah lay in a deeply recessed harbour. There was the *Windward* at anchor in calm waters, undamaged, sails furled, looking as though it had not moved in months. The captain, a short, compactly built Newfoundlander named Sam Bartlett, had been hoping that another ship would come bearing someone, anyone, who had the authority to release the *Windward* and its crew from their obligation to the Pearys and the expedition.

The mate of the *Windward* was Robert Bartlett, the captain's cousin. Dr. Cook introduced me to them. They had heard of Francis Stead and offered me their condolences. They lived in Brooklyn, they said, but often spent their summers in Newfoundland. I wondered how long it would take for them to spread the word about me once the expedition ended.

The ships were moored side by side, tied fast with ropes. Where their gunwales met, a gangplank with rails of rope was put in place. Like the *Erik*, the *Windward* was a sealing ship. The two were so similar they might have been sister ships, their bowsprits like a pair of tusks.

"Where is Peary?" said Dr. Cook. Captain Bartlett pointed to one end of the rocky beach, where a tupik stood in the lee of a hill. Peary, he said, was in a bad way. He had not left the tent in more than a month. The only person who had seen him in that time was his black manservant, Matthew Henson, who even now was sitting on the ground a few feet from the entrance to the tent.

The Eskimos, saying that Peary was "asleep," had been keeping their distance from his tent, as had the crew of the *Windward*, some of whom, on the first day of his confinement, had made the mistake of asking him through the tent when he planned to sail for home. Peary had calmly replied, Captain Bartlett said, that the next man to ask him that question would be shot.

As for Jo Peary, she and six-year-old Marie were in their quarters, neither of them having seen or spoken to Peary since Mrs. Peary found out that he had fathered a child by an Eskimo woman. She had learned this from the woman herself, who, when Mrs. Peary met her, was bearing Peary's child on her back. The child, a boy, was unmistakably Peary's, his hair as red and eyes as blue as his father's. The woman, whom Mrs. Peary described as "a creature scarcely human," seemed to think, she said, that simply from having borne children by the same man, the two of them were "colleagues."

Mrs. Peary had come to Greenland expecting a six-week summer stay. She had been stranded for thirteen months at Etah, and she and Marie had already been five months away from home by the time of their arrival.

When told through their door that a ship come to rescue them was just now steaming through the narrows, Mrs. Peary had replied that she had seen it through the porthole window but was staying below because she wished to speak in private with the leader of the rescue expedition.

"Commander Peary's mother passed away in his absence," Dr. Cook said. "I'm sure that in spite of their disagreement, Mrs. Peary will want to tell him herself."

The captain took Dr. Cook below deck on the *Windward*, saying he would wait outside the door while the doctor spoke with Mrs. Peary.

About twenty minutes later they came back up on deck, Mrs. Peary behind them, emerging for what might have been the first time since the *Windward* had sailed from Philadelphia, her expression that of someone well accustomed to being stared at. She was dressed as though for a chilly day at Coney Island. She wore a long serge skirt, a waist-length cloak that buttoned up the front, a flat cap with a spotted veil beneath which she had her hair, which must have been very short, tucked completely out of sight, so that it looked as though she had no hair at all. She was very thin. Her face, unframed by hair, seemed especially so, her jaw lines forming a sharply defined V whose forks ended in deep hollows beneath her ears; her neck was so slender that on the back it was furrowed down the middle.

She exuded many forms of aloofness all at once: that of a woman from the coarse company of men; that of a person of social standing from the company of people who neither had it nor understood its value; that of an expeditionary at the mercy of a crew than which there had been none worse in the history of maritime travel; that of a white woman among Eskimos, to whose level she would never sink no matter how long she was stranded with them in the Arctic. I remembered Aunt Daphne, ten years ago, looking at the photographs of Mrs. Peary that were taken on the North Greenland expedition. "What an extraordinary woman she must be," Aunt Daphne had said.

Aloof. Extraordinary. Incongruous. It was as if Dr. Cook and Captain Bartlett had brought up with them from below a prisoner whose time to prove her usefulness had come at last.

There was nothing in her manner, nor in Dr. Cook's, to suggest how well they had once known each other. They might have been two people who had, some years ago, exchanged a few words at a dinner party. Yet they had lived at close quarters for eighteen months on the North Greenland expedition, for much of that time at Redcliffe House, to which they had been confined by storms for weeks on end with nothing dividing them but a makeshift curtain. I suspected that that curtain had been put up not just to give a husband and his wife some privacy and to separate the leader of the expedition from his subordinates, but also to separate the Pearys from their social inferiors. I did not doubt, looking at Mrs. Peary, that even throughout the long months of the Arctic night, she had managed, because of her gender and because of the difference in their social status, to maintain this distance, this air of formality, between herself and Dr. Cook. There was the suggestion, only slightly less pronounced on his part than on hers, that the moment they met below deck, Dr. Cook had ceased to be the leader of an expedition come to rescue her and had resumed his former role as her attendant.

We watched as, with Dr. Cook, she was rowed ashore by two crew members. She and Dr. Cook walked up the beach towards the tent. About a third of the way there, Dr. Cook stopped and Mrs. Peary went on by herself.

She walked down the beach in what might have been a silent, decorous protest against all that was primitive and backward—against her circumstances, the latitude, the landscape, the natives, the structure in which, inexplicably, her husband had of late been living.

When she raised the flap of the tent and went inside, Dr. Cook sat down on a rock to wait. More than an hour later, Mrs. Peary re-emerged. Dr. Cook fell in beside her. They walked some distance, perhaps until they were sure that Peary could not overhear them, and then stopped. They spoke for a long time, face to face, Mrs. Peary with her back to the harbour. Then she turned abruptly away from Dr. Cook, as though he had said something that displeased her. He fell in beside her again, and they walked the remaining distance to the boat.

They were rowed out to the *Windward*, where Mrs. Peary, her face as blank as before, went below deck to her quarters. She had told Dr. Cook that the expedition had been without a medical officer for months now, the man who had filled that role, a Dr. Dedrick, having been banished from Etah by Peary, who suspected him of trying to sabotage the expedition by tampering with his caches of supplies and undermining him with the Eskimos. Dr. Dedrick was now a few miles up the coast in a smaller village, the two men engaged in a long-distance standoff, each having vowed not to be the first to go back home—Peary because he believed that in his absence, Dedrick would make his own bid for the pole, and Dedrick because he knew what a torment his presence in Greenland was to Peary (tormenting Peary having become for him the last remaining purpose of the expedition). For so long pointlessly, uselessly marooned, unable to sustain any real belief in the existence of the outside world, each man could conceive of no greater ambition than to outlast the other. Not even the presence of his wife and child could divert Peary from his pursuit of the consolation prize of beating Dedrick, though he continued to pay lip service to the notion that once the snow returned, he would resume his quest for the pole.

Minutes after being told by his wife of his mother's death, he had started in again about Dedrick. She had told him of his mother's death half a dozen times, and each time he wept for a while, only to return to his obsession as if he had forgotten not only what she said but the very fact that she was there.

Dr. Cook went ashore again the next day and, escorted by Matthew Henson, walked down the beach to the tent and went inside.

Hours later, when he returned, he went to Mrs. Peary's quarters and told her that she had to do all she could to convince her husband to return home immediately, there being no chance that he would survive another winter in the Arctic. Mrs. Peary replied that she had tried a thousand times to convince her husband to leave and there was no point in trying again while he was in his present state—and that, at any rate, it fell to Dr. Cook to change her husband's mind, since the Peary Arctic Club had sent him there to bring her husband home.

"At times," Dr. Cook told me, "Peary thought I was Dedrick, and poor Henson had to keep him from attacking me. He submitted to a medical examination, though he seemed barely aware that it was taking place and ignored me when I asked him to report his symptoms.

"When I was finished, I told him that he would go exploring no more, and that, if he did, he would surely fail, for his body was such that to push it any further might prove fatal. I would not have been so blunt except that it seemed the best way of convincing him to leave."

Peary, Dr. Cook said, was haggard and wasted. His skin was hard in texture and hung from his bones in baggy folds. All that were left of the eight of his toes that because of frostbite had been removed some years ago were painful stubs that refused to heal. He had paid a great price for his falling-out with Dedrick. He had eaten almost nothing in weeks, and had not been eating properly for at least a year, forgoing the fresh meat offered to him by the Eskimos in favour of canned food.

"His pallor is morbid," Dr. Cook said. "There is an absence of expression in his eyes, as if he knows that for him, the game is up. But he would rather be misperceived as having died trying than perceived as having given up. I told him that he would never travel over ice and snow again, that without big toes the use of snowshoes was impossible. 'Don't tell anyone about my toes,' he said, like a child who dreaded being teased. He really does want to keep the state of his feet a secret, especially from the Peary Arctic Club. He said he would stay in the Arctic one more year, make one last push for what he called 'the biggest prize the world has yet to offer.' I tried to persuade him that for him to stay another winter in the North in his condition would be madness, but he started in again on Dedrick."

"What should we do?" I said.

"We will wait," Dr. Cook said. "It may be that he will change his mind."

So began our strange vigil at Etah.

· CHAPTER EIGHTEEN ·

EVERY DAY, HENSON SAT MOTIONLESS FOR HOURS ON A ROCK near Peary's tent, staring out across the harbour, his hands on his knees, as though he was awaiting the arrival of yet another ship, another expedition led by someone more persuasive than Dr. Cook. Now and then he would jump up and go to the tent, presumably when Peary called to him, though I did not, by day, hear Peary's voice. He carried things to the tent and carried things away, including enamel bowls whose contents he discreetly dumped in the water near the talus of the cliff. He washed Peary's clothing and bed linen in a nearby stream and spread them out on the rocks to dry. The Eskimos regarded him with great deference and were quick to provide him with anything he asked for, especially if he said it was for Peary.

The two ships, moored together, rose and fell as one—one double-hulled, double-decked, double-masted vessel.

By mid-afternoon, the sky was such a pure deep blue I could sometimes see the stars. I thought it was just an illusion until I mentioned it to Dr. Cook, who said that at one time his eyes had been good enough to make out stars at this latitude and time of day.

"The anomaly of summer," Dr. Cook called what in New York might just have passed for early spring. Here there were ten months of winter and two months into which the other three accelerated seasons were compressed.

Each time I breathed in, even on the warmest days, the air went down inside me like a gulp of ice-cold water, seeping through into parts of my body that I had never felt before.

Massive, melting chunks of ice littered the shore like the wreckage of some all-white fleet of ships.

The Eskimos, those who were well enough, worked ceaselessly in preparation for the winter. Wood was so precious in this treeless, scrubless place that it was rare for them to light a fire at this time of year. They traded furs for wood, mystified as to why the whites would value something as commonplace as fur over something as rare as wood. Some spent their days salvaging wood left behind by other expeditions—abandoned shacks and rowboats, broken masts and spars, foot-thick planks like the ones that reinforced the *Erik's* hull.

Every day, the Eskimos and some of the crew took up the coast to the walrus grounds the paying passengers who had not gone ashore farther south. All morning, all afternoon, we heard the sound of distant rifle shots. According to Captain Blakeney, the sons of the backers shot everything that moved. They came back to Etah in whale boats sunk to the gunwales with the weight of furs and tusks. They beached their boats just as the sun was going down, then retired to their bunks, eating and drinking from the private stock they had brought along.

Every night in the captain's cabin, Dr. Cook and I lay awake, talking, discussing the books I was reading. I was constantly aware that Mrs. Peary and Marie were just a few feet away in their quarters, Captain Bartlett having relinquished to them his cabin, whose location corresponded exactly to ours. The thickness of two hulls and the foot or so of space between was all that separated me from the *Windward*. Dr. Cook's bed was on the side of the *Erik* that faced the other way.

I imagined Mrs. Peary and Marie on the *Windward*, lying awake, the night silent except for the lapping of small waves against the hull and the murmuring of voices from the other ship. At times, it was clear from Mrs. Peary's voice that she was reading to Marie. Frequently, it sounded as if Marie, with prompting from her mother, was memorizing prayers.

Dr. Cook, speaking softly so as not to wake the Pearys or be overheard by them, would tell me what Peary, as he lay on the floor of the tent, had said to him, or accused him of, that day.

He said that Dr. Cook had "betrayed" him.

"Dr. Stead, Dr. Cook, Dr. Dedrick," Peary said. "It is my fate to be betrayed by doctors." Exactly how Dr. Cook had "betrayed" him he did not say.

"He is often delirious," Dr. Cook said. "He believes that I have been sent here to replace him. I assured him that he was mistaken, that I will leave with him on the *Erik* as soon as he agrees to go. I told him he could go to the *Erik* if he wished and satisfy himself that I am not prepared for winter travel. 'I have everything you need,' he said. 'You will use my gear when I am gone. If I go to the hold, you will close the door behind me.'

"He lies there wide awake," Dr. Cook said, "staring at what he can see of the sky through the opening in the top of the tent. I tell him that it would do him good to read, that it would help him concentrate his mind, but he ignores me. That is the last thing he wants, to concentrate his mind. He sometimes writes in his journal, but I have no doubt that he writes the way he speaks."

I imagined it, Peary staring up at a dot of clear blue sky or at passing clouds or birds, staring night after night at the same cluster of stars, the same fragment of a constellation from which, with his knowledge of astronomy, he was probably able to imagine the entire dome of heaven. It must have seemed that it enclosed no one else but him.

"Can he not be moved against his will?" I said. "It is clear, from your description, that he is past the point where he can judge what is best for himself or his family."

"What seems clear now," Dr. Cook said, "would not seem clear when we went back home. Not to Peary, probably not even to Mrs. Peary or to the members of the Peary Arctic Club. Perhaps not even to you and me. Looked at from home, nothing that happens up here seems clear. Any member of either crew whom he could prove defied him could be charged with insubordination or even mutiny."

Peary could not be taken back against his will unless it was absolutely certain that nothing less than doing so would save his life. Bridgman had put that in writing for Dr. Cook so that there would be no misunderstanding. "Absolute certainty," said Dr. Cook. "I cannot say with absolute certainty that the sun will rise tomorrow."

For a while to be a famous failure and after that to be forgotten—this was Peary's greatest fear, said Dr. Cook. "He worries about his obituary appearing in the papers thirty years from now. He imagines people who have never heard of him reading that, in his day, he was considered the man most likely to make it to the pole."

I could not help wondering if Peary's state was an indication of what lay in store for me and Dr. Cook. Might that be him or me one day, pent up in a tent for weeks, resisting rescue, ignoring some man who was trying to steer us through the shoals of our delusions?

Peary was thousands of miles from the pole. At no time on this expedition, which now was three years old, had he even reached the polar seas. Could it be, I asked Dr. Cook, that the pole really *was* unreachable?

"You should not jump to conclusions about Arctic exploration based on what you have witnessed here," said Dr. Cook. "I have never seen an expedition reduced to such a state as this."

Only at night did I hear Peary's voice.

"Henson," Peary would roar over and over until Henson reached his tent. Most of us, the dogs included, became accustomed to it, the night sound of Peary roaring Henson's name, as if at the far end of the beach was located the warren of some nocturnal, sedentary creature given to asserting its existence by bellowing that two-part sound, the second syllable louder and more stressed than the first—"Hen-SONNNN"—drawn out more and more with each repetition, until the bellowing abruptly ceased. Peary's voice, even at its loudest, had a note of resignation in it, as if he was a pain-wracked patient screaming for a nurse he knew would never come.

Often, as Peary was roaring for Henson, I heard Marie calling out to her mother on the *Windward* and then Jo Peary's soothing voice.

What explanation could Mrs. Peary have devised to reassure the little girl that, in spite of his roaring out to Henson in the middle of the night like that, there was nothing wrong with her father?

Mrs. Peary, Dr. Cook told me, had cut her hair short to minimize the chance of catching lice. Marie, however, had protested so at the prospect of having hers cut that Mrs. Peary had relented. Mrs. Peary was determined to keep her child's hair free of lice, as if that hair, being the last thing left untainted by their stay at Etah, was symbolic to her of the world to which they would soon return.

Once a day, Marie would appear on the deck of the *Windward* with her mother, holding her hand, blinking at the brightness of the sunlight and the water. If Mrs. Peary, in this setting, looked incongruous, the little girl was not far short of an apparition. She wore a frilly white hat tied in a bow beneath her chin, had long, well-tended ringlets of red hair that rested on her shoulders. She had variously coloured knee-length coats but always wore white gloves and carried an unfurled sunshade with which she prodded at things on the beach.

When they were rowed ashore for their daily walk, Marie would look down the beach at the tent, but she never complained when Mrs. Peary turned her the other way. Her mother must have explained her father's long confinement in the tent in some way that satisfied Marie, though I could not imagine what it was.

In her black stockings and buttoned boots, she made her way along the beach beside the caped, parasol-toting Mrs. Peary. Sometimes the Eskimos, clad in light pelts and furs and moccasins, all with the same shoulder-length tangled mass of black hair, would come down from their tupiks on the hill and follow in a train behind the Pearys, chattering and laughing, some of the women bearing babies on their backs. Among those who would follow behind them, every bit as unselfconscious as the others, was Peary's Eskimo wife, Allakasingwah, with her son, himself an exotic, papoosed on her back. Allakasingwah, with the boy on proud display in her papoose, seemed to me, and I suspected to Dr. Cook, like some sort of native parallel of him and me. "I can assure you," he said, "that when they go back to America, neither of the Pearys will speak of Allakasingwah and her son. The list of things that members of the Peary Arctic Club have had named after them by Peary will never include an illegitimate half-Eskimo."

Jo Peary was resigned to their presence and paid them no special attention. As Mrs. Peary knew a little of the Eskimos' language and they knew a little of hers, they were able to communicate. Mrs. Peary smiled but stayed close by when the Eskimo children gathered round Marie to gaze at her hair and the frills of her hat. If they made to touch her, Mrs. Peary would rap their hands with her parasol, at which they would laugh.

Unlike those of white adults, Marie's face was close enough in height to theirs that they could scrutinize it. They peered closely at her pale complexion as if they believed that behind it, masked by it, was a face just like theirs. Marie submitted to their curiosity with the same mixture of obliviousness and patience with which a good-tempered pet will submit to the ministrations of strangers. It was as if Miss and Mrs. Peary had been acquired by the Eskimos for the purpose of extended observation.

How much of all this, I wondered, will Marie remember years from now? How much of it does she understand? She had been here more than a year now, had wintered here on board the *Windward* while it was dark for months on end. What a task it must have been for Mrs. Peary just to keep her occupied, to structure her days, to prevent her from becoming bored and despondent. And to disguise her own anxiety so that her daughter did not catch it, did not suspect what a predicament they were in. What a winter they must have had, pent up in the ship throughout four months of night, confined to their smokey, lantern-lit room, scarcely able to hear each other speak above the screeching of the wind, the creaking of the masts.

Yet here she was, the little girl, looking not too much the worse for wear, thinner than she would have been if she was home, though not so thin as Mrs. Peary, who no doubt had gone without food sometimes or got by on less than usual so Marie would not be hungry. Compared with me, young Marie was a seasoned expeditionary.

Sometimes, while Marie was in the care of Matthew Henson, Mrs. Peary would walk about the village on the hill with Dr. Cook and me. Her hands beneath her cloak, head slightly inclined, she nodded as he gestured here and there. He might have been the local governor, she a monarch paying a brief visit to the most far-flung region of her kingdom, observing, surveying the most primitive of her subjects while Dr. Cook spoke of the possibilities for betterment and progress.

Dr. Cook introduced me to Mrs. Peary as the son of Dr. Stead. She had spent as much time with Dr. Stead as with Dr. Cook on the North Greenland expedition, at the same close quarters, with nothing between him and her but that symbolic makeshift curtain. But all she did was nod politely at me as if she was hearing the name of Francis Stead for the first time. I think she was so wearied with her husband's quest, so worn down by her thirteen months at Etah, that she could no longer even pretend an interest in anything but going home. The presence of someone to whom all this was new and exciting, whose sojourn in Etah had just begun, she seemed to find almost unbearable. She would let nothing divert her from her one sustaining thought— that soon she and her daughter, and hopefully her husband, would be leaving, and none of them would ever set eyes on what she called "this wretched place" again.

I occasionally accompanied Dr. Cook when he made his rounds of the tupiks. There were about two dozen of them arranged in a cluster—haphazardly, it seemed to me, though there may have been a pattern that I could not discern. The village was a constant frenzy of activity. The Eskimos worked as though the sky had cleared in the midst of a storm that had lasted for years and would soon return some night while they were sleeping. The men scoured animal pelts, some with knives for which they had traded furs, others with sharp-edged stones through which they had painstakingly carved grips like those of saws. The women sewed the pelts together with large needles carved from walrus tusks, threading them with rawhide as thick as the laces of my boots.

As he did with the residents of Brooklyn and Manhattan, Dr. Cook observed the Eskimos in a manner that somehow combined detachment and sympathy, moving about among them slowly, as if a sudden movement or even a brisk manner would scare them off or earn him their mistrust. He spoke quietly to them, inquired of their symptoms, smiling no matter what they replied so as to assure them that their answer boded well for their recovery. They wore sheepish grins, as if their illnesses were forms of misbehaviour, as if they were sorry for putting him to all this trouble.

Many of the crew members of both ships preferred, for various reasons, to spend their nights on shore. They slept in tupiks, luxurious accommodations given that on the ship, they had no quarters and merely bunked down each night wherever they would not be underfoot. On shore, there was space, peacefulness and quiet, fresh air, food and water, and, for those who wanted it, the company of women. Dr. Cook told me that there was no sexual jealousy among the Eskimos. Nor was a pregnancy ever regarded as anything but a cause for celebration.

"I suppose," he said, "they would be greatly amused to know the truth about us and the lengths to which we go to keep it secret. It mystifies them, this race for what they call the Big Nail. They place no importance whatsoever on its discovery, had never heard of it until they met the first explorers. They will think no more highly of the man who gets there first than they do of any other man. Yet they take care of us while we are in their country, as if they are to blame for its hazards and therefore must protect us from them. They cannot conceive that another race's capacity for evil might be greater than their own. Some of them will die trying to keep Peary alive if he remains another winter. He knows this, yet insists on staying anyway. Whoever makes it to the pole first will owe a greater debt to the Eskimos than he owes to his captain, his crew and his backers put together."

Despite extolling the character of the natives, he slept apart from them at night, going back to the ship instead of sharing a tupik with one of the families as they were forever urging us to do. On the *Erik* at night, he would jot down in his notebook his observations of them, add new words to the Eskimo dictionary he was compiling.

One day, as I was walking through the village, I was surrounded by a group of Eskimo women and children. The women were laughing so hard they were clutching their stomachs. Two of them stood on either side of me, took me by the arms and began to pull and push me towards one of the others, a young woman roughly my age. I resisted, my heals ploughing furrows in the dirt as I moved towards my intended. She was laughing, clearly my partner in neither embarrassment nor reluctance. What might be expected of me once we were face to face I had no idea. I began to struggle even harder.

"They are only playing with you," a voice I recognized as Dr. Cook's said behind me. At the sound of his voice, they released me and ran away laughing. He clapped me on the back and walked on past me with a briskness meant to minimize my embarrassment.

I thought about the incident later that night as I sat on the deck of the *Erik* with Dr. Cook. I was not sure that they had only been playing with me. I wondered if they had meant me to understand that she would be receptive if, later on, after dark, I sought her out.

From time to time each day, I looked down the beach at the tupik. I was finding it ever more difficult to believe, in spite of hearing him night after night roaring Henson's name, that Peary was inside it, or indeed that anyone was. Standing on the deck of the *Erik*, I had seen from within the tupik after dark no lights, no lantern, no smoke from a campfire, not even on cold nights when it rained. I had not seen so much as Peary's shadow, day or night, through the walls of the tent.

Some days, it seemed that the purpose of the rescue mission had been forgotten altogether, that the tent in the shadow of the cliff had been forgotten by all but Dr. Cook and Matthew Henson.

It was as though Peary was quarantined, the rest of us waiting for Dr. Cook to declare him cured and non-contagious so we could take him home.

Dr. Cook went day after day to Peary's tent—sometimes several times a day—only to emerge each time in ever-more-obvious frustration, striding away from the tent in long, savage strides.

It began to feel like we were waiting not for Peary to emerge from his tent, but for word that he was dead.

"Peary knows you are here," said Dr. Cook one night. "Henson told him so that he would not find out some other way. If Peary was in his right mind, your being here would bother him no more than it bothers Mrs. Peary. But you are now in the stew of his delirium like all the rest of us, you whom he has never met. Don't worry. You are not a primary ingredient as far as I can tell. He mentions Francis Stead more often than he mentions you."

It occurred to me that I might well leave Etah, go back to New York, without ever having seen Peary, having only heard him at night, roaring out what might have been the only word he knew. It was also possible, even likely, in that case, that I would never in my life see Peary. It seemed absurd that having come all this way, I might leave without even having set eyes on him. I considered walking down the forbidden stretch of beach to poke my head in through the tent just for one brief look at him.

One night on the *Erik*, after Peary had been roaring Henson's name for an unusually long time, Dr. Cook jumped out of bed and began to pace the cabin. "Where in God's name is Henson?" he all but hissed at me, whispering to keep from waking Mrs. Peary or Marie, though I was sure that they had already woken up. "Can he not hear Peary calling for him? Does he not realize the effect it must have on Peary's wife and child?"

At last the shouting stopped, but Dr. Cook could not get back to sleep.

"My motives for leading this rescue mission are not as pure as I have led you to believe," he said. "It will help my own cause immeasurably if I bring the Pearys safely home."

"I know," I said. "It's only natural to think about such things."

"The outcome of this expedition will affect my standing in the Peary Arctic Club, and my chances of getting up an expedition of my own. It weighs on my mind that his wife and child are depending on me to bring him home. But I also wonder what people will think of me if I leave him here and he does not make it through the winter." He cast a momentary glance in the direction of the *Windward.* Our porthole faced theirs, so both were covered with small curtains.

"When I told her I might eventually have to insist that we leave, with or without him, Mrs. Peary reminded me that I was sent here to save his life. 'I am trying to save his life,' I told her, 'but I was also sent here to bring you and your daughter back.' She offered to give me written permission to remove him from the tent and put him on the ship against his will. I told her that unless he agrees to go, we must leave him here. The crews of both ships are depending on me to bring this rescue expedition to an end, one way or another, before it is too late in the season to make a run for home. Perhaps they should have sent someone else, someone he would not feel so threatened by. Someone with the courage to defy him."

"You are right not to force him to go home," I said. "Mrs. Peary should not have asked you to."

"I told Peary today that I would not feel I had done my duty to the Peary Arctic Club unless he returned with me. 'It is, as you say, Doctor,' he said, 'the *Peary* Arctic Club. Not, unfortunately for you, the Cook Arctic Club. Not yet, anyway. You must first rescue me before you can succeed me. If you bring me back, you will be their favoured one. Who better to succeed Peary than the man who saved him, the man who did what Peary could not do—brought Peary home.'"

"You should try to sleep," I said.

"The Pearys are in a fix, and I wish to help them," he said. "But so, too, am I in a fix, one that I should have foreseen. I thought that Peary, if he was alive, was awaiting rescue, that the *Windward* was lost or disabled. I know I should not see myself as the victim of this piece, but it seems that whatever I decide, I risk paying a great price. If I order Peary removed from the tent and put on board, he will tell the world that if not for me, he might have made it to the pole. He will be spared the humiliation of being rescued with his wife and little girl. He could ruin me with the Peary Arctic Club. Some of them would be only too glad to think the best of him and the worst of me. He could have me charged with insubordination, even mutiny. I think he would be quite happy if I forced him to leave. It may be the very thing he has been waiting for all this time. But if I leave him here and he dies, I will be blamed for deserting him and he will be remembered as a hero."

He looked again at the curtain-covered porthole, then turned over on his side, facing the wall, staring at it, I was certain. For a long time I watched him as he lay there motionless.

One night, I was awakened in my bunk on the *Erik* by the sound of sled dogs barking on the hill. I had been listening to them for some time before I realized that they were barking in response to the voice of a man far below them on the beach. I couldn't make out what the man was shouting or where he was in relation to Peary's tent. The words, though unintelligible, had the cadence of English. The man was shouting, but not angrily, his tone that of a man making customary small talk with a distant neighbour. I would not have been surprised to hear it answered by a like-sounding voice from farther down the beach, but the only answer was an echo that rolled round and round like a marble in the bowl of the harbour. Was it Peary, amusing himself with echoes, perhaps even mistaking the echoes for replies? Peary having a reflective conversation with himself? I thought of going up on deck, but I knew there was no moon. On moonless nights in Etah, nothing was visible except the stars, a host of lights that illuminated nothing.

· C H A P T E R   N I N E T E E N ·

THE DAY AFTER I HEARD THE VOICE, THE SEVENTEENTH DAY OF
our anchorage at Etah, Dr. Cook and I were talking on the deck of the
Erik when we saw several Eskimo boys running uphill towards the
tupiks, shouting, "Pearyaksoah! Pearyaksoah!" We looked down the
beach at Peary's tent.

Henson was standing just outside the doorway, clearly waiting for
someone to emerge. I wondered if Mrs. Peary might be in there, or if she
was in her quarters on the *Windward*. Henson peered inside, then stood
erect again. I was now sure from Henson's posture and air of anxiousness
that it was Peary he was waiting for. The Eskimos came running from
their tupiks and gathered on the hill to watch. Crew members from
both the *Erik* and the *Windward* came up on deck or stopped working
to stare at Peary's tent. Those who were on the beach did likewise.

I looked back at Henson just in time to see Peary stagger regally
into the light, his legs wobbling but his upper body ramrod straight, his
hands behind his back as if he had emerged from his tent for a customary stroll about the beach.

At first, there were shouts of greeting and celebration among the
Eskimos, but they did not, as I half expected they would, run down the
hill to greet him. The shouting stopped abruptly. The initial euphoria
having subsided, they had looked more closely and were dismayed by
what they saw. I wondered what he had looked like when they saw
him last. Some of them, as if to spare him the indignity of being seen
in such a state, went back to their tents.

Peary looked towards the harbour, stood for some time staring at the ships, one of which had not been there when he last looked out.

He was, it seemed, trying to project the image of a frail but past-the-worst-of-it, improving convalescent. He was wearing winter moccasins that came up past his knees. Thicker-soled than summer ones, they enabled him to stand on the rocks despite his injured feet.

With his hands still behind his back, so that his arms looked like a pair of folded wings, he began to make his way over the beach rocks, as much through them as over them, shuffling his feet, scuffing as though, shod in slippers, he was crossing a newly waxed floor. He moved his legs, which were bent at the knees, faster than normal to keep himself from falling.

I felt certain that he would pitch forward onto the rocks before he could reach the rowboat in which two crew members were waiting. Dr. Cook had to have thought the same thing, for he shouted to the men of the *Erik* to lower the rowboat so that he could go ashore. Henson, who must have heard him, put up his hand, and Peary shouted, "STOP," the second word I had ever heard him speak.

"All right. For the moment, we will wait," Dr. Cook said.

Peary towered by at least a foot over Henson, who walked beside him, discreetly solicitous, glancing sideways at him now and then, ready to support him should he begin to fall. He had clearly been instructed not to touch him unless absolutely necessary.

Peary wore a black peaked hat, a black double-breasted watchcoat and thick black woollen trousers.

It seemed that the only sound in all the world was the distant clattering of those rocks beneath his moccasins. Stretching behind him almost to his tent were the jagged pair of furrows he had ploughed with his feet. Then I heard another shout and, looking towards the other end of the beach, saw Mrs. Peary and Marie, Mrs. Peary walking as quickly as she could without dragging the little girl behind her. They were much farther from the rowboat than Peary. It was as though a race was taking place, with Mrs. Peary trying to make it to the boat before her husband did. She was urging Marie to walk faster, now and then looking impatiently behind her, clearly hoping to intercept her husband before he reached the boat, as if she somehow knew what his intentions were and meant to keep him from announcing them to Dr. Cook.

From the quarterdeck, we watched in silence this convergence of the Pearys—watched Peary, whom Jo and Marie hadn't seen on his feet in months, lurching down the beach like some black, weird-gaited bird with Henson at his side.

What *does* he want? I wondered.

Dr. Cook placed his hand very lightly on my shoulder and left it there, all the while looking at Peary, who, it was now apparent, would reach the rowboat long before his wife and daughter did. Dr. Cook's hand tightened on my shoulder the closer to the boat Peary drew, as though he thought I needed reassurance. The crew members, and the passengers who had come up from below, were now gathered in twos and threes behind us, whispering among themselves.

As Peary and Henson reached the boat, Henson and one of the crewmen helped Peary climb aboard. The crewmen pushed the boat into deeper water and began to row at a furious pace, doubtless ordered to do so by Peary, whose back was to the shore. He did not so much as glance over his shoulder to acknowledge his wife when she shouted something to him that I could not make out. Mrs. Peary and Marie stopped walking and for a few seconds watched the receding rowboat, until Mrs. Peary called out to Dr. Cook to send a boat for them. Dr. Cook complied, so that even as Peary's boat was drawing closer to the ships, another was setting out from them for shore.

Peary, sitting, held himself as rigidly, as upright, as he had while he was walking down the beach, head motionless, hands on his thighs.

I could see his face clearly now. It was a strange cherry brown colour, the combined effect, I guessed, of the elements and the deficiencies of diet. He must have shaved or had Henson shave him. He had a neatly trimmed Vandyke beard and a florid moustache, both bright red and all the more conspicuous because of the unvaried colour of his clothes.

His long frame served only to exaggerate his emaciation, as did the layers of clothes that he was wearing to disguise it. Even with others underneath, his outer clothes were far too big for him. The shoulder seams of his overcoat were just above his elbows. The wind gusted for a moment and his trousers became a pair of flags, so that I could see the stick-like outlines of his legs. I mentally compared the man advancing towards me with the one I had so often seen in photographs. His normal weight, of which I guessed he had lost more than one-third, was two hundred pounds. Newly coiffed, neatly attired—albeit in clothes that were all but rags—a physical ruin, he might have been the commander of some long-besieged army who had come out to offer to the enemy a ceremonial surrender. I would not have been surprised, once he came on board, if he had taken from Henson and presented to Dr. Cook some symbol of surrender like a sabre or a folded flag.

And perhaps that is it, I thought. He has come out to tell Dr. Cook that he has changed his mind. This is the formal end of Peary's final expedition. He wants to make the announcement standing up, looking down at Dr. Cook, not lying on his back half delirious in a tent he hasn't left in months. He means to put as splendid a face as he can on this defeat. And he *had* looked splendid, a towering, tottering wreck of a man, moving with a lurching grace along the beach, and he looked splendid now as he sat there in the boat, the epitome of military impassivity and composure. The boat that had been sent from the *Erik* for his wife and child passed within ten feet of his, but he gave no sign of having noticed it.

Dr. Cook's hand tightened yet again on my shoulder. He seemed to be saying that just as Peary had Henson by his side, he had me.

I lost sight of the rowboat as it drew up on the far side of the *Erik*. I watched two crew members crank the winch, the ropes creaking with the weight. And then the boat came slowly into view—or rather its four occupants did, so it seemed that they were levitating, especially Peary, who, as the boat rose side-on to it, did not so much as glance at the ship but stared straight ahead, sightlessly ahead, it seemed. He might have been in such a trance he did not know the ship was there.

Henson helped him from the boat and onto the deck of the *Erik*. Peary turned to face us, slowly shifting his body and his head at the same time, as though he could not move his neck. He began to walk towards us, and when he and Dr. Cook were perhaps ten feet apart, Peary extended his hand. Dr. Cook withdrew his from my shoulder, stepped forward quickly as if to spare Peary the effort of walking those last few feet and took his hand.

Peary smiled and, looking about, made an expansive gesture with one arm, but he said nothing. Anyone looking at a photograph of the scene would have assumed that the *Erik* had just arrived, that Peary had rowed out from shore to welcome Dr. Cook to Etah and they were now exchanging such pleasantries as were customary when two gentlemen met on board a ship so far from home.

With Dr. Cook following Peary's lead, they talked as if, after a long and unavoidable delay that they had tacitly agreed not to mention, they were meeting for the first time.

"Summer in the Arctic," Peary said. "We have not been here together, Dr. Cook, since 1892." His voice, though powerful, quavered.

"I have not been here at all since then," said Dr. Cook.

"I could not stand to be away from it for so long," said Peary.

Dr. Cook watched Peary closely. Peary still stood fully erect, head motionless, hands behind his back—the very model of composure, it seemed, until I saw that his eyes were darting about like those of a blind person, as if he were attending to a host of inner voices. The pain of standing on feet from which all but two toes had been removed, on stubs that he had never rested long enough for them to heal showed in his face, even in his glazed-over, darting eyes. But he did not wince or move his weight from foot to foot.

"Have you changed your mind, sir? Will you be with us when we leave for home?" said Dr. Cook.

"I am afraid not," said Peary, flashing a smile that pulled the skin on his face so tight it shone like it was waxed. "Of course you will see to it that Jo and Marie are returned home safely." At the mention of their names, I looked towards shore and saw that their boat had nearly reached them.

Dr. Cook stepped forward and, looking up at Peary, spoke in a voice much lower and more tender than before. "Sir, I fear that unless you leave with us, they will suffer the permanent loss of a husband and a father."

"We will make one more dash for it," said Peary. "If we do not succeed this time . . . well, there will be other times."

Dr. Cook looked appealingly at Henson, who neither spoke nor looked away, though there was no defiance in his eyes. I heard the boat bearing Mrs. Peary and Marie being pulled into the water.

"I thought I had your loyalty, Dr. Dedrick. I foresaw you being my medical man on all my expeditions. Associates for life. I can't think why such a small thing would have meant so much to you."

"Lieutenant Peary, I am not Dr. Dedrick."

"Indeed you are not," Peary said, as if he had not said "Dedrick," as if he had not for a second mistaken one doctor for the other. "Compared with Dedrick, you are a saint, Dr. Cook. The man is such a cur."

"I must be absolutely frank with you, Lieutenant Peary," said Dr. Cook, his voice almost a whisper. "It is not the risk of death but the certainty of it that I am warning you against. Sir, you suffer from an illness for which you are not to blame, an illness that is preventing you from thinking clearly. No one is conspiring against you. No one wishes you any harm. We are here to help you. I know it is hard to let someone else be the judge of what is best for you, hard to know when you need to entrust yourself to someone else. But I ask you to try to honestly assess your present state, and having done so, to trust me, to trust your wife and all the men who have sacrificed so much for you on both these expeditions. Will you let us take you home?"

As Dr. Cook spoke, Peary smiled, as if to say that mere words could not deceive him. He also smiled when *he* spoke, as if he believed that the real meaning of *his* words was lost on Dr. Cook.

Dr. Cook and Peary continued in this fashion for some time, Dr. Cook speaking gently, Peary smiling.

Dr. Cook stopped speaking when he heard Mrs. Peary's boat

being winched up on the far side of the *Windward*. Peary went on smiling, his head cocked, eyes darting about as if the inner voices had begun again.

Mrs. Peary and Marie stepped onto the deck of the *Windward*. Marie, after a brief glance at her father, went straight below deck. Mrs. Peary crossed over from the *Windward* to the *Erik*, ignoring the rope rails of the gangplank. Dr. Cook looked at her entreatingly, then glanced sideways at Peary. "Mrs. Peary—" he began.

"Bert knows how I feel," she said softly. But then she stepped forward and, standing on tiptoe, as though to kiss her husband's cheek, whispered something in his ear.

Peary bowed his head slightly, as if he might relent or were trying not to cry. But then, as though rousing himself from a spell of dizziness, he drew himself to full height again and shook his head.

"All else but this criminal foolishness I can forgive," said Mrs. Peary. "Come home with me and Marie, and when you have got your strength back, you can try again."

"I have merely had a fever, Dr. Cook," Peary said, "a fever that has now passed and my comportment during which no fair-minded man would hold against me, especially as I am unable to remember it."

"You have not had a fever, sir," Dr. Cook said, at last losing his patience. "Nor has your affliction passed. You have pushed your mind and body beyond their limits. Both have broken down. I have been sent here by the club to bring you home."

"Yes. By the *Peary* Arctic Club. Not, unfortunately for you, the Cook Arctic Club. Not yet, anyway. You must first rescue me before you can succeed me. Who better to succeed Peary than the man who saved him, the man who did what Peary could not do—brought Peary home." The exact words he had spoken before. He must have memorized the speech and forgotten he had already delivered it.

Perhaps he wanted to be rescued by force. Perhaps it had occurred to him that if Dr. Cook were to rescue him by force, all his problems would be solved. Perhaps, even now, he was waiting for Dr. Cook to order the crew members to seize him and confine him to his quarters.

It might have been for this reason that he had insisted on meeting with
Dr. Cook on the *Erik* instead of on shore. How easy it would be, here,
to bring all this to a head at last, to tempt Dr. Cook to have him taken
below with a minimum of embarrassment for everyone. Far preferable
to the scene—the spectacle—that would take place if he had to be
removed from his tent against his will and rowed out from shore,
humiliated in front of everyone, including the Eskimos.

"Dr. Cook," Peary said, "I intend to win for myself and for my
countrymen a fame that will last as long as human life exists upon the
globe. The winning of the pole is for all time."

He turned to Mrs. Peary.

"Jo, my dear, will you place a rose for me on Mother's grave?"

She turned away from him and walked back to the *Windward*,
where, without so much as a backwards glance, she went below.

I looked at Dr. Cook, wondering if he would relent and relieve
Peary not only of command of the expedition, but of responsibility for
his life and death.

Dr. Cook extended his hand.

"Good luck, sir," he said, raising his voice almost to a shout.

Peary slowly raised his hand and shook Dr. Cook's. He looked
grimly resigned, whether because he had failed to unnerve Dr. Cook
or simply because the matter of his fate had been resolved at last I
couldn't tell.

Captain Bartlett came forward and held out his hand, and Captain
Blakeney after him, both wishing him good luck. In no time, the crews
of both ships were queueing up to shake Peary's hand. It was a moving sight, one which, I noticed, his daughter was watching from the
deck of the *Windward*, to which she had returned without her mother.
Like the relatives of a man who the next day was to undergo an operation that it was almost certain he would not survive, they filed past,
saying, "God bless and good luck, sir," many of them, like me, not having set eyes on him until just minutes before. Henson looked at Peary
and then at the long line of men. He must have doubted that Peary
could stay on his feet long enough to shake every hand.

When all the others had shaken Peary's hand and, except for the two who began preparing the rowboat for Peary's return to shore, had gone below deck, Dr. Cook, his hand in the crook of my arm, led me forward.

"Lieutenant Peary, this is Devlin Stead," said Dr. Cook. At that instant, Marie called out to Dr. Cook, and Dr. Cook turned away from us and hurried to the *Windward,* where the little girl still stood, unattended by anyone.

"Stead's boy," Peary said as he took my hand and so abruptly pulled me towards him that I almost fell. His eyes stopped moving. Neither a Stead nor a boy, his tone made me feel like saying. He must have seen that flash of defiance in my eyes.

"You have yet to see the Arctic, Mr. Stead," he said. "Do not let yourself be drawn to it by the few weeks of idleness you have spent here in the summer."

I could think of no response.

"I know the sort of stuff that you are made of, Mr. Stead," he said, lowering his voice, and I was convinced he was about to tell me that he knew of my relationship to Dr. Cook. "Stay home, boy. Stay home, or someday you will wind up like your fool of a father."

Peary adjusted his grip on my hand, which in size was like a child's compared with his, and squeezed it with such force I thought that he was using me to keep his balance, to keep from falling forward, and that it was only by coincidence that he had brought his face so near to mine. I pushed back in an attempt to steady him, but Peary, whom I must have outweighed by forty pounds, did not budge. He gripped my hand still tighter, pushed his own farther back on mine, on one side past the thumb, on the other almost to my wrist, so that neither our fingers nor the palms of our hands were touching and my hand lost all ability to return his grip. Determined not to cry out or pull away, or to ask for the help of Henson, who appeared to be watching the crewmen prepare the rowboat, I felt as though my hand would break, as though its bones, in the vise of his, would shatter like a pouch of icicles. Even this close up, his eyes were glazed over as though he were focused inward on some thought or image goaded on by which he was squeezing what he no longer realized was another person's hand. His cherry-coloured skin was uniformly calloused. It was the closest I had ever been to another man's face. His breath, which I feared would be unpleasant, smelled of peppermint.

"Your mother," he said, "was buried in the clothes she was wearing when they found her, buried dripping wet in a graveyard in St. John's. Your father lies entombed, preserved in ice, not far from here, where he will go on smiling his idiot smile long after his hell-dwelling soul has ceased to burn." My legs went weak as Peary, groaning from the strain, squeezed even harder.

Dr. Cook suddenly appeared and brought his forearm down like an axe on Peary's.

It seemed that at the sudden severance of our hands, Peary completely lost consciousness. He did not drop to his knees. His legs did not buckle beneath him. He simply began to fall forward, his head making a top-heavy pillar of his body, his arms limp at his sides. I saw that as he was facing a set of steps that went below, he would have to go well past the horizontal, would have to fall more than his own height of six-foot-three, before, face first, he hit one of the wooden ledges.

Several things happened at once. Dr. Cook lurched forward, intending, it seemed to me, to interpose himself between Peary and the deck. Henson, as if he thought Dr. Cook's intention was to attack Peary, hurled himself at Dr. Cook, hitting him with a force that sent them both reeling deckwards in opposite directions. I stepped in front of Peary just in time to have him land on me, just in time to see his head bearing down on mine, which I turned away so that the underside of his chin fit quite nicely on my shoulder, and for a while there was nothing but that holding him up. I tried to hold him under the arms, but my right hand hurt so much I couldn't grip him with it. I threw my arms around his waist, pinning his arms to his sides, and tried to support his weight by digging into the deck with my feet, my left one planted at an angle behind me, my right one forward. The left foot slipped, gave way, so that I was forced to walk in reverse to keep from falling. In this manner—pedalling backwards across the deck, hugging Peary to me, his feet dragging, toes down—I travelled perhaps twenty feet, impelled by Peary's dead weight until I fell at last, brought up against the gunwale shoulders first, my head snapping back, Peary on top of me, laid out prostrate on me in a lifeless bundle as if we had been dancing and had dozed off in each other's arms.

I thought that would be the end of it, but as I tried to move Peary forward, move away from the gunwale, something snapped in my already injured right hand. Instinctively, I withdrew it, whereupon I lost my hold on Peary, who, being so tall, struck the gunwale at waist height and pitched forward in a perfect somersault. Again instinctively, I grabbed at him with my right hand, caught hold of the heavy collar of his watchcoat and, with my left hand and my legs braced against the gunwale, kept him from pulling me over with him. He was dangling, still unconscious, between the two ships, just off to one side of the gangplank. If I released him, he would fall forty feet into the water, probably striking one or both of the hulls on the way down, and then would sink beneath the hulls, where it would be impossible to rescue him.

Peary swung slowly back and forth, insensible to his predicament, eyes closed, mouth slightly open. Just as it occurred to me how strange it would be if he awoke while hanging in mid-air like that, awoke to find himself no longer on deck, no longer squeezing my hand, but suspended between the two ships, between life and death, he did just that.

There was a fluttering behind his eyes and then they opened. At first, all they registered was a look of dazed confusion, as if he knew that something was wrong, that he had never, upon waking, felt like this before. And then there was a sudden look of alarm as it dawned on him that he was hanging in mid-air above the water. As yet, I think, he did not realize that it was a man's arm he was hanging from, let alone whose arm it was.

Finally, his eyes focused on my hand, which was above him, for his coat was pulled up so far that he wore it like a cowl and anyone watching from either side of me would not have known who the coat contained, who it was that was hanging from my hand like a drowned man whose water-weighted body I had fished up from the sea. He looked at me as if he thought I was in the act of throwing him overboard. He had woken up not *from* a nightmare, but *into* one. He brought up his hands and grabbed hold of my coat collar as if he meant to pull me over with him, though the only effect of this was to lessen the strain on my arm.

Then the manner of his struggling changed. He seemed to be trying not to pull me in with him, but merely to free himself. He tried with both his hands to pry himself loose from the single hand that held him by the collar of his coat. I would not have been able to hold onto him if it had gone on much longer.

Henson, Dr. Cook and the two crewmen all at once surrounded me, and there followed some flurry of commotion to which I was too exhausted to attend. "It's all right, Devlin," I heard Dr. Cook say, but unsure of what this meant, I did not release my grip on Peary's coat. I might have passed out momentarily. I heard the passengers and crew. Later, I would imagine what they saw: Henson and Dr. Cook bent over me as I lay beneath Peary, who might have tackled me in full stride. Henson and Dr. Cook trying to pry the still-limp Peary from the grip of both my hands. When I realized that Peary and I were safe, that the other two men had hoisted him over the rail only to have me pull him down on top of me, I let him go.

Of what could this scene possibly be the aftermath? The others must have wondered. Peary's head was beside mine, his forehead on the deck, nestled into it as though he was peacefully napping. At some point, his hat had come off. It was probably floating on the water between the ships. All I could see was the blue sky, though I heard, from every direction, the hubbub of voices.

"What happened? Who's hurt?"

Peary began to stir, muttering something unintelligible as though whispering some parting insult in my ear. As he supported himself on one arm, Henson, Dr. Cook and several others helped him off me.

"You should not stand up so soon, sir," Henson said, but Peary, shaking his head, rose to full height as others began to help me up. I was winded and my right hand was of no use it hurt so much. I saw Peary shake free of the hand Henson held beneath his elbow.

I tried to open my hand to flex the fingers and see if anything was broken, but the pain, a deep bone pain pulsing from my shoulder to the tips of my fingers, was such that I could not. I cradled my right arm in my left, which focused the pain in my forearm. My legs still unsteady, I thought I would be sick.

Peary gripped his right forearm where Dr. Cook had struck it, closed his eyes. I looked at Dr. Cook, who seemed to be preparing himself to have it all out. He stared at Peary, who looked as though he might faint again.

"What happened here?" Captain Bartlett said as the others crowded round.

"Lieutenant Peary—" Dr. Cook said, drawing a deep breath, but Matthew Henson cut him off.

"Lieutenant Peary fainted," Henson said. "And as he went over the side of the ship, Mr. Stead here caught him and held him with one hand until Dr. Cook and I could pull him in."

Captain Bartlett looked at Peary, who remained as before, swaying slightly, eyes closed. There was no chance that the captain was going to ask Peary to explain himself. He looked at Dr. Cook.

"We—Henson and me—we stumbled over each other trying to get to Lieutenant Peary," Dr. Cook said. "Devlin got there first and grabbed him by the coat as he was falling, and he held onto him until we could help him pull Lieutenant Peary back on deck."

"Is that what happened, Mr. Stead?" said Captain Bartlett.

"Lieutenant Peary would have been badly hurt, or worse, if not for Mr. Stead," Henson said, looking nervously around as if he was unsure if anyone besides the principals had seen what happened. Someone had, but it was not the two crewmen who manned the rowboat, for they looked as mystified and surprised as everyone else. It was Marie Peary, who was still solemnly watching from the deck of the *Windward*. There was no sign of Mrs. Peary.

"Is either one of you hurt?" said Dr. Cook.

Peary, still clenching his arm, shook his head.

"Are you all right, Devlin?" Captain Bartlett said. He had never called me by my first name before.

"I think I sprained my hand," I said.

"I will see to Mr. Stead's hand," said Dr. Cook.

"All right, then," Captain Bartlett said. "Lieutenant Peary is greatly in your debt, Mr. Stead. I'm sure that someday, when he is feeling more like himself, he will thank you for helping him."

The agitation of Peary's eyes resumed as suddenly as it had stopped. *Stay home, boy. Stay home, or someday you will wind up like your fool of a father.* It had sounded as much like a threat as a warning or a prediction.

Dr. Cook led me away from Peary, at whom I looked over my shoulder. Peary, without crossing one foot over the other, taking tiny steps, turned around, with Henson beside him, even closer than before, and the two of them made their way towards the rowboat.

Peary and I might just have fought a duel in which both of us had been slightly wounded and were now being attended to by our seconds.

In spite of what had happened, in spite of my arm, I could not resist watching Peary's return to his tent. In the boat, he sat as before, now with his back to us, ramrod straight.

On the beach, he fell forward once but caught himself with his hands before he hit the ground. Shoulders now hunched, as if he were calling on his last reserves of strength, Peary continued towards his tent with Henson all but facing him. He walked without even a token effort to lift his feet from the ground, shuffling through the rubble in his moccasins. Dr. Cook shook his head as Peary, while Henson held the flap, bent over as though bowing deeply to someone inside the tent. Henson pulled the flap closed before I could see if Peary fell.

Dr. Cook took me below on the *Erik*, where he examined my hand and arm, palpating them gently with his fingers, noting when I winced.

"The main bones on both sides of your hand are fractured," he said. "Your wrist, too, but not badly. I won't know for certain until we get back home."

He went about fashioning a sling and an ice pack, which he hoped would reduce the swelling. He taped the pack, which had a kind of pouch to hold the ice, to the back of my hand.

"You won't be climbing the mast on the way home," he said. "No more ice piloting for you. At least not on this expedition."

"Thanks for helping me," I said.

"I would have intervened sooner if I'd been watching. It's an old trick, what he did with your hand—one with which I'm sure he knew you were not acquainted. If you hold a person's hand the right way, he can't squeeze back."

"I was surprised at how strong he was."

"He *is* strong. But it has more to do with where you grip the hand than with how hard you squeeze it. A boy who knew what he was doing could have brought Peary to his knees."

"I hope what you did doesn't get you into trouble."

"It won't. Henson kept us all out of trouble, though I'm sure that it was only Peary he was thinking of. If Peary survives, he will either hold to Henson's version of what happened or, more likely, pretend that nothing did."

"Marie saw what happened," I said.

"I know," Dr. Cook said. "But I doubt that she understood much except that her father was in danger for a while."

"She might have seen you strike Peary's arm."

"It doesn't matter what she saw or what she tells her mother. Henson's story will hold up."

"Did you hear what Peary said to me?" I said.

Dr. Cook shook his head. I told him, repeated it word for word as I was certain I would be able to do forty years from now. *Your mother was buried in the clothes she was wearing when they found her, buried dripping wet in a graveyard in St. John's.*

Dr. Cook turned away from me and sat on the edge of his bed. "Only a fevered mind," he said, but his voice trailed off.

"He said my father was buried in the ice," I said. "Surely he knows you are my father. He told Francis Stead you were."

"He strongly suspects it, of course," said Dr. Cook. "But I have never talked to him about it."

He rose suddenly, put his arms around me and hugged me to him as much as my injured arm would allow. I hugged him back with my left arm. When he stepped back from me, his eyes were glazed with tears. "You are your mother's son," he said. "But also mine."

Later that day, Mrs. Peary and Marie paid a long visit to Peary's tent, taking with them some presents that they told him not to open until Christmas. It was clear, when they returned to the *Windward*, that Marie had been crying. Aside from her red and swollen eyes, however, she wore the same look of grim composure as her mother.

At night, in my bunk, I wondered what I was to make of Peary's words, his particular choice of words. *Your mother was buried in the clothes she was wearing when they found her, buried dripping wet in a grave-yard in St. John's.* Surely he had no idea what my mother wore when she was buried.

"You acted quite heroically, you know," said Dr. Cook. "He may never admit it, not even to himself, but he owes you his life."

"It seems like a strange way to end my first expedition," I said.

"All expeditions have strange endings," Dr. Cook said, "because they all end with a return to civilization. You'll see what I mean. The world we are returning to will never again seem to you as it did before we left."

We stopped talking when we heard Marie crying on the *Windward*. We heard the murmur of Mrs. Peary's voice, more subdued than usual, as if not even to comfort Marie could she put aside her own preoccupations.

I fell into a dream-filled sleep, the throbbing of my hand incorpo-rated into every dream. I shook hands with a succession of firm-gripped men—among them Peary, Uncle Edward, Francis Stead, Dr. Cook—all of whom wished me good luck as if they believed that no amount of luck could save me. The dream moved on. I was look-ing over the side of a rowboat at a dead man who was floating just beneath the surface, his clothing buoyed up by the water, his coat pulled halfway around his head, which was tilted back as though he had spent his last moments peering up through the water at the sky. Then I was holding onto my mother, who was submerged and whose face, as I looked down at it, was peacefully composed. Before I could pull her out or was forced to let her go, the dream moved on again. Next, I was standing face to face with Francis Stead, who suddenly tried to throw me overboard. We struggled, and it was Francis Stead who went over. A second later, he confronted me again and this time *I* went over, but I woke up before I hit the water.

When I woke up for good, I was more tired than if I had not slept at all.

Dr. Cook made his last rounds of the tupiks on the hill, bidding the Eskimos goodbye, giving them as much medicine as he could spare.

He told me that Peary and Henson would soon be going northwest with a number of Eskimos to Peary's winter quarters. Charlie Percy, the steward of the *Windward* and the closest thing to a medical officer among the crew, would go with them. Dr. Dedrick was, as stubbornly and pointlessly as Peary, staying on in Greenland until next summer, but he planned to keep his distance from them.

From the winter quarters, once the snow pack was right for sledding, they would set out for the polar seas and then across the seas to the pole. That, at least, was the plan. Dr. Cook said that if Peary left his winter quarters, he would be dead within a week. Men were going to risk their lives, he said, to indulge this delusion of Peary's that he was still strong enough to reach the pole. Henson, Percy and the Eskimos were going with him so that in his last days, when death was certain, when even he was forced to admit that he had failed, he would not be alone.

All hands were on the decks of both ships just after noon. As the crews raised the gangplank and unmoored from each other the *Erik* and the *Windward*, I looked at the beach, on which there was nothing now but Peary's tent and Henson's smaller one, nothing in the prospect to indicate what century this was or that any white man had ever set foot here. There were no crew members, nor any of their tools and equipment; no rowboat pulled up on the sand; no coloured clothing spread out on the rocks to dry. The flags of America, Canada, Denmark and Newfoundland had been removed. How improbable it seemed that along that beach, little Marie Peary had walked with her mother, apeing the way she twirled her parasol, and that I had, one warm day, sat against a flat rock in the sunlight, reading the books assigned to me by Dr. Cook.

When Charlie Percy climbed into the boat to go ashore, Marie Peary said, "Take care of my father, Charlie." Percy, a tall, shy young man from Brooklyn who had instantly accepted when Henson invited him to stay behind, assured her that he would.

In my hand, I felt not only pain but the ghost of Peary's grip. How strange it would be if I could still feel it when I heard that he was dead.

As the two ships separated and the *Windward*, powered by its diesel engine, led the way towards the narrows, Captain Blakeney blew the *Erik's* whistle three times in farewell. Captain Bartlett blew the whistle of the *Windward* three times in response. The Eskimos had congregated on the beach to watch us leave. They waved and shouted. Among them was Charlie Percy, but there was no sign of Peary or Matthew Henson.

Jo and Marie stayed below deck as we bade the Eskimos goodbye.

"What really happened, Mr. Stead?" a young man named Clarence Wyckoff asked one day as we were sailing home. He grinned as if to say, We all know it was not like Dr. Cook and Henson said. I knew Wyckoff and his father were members of the Peary Arctic Club.

"Lieutenant Peary fainted," I said, "just after we shook hands. He went over the side and I caught him. That's all. Just like Henson said."

"It will wind up in the papers, you know," he said. "I'll make sure of that. So will Herbert Bridgman. You saved Peary's life. There will be reporters waiting for us when we dock. There always are."

My first thought was that Aunt Daphne would soon know where I had gone.

BOOK FOUR

· CHAPTER TWENTY ·

"YOU NEED NOT TALK TO THE REPORTERS," DR. COOK TOLD ME IN the cabin. "In fact, Bridgman would be quite upset if you did. The two of us will meet with Bridgman and give him Henson's version of what happened. It is always like this in the aftermath of expeditions. Things that up north seemed very clear become so mixed up in New York that in the end no one knows who did what."

In New York, by the time Dr. Cook and I met with Bridgman, there had been stories about me in the papers—not prominent ones, but sidebars to the stories that recounted the rescue by Dr. Cook of Jo and Marie Peary; the ones that gave the present location of the expedition and a gilded view of its chances of success. I was said to have saved an "ailing" Peary from near-certain death, in the process suffering a "severely fractured arm."

The testimony of crew members and passengers was quoted at length. They spoke as if they had seen with their own eyes everything that happened. They said I had screamed with pain while holding onto Peary with my broken arm.

"The stories are Bridgman's doing," Dr. Cook said. "He wants to draw attention away from the failure of the expedition and Peary's physical state, not to mention his feud with Dr. Dedrick."

He assured me that it would be pointless to try to convince the press that they were exaggerating what had happened.

Other pieces followed, providing yet more fanciful details. When it became common knowledge that Francis Stead had once served with Peary, and I had supposedly joined the expedition so I could set eyes on my father's final resting place, the story gained extra prominence. It was no longer a sidebar.

This, Dr. Cook said, was the "special slant" that the papers had been looking for.

I was interviewed by several reporters, one of whom described me as "humble, self-effacing and taciturn."

"One can see," he wrote, "from his unflappable manner how he was able to maintain his composure and provide assistance to Lieutenant Peary under what, for one so young, had to have been the most difficult of circumstances."

I played down my supposed heroism to a point just short of denying that I had done anything for Peary, but the reporters would not have it. In every photograph of me that appeared in the papers, my arm in its sling was conspicuously visible. I told the reporters that it was only my hand that was broken, but they kept referring to my "badly broken arm."

"Why don't you simply take the credit you deserve?" said Dr. Cook. "There is no doubt that you saved his life."

"I suppose it's because of what he said to me," I said. "And because he told Francis Stead that you were my father. I would rather that people not dwell on my having saved someone who would do such things. Besides, I could not have saved him without your help and Henson's."

"It would do no harm if you simply give the papers what they want, which is the story, in your words, of what *you* did. Has it occurred to you that we might use all this to our advantage? It seems that Bridgman and the members of the Peary Arctic Club do not blame me for returning from Greenland without Peary. But all that may change if Peary dies."

I relented. I was, as *The New York Times* put it, "finally forthcoming." I described in detail to one of the *Times*' reporters everything that happened after Peary fainted.

A short sketch of my life was included with the story. Born and raised in Newfoundland. Son of Francis Stead, who was now referred to as "a former colleague of Lieutenant Peary's, a medical officer who was tragically lost on the North Greenland expedition." Came without prospects to Manhattan, where, by sheer coincidence, he met up with Dr. Cook, member of the Peary Arctic Club, leader of the rescue expedition and likewise a former colleague of Peary and Francis Stead's on the North Greenland expedition. "It started out for Mr. Stead as a pilgrimage to the bleak northern land where his father disappeared. In 1892, when Devlin Stead was just twelve, his father went to Greenland with Lieutenant Peary and Dr. Cook. Tragically, he did not return. To join those two great explorers, Peary and Cook, to walk where his father had walked, has been for Mr. Stead a life-long dream. Who could have known how that dream would end? That the young man whose father lost his life in Greenland so long ago would wind up saving the life of the great explorer under whom his father served."

It seemed that every day some new embellishment appeared: the long line of men shaking Peary's hand and wishing him good luck on the eve of their departure from Etah; Peary "chatting" with each of them despite being so exhausted; Peary collapsing as he and I were talking, with me catching him as he went over the rail, shouting through gritted teeth for help, refusing to drop a man who weighed so much more than I did.

The papers did nothing more than hint obliquely at Francis Stead's abandonment of his wife and child and the circumstances of his death. They made no reference to my mother's death except to say that she had died when I was six. Almost nothing was said of Aunt Daphne and Uncle Edward, who were referred to only as "the aunt and uncle by whom Mr. Stead was raised," which somehow made it sound as if they had had many children of their own, as if I had grown up in a household so swarming with their offspring that I had more or less been left to raise myself, thereby developing the hardihood and quick-thinking resourcefulness that in Greenland had so well served me and Lieutenant Peary.

"Wherever Mr. Stead is," *The Times* story read, "Dr. Cook is sure to be close by, attending to his protégé. Those who know them say that they were like this from the start, that there was a familiar, collegial air between them that made their just having met seem inconceivable. Dr. Cook explains this by saying that he was so close to Mr. Stead's father that when, by chance, he met his son, he felt as though they had been friendly associates for years. What father would not regard with envy the closeness of these two, would not wish from his son the same measure of dutiful obedience as that accorded Dr. Cook by Mr. Stead?"

CHAPTER TWENTY-ONE

Dear Aunt Daphne:

As you will have read by now in the St. John's papers of my involvement in the rescue expedition that was sent to Greenland in search of Lieutenant Peary and his family, the time seems right for a full disclosure of my whereabouts and plans.

Up to the point of my strange and chance encounter with Lieutenant Peary, I was really little more than a guest of the leader of the expedition, Dr. Frederick Cook, whose personal assistant I have been since shortly after arriving in New York.

As you know, both Lieutenant Peary and Dr. Cook were members of the North Greenland expedition of 1892, from which my father disappeared. Lieutenant Peary was its commander, Dr. Cook my father's fellow medical officer.

Dr. Cook and his wife, Marie, have been kind enough to put me up in the unoccupied wing of their house in a part of Brooklyn known as Bushwick. I am very well provided for, wanting for nothing except your own dear company, which I have greatly missed these many months.

I realize that, what with all that happened to my father and mother, the idea of my taking part in polar expeditions and associating with a polar explorer with a view to becoming one myself must be very troublesome to you. I can think of no way of putting your mind completely at rest on this score, since you are as well-

acquainted as I am with the perils of exploration. I have chosen my vocation not because it was my father's, not to redeem his reputation or to complete what he began. I am drawn to Dr. Cook not because he knew my father or because he took part in my father's last expedition. That Dr. Cook is, to some degree, my inspiration I happily admit, but not even he could have inspired me to become an explorer were I not predisposed by nature to become one.

I could not make you understand in a thousand letters how much Dr. Cook's kindness and tutelage have meant to me. I have spoken to Dr. Cook about you and Uncle Edward, and he has asked me to assure you that I will not participate in any venture for which, in his judgment, I have not had adequate preparation.

I have changed somewhat in the short time since I left home. There is much that I must put behind me. As no one better understands than you do what I mean, I hope you can forgive my manner of leaving, which, though regrettable, was necessary.

I will not presume to hope to receive your blessing on my choice of careers. Nor is there any chance that I will receive it for what I am about to ask.

You may think it ungrateful, even treacherous, of me, but I must ask that you allow me to try to make my way without your help. Indeed, I must insist upon it. For so long, you were all I had. If not for you, I would have become what other people thought I was. Your love kept alive in me the faint hope that someday someone else might love me too. I so came to depend on you that I will never gain my independence except by being, for how long I do not know, completely apart from you. It is not your nature but mine that makes this necessary. Were you here, so that I could daily see your face and hear your voice, even were you to write frequently to me and I to you, the result would be one that, though you did not intend it, I would, because of my own faults, my own deficiencies, be unable to prevent.

When I have remedied these deficiencies of mine, when I can return your affection without detriment to either you or me, I will let you know. Please believe that I long for that day, that I wish I was writing now the letter I will write to you when that day comes.

It pains me to say that for a while, we must not see each other and must not correspond. I look forward to reading your reply to this letter, and to the day when I can write to you again. Please trust my judgment in this and know that it signals no lessening of my affections for you.

Love,
Devlin

My darling Devlin:

I expected that, sooner or later, word of your whereabouts would surface, but I never imagined that it would be in the newspapers, that in the papers I would learn where you have been and how you have been occupied since you left home.

They have run several recent photographs of you, which, after our long separation, should make you seem closer to me, yet do the opposite. They make you seem so distant, so foreign, as if you have no past, or have one in which I played no part. You look as though, for you, far more than fifteen months have passed. How strange it was, after not having seen you in fifteen months, to come upon those photographs. It did not seem right that I was learning of your exploits just as people who had never heard of you before were doing. It seemed that these stories and photographs were notice that you would never write to me at all.

Can you imagine with what joy and relief I received the envelope that bore your name and return address? Oh, how I miss you, Devlin. How I wish that you were here so I could hold you in my arms. I do not hope, by saying such things, to cause you any torment, or to castigate you for doing what you still believe was right. But how pointless it would be to write to you and not tell you how I feel.

It would seem from your letter that you have changed much in the short time since you went away. I can think of nothing to attribute it to but the influence, whether good or bad, of this Dr. Cook, whose name, in the papers, figures in every paragraph that features yours.

I must confess that while I was glad to hear you are prospering, I was dismayed to hear which profession you have chosen, for it seemed to me that of all the world's professions, it should have been the one least likely to appeal to you. I do, as you predict in your letter, find your choice of this vocation troublesome, and I wonder if it can really have as little to do with your father as you seem to think, especially as your new associate was a colleague of your father's and a member of the expedition on which he was lost. Can all this be mere coincidence?

You are right, I suppose. There is much that you must put behind you, though I fear that you can no more forget the past than you can change it. I do not fully understand this quest of yours, nor why you think it more likely to succeed if, however temporarily, you exclude me from your life. However, I sense that to try to change your mind or to ask you to explain yourself at greater length would not advance my cause, which is to keep to a minimum the amount of time that must pass until we meet again. I would almost consent to this interval being a protracted one so long as it was fixed, not indeterminate, indefinite, as it is now, for I cannot help fearing that this yet-to-be-determined date may never come.

I am very proud of you, and not at all surprised that you risked yourself to save another without any expectation of reward. You may think this insincere coming from someone who showed imperfect faith in you. But my faith in everyone, myself included, is imperfect.

I do not wish to strip you of your new-found self-confidence. I do not wish to make you doubt yourself, though it seems to me that what is really self-knowledge is often mistaken for self-doubt. But I worry that you are far too hastily putting things behind you, that you are not ready to live in New York, or to be an explorer, or to throw in your lot with a man like Dr. Cook. What I mean by "a man like Dr. Cook," I hardly know.

I am happy to hear that you are well, and well provided for. But I have my doubts about this Dr. Cook, whom you so unreservedly admire and with whom you have become so close. Judging by the papers and your letter, he seems to be no less devoted to you than you are to him, which is perhaps what concerns me most—that he, a grown man who should no longer be prone to forming impulsive attachments, should have become so devoted to you in so short a time. If you had allied yourself for the same purposes with someone your own age, I would be concerned but not surprised.

Perhaps you will dismiss my concern as mere jealousy, some measure of which I am willing to admit to. He has the pleasure of your company, but I do not. You may think I would dismiss out of hand anyone who encouraged and pledged to help you realize an ambition of which I disapprove. Again, you would not be altogether wrong. Or you may think my concern unflattering to you, as good as saying that I cannot imagine how you, in particular, could so rapidly inspire such devotion in anyone. In this case, you would be altogether wrong.

I thought you might like to know, if you do not already, that there is no hint in the local papers that you were ever looked upon as anything but "shy." And everyone speaks of you as if, all along, they knew that you would do great things. Suddenly everyone talks to me about you, wants to know how you are doing and when you will be coming home—that you should be so popular now that you are gone! It all seems so perverse.

I cannot keep this letter from rambling. I feel as though I must cram everything into it, since it may be the last letter of mine that you will read for quite some time. It almost freezes my pen to think that I have but this one chance to prepare you for your setting forth.

I cannot think what interest of Dr. Cook's it would serve to convince you to pursue a life for which he knew you to be ill-suited and by nature disinclined. Perhaps he is merely acting out of an impulsiveness that a man his age should be able to resist. But it seems far more likely to me that his motives are in some way dishonourable. If, by voicing these concerns, I make myself out to be just the sort of suffocating guardian from whom you feel you must escape, then so be it. I would be remiss if I did not say that this sudden alliance he has formed with you does not seem right.

I do not know Dr. Cook except by reputation, which is described by the papers as "untarnished." Yet they say that he will not allow you to be interviewed alone, that he is as watchful and protective of you as a mother cat is of her kittens, that he fields or diverts from you any question requiring an answer of more than one word, and that even that one word must first, by an exchange of looks, be cleared with him before you say it.

I cannot help wondering why this man, whom you esteem so highly, will not allow you to speak for yourself. What harm does he think will come of it? What is it that he thinks you need protection from?

It seems that this man is all things to you. Patron. Sponsor. Mentor. Guardian. Friend. In some of the papers, he is referred to as your "manager." I do not like the sound of that. I would say that he was trying to gain something for himself, except that he seems to have been as protective of you before the rescue expedition on which you rose so unexpectedly to fame as he is now.

I tell myself that perhaps Dr. Cook merely wants to advance the cause of a young man whom he senses has been kept back through no fault of his own. Perhaps I should be grateful that hardly had you left home than your "possibilities" were spotted by a man as shrewd as the papers make him out to be. "Shrewd." "Unaffected." "Reserved." "Reflective." "Watchful." "Generous in his estimations of others." "Laconically modest about his own accomplishments." "A likeable, open-hearted man to whom one is immediately drawn." A word critical of him is nowhere to be found. Yet I distrust him.

Perhaps because of the photographs I have seen of him. At first glance, they seem undamning. I know you will think it absurd of me to read so much into photographs, to blame a man so much for having had his picture taken. But I see the two of you in those photographs, and I do not see in your eyes what I see in his. I look at his eyes and think, Here is a man whose true nature no one knows.

This assessment of him is all that I can really give you by way of warning or advice.

It would be pointless for me to write to him. A charmingly evasive reply is all I would get in return, if he answered me at all.

I feel as though I should hire someone to go to New York and bring you by force back home where you belong. At the same time, I fear that if I meddle in your life, you will make my exclusion from it permanent, which I could not bear.

I must have some word from you—I must—or the days to come will be more difficult to endure than the past fifteen months have been.

Surely it would do no harm for you to write to me from time to time, simply telling me of your whereabouts and plans. Otherwise, I will have no knowledge of you except what I can gather from the papers. I believe I have done nothing to you that would make me deserving of such treatment.

I hate how this letter sounds. I cannot make it sound like me. I do not know what tone I should take with you. I cannot make you understand, in a letter, why I am so afraid for you. You are too young, Devlin. Through no fault of your own, you are younger than your age. You are not ready. I wish, my sweet, my darling Devlin, that I could convince you not to go where you are bent on going. Please, please come back home instead. Surely the advice of someone who loves you and has known you your entire life should count for more than whatever you have heard from Dr. Cook, who cannot possibly know you as I do.

*Be careful, Devlin. Do not do anything simply because some-
one else desires you to do it or may think less of you if you refuse.
Follow your true heart in all things. It is not infallible, but it is
yours.*

*I wish I could go on writing this letter forever. Knowing that
you will read it makes me feel as though I am speaking to you now,
as though you are here but must soon leave and it will be a long
time before you can be with me again.*

*Imagine that I am always with you, always able to hear you if
you speak to me, always answering if only you remember me.*

Love always,
Daphne

I was at first taken aback by Aunt Daphne's distrust of Dr. Cook.
But there is so much that she does not know, I told myself. If she knew,
she would understand.

Shy. Could it be that that was all that most people ever thought I
was? I so wished it was true that it seemed momentarily possible, that
the whole thing, my childhood, had been a protracted misunderstanding on my part, that if I was to return home I would be celebrated by
people who had all along thought shyness to be my only shortcoming.

I told Dr. Cook that I had written her but showed him neither my
letter nor her reply, saying only that I had told her it was necessary that
we not have any contact with each other for a while. I said that I
would keep her informed of my whereabouts and plans so that she
would not be forever in suspense.

· CHAPTER TWENTY-TWO ·

DR. COOK AND I WERE FÊTED IN NEW YORK SOCIETY AS A TANDEM of heroes, Dr. Cook for rescuing Peary's wife and child, and I for what became known as "Mr. Stead's encounter with Lieutenant Peary."

"There is no way to resist it," said Dr. Cook. "They have chosen you to play a part. This is the sort of story they love: an unknown young man saving a famous old man's life."

"It's being made to seem as if I am fond of Peary that I don't like," I said.

"Look," he said, "you do not have to lie to them. Tell them about climbing the mast and standing in the pilot barrel. Tell them about the iceberg. Tell them about the fiords and the glaciers and what they sounded like at night. Tell them about the walrus and the narwhal. That is the sort of thing they want to hear. You cannot control the manner in which good fortune comes your way. But it would be foolish to refuse it."

There came our way an invitation. We—that is, Dr. Cook, his wife and I—were invited to the Fall Ball, which took place every year at the Vanderbilts' on the Hudson, where Frederick W. Vanderbilt and his wife lived in an Italian Renaissance mansion whose expansive grounds in Hyde Park overlooked the Hudson River.

Not only would every member of the Peary Arctic Club be there, Dr. Cook said, but they would be outshone by the other guests, "the absolute upper crust of New York society."

Mrs. Cook, telling her husband that she did not wish to "spend time with people who will regard my every word and deed as confirmation of the opinion they held of me before we met," asked him to decline the invitation on her behalf. He wrote the Vanderbilts that at the time of the Fall Ball, his wife would be visiting her sister in Washington.

Dr. Cook took me to a tailor and had me fitted for "white tie and accessories." White tie, it turned out, really meant vanilla tie—vanilla so that it could be seen against the white background of the shirt. I was also fitted for a vanilla-coloured vest, and a milliner fashioned a removable white silk lining for my top hat. After the purchase of a long white silk scarf and a pair of white silk gloves, I was, sartorially speaking at least, ready to meet the Vanderbilts.

We drove to the house in Dr. Cook's horse and carriage, Dr. Cook being loathe to risk having the unreliable Franklin break down in the Vanderbilt driveway in front of all the other guests who owned motorcars but regarded them as toys.

We had a long time to talk as the pair of horses clopped along, the sound of their hoofs making our voices unintelligible, Dr. Cook assured me, to the driver, whom Dr. Cook had hired because, in the eyes of the people I was about to meet, it would not do for us to drive ourselves.

"It is well known that by the time of the North Greenland expedition, your parents were estranged," Dr. Cook said. "No one will mention this to you. It is highly unlikely that anyone will mention your mother at all. They will expect, on this one matter at least, the same sort of tact from you. With your father, things are somewhat different. They will expect you not to mention your father until, by doing so themselves, they invite you to.

"It is, in part, the story behind your story—the story that will never appear in the papers and that they will not allude to in your presence—that fascinates them. They see you not only as the strong, quick-thinking, promising young man the papers make you out to be, but also as a somewhat mysterious, possibly 'haunted' young man with a tragic past. That you are following the vocation that brought so much unhappiness to your mother and father intrigues them. You are now among those whom they believe to be worth watching, as I once was. I do not mean that I am now regarded as uninteresting, but it is thought, in many quarters, that I am unlikely at this point to exceed my past accomplishments, unlikely to do anything surprising; that I will continue to distinguish myself in the second rank of exploration. I should add that I am not so regarded by other explorers or those who follow exploration closely.

"The front rank of American explorers is a front rank of one. It contains no one else's name but Peary's. No explorer in history has been more 'backed' than he has. The uninformed, by whom he is regarded as our explorer laureate, appointed to his position of pre-eminence for life, have given no thought to who should succeed him.

"That someone must soon succeed him—that he is, however unwillingly, about to step down—they do not know as yet. Nor should we so much as hint at it tonight. Do not say a word to them of Peary's condition. If they ask you what you think his chances are of reaching the pole, tell them that if any man, after three years in the Arctic, still has strength enough to make it to the pole, that man is Peary.

"You should say nothing even faintly critical about him. We should seem to be Peary's admiring rivals, his gentlemen competitors.

"They will watch you, Devlin, not so much to see what you make of yourself as to see what life makes of you, to see what becomes of you."

"I had hoped to make a new beginning here," I said. "Now it seems that I am regarded in New York as I was in St. John's: as being fated to wind up like my parents."

"No, no, it is just the opposite. They do not know what you are fated for because most of them do not believe in fate, not really. Americans, even those who not only value social standing but believe it is fixed, immutable, do not like to think in terms of fate. There is, I know, a contradiction there, but they could not be bothered to acknowledge it. Americans like to think that anything is possible, that ours is a country of limitless opportunity for all. One cannot believe that *and* believe in fate."

"I think you are exaggerating the degree of their interest in me."

"I assure you that I am not. How long it remains at its current level to some extent depends on you. But they will always be watching now to see what becomes of you. They like to bring in people like you and me as guests—not just into their houses, but into their lives. But guests are all that we will ever be. It is important to remember that."

"I would like it if, at some point in my life, I could just fit in somewhere, not seem like such an oddball," I said.

"Well, do not try to fit in among these people. Do not try to act 'properly.' Do not be anxious because you do not know the rules of polite society. Among the people who wish to meet you, it is universally *assumed* that you do not know these rules. They would be disappointed if you did. The last thing they want you to be is one of them."

"What *do* they want me to be?"

"Yourself."

"But I am not what they think I am."

"Perhaps not quite what they think you are. But you are rougher around the edges than you realize. You will soon see what I mean."

"Now you have me terrified."

"They will love your accent."

"I didn't think I had that much of one."

"My dear fellow, you have a brogue so thick it would blunt a butcher's knife."

We drove up a well-lit driveway overhung by massive oaks and pulled up behind some other vehicles at the foot of a set of limestone stairs that fanned out widely at the bottom like the train of a wedding dress. We disembarked and, as our carriage was led away, ascended the stairs to a double-storied portico, on each side of which there were two massive fluted columns that supported an entablature whose centre-piece, though it reared above me, I could not make out.

We were relieved of our scarves, gloves and hats just inside the door, swarmed by taciturn footmen who simply waited to be handed articles of clothing. If not for Dr. Cook, I would not have known when to stop, what to give them and what to keep.

The moment I left the vestibule, I had to resist the urge to turn sharply right, to where I knew the business room to be.

We were led by a short, scarlet-complexioned butler through the vestibule into the entrance hall and then upstairs to the enormous reception hall, a circular room at the heart of the house from which a dozen doors, now closed, led off to other rooms. As we climbed the bronze-work stairs, I put my left hand on the balustrade, only to withdraw it when I saw that the rail was encased in velvet of which only the light side showed, as if it had never been touched, never brushed against the grain. I looked at the mark left by my hand, the only such blemish the whole length of the balustrade, and, resisting the urge to turn back and erase it, hurried on.

Dr. Cook and I joined a receiving line, in which, I was relieved to see, were Clarence Wyckoff and some of the other passengers from the rescue expedition.

We had been waiting a couple of minutes, the line moving slowly, when Wyckoff glanced over his shoulder and saw us.

"Dr. Cook and the doughty Mr. Stead," Wyckoff said, and everyone in front of and behind him turned round to look. There was an outbreak of applause, led by Wyckoff, to which even Dr. Cook seemed unsure how to react. He smiled and bowed slightly, as if he believed Wyckoff were being playfully ironic. I did likewise.

"How is the arm, Mr. Stead?" Wyckoff said. The arm. The arm that saved Lieutenant Peary, the arm we have all read and heard so much about, he might have said by the way people looked at my arms, both of them, as if, now that I no longer wore a sling, they were unsure which was the special one.

"Much better," I said. Instinctively, I flexed my right hand slightly, and now all eyes were on my right arm, people nodding and murmuring as if it was apparent to them, as it could never be to people who had not seen it with their own eyes, how such an arm could have saved Lieutenant Peary.

It seemed strange to think that at that moment, Peary was still up north, somewhere in Greenland, facing such hardships and privations as none of us but Dr. Cook could even begin to understand. He was facing almost certain death, while there I was in Manhattan being celebrated for having saved what little remained of his life—there were we all, lining up to meet the Vanderbilts and partake of their lavish hospitality, speaking with such cheerful ease of Lieutenant Peary, who by that time, along with Matthew Henson and Charlie Percy, might have been dead.

Dr. Cook, who had met the Vanderbilts before, stepped aside after a short exchange of pleasantries to introduce me. But before he could say my name, Mr. Vanderbilt put his hand on my left arm.

"This must be Mr. Stead," he said, as if he had not heard Clarence Wykcoff's butler-like announcement of Dr. Cook and me.

"How do you do, Mr. Vanderbilt?" I said, extending my hand, which he took in both of his, giving it a gentle squeeze.

"Very well, young man. Very well," he said. "I can now tell my friends that I shook the hand to which Lieutenant Peary owes his life. It was a great thing you did, a great thing that will never be forgotten."

"Thank you, sir," I said.

He introduced me to his wife, who smiled and held out her gloved hand to me palm down. For a moment I was mystified, then I realized that I was meant to kiss it, which I did. I must have been looking elsewhere when Dr. Cook had done so. I had never kissed a woman's hand in my life. Should I bend to kiss it or raise it to my mouth, or both? Both, I decided. That there were no gasps of disbelief or disconcerted looks, I knew to be no indication that I had done it properly.

"We are all very proud of you, Mr. Stead," she said. "You might not have been born in New York, but when anyone who lives here does something great, we shamelessly claim him as our own."

After exacting from us a promise that at some point during the evening, Dr. Cook and I would tell them all about the rescue expedition, the Vanderbilts turned their attentions to the guests behind us.

Dr. Cook and I were admitted into the main chamber of the reception room.

The room was lit by a row of identical, evenly spaced, globe-like chandeliers. I would later count six of them, though from where we stood, they all blended into one, as if a massive, sparkling, horizontal beam of glass was hanging from the ceiling. Whatever furnishings the room normally held had been removed, except for the reproductions of several Greek busts and statues, each of which stood on a pedestal in a grotto-like recess in the walnut-panelled walls.

Along the walls innumerable armless chairs sat side by side, all with red plush seats and upright wooden backs. Most of the chairs were empty, but I imagined them all occupied, everyone sitting around the edges of the great room, solemnly surveying their fellows across the way as if the occasion was not a ball but a multitudinous assembly at which matters of great importance were to be discussed.

Each half of the room was a mirror image of the other. Anyone entering by the opposite door would have seen exactly what we had, including the double doors themselves, flanked by the same Ionic marble columns. The doors at the opposite end were closed, and on a slightly raised dais in front of them, an orchestra was gathering.

Dr. Cook inclined his head towards me, about to give me some instruction, I assumed, but before he could speak, a woman emerged from the teeming throng of people on the floor, holding out her gloved hand, which he kissed.

"How nice to see you, Dr. Cook," she said.

"And you, Mrs. Frick," he said.

I guessed that Mrs. Frick was in her mid-fifties. She wore a large green feather in her hair and the mock décolletage favoured by older women who thought the bare-shouldered style no longer flattering to them—an opaque, flesh-coloured mantle from which, at the height of her bosom, her black gown depended. After we were introduced, she took my arm.

"I wonder if I might borrow you, young man," she said. "There will not be enough time for everyone to meet you both, though of course they would like to, so we have decided to split you up. I'm sure Dr. Cook can fend for himself?"

Dr. Cook smiled at her and nodded, and just as Mrs. Frick turned away, he smiled reassuringly at me.

Both hands on my upper arm, she led me along the edge of the guests, past punchbowls swimming with cherries and wedges of lemons and limes. We surveyed what might have been a foods-of-the-world display, including a sculpture of Neptune fashioned from whole salmon with jets of water spouting from their eyes. Somewhere beneath all those fish there had to have been a fountain, but I could not make it out.

She took me to the nearest available pair of chairs, where we sat down. Still holding my arm, sitting side-on to me and looking at the floor as if to do so helped her to formulate her words and to hear my answers, she said she expected that I had not often had to "endure" an event like this one. Before I could object to the word *endure*, she told me she planned to make the evening as painless for me as possible.

"I will take you around and introduce you to those people by whom you are least likely to be bored. Of course, no one will mind if you do not wish to dance—"

"But I would like to dance," I said. "I would like it very much."

"Then you've danced before?" she said, still staring, as if the better to appraise me, at the floor.

"Yes," I said. "Many times. I'm thought to be quite a good dancer."

"That's wonderful," she said, though clearly she was wondering if I meant the same thing by *dance* as she did.

She introduced me to a great many people, never allowing me to stay long in one place, steering me away from people she said she had already introduced me to, though I could not remember having met them. Looking about the room, I could not remember having met anyone. But Mrs. Frick, I was certain, was keeping track and, even had there been five thousand guests in the room, would not have made the mistake of introducing me to the same one twice.

I was congratulated over and over for having saved Lieutenant Peary's life.

A number of young women who looked to be unescorted stood

in a semi-circle near the wall, all talking at once, it seemed, though they stopped talking and smiled when they saw me staring at them.

Mrs. Frick led me over and introduced me to each of them in turn. Though they were my age, they had an assurance about them, an ease of manner, that even Mrs. Frick did not possess.

"Devlin Stead, the young man you have all heard so much about," Mrs. Frick said.

"How do you do, Mr. Stead?" they said one after the other, and one after the other I kissed their gloved hands, which they offered to me until the repetition struck me as absurd, though they betrayed not the least embarrassment.

"Mr. Stead says he is thought to be quite a good dancer," Mrs. Frick said. "Perhaps you should include him on your dance cards."

There was a chorus of "Yes, indeeds," and much scribbling on cards that seemed to appear from out of nowhere and just as quickly disappear.

Except for the colours of their evening gowns, the women at the Fall Ball were dressed almost as uniformly as the men. Their gowns were décolleté, cut very low to just above the cleavage, so that the bare necks, arms, shoulders and upper backs of women were distractingly everywhere.

It was as if they were all wearing the same form-fitting, ideally complected, skin-like fabric, chosen because it would show to best advantage beneath the chandeliers of the Vanderbilt ballroom.

Through it faintly showed the shapes of collar-bones and shoulder-blades, though *clavicles* and *scapulas* were the words that came to mind, delicate, fragile words better suited for describing the frames of girls like these than *bones* and *blades*.

Many of the women wore chokers that seemed to be pinned to them by brooches that fit snugly in the hollows of their throats. Almost all the women clasped, at waist height with both hands, small mesh bags made of tightly interwoven metal links. Some were silver, some gold. A couple of the women sported beau-catcher curls in the middle of their foreheads.

"Step-step-close, step-step-close," I kept repeating to myself. What a fool I had been to boast of my proficiency at something I had not done in years. It had been second nature to me at one time, requiring little more effort, little more concentration, than walking. For all I knew, the sort of dancing that Aunt Daphne had taught me had gone out of fashion everywhere but Newfoundland a hundred years ago. What if, in this time of invention, someone had dreamed up a new kind of dancing?

To my relief, the orchestra, when it began to play, did so in my accustomed three-quarter time.

One of the young women Mrs. Frick had introduced me to approached us.

"Mr. Stead," she said.

"Miss Sumner," said Mrs. Frick.

"Thank you, Mrs. Frick," Miss Sumner said. "I have only a few new names to remember. Poor Mr. Stead has hundreds." She held out her arms to me. I took her hand, and we began to dance.

Miss Sumner. Having for so many years been deprived of fellowship, I was almost overwhelmed now to be faced with this open-armed young woman, who might have been appointed to dance with me as a gesture of propitiation. The meaning of her smile might have been that, though I had been wronged, I should regard the past as past, there being no remedy for it but to keep it from determining my future.

In one way, I had broken free into the world the instant I leapt into that rowboat at the foot of Signal Hill, had been making my way further and further into it since then. But here, it seemed, was my official, ceremonial welcomer—not Dr. Cook, not Clarence Wyckoff or the Vanderbilts, but this young woman whose first name I did not know and who had no idea, any more than did the other guests, perhaps including Dr. Cook, how momentous an event this was for me. It was as though I was being exonerated of a crime of which I had been presumed guilty for so long that I had come to *feel* that I was guilty of it. I felt so many things at once—relief, self-pity, gratitude, resentment, curiosity, arousal—that there rose up in me what I was almost too late in realizing was the urge to cry. I hoped that the struggle to suppress it did not show.

I was not used to being watched while I danced, let alone surrounded by other dancers, but I soon grew accustomed to it. At first, Miss Sumner felt like an annoyingly altered version of Aunt Daphne. Everything about her seemed slightly off, but she seemed not to notice my annoyance and gradually it passed. I had never been this close to any woman but Aunt Daphne before, had never been allowed so close a look at any woman's bare arms, neck, shoulders and back before. I spoke only when she spoke to me, or rather only when she asked a question, which she did repeatedly, as if word had gone out from Mrs. Frick that nothing less than a question would draw any sort of response from me. I felt like I was being interviewed. Not that I minded. I tried to answer such unanswerable questions as "What is Greenland like?" To elaborate beyond yes or no my replies to such questions as "Did it hurt when you broke your arm?"

The second woman I had danced with in my life and the first one not related to me. The first one of the latter kind to whom, under any circumstances, I had been this close. It seemed a miracle, this young woman's face, her eyes, her nose, her lips almost touching mine. The smell of her perfume. The smell of her hair. The soft, pliant feel of her upper back beneath my hand, the part of her back that exactly corresponded to her left breast. The wonder of moving in concert with a woman, her body moving in willing sympathy with mine.

She seemed impossibly poised. Nowhere on all the bare parts of her was there so much as a hint of high colour. I had always, when aroused, felt as though my own body was mocking me, mocking the idea that for me women would ever be anything more than things to be gawked at from afar, material for fantasies of which I could never bring myself to make practical use, knowing how I was regarded by the girls and women who inspired them.

Fresh from my long-imposed solitude, I could not believe that after Miss Sumner, another woman would dance with me, and after her another—that I was being sought after.

I felt that I had spent my life in a cell, and that, though it still contained me, though I was not yet free to leave it, I was at last being allowed visitors, a steady stream of whom were filing through to meet me.

I was soon able to gauge in seconds the distinctive rhythm of each woman. There were some good dancers among them, but most of them danced as though performing by rote some necessary and painstakingly acquired social skill.

It seemed to me that there was something frank, generous, almost wanton in the way the young women held open their arms as they prepared to receive me.

My hand still warm from the last hand I had held, I took hold of another—my shoulder still warm from the last hand that had rested there, another one was placed upon it—and the whole thing began again, a new pair of eyes to look into, a new face close to mine, a new voice issuing from lips that I could not stop staring at or wishing I could kiss. Men and women could not touch like this in public, could not converse at such close quarters except when they were dancing. Hurray for dancing, which conveyed this strange but wonderful exemption.

Sometimes, if I looked long enough at the other dancers, all I saw were the bared upper bodies of the women, a teeming fleet of marble busts, as if the sculptures in the hollows of the walls, having left their pedestals, were gliding about in perilous proximity.

The women seemed to find it both charming and also faintly amusing that someone so uncultivated, someone who looked like he could not have *named* the other social graces, had become so masterful at one of them. I saw that they were intrigued, but that they could think of no way of asking me to satisfy their curiosity that would not offend me.

An account of the Fall Ball and my part in it would appear the next day in the society pages of the papers under the bylines of people who had attended the event and whom I had taken to be guests, among them Mrs. Frick, who listed, in the order in which I danced with them, every one of my partners, pointing out whose daughters they were and to whom of note they were otherwise related. Me she would describe as "taciturn but self-composed, a trait he seems to have learned from Dr. Cook; a marvellous dancer, his manner of becoming which was the subject of much debate among his charming partners; deceptively frail-looking, almost delicate, except for his eyes, which are those of a young man well used to roughing it."

Between dances, I could think of nothing to say to the young women who surrounded me. I tried to affect an air of laconic modesty, as if I was not tongue-tied but was staying silent merely to impress upon my admirers that altogether too much fuss was being made over me for having saved Lieutenant Peary's life.

I soon realized that it didn't really matter what I said or did, so eager were they to meet an explorer, so determined to find him interesting and thus make it a greater distinction to have been among the first to meet him. They spoke as if I had been an explorer before the rescue expedition, had merely come to prominence by rescuing Lieutenant Peary—that being my most significant accomplishment, but by no means my first.

From time to time, I saw Dr. Cook watching me, taking time out from conversations with men I assumed to be backers to throw my way a worried glance, which, when our eyes met, turned into a smile. He was not dancing, no doubt because it was primarily the men he was hoping to impress.

"Explorers are so often in peril that for one of them to save another's life is commonplace," I heard myself saying. This was met with a chorus of protest led by Mrs. Frick, who sounded mortified that I had committed this social gaffe while in her custody.

"There is nothing commonplace about a man your age saving the life of a man like Lieutenant Peary," loudly said an especially distinguished-looking middle-aged man who until now had been watching from the margins of the group that surrounded me.

"I am Morris Jesup," he said. The others parted as he extended his hand to me. "President of the Peary Arctic Club. Young man, you performed a service not only for Lieutenant Peary and his family, but for all of us and for this country, too. Lieutenant Peary is a national treasure whom, if not for you, we would have lost. There is every reason to believe that you will be officially rewarded for your actions. By way of recommending you for the Harding Medal, I have sent to the navy the testimony of several men who witnessed what you did. The Harding is one of the highest honours the navy can bestow for service to this country."

Everyone within earshot burst into applause as if Jesup had just pinned the Harding Medal to my chest. There were further eruptions as news of what Jesup had said moved from group to group throughout the hall.

Jesup looked at me, as if to say that to belittle my heroism was to belittle the object of it.

I looked around in search of Dr. Cook, but he was nowhere to be seen. I felt foolish for having tried to speak like the seasoned explorer they were all pretending to believe I was—for having spoken with such transparently false modesty in front of a man as important as Jesup was to Dr. Cook's ambitions, a man in a position to be even more aware than the others how absurd it was for me to have held forth as though I was a representative member of the fraternity of explorers, who daily saved each other's lives as matter-of-factly as they put on their hats and coats.

"Mr. Stead. I believe we are third cousins. Or something. I've never understood how such things work, have you?"

"I don't believe we've met," was all that I could think to say to the young woman with whom I was dancing.

She smiled. "Of course we have," she said. "This is our second dance."

It was Miss Sumner, the first woman with whom I had danced.

"Miss Sumner," I said. "I'm sorry, I—"

"Kristine Sumner," she said. "Lily Dover's daughter? Dover was her name before she married."

For a moment, it was as though I was dancing with the Lily of Dr. Cook's letters and conversations, the Lily because of whom my mother and Dr. Cook had met. The Lily who, while they were falling in love, had been their chaperone, the third whose constant, patient presence had been a diversion, keeping people from noticing the courtship that was taking place beside her. For a moment, it was as if my mother was close by—as if, were I to look around, I would see her standing next to Dr. Cook, the two of them not touching, watching while I danced with Lily's daughter, their secret safe.

"You seem distressed, Mr. Stead," Miss Sumner said. "I would hate it if, having danced so well with all the others, you fell on your face while dancing with me. Everyone would think it was my fault."

"I'm sorry," I said. "I was not expecting to meet . . . a relative tonight."

She laughed, as if some trait that I was amusingly unaware of had just shown itself. It was a wonderful, unselfconscious laugh. Kristine. A name at last.

"My mother came to visit yours," I said. "Here, in Manhattan."

"Oh, I know all about it," Miss Sumner said. "She was engaged, soon to be married, and my mother insisted that she come and see Manhattan before she settled down."

I waited to hear what else she knew. Despite Dr. Cook's assurances that Lily did not know I was his son—that my mother had written to her saying that she had changed her mind about Dr. Cook and would marry Dr. Stead as planned, only sooner—I had often wondered if Lily Dover had guessed the truth, guessed it when the wedding was moved up and my mother so soon after announced that she was pregnant. Had she guessed what she had no way of proving, and what my mother, if she wrote to her about it, had denied? Probably not. If Lily jumped to any conclusion, it would have been that my mother had consummated her marriage in advance, conceived a child with whom she was already, if unknowingly, pregnant when she met Dr. Cook. Dr. Cook had never seemed concerned about Lily, about what she might know or suspect.

I wondered if Miss Sumner knew, if her mother had told her, about my mother and Dr. Cook and the part she had played in their short-lived and secret romance.

"What did your mother tell you about mine?" I said. "I was so young when my mother died that I hardly remember her. All I know about her is what other people tell me."

"She talks about her a lot," Miss Sumner said. "Especially now, what with you having become so famous. 'Amelia's boy,' she calls you, as if you are nine years old. 'There's another story in the paper about Amelia's boy,' she says."

Lily. Amelia. I remembered Dr. Cook recounting his story by the fire in the drawing room, saying their names. Again, it was as if my mother was close by, as if she was at the Fall Ball as Lily's guest, as was Dr. Cook. A seemingly innocent threesome, with Dr. Cook taking turns dancing with the two women—of whom Lily, having no engagement ring, was the eligible one, the one in whom it was presumed that Dr. Cook was interested.

I was startled from this revery when I noticed that Dr. Cook was looking at me from across the room. He nodded but this time did not smile, which made me suspect that he knew who I was dancing with.

"Has your mother ever met Dr. Cook?" I said, regretting it instantly.

"Not to my knowledge," Miss Sumner said. "Why do you ask?"

"Oh, no reason really," I said. "Dr. Cook was . . . Dr. Cook lived in Brooklyn at the time."

"Not everyone who lives in Manhattan knows everyone who lives in Brooklyn," Miss Sumner said, looking appraisingly ironic.

"No, of course not," I said. "I was thinking of the way it is in St. John's. Where everyone knows everyone, I mean."

Miss Sumner nodded and smiled quizzically.

I imagined Miss Sumner telling her mother, telling Lily, about my odd question. Would Lily guess that Dr. Cook had told me everything? She might already have assumed he had from the mere fact of our being associates.

"Is something wrong, Mr. Stead?" Miss Sumner said.

"I'm a little tired," I said.

"You do look tired," she said. "And people are starting to leave anyway."

We drew apart.

"I hope I see you again," I said.

She smiled and seemed to suffer a rare loss of composure.

"Yes. I hope so, too," she said.

I rejoined Mrs. Frick. We searched for Dr. Cook and found him near the wall surrounded by a semi-circle of young men and women.

"Some say that the age of exploration is nearly over," a woman was saying as I walked up to them. "They say that the parts of the world that have yet to be reached cannot be reached, and that there is therefore nothing left to be discovered."

"I cannot imagine any quest, no matter how challenging, being abandoned for good," said Dr. Cook. "I cannot imagine that mankind will be content to leave some parts of the globe forever undiscovered, forever known to be there but never seen, never walked upon."

There was a murmur of assent among those who were gathered round, the young women nodding and smiling at each other as if Dr. Cook had just said, with unusually fine eloquence, something they had long believed.

Upon seeing me, Dr. Cook bade his audience good night.

"Come, Devlin," he said. "Let us join the leaving line."

As I walked beside him, he took my arm and inclined his head.

"Are you all right, Devlin?" he whispered.

"I'm fine," I said, looking at him as if to prove it. He did not look at all reassured. I remembered that, between waltzes, Mrs. Frick had seemed concerned about something that delicacy forbade her from mentioning, but the nature of which she seemed to think I would eventually guess from the way she looked at me. I had been unable to imagine what it was. Now I knew.

I suddenly realized, suddenly *felt*, the state I was in. I hoped it was only now that this unprecedented evening was ending that my body was beginning to deal with its effects, only now that I was coursing with relief at having made it through without catastrophe that my body, too, was letting down its guard, having up to this point been perfectly concealing its distress. But I feared that this was not the case. I feared that for hours I had looked as awful as, judging by the way I felt, I had to be looking now. My head was pounding as if my heart had switched places with my brain. My whole body was throbbing. Dr. Cook could have taken my pulse by touching me anywhere. All of me throbbing and faintly trembling the way my arms did sometimes after I had carried something heavy. Drops of sweat trickled down through the hair on my temples onto the sides of my face and others made their long, cool way down my back and chest, so that I knew that if I leaned against anything, my shirt and jacket would be soaked.

For how long had I been like this? My very wrists were flushed deep red. So must my neck and throat have been. As for my face, I dared not glance at a mirror. I could all too easily imagine that startled, furtive moment of self-recognition as I realized that the unfamilar, blood-gorged face with the swollen, sunken eyes and the glistening, livid cheekbones looking back at me was mine. I did not want to see what other people saw, had been seeing all evening when they looked at me, or would see in the eternity that would pass from now until we left. I looked at my hands. They were so damp I must have stained the gloves and gown of every woman I had danced with. Yet Miss Sumner had danced a second with me and had said with such sympathy that I looked tired. A kind understatement.

"Let's get you home," said Dr. Cook. I looked at him. He sounded concerned not with what others might think of my appearance or with what sort of impression I had made, only with taking proper care of me. I could not imagine ever being clear-headed or normally complected again.

"You poor man, Mr. Stead," said Mrs. Vanderbilt. "What an ordeal I have put you through. You look as though my hospitality has taken a greater toll on you than all the months you spent in Greenland. How like an explorer to be more at home in the Arctic than in some fancy Hyde Park house."

"Oh no, I enjoyed myself immensely, Mrs. Vanderbilt," I said, so fervently that she laughed, as if here at last was the guileless enthusiasm she had been expecting from me.

"I hope you will not consider it too much of an imposition if we send you yet another invitation sometime soon," she said.

"I would love to come again," I said.

She turned to Dr. Cook, said something to which he replied at length, though I could not make out a word.

As I descended the winding, velvet staircase with Dr. Cook, it briefly crossed my mind that I was walking away from a world of which I had had my single, token glimpse, a world that from then on I would know was there but would be barred from, this evening having been a kind of prize that I could win but once.

To the others who were strolling down the staircase with us, such events as the Fall Ball were customary. Here were Dr. Cook and I, affecting the manner of people who had no reason to think that invitations to such events would ever cease to come their way. There, waiting for us behind the servants who held our gloves and scarves, was the open door through which we would walk as casually as those who knew they would soon have occasion to walk through it again, as if there stretched before us an endless number of descents down the stairway of this house and others like it. I looked at Dr. Cook, but clearly no such thoughts were on his mind.

"The evening went very well," he said. "More people know the truth about Peary than I realized. Some of it, anyway. They know that this expedition is his last, even if they still believe it might succeed. I was many times asked about my own plans. One member of the Peary Arctic Club referred to me as the 'prince regent of American explorers.' Some of the others heard him and did not look displeased. It would seem that all that is required of us now is patience. We need not even pick the apple. We need but let it fall into our hands."

It heartened me to hear him so exhilarated and speaking with such calm conviction about the future, his mind perhaps free of all the doubts and torments he had poured out to me in his letters and in person.

The evening *had* gone very well. Kristine. Should I have called her by her name after she told me what it was. I had not told her that my name was Devlin. Doubtless she knew, but that was not the point. I thought of Dr. Cook crossing back to Brooklyn after his first meeting with my mother, thinking about how strange and wonderful it was that at a posh party for graduating doctors to which he had dreaded going, he had fallen in love.

"It was wonderful," I said. "I had no idea what it would be like."

"Remember what I told you," he said. "In that world, we are only visitors, only guests. It is not just a matter of money."

"I danced with Lily's daughter," I said. "Miss Sumner."

"Kristine Sumner," Dr. Cook said. "She is a marvellous young woman. Much like her mother."

"I might have made a mistake," I said. "I wondered if she knew that you had met my mother. And so I asked her if her mother had ever met you."

Dr. Cook was silent for a while, as if he was thinking through the possible consequences of my question.

"No harm done, I'm sure," he said. "I would forget all about it if I were you."

But he did not speak again as we drove home.

I could still feel the women I had danced with, still feel an extra warmth where they had touched me, a memory of them in my hands and on my shoulder that I hoped would never fade.

Later, when I got into bed and lay down, it felt as if a gloved hand was clasping mine and another resting lightly on my shoulder. And then, when I closed my eyes, it seemed that I was dancing, as if that oft-repeated motion was so imprinted on my mind it must continue in defiance of my body, which I kept completely still, hoping my mind would follow its example. I thought of Kristine, my hands on her and hers on me. I danced faster and faster, the room—the world—spinning about as though I had had too much to drink, though I had not drunk at all. I had to open my eyes and sit up in bed to make it stop.

· CHAPTER TWENTY-THREE ·

SOMETHING ABOUT THE DAKOTA UNSETTLED ME, SOMETHING beyond the obvious eeriness of all that shrouded furniture and all those empty rooms.

Late almost every night, I heard footsteps in the hallway. Several times, venturing out of my room, I found the doors of the drawing room closed. Sometimes I saw a light beneath the door, sometimes only what I knew to be the flickering light from the fireplace. Occasionally, though I smelled the smoke of Dr. Cook's cigars, there was no light at all.

One night, the drawing-room door nearest to my room was closed, but the other was slightly open. There was a diagonal, flickering shaft of light on the floor of the hallway. I could hear the crackling of wood in the fireplace.

Remembering that Dr. Cook had told me that I should regard an open door as an invitation to join him, I was about to do so when I heard the voice of Mrs. Cook, her tone upbraiding, plaintive, though not until I went a few feet closer, where there was nothing to hide behind, could I make out what she was saying.

"When will Mr. Stead be moving out? I mean, he can't live with us forever. He is a grown man. Should he not find a place of his own, a life of his own—"

"My dear, he comes from a place so unlike, so much smaller than, New York that he is not yet ready to strike out on his own."

"When *will* he be ready?"

"I don't know. You hardly see him from one month to the next, so I don't see why—"

"I hardly see *you* from one month to the next. Because of him."

"You're exaggerating. You mustn't blame Mr. Stead if you feel that I have been neglecting you."

"If I *feel* it? It is like night and day," she said. "You have not been yourself since he arrived."

"That's not true. I've always been preoccupied."

"Since he arrived, you have acted like you are under a spell."

"It has nothing to do with Mr. Stead. There was a lull in exploration that happened to end not long after Mr. Stead arrived. Sheer coincidence. You know what I'm like when I'm planning for an expedition or just back from one."

"Planning expeditions. Away on expeditions. Recovering from expeditions. There is no time left for anything else, except gallivanting about with Mr. Stead."

"Please, Marie, keep your voice down."

"You are not the same man as you were. I feel that I no longer have a husband, that my child no longer has a father."

I felt as though I was hearing an argument between my mother and Francis Stead, as though I was back in their house on Devon Row, just an infant whom they thought could not understand what they were saying.

"I told you before we were married that I would often be away—"

"Being left alone when you are away is one thing. Being left alone when you are here is something else. Being ignored. Avoided. Having your excuses relayed to me by the servants as if we live in different houses."

"I have not had an assistant before. That is all that is different. It is only natural to spend time with one's assistant."

"I wish it was only a question of how much time you spend with him. But your whole manner with me and the child has changed. You used to have a playfulness, a tenderness about you. Now you seem so formal, so cold. Going through the motions. I have always known that you would never love me as you loved the first Forbes girl—"

"My darling Marie—"

"But I believed that you felt a great affection for me that might one day turn into love."

"Marie—"

"I do not know how this Mr. Stead has changed you so quickly for the worse. I know only that he has, however irrational that seems. I wish you had never met him. But all this can be fixed so easily. Find him a job, a place to live. Is that asking too much? Is that too much to do for the sake of your own wife and family?"

"Marie, this is absurd. I will not have all of New York and half the world wondering why I so suddenly parted ways with my heroic protégé, as the papers like to call him. You know how I feel about you—"

"Then why will you not prove it by doing what I ask? We will find you a new assistant, one who need not live with us—"

"*No.* I will not dismiss a perfectly able young man. I will not deprive him of his preferred way of supporting himself just to indulge this strange jealousy of yours."

"I just don't understand, Frederick. You have always been so indulgent of me in the past, even when I did not deserve it. But on this one matter you will not relent, even though it is clearly making me unhappy. Doesn't my happiness matter to you any more?"

"Of course it does. But I do not wish to start a precedent by indulging this irrational animosity of yours. I will not cast away from me everyone whom, on a whim, you find unsuitable or feel threatened by in some inscrutable way."

I felt sorry for her and guilty for the trouble my presence in the house was causing her. Libby Forbes, Dr. Cook's dead first wife. She thought it was by the memory of Libby Forbes that he was haunted, that *she* had been his one true love.

"Goodnight, Marie. We will speak more about this later if you insist, but for now—"

He was still speaking when she left. The heavy door swung

outward. She must have shoved it with both hands. If not for that door, she would have seen me. By the time I saw her, she was receding down the hallway, marching with head and shoulders thrown back in defiance, as if she believed that Dr. Cook was watching her.

I waited until Mrs. Cook was out of sight, until I heard a distant door opening and closing.

I went to the open door of the drawing room. Dr. Cook was sitting on the edge of the sofa, hunched over, his forearms on his thighs, a half-smoked cigar unlit in his left hand as he stared into the fire. He looked up irritably, perhaps thinking that his wife had returned, but smiled when he saw that it was me.

I went into the room, closing the door behind me. I sat in the armchair in which Mrs. Cook must have sat, for it was still warm. I pictured her there, imploring him across the distance of several feet.

"I overheard. By accident," I said. "I saw that the door was open. When I realized that your wife was with you, I was afraid to go back to my room in case she heard me."

"I would have told you anyway," he said. "Just in case she approached you. It might be best to keep your distance from her for a while." The only way we would meet was if Mrs. Cook stopped keeping her distance from *me*, but I did not say so.

"If my being in this house is making her unhappy—"

He shook his head. "It wouldn't make any difference now if you moved out. No difference to her, I mean. She would still think I was not the man she married. I would still be what she calls preoccupied. Which is, in part at least, a euphemism for something else."

Though I was fairly certain I knew what he meant, I said nothing.

"I have been avoiding her," he said. "I do not plan to do so forever, but for now..." He shrugged. "My mind is...I can think of no woman but your mother, Devlin. I can think of no *thing* but your mother and what might have been. For you. For me. For her."

"I think it is wrong," I said, "unfair for you to blame yourself so much for what you did. You were young. Younger than I am now. I might have done the same thing. You had no way of knowing what the consequences would be. And you were not responsible for the actions of Francis Stead or my mother. Most people would have done what they did."

Dr. Cook stood up quickly, as if he could not bear to hear another word.

"I don't just *blame* myself. I also feel sorry for myself, pity myself for having to suffer the consequences of my actions. Your mother I cannot have. I have Marie, of whom I am fond but, were she not rich, would not have married."

"I don't believe you mean that," I said. "You can forgive everyone, make allowances for everyone, understand everyone except yourself. You speak with more contempt of yourself than you do of Peary. Two of the three people you betrayed are still alive. You and me. It is not too late for us. That you are my father means more to me than anything. It doesn't matter that no one else knows that I am your son."

He shook his head.

"It does matter," he said. "Someday you will understand how much it matters." He walked over to me and, with one hand, gripped me where my neck and shoulder met. "You are becoming more and more like her," he said, then quickly left the room.

The Dakota. These were the empty rooms of the life that might have been, the alternative life that Dr. Cook visited from time to time. It seemed that my mother was in the Dakota—there by the investiture of Dr. Cook, there even when neither Dr. Cook nor I was there, pursuing by herself some ghost version of the life she might have led.

I felt this most strongly whenever I returned to the Dakota. It was as if she was in a parallel, not quite perceptible Dakota, a much lived-in one in which there were no sheets on the furniture and the rooms were filled with voices—hers, Dr. Cook's, mine and those of the other children they might have had.

At night, when Dr. Cook was in the drawing room and I was in my bedroom, it seemed that two-thirds of the cast of this other life had been assembled—that the Dakota was occupied by an impaired, adulterated version of this other life, an almost mockingly disfigured fragment of it, a marred and silent simulacrum.

I could not help feeling sometimes that it only seemed that I had come here of my own accord; that, in fact, I had been brought here to play the very role that I was playing; that Dr. Cook had had this very thing in mind when he first wrote to me, had foreseen these nights in the Dakota, this simulacrum of the life he had turned away from. Me, a grown man, sleeping in the room down the hall from the one in which he stayed up late, forbidden, as though I was a child, to knock on the doors of the drawing room if they were closed. I was a constant reminder to him of her absence. She was never more palpably absent than when he and I were together.

There were times when I heard his voice and thought he was again arguing with Mrs. Cook, only to find upon opening my door that both of the doors to the drawing room were closed. His tone was mildly disputatious, but he spoke at too low a volume for me to make out what he was saying.

"I heard you talking the other night when the doors were closed," I said one day.

"Just thinking some things through," he said. "I find I think better when I think out loud." He smiled. "Though of course other people find it off-putting. I'll try not to raise my voice from now on."

"What were you thinking about?" I said.

"Oh," he said. "Expeditions, mapping routes, supplies, that sort of thing."

That sort of thing. I knew he did that sort of thing in silent, intense absorption in his study, poring over maps and charts and logs that he was unlikely to remove from his study, and that he could not have spread out properly in the drawing room as there were no large desks in it, draped with sheets or otherwise. But I said nothing.

I at first fancied that these drawing-room monologues were addressed to my mother, but I soon realized that the tone did not seem right. Always he spoke in that same, faintly disputatious way as when I had first heard him, not the tone you would take with a lost lover from whom you hoped for solace, guidance or forgiveness. It seemed that he was arguing both sides of some question—perhaps, as he said, thinking things through, playing devil's advocate to himself. Or rehearsing a momentous meeting with the backers, with Morris Jesup, with Herbert Bridgman and the members of the Peary Arctic Club.

One night, his voice rose every few minutes to a shout, as if he were giving himself a good dressing-down, enumerating his misdeeds, castigating himself, shouting with exasperation as you might at someone who committed the same misdeed over and over.

He often spent the entire night on the sofa. "Dozed off," he'd say whenever I encountered him as he left the drawing room, as if it was never his intention to stay there longer than it took to "think things through."

Still wearing his clothes from the day before, he looked dishevelled, sheepish, his shirt rumpled, his hair standing on end. He would hurry to the Cooks' for a quick bath and a change of clothes, and half an hour later, he would begin receiving patients in his surgery.

Sometimes, when I was on my way from the Dakota to my office in the Cooks', I saw the little girl, Ruth. She would stare solemnly at me from the doorway of the other drawing room until I waved to her or said hello, at which point she would run from the room and down the hallway.

What she thought of the continuing presence in her own house of someone her mother regarded with such dread and disapproval, I could not begin to imagine. Her mother did not want me there, and yet I remained. Her father insisted that I stay and spent more time in my side of the house than he did in theirs, more time with me than he did with her. What, she must have wondered, could this mean?

· CHAPTER TWENTY-FOUR ·

LIEUTENANT PEARY, ALONG WITH MATTHEW HENSON, CHARLIE Percy and Dr. Dedrick, returned from Greenland in the summer of 1902.

Peary, refusing all requests for interviews, ignoring, in public at least, Dr. Dedrick's accusations that he had withheld food and medicine from the Eskimos in his employ, some of whom as a result, did not survive the winter, went to Washington, where he was assigned to the Navy Yard. It was widely believed that in its quarters, he would spend the rest of his career, scuffing about, barely able to walk, let alone try again to reach the pole.

It was said that he planned to spend his summers away from the heat of Washington in a Cape Cod house on Eagle Island, off the coast of Maine. He renewed my modest fame when he published in the Eastern Seaboard papers a note of thanks, a copy of which he sent directly to me.

Mr. Stead:

I wish to thank you for the part you played in minimizing the effects of the accident I suffered last summer in Greenland on the rescue vessel that was sent to retrieve my wife and child.

*   I confess that, having fainted because of some passing malady, I remember nothing of the incident except what others have told me. By their account, you acted without hesitation, lending me*

assistance at some risk to yourself and incurring a minor injury, which I am told has healed.

I will be forever grateful to you and wish you well in your own endeavours. I am told that you have chosen exploration as your field. There is no greater one. It may be that our paths will cross again.

Yours sincerely,
Lt. Robert Peary

"It is pure Peary," said Dr. Cook in the drawing room, holding a newspaper copy of Peary's letter in his hand. "He wisely waited until he was fully lucid to write it. Does he really think people will believe that in four years in the Arctic, he suffered nothing worse than a 'passing malady'? He remembers nothing and is therefore not obliged to describe what happened. He has thanked you only because he had to. He has heard of how you were celebrated in New York and elsewhere during his absence. He has to thank you publicly. He would seem churlishly ungrateful otherwise. He wishes people to think that this is how explorers write to one another. That they are men of action, and therefore men of few words, not given to effusiveness no matter what the circumstances. Just as stoically as they endure, so do they stoically give thanks. By way of thanking you, he implies that he will lead further expeditions to the Arctic, that his days as an explorer are far from over. Well, the public may believe it, but those in the know will not. Peary will never officially declare that his day is done. Nor will anyone else presume to do so on his behalf. Not until after it has happened will most people notice that the torch has been passed. To see this letter in the paper, to know that people are reading it and being taken in by it, and to be unable to answer it—"

He stopped speaking and faced the fire. I was surprised to see him so upset.

"I don't think anyone will be fooled by this letter," I said.

Dr. Cook did not reply. He slowly tore up the paper he held in his hand and fed it to the fire piece by piece, as if he was burning the only existing copy of Peary's letter, as if this ritual burning of it would somehow prevent readers from being taken in by it.

I replied in private to Peary. At Dr. Cook's urging, I wrote as euphemistically as Peary did, saying that it was an honour to have "helped" him, especially as he and Francis Stead had once been "colleagues."

· CHAPTER TWENTY-FIVE ·

SOMETIMES AS WE CROSSED THE BRIDGE THE WIND SMELLED faintly of the open sea, reminding me of my first crossing from Newfoundland to Nova Scotia, of a childhood that seemed more unreal as each day passed.

I began to notice the city again, having stopped doing so for some time, so caught up was I in my new-found popularity.

It seemed that there were no locals in Manhattan, no one who was so accustomed to the city that he didn't stop to gawk at it. Everyone gawked as though they had just arrived from somewhere else, which in a way they had, given the pace at which the city was remaking itself.

It was not just one makeover that was taking place. Manhattan was not just one city but dozens of overlapping ones. Just when the barest glimpse had begun to take shape in your mind of what one of these cities would look like a year from now, the plans for that city were discarded in favour of new ones. Half-finished buildings were demolished. Builders of one block looked as if they had no idea what would rear up from the rubble of the one beside it.

The men who walked the iron beams high above the ground stood staring off into space, dangerously transfixed by the progress of a building greater than theirs that was going up many blocks away, too far for them to make out the men or even the machines that were making it, so that it must have seemed to be climbing skyward by some means of self-construction.

Week by week, month by month, the frieze of Manhattan, of

which we had so fine a view from Brooklyn, changed. A partial view of a building, a conspicuous sliver of yellowed stone that I had grown accustomed to, was there one day and gone the next, the gap it left soon filled in with a different colour. The silhouette of the skyline changed as though a child was rearranging it at random, moving and removing building blocks, topping them with attenuated steeples that rose up so far they stood out by themselves against the sky.

At night, Dr. Cook and I drove past building sites where steam-powered cranes stood immobilized like mechanical giraffes, where massive steam-shovels sat in silence. From some of the cranes, iron girders that, when work stopped, had been on their way to out-stretched hands hung suspended in the air, high above us. Some of the shovels were crammed with debris. It was as if the city, in the morning, would not slowly come to life, but would reanimate abruptly. Everything and everyone that had stopped in mid-motion would, as though at the flick of an electric switch, resume their motions. All that dispelled this illusion was the absence from the machines of their operators, an absence that at this time of night could only be inferred, since it was too dark to see inside the cabs.

It seemed that the streets were still faintly ringing with the din that had died down hours ago and would soon start up again. To the city, Dr. Cook said, darkness was a recurring, cyclical inconvenience, an imposed respite from activity and progress, a problem that no doubt would soon be solved by some invention. As he explained to me how steel-frame construction had revolutionized architecture and trans-formed the look of cities, how steel frames and elevators were making it possible to erect buildings three and four times taller than the tallest ever built before, I stopped listening.

It seemed that everything that before had made me uneasy about the city reassured me now. The ongoing erasure of the past, the prospect of an unknown, unfixed future, appealed to me. Perhaps it was because I had seen the people who were behind it all—men who seemed to know what they were doing, and who, after all, were merely men, boyishly impressed by explorers and adventurers, not the sinister-seeming tyrants whose caricatures appeared in all the papers, not the poor-exploiting, arch-villainous tycoons in some editorials and printed sermons.

Now when I ran my errands for Dr. Cook, I was not directed to the "rooms on the right" just inside the front doors, the business rooms of the great houses of Manhattan. I was invited into the parlours, and sometimes the libraries and the drawing rooms, of the members of the Peary Arctic Club, who seemed to want to do little more than beam at me approvingly.

The city never failed to set Dr. Cook going, talking, expostulating. It was now the fashion, he said, owing to Peary's futile four-year expedition to the Arctic, to believe that the North Pole could not be reached.

As no one but Peary was legally allowed to write about the expedition, no one knew just how little it had accomplished, which Dr. Cook said was just as well. If it was known just how complete a failure it was, no one would ever put another cent towards an expedition to the North.

Now all the talk was of the South Pole, which Dr. Cook said no longer interested him. It had been established that it was a fixed point in the middle of a great landmass, an ice-covered continent, and therefore would be easier to reach than its ever-moving opposite "atop" the world.

Much was being made of the duration of Peary's expedition. "Four years," people said. "Not even in four years could Peary make it to the pole." As if to say that if Peary could not do it, no one could.

"I have always known that his success would mean my failure," Dr. Cook said. "But now it seems that even his failure means my failure. Four years. If only they knew how much of that time he spent trying for the pole and how much he spent huddled in tents and huts and tupiks and igloos in a state of such despair that he was indifferent as to which of death or rescue found him first.

"Now that he is out of the running, Peary is *eager* to promote the idea that the pole cannot be reached. He seems to have settled for the consolation prize of being remembered as the man who *proved* it was unreachable.

"Not even as much money as I would be willing to accept from Marie could outfit me for an expedition to the pole. The backers have lost interest in the North for now. It seems there is not one of them who does not already have his name on some cape or bay or inlet that Peary blundered onto in his quest to reach the pole. I tell myself that in time they will want something new named after them, and their interest in the North will be revived.

"I know how bitter, how cynical, that sounds. But as I said at the Vanderbilts', to turn away forever from the pole, to content myself with simply knowing that it's there, eternally, affrontingly unreachable, but *there*, to join with Peary in setting for the cause of exploration such a precedent of failure and defeat—all this seems unthinkable. The compass of fashion will spin round for us again. The needle will be dead on north again someday, Devlin.

"For the moment, I have found for us a lesser but still intriguing goal, one that will keep us fit for polar travel and our names in the papers and before the backers. Not long ago, a mountain in Alaska was surveyed at 20,300 feet, the highest point of land in North America. I am going to climb it with your help. I am going to be the first man to reach the summit of Mt. McKinley. It can be done in a single season and will not keep me apart from Marie for as long as a polar expedition would, which should placate her somewhat. And we may learn something from it that will make our achievement of the greater goal more likely."

Dr. Cook and I were invited to other society balls and gatherings. Each time, he had to make up some excuse for the absence of Marie. None of these functions seemed to me to be quite as splendid as the Vanderbilts' had been, perhaps because I was growing accustomed to socializing, taking for granted both my desirability as a guest and the company of others, as if I had never craved companionship, never in my life been bereft of it.

I was disappointed by any gathering that Kristine did not attend. Whenever she spotted me, she smiled and we made our way towards each other. We spent entire evenings dancing and talking, so that Kristine was often teased for monopolizing me. "She is quite fond of you, Mr. Stead," Clarence Wyckoff said. He peered closely at me. "My God," he said. "I've never seen anyone turn so red in my life."

I was invited out so frequently that I began to encounter other people I had met before, old men and women, young men and women, all of whom seemed no less pleased to see me than they had been the first time.

If they felt that Peary's letter was lacking in graciousness or gratitude, or that its tone was in any way inappropriate, they did not say so. What an honour for me it was, they said, to have such a man as Lieutenant Peary thank me in public for having saved his life. And what a pity it was that Lieutenant Peary did not live in New York but was bound by his naval career to "horrid" Washington. How marvellous it would have been for he and I to appear together in public.

When asked what "adventure" Dr. Cook and I were planning next, I told them we were going to attempt to climb Mt. McKinley in Alaska—the tallest peak in North America—no serious assault of which had yet been made, since it had only recently been "discovered" and surveyed, though the natives of Alaska had known of it for centuries.

"But what about the Arctic poles?" some of them asked. "Is it true that they cannot be reached?" I assured them that Dr. Cook and I had not abandoned our quest to reach one or both of the poles, but the climbing of McKinley could be accomplished in one season, one summer, such as the one that we had spent in Greenland. It would, Dr. Cook had said, be good training for me, better than embarking so soon in my career on a polar quest that might last for years, and for which I might not be physically or psychologically prepared.

Had I done any mountain climbing before? Just the normal amount required of anyone who lived in Newfoundland, I joked, but I was taken seriously, everyone nodding as if they knew just what I meant, just how skilled a climber I had to be from the simple fact of having grown up where I had.

I told them that I would climb as much of McKinley as Dr. Cook would let me, or as much of it as I was able, whichever came first. "The climbing of McKinley," I said, quoting Dr. Cook, "is just a temporary detour on the way to the greatest prize of all."

I received looks of wonder and admiration as I described the preparations Dr. Cook had made. I did not mention that his main backer for this expedition was his wife, or that the American Geographical Society, of which Peary was the president, had been among the many bodies that had refused his request for funding. Or that the Peary Arctic Club had made only the token contribution of an aneroid barometer that measured altitude and a pocket sextant.

We travelled by train to the Pacific Northwest, leaving New York on May 26, 1903, accompanied by several of the usual "gentlemen adventurers" whose fathers paid Dr. Cook to take them with him.

I saw, for the first time, the great expanse of America, most of which was still unsettled and was thought likely to remain that way forever. On a steamer called the *Santa Ana*, we sailed up past Vancouver Island, entering the Inner Passage, negotiating the desolate islands of Alaska, stopping at Juneau, Sitka, Yakutat. It was the route taken by those who had travelled to the Klondike in search of gold, said Dr. Cook.

We reached Tyonek on June 23, there debarking with our pack-horses, which were left to swim ashore to Cook Inlet, after which they were so exhausted as to be of almost no use to us.

Not until August 21 did we establish a base camp at the foot of Mt. McKinley, after two months of sometimes dangerous but mostly tedious travel through the dense, mosquito-infested bush of the Alaskan wilderness.

The climb itself seemed anti-climactic, would have seemed so even had it been successful. For two weeks, the seven of us completed what was little more than a steep walk to an elevation of about seven thousand feet, just above which the largest of McKinley's glaciers began. From there, Dr. Cook and a journalist named Robert Dunn went on alone, reaching a height of 11, 300 feet before they were forced by unscalable walls of ice to head back down.

Dr. Cook and I were back in Brooklyn by the end of December, with Dr. Cook telling reporters that he would have another go at Mt. McKinley, perhaps the following summer.

For me, it had been little more than a long, if arduous, camping trip. Compared to polar exploration, mountain climbing seemed to me a waste of time and money. When I said as much to Dr. Cook, he merely urged me to be patient.

We were celebrated in the Brooklyn and Manhattan papers for our attempt at McKinley. Dr. Cook convinced me not to belittle the expedition or my part in it. Robert Dunn published a frank, unvarnished account of our adventure in a magazine called *Outings*, highlighting the petty bickering that had taken place among the members of the climbing party.

Dr. Cook was at first convinced that his reputation was ruined, but all that the public cared about and fastened upon were the hardships we endured and the obstacles we overcame. A trip by raft down an uncharted glacial river was the highlight. While Dr. Cook and Dunn piloted the raft, the rest of us took turns pulling from the water men who had fallen overboard. I was plucked out twice, gasping for breath because of how cold the water was. Several times, I helped pull others out. Whenever I remembered my two plunges into that icy green water, I thought of my mother and fancied I had some idea of what her final moments had been like.

Dunn did not make me out to be any more or less heroic than the others, only describing me as "slavishly devoted to Dr. Cook, whose side he took in all disagreements and whose orders he obeyed no matter how foolish they appeared to the rest of us to be."

I had written to Aunt Daphne of our plans to climb McKinley and wrote to her again upon returning to New York.

Dr. Cook spent fewer nights in the Dakota than he had before the expedition to McKinley. One night, when he did come to the drawing room, he told me that his wife was four months pregnant.

Mrs. Cook gave birth to a healthy girl whom they called Helen. When she was two weeks old, I was, to my surprise, invited to the Cooks' to see her. Mrs. Cook was in the parlour, the baby in a basket on her lap, a bundle of plaid within which Helen was sleeping, no part of her visible except her tiny, pinched red face.

"She's very pretty," I whispered.

I had spoken with real affection at this first sight of my first sibling, my half-sister. Helen. I had spoken so tenderly that Dr. Cook, as if by way of reminding me to be discreet, backed away and sat in a chair across the room. But Mrs. Cook smiled at me as she never had before.

"Who do you think she looks like?" said Mrs. Cook.

I might have said, "She looks like me." The words sounded in my mind. She was too young, too small to look like anything except a baby, but I said I thought she looked more like her mother than her father. Mrs. Cook smiled warmly at me again.

· CHAPTER TWENTY-SIX ·

"I HAVE NOTICED SOMETHING UNUSUAL ABOUT YOU AND DR. Cook," Miss Sumner said.

I tried not to look as taken aback as I felt.

"There is a strange kind of awkwardness between you," she said. "You seem uncomfortable in each other's presence. You always stand slightly farther apart from each other than other people do. I have seen boys do this who wish to make it seem that they are unaccompanied, that it is pure coincidence that their mother or father is standing beside them. Yet when the two of you are separated, each of you is constantly looking about in search of the other. The strangest thing of all, however, is this: you do not *call* him anything. You just look at him and speak, as if you remember his face but not his name. And as if to compensate for this, he uses your name too frequently, sometimes saying it twice in a single sentence. Devlin, Devlin, Devlin. It sounds unnatural somehow. And each time you re-encounter one another, you look as though it is all you can do to keep from shaking hands."

She had to have been attending to us very closely, or been uncommonly perceptive, to have noticed so much. There was a familiarity about her, an appealing presumptuousness that at gatherings seemed out of place. On this occasion, it disarmed me.

I did not know how to reply to her. By whom else, I wondered, were Dr. Cook and I being so closely scrutinized?

"I was not aware of any awkwardness between Dr. Cook and me, Miss Sumner," I said. "Though perhaps I will be from now on."

"Oh, dear," Miss Sumner said. "I fear that I have spoken out of turn."

"You mean, you *hope* you have," I said.

She smiled and raised her eyebrows in a kind of mock tribute to my wit.

"You haven't spoken out of turn," I said. "It's just that I think you're mistaken. There really is no awkwardness between him and me."

"I have a confession to make," she said. "I have been watching you and Dr. Cook this evening. Because of something my mother said."

She looked intently at me, as if she had hoped by her remark to provoke me into some sort of admission.

"You are blushing," Miss Sumner said.

"I often blush," I said. "As someone who watches me so closely ought to know."

"I asked my mother if she had ever met Dr. Cook," she said. "I did not tell her why I asked—that is, I did not tell her that *you* had once asked *me* if she had met him. I was, if you'll forgive my saying so, a little more tactful, a little less blunt, in my approach than you were. I told her that she really had to meet you and Dr. Cook sometime, since she once knew your mother. 'Of course,' I said, 'you may already have met Dr. Cook. He seems to know everyone you know. It hardly seems possible that your paths haven't crossed.' Then my mother said something very surprising. She said that she *had* met Dr. Cook, but that it had been before they started moving in the same social circles. She met him many years ago, she said, when he was, as she put it, 'even younger than Amelia's boy.' She said that her encounter with him was such that even after all this time, she did not wish to repeat it. Now what do you make of that?"

"I cannot imagine," I said, "why anyone, having once met Dr. Cook, would not wish to do so again. Perhaps your mother has mistaken him for someone else."

"My mother is barely fifty," Miss Sumner said. "Not nearly old enough, I should think, to make a mistake like that."

"I cannot answer for your mother," I said. "I am sorry that she somehow formed the wrong impression of Dr. Cook."

"She said," Miss Sumner said, "that they still move in the same social circles, but that each of them makes sure not to cross paths with the other. She said that given how devoted you are to Dr. Cook, it might be best if she not cross paths with you as well. Then she absolutely refused to say anything more on the subject. Can you imagine? She ... she incites my curiosity and then absolutely refuses to say another word. 'If you did not intend to finish your story, Mother,' I said, 'then why did you begin it in the first place?' Then she drew in her horns. She said that she had spoken foolishly, that she had been exaggerating. 'I want you to forget that we ever spoke about this matter,' she said. 'And please don't speak to Amelia's boy about it.' Can you imagine? 'I want you to forget.' As if I could. As if such a thing were possible. When she was speaking of her 'encounter' with Dr. Cook, she became quite animated. If I didn't know better—if I wasn't certain that my mother's parents would never have allowed it—I would have sworn that they had once been sweethearts or something, and that he had thrown her over for another woman. There must once have been some unpleasantness between them. I don't suppose you know what it was."

I shook my head but could not look her in the eye.

"What with your strange question on the one hand and her strange answer to mine on the other," Kristine said, "the two of you have driven me to distraction. And now here you are standing in front of me, turning all sorts of colours, which you would presumably not be doing unless you were withholding something from me."

Surprised by her sudden change in tone and the volume of her voice, the abrupt switch from coy playfulness to exasperation, I realized that she was genuinely distressed. I looked about to see if anyone had noticed when she raised her voice. A few people were looking our way, but I did not see Dr. Cook.

"I can't imagine," she said, "what it can be that I have stumbled upon, why you and my mother insist on being so mysterious, as if there is something, some knowledge, from which I need to be protected."

"Really," I said, "I know of nothing from which you need to be protected. There *is* nothing. I know nothing about any sort of 'encounter' between your mother and Dr. Cook. I asked you that silly question at the Vanderbilts' because I was stuck for something to say, that's all. I might just as easily have asked you if your mother knew Lieutenant Peary. Or General Armstrong Custer."

She laughed.

"I do not believe you, Mr. Stead," she said, "though it is true that you are often at a loss for words. Let's not talk any further about such things. If you are not too terribly annoyed with me, I would very much like it if you asked me to dance with you again."

We danced, and I was not annoyed with her. I reminded myself of what Dr. Cook had advised me to remember—that I was merely visiting this world of hers. Could it be that I was merely visiting Miss Sumner, merely visiting her arms, her hand, which it seemed to me was holding mine more tightly than usual? My hand was merely visiting her back. My eyes merely visiting her eyes. I wondered what it would be like if my lips paid hers a visit.

I did not tell Dr. Cook what she said to me, what her mother had said about him. Just why her mother had said what she had I could not understand. According to Dr. Cook, she believed that it was my mother who had ended their romance. What could so have turned her against Dr. Cook? Perhaps she had disapproved of his courting a woman who was engaged to be married, but then it was she who had helped them cover up their courtship. Perhaps she was ashamed now of the part she had played and did not wish to be reminded of by meeting Dr. Cook again.

CHAPTER TWENTY-SEVEN

SCEPTICISM ABOUT THE VALUE OF POLAR EXPLORATION WAS STILL rampant after our attempt at Mt. McKinley. The one explorer who seemed to be exempt from it was Peary, who had risen to his new rank of commander on the basis of seniority, the openly hostile navy admirals being scornful of the notion that polar exploration could be construed as service to either the navy or the country.

Peary, Dr. Cook learned at a meeting of the Peary Arctic Club, had been voted the backing for yet another ship, and he would try for the North Pole again starting in the summer of 1905. "You'd think," Dr. Cook said, "that all that had kept him from succeeding the last time was the *Windward*." But he appeared to take the news of what seemed to me to be a major setback for him surprisingly well.

"There is a general feeling," he said, "that it would not be right if his disastrous four-year expedition proved to be his last. He is being allowed one last chance, not to make it to the pole, but to save face, to go out on the proper note. He has fooled the money-men again. And he has named his ship the *Roosevelt*. The president believes Peary to be as fine an example of American manhood and the 'hardy virtues' as can be found—next to himself, of course. While Peary is failing yet again to reach the pole, I will be making my way to the top of Mt. McKinley. And when my success is set beside Peary's failure, there will be no question as to which of us is America's foremost explorer." It sounded hollow, almost desperate.

In the summer of 1905, Peary steamed from Smith Sound to Cape Sheridan in the hopes of making it to the northernmost tip of Grant

Land before proceeding from there by sled to the pole. He was soon beyond the range of the farthest-flung telegraph station, so there was no telling how much progress, if any, he was making.

Dr. Cook began making plans for his second try at Mt. McKinley, which was to take place in the summer of 1906, almost exactly a year from the date of Peary's departure for the pole.

Peary's exact whereabouts were unknown when Dr. Cook and I set out for Mt. McKinley with an entirely different climbing party than before, including one highly experienced climber named Herschel Parker, a physics professor from Columbia University. This second attempt was again being funded by Mrs. Cook, and by an advance from *Harper's Monthly* magazine for the exclusive rights to our story, which Dr. Cook had been asked to write.

We again crossed the American continent northwest by train—again travelled the same Klondike boat route to Tyonek, endured the same hardships, overcame the same obstacles as before, so that I could not help thinking of the backer who was quoted in the papers as having asked what the point was of "giving money to explorers to enable them to re-enact their failures."

We travelled on slush-thick streams that were fed by melting glaciers. We completed the same steep hike to about seven thousand feet as before, at which point the real moutain climbing began and it became apparent who the real mountain climbers were.

I was not much interested in McKinley, and so was not disappointed when Dr. Cook told me that I would not be among those to attempt the summit.

One of our group, William Armstrong, at the first sight of snow on Mt. McKinley, declared that he would "rather jump from the Brooklyn Bridge than climb McKinley above the snowline."

Informed by Dr. Cook that the chance of anyone making it even close to the summit were slim, Professor Parker also turned back. The rest of us were still on the mountain when he was halfway to New York on the eastbound continental.

Dr. Cook chose from among the remaining members of the party a man named William Barrill to be his lone companion on the climb from the snowline to the summit. They left base camp on August 27, fully expecting to fail, and returned on September 22 with the news that they had reached the top. A photograph, taken by Dr. Cook, of Barrill standing at the end of an upward-sloping set of footprints in the snow and holding the American flag on the summit of Mt. McKinley was printed in *Harper's* shortly after we returned to Brooklyn in the fall. Herschel Parker dismissed Dr. Cook's accomplishment as "merely a feat of endurance having no scientific value."

But Dr. Cook was otherwise celebrated as a hero. Peary, his exact whereabouts unknown, was still up north.

Dr. Cook was suddenly in great demand as a lecturer and dinner guest, as was I suddenly in great demand as what the papers called his "precocious sidekick." Wherever he spoke, wherever we went, he said he could not have reached the summit of McKinley if not for me, the only member of the climbing party, including Barrill, who had never doubted him.

As before, I felt that I had merely taken part in an extended camping trip. But I knew that it would diminish his accomplishment to make light of my own contribution to it, so I accepted his compliments with what was taken to be my "characteristically laconic modesty," even though I suspected myself capable of getting lost in Central Park, my promised tutelage at the hands of Dr. Cook having not yet begun.

I was eager to begin what I considered to be our real quest, a quest on which, as it would involve no climbing, Dr. Cook would have the time to explain his methods and strategy to me, and I could be of real assistance to him.

Peary returned after yet another failed attempt to reach the pole, the *Roosevelt* so badly damaged that it had to be moored in Philadelphia for fear it would sink on its way back to its home port of New York.

· C H A P T E R T W E N T Y - E I G H T ·

D R. C O O K C A L L E D M E T O H I S S T U D Y. H E S A I D T H A T O N
December 15, the National Geographic Society would be holding its
annual banquet in Washington, D.C., and he and I had been invited.
Aside from explorers from all over the world, there would be senators,
congressmen, ambassadors.

"And who do you think has been chosen to be the guest of honour?" he said, beaming at me. "Who do you think is to receive the
first-ever Hubbard Medal for exploration, a three-inch-wide gold disc
embossed with a map of the world?"

"It must be you," I said, and suddenly his expression changed.

"Yes," he said, "it must be. In the sense that it *should* be. But it will
not be me. It will be Peary. And we shall be on hand to see him get it."

We went to Washington for the National Geographic Society
banquet, which was held in conjunction with the Eighth International
Geographic Congress. Dr. Cook was invited to present three papers,
the only member invited to give more than two. Peary was chosen to
be the president of the congress *and* the guest of honour at the closing banquet.

In Washington, snow fell straight down in large, wet flakes. The
city was like some playful simulation of the Arctic, the snow laid on for
the amusement of the delegates. Men wearing light coats or none at all
strolled about beneath umbrellas, hopping from one bare patch of
sidewalk to the next in summer shoes.

It was only the second large city I had visited, so Dr. Cook showed me about before the conference began. A city of monuments and massive statues. Grave-looking Lincoln seated with his hands gripping the arms of his chair, his manner that of someone who hated nothing more than to have his likeness taken. Thomas Jefferson. Lincoln and Jefferson were each several storeys high, contained on all sides but one by buildings that imitated those of the republic after which this one had been fashioned. The White House. And nearby, the modest house where George Washington had lived when he was president. The dome of the Capitol Building. We crossed the grey, slow-moving Delaware to Virginia, to Arlington Cemetery, whose scores of white crosses I at first could not make out against the snow, endless fields of wooden crosses marking the gravesites of Americans who had died in wars—the Revolutionary War, the still-remembered Civil War, which ended the year that Dr. Cook was born. Then it was back to Washington, the snow-covered whole of which seemed commemorative of something, though I could not say exactly what.

New York was New York, the mythical America of picture books, but Washington, said Dr. Cook, was the real America. I did not understand what he meant.

America, he said, was a country that, although young, paid tribute to its own heroes, not the long-dead ones of a mother country its citizens had never seen. Self-orphaned from an empire whose opinion of it did not matter to those few who knew what that opinion was. *Tabula rasa.* America had wiped the slate clean and begun again. Never before had a nation grown to greatness as fast as this one had.

"It is wonderful," said Dr. Cook. "Or terrible. I cannot decide."

My mind was reeling by the time we arrived back at the New Willard Hotel, where the congress was taking place and most of the delegates had rented rooms. Mine was next to Dr. Cook's.

Peary, who lived in Washington and was to give the opening address to the congress, sent word that he was sick. Herbert Bridgman spoke in his place, delivering a rambling speech that was largely a summary of Peary's accomplishments to date.

Word went about that Peary was not sick—that in spite of being its president, he planned to visit the congress but once and that was at the closing banquet, where he would be the guest of honour. Speculation began as to why Peary was staying away.

There were stories that he had been seen wandering slowly about the grounds of his house arm in arm with his wife, wearing a dressing gown and looking as though he could not have walked without Mrs. Peary's help.

Soon the congress was rife with rumours that in his acceptance of the Hubbard Medal at the closing banquet, Peary would announce his retirement from polar exploration. Some said that the choice of Peary as the congress president was an outgoing honour bestowed on the *éminence grise* of expeditionaries, who, after a lifetime of distinguished service, would announce, having made it known to the congress months before, that he was retiring.

Some said that he had for months been preparing his speech, trying to find exactly the right note on which to renounce his quest for good. As for the Hubbard Medal, it was to be given in honour of the retirement about which Peary was said to have confided in a few select members of the Peary Arctic Club, including Morris Jesup and Herbert Bridgman.

"The minting and awarding to Peary of a new medal at this stage in his career can mean only one thing," said Otto Sverdrup. "I do not know why I did not think of it before."

It was even said that Peary was going to name the American whom he thought was most likely to be the first white man to reach the pole, and that his doing so would be tantamount to naming his heir, his replacement, who would be accepted as such by the Peary Arctic Club.

No one was more dismissive of these rumours than Dr. Cook. Before and after each lecture we attended at the congress, other delegates huddled about us, including explorers such as the Italian Umberto Cagni, whose farthest north Peary had bettered by a fraction in 1905.

"What do you think, Doctor?" Cagni said on the afternoon of the first day. "Will Peary give up now that he holds the record?"

"Commander Peary would never choose to announce his retirement at an event like this," Dr. Cook said. "If I were retiring, I would not do so at a congress of explorers of which I was the president, would you? One surrenders as discreetly—as privately—as possible, not in front of all one's peers and rivals, not to condescending fanfare and unwanted sympathy."

"What do you think, Mr. Stead?" Cagni asked me. "You from whose strong arm Peary hung between life and death. What is your hunch about this?"

"Commander Peary is the second most determined man I have ever met," I said. "He will retire someday. His most recent voyage might have been his last one, but we will never hear it from *his* lips." Dr. Cook gave me a look, as if to remind me that I should not be critical of Peary in public.

"Spoken like a true protégé," said Cagni, clapping me on the back.

But the other delegates, many of whom had never met Peary, vigorously disagreed, repeating what they said they had been told by members of the Peary Arctic Club.

The Norwegian Roald Amundsen, with whom Dr. Cook had tried for the South Pole on the *Belgica*, was among those who thought Peary would announce his retirement.

"I think Commander Peary's wife has convinced him," Amundsen said, "that this way of doing things is best. No—what is your word for it?—no ambiguity. No doubts. Why not fanfare? The more fanfare, the more fuss, the less like a defeat his retirement will seem."

Dr. Cook smiled as if in fond recollection of the many deeds whose motives the soft-spoken Amundsen had misconstrued because of his too-innocent, too-generous view of human nature.

"My dear friend," Dr. Cook said, "it is not in Commander Peary's nature to take direction from his wife in matters such as these. Nor is it in his nature to admit defeat, publicly or otherwise. Even at Etah, during his long confinement in his tent, when he was so delirious that I feared he would lose his mind for good or even die, he did not speak of defeat or retirement, or the wishes of his wife. We would all, if we followed the wishes of our wives, retire from exploration at this very instant, would we not?"

Everyone laughed, but the rumours persisted and the huddle of explorers, reporters, diplomats and politicians around Dr. Cook and me grew larger with each passing hour of the congress.

We were told of delegates who claimed to have heard from Herbert Bridgman that Peary was practising his farewell speech at home, trying it out on his wife and a few close friends, among them a well-known writer who was helping him revise it. Others said that a copy of Peary's speech had been obtained by some reporter on condition that his paper not print it until after Peary delivered it in person.

"They say that you are mentioned many times in this speech," Amundsen told Dr. Cook. "They say that it is you who will be tapped with Peary's sword. They say that he as good as names you as his successor. Who else could he name? What American would be more deserving of the honour, especially as you saved his wife and child, and Mr. Stead saved him?"

But Dr. Cook only smiled and shook his head, as if the coming banquet address held no suspense for him, however taken in by rumours the rest of them might be.

"There must be some reason that Peary is staying away," Cagni said. "I believe it is because he wants the drama to build. He wants us to do exactly what we are doing: talk about him for days, speculate. And then at the end, the big moment comes, and he appears at last to get his medal and to bid us all goodbye."

On the evening of the third day of the congress, after we had finished dinner, Dr. Cook invited me to his room in our hotel. I sat in an armchair, but he went to the window and looked out at the snow-covered street.

"It seems that it is true, Devlin," he said.

"Peary is finished?" I said, half expecting him to tell me not to be absurd.

"Bridgman himself has shown me the text of Peary's speech," he said. He turned around to face me. He smiled when he saw the look on my face. *His* face was flushed, completely at odds with his voice, which had the noncommittal, faintly reassuring tone of a doctor addressing a patient.

"I know," he said. "I could not believe it at first, either. Even Bridgman was shocked. It seems that until the congress began, Peary had told no one except his wife. Even Morris Jesup did not know. We are to keep this information to ourselves. In the speech, Peary recommends me as his successor. All the members of the Arctic club have assured Bridgman that they will pledge me their support."

"That's wonderful," I said.

"Bridgman has convinced the congress to change the speakers' schedule at the banquet. They have asked me to give the closing remarks. Bridgman says that, symbolically at least, this will be my acceptance speech, my inaugural address, in which I should pay fulsome tribute to my departing colleague. All the waiting is over, Devlin. At last. I feel relieved, of course, and elated. But also terrified. The main task of my life will soon begin. There can be no more rehearsals for us from now on. No more Mt. McKinleys. I knew I would not reach the South Pole, so it did not seem when I fell short that I had failed. But now . . . now everything will be different."

"When did this happen?" I said. "When did you meet with Bridgman?"

"When I left the hotel dining room during dinner. While you were talking with Amundsen."

"You were gone only fifteen minutes at the most," I said.

"Yes," he said. "Fifteen minutes. The lives of greater men than me have changed in much less time than that."

"You were so sure that they were wrong," I said, laughing. "So sure that it was all just gossip."

He extended his hand to me, and I stood up to take it.

"Congratulations, Devlin," he said. I hugged him, still laughing, giddy with this sudden windfall.

CHAPTER TWENTY-NINE

THE WAINSCOTED WALLS OF THE BANQUET HALL OF THE NEW Willard Hotel were hung with bunting, semi-circles of red, white and blue. The four hundred guests would sit at twelve long, mead hall-like tables on which crystalware, silver cutlery and white bone china sparkled beneath a constellation of chandeliers. Dr. Cook and I would sit near the head of table number six, twenty feet from the centre of the dais where Peary was to give his speech.

That morning, the papers had proclaimed: "PEARY TO BID FAREWELL TO EXPLORATION"; "PEARY TO RETIRE AT EXPLORERS' BANQUET"; "PEARY: NORTH POLE UNREACHABLE." All the papers referred to an unnamed source within the Peary Arctic Club. In the very brief stories that accompanied the large headlines, no mention was made of Dr. Cook or the rumours that Peary would recommend as his successor the man who had saved his wife and child.

Bridgman, Amundsen told us, had been unable to resist showing Peary's speech to others besides Dr. Cook, who had been sensibly discreet. I, too, had told no one, but it seemed that Amundsen was right, that everybody "knew." Peary was only nominally the guest of honour. It would soon be revealed that the true guest of honour was Dr. Cook.

I was, unlike Dr. Cook, unable to conceal my excitement. I looked so openly expectant, was such a picture of youthful anticipation, that everyone who looked at me could not help smiling. I rendered pointless, almost comic, Dr. Cook's contained, reserved manner. Standing there beside him, I was like a caricature of his inward self, the self that he thought he was concealing from the world, but that was following him about the room like a mime whose presence he was unaware of.

There was no sign of Peary yet, though it seemed that almost everyone else was there, including more than twenty senators and twice that many congressmen.

"There is much talk about you, too, Devlin," Amundsen said. "For the first time ever, Peary and the young man who saved his life will meet in public."

I was anxious, for there was no telling when Peary might appear at my side, hand extended to shake mine a second time while all around us people gaped. I tried to prepare myself, knowing that if he took my hand, I would recall the first time when he all but crushed it in his, when he spoke about my mother and Francis Stead as though he was casting their curse on me. I had rehearsed a few pleasantries and was prepared to keep smiling for as long as our conversation lasted.

The unmistakable sense in the room that something momentous was imminent grew more palpable as the time for the start of the banquet approached.

"It is as Captain Cagni said," Amundsen told us. "Peary plans to go out in such a way that it will never be forgotten. I dare say he is in the hotel somewhere, waiting until the last moment." Amundsen examined Dr. Cook's face closely, hoping that now, on the brink of the announcement, he would admit that the rumours were correct. Dr. Cook shook his head and smiled. "I think you and Peary must be in this together," Amundsen said.

A phalanx of trumpeters blaringly announced that the serving of dinner would soon commence. But there was still no sign of Peary.

Herbert Bridgman went to the head table and announced from the dais that Commander Peary was unavoidably detained but had insisted that dinner proceed without him. There were many shouted protests, but soon the delegates and guests began to search out their seats at the tables.

As dinner began, Dr. Cook sat there, unable to do anything but smile and nod when people spoke to him.

"This is taking suspense too far," said Cagni. "Peary is the congress president and the banquet's guest of honour. What can he be up to, Dr. Cook?"

Dr. Cook smiled as if all was going according to plan.

The middle four settings of the head table were still unoccupied an hour later. The guests cast glances at the head table and at Bridgman, shaking their heads as if they were not only puzzled, but considered this behaviour of Peary's to be bad form. And why were *four* settings unoccupied? Two were for Peary and his wife, but what about the other two? The president of the National Geographic Society and his wife were sitting to the right of the empty chairs, a senior senator and his wife to the left. It seemed that everyone but the Pearys was accounted for.

Several delegates wandered up to the head table and passed a word with Herbert Bridgman, who faintly shook his head and was clearly trying not to show how mortified he was. He looked genuinely baffled.

How, those people who were seated with Dr. Cook and me wondered, could the Hubbard Medal be presented without Peary? Speculation began that perhaps he really was sick—sicker even than those who had believed this explanation for his absence from the congress had imagined. I looked questioningly at Dr. Cook, who faintly shrugged.

The last of the dessert dishes were being cleared and it seemed that most of the guests had resigned themselves to not setting eyes on Peary that night when the large front doors of the banquet hall were ceremoniously opened by two white-gloved butlers. A lone man dressed in scarlet livery stepped into the room.

"Ladies and gentlemen," he shouted, "the President of the United States of America and the First Lady, Mrs. Roosevelt."

As if it had followed the president to the hotel from the White House but was not allowed into the banquet room, an unseen brass band struck up "Hail to the Chief" somewhere outside the room.

Like an apparition, Teddy Roosevelt and his wife appeared, walking arm in arm, encircled by aides and a two-man colour guard, the beefy president looking uncomfortably crammed into his tuxedo, the overhead lights reflecting in his monocle, which glittered like a brooch. His wife wore a long white dress that flared out slightly at the hem. Her ample form was contained by a tightly tucked bodice from which a slight pouch depended, and she wore around her shoulders a long white fur boa that extended almost to the floor. Her flat, dark hat looked like an extension of her hair, so that it seemed the hat had earflaps, as if she and the others had made the trip from Pennsylvania Avenue on foot through the snow.

The Roosevelts were followed by the Pearys, Peary in full navy uniform. Restored to what I took to be his normal weight, he looked almost nothing like he had at Etah. He carried his hat beneath his arm. His red hair and florid red moustache were newly coiffed. The front of his jacket was festooned with medals and ribbons, its back almost comically bare by comparison. Mrs. Peary's expression seemed to say that at last exploration had yielded something of which she wholeheartedly approved. She wore a flowing dinner gown made of some filmy, gauze-like material, with a narrow frill of transparent lace at the neck and loose transparent sleeves. The skirt, which dragged the floor, was edged with several layers of lace flounces. The dress had a wide waistbelt with a chatelaine bag, a silver-chain purse and, hanging lowest of all from the belt, a thin lorgnette, as if she intended from the head table to examine the assembled guests as one might the cast of some expansive opera.

Peary shuffled along like a man whose toes were bent beneath his feet. It might have been Peary's peculiar, pathetic gait that broke the spell that had fallen over everyone as the foursome arrived, for at last the guests rose to their feet with much scraping of chairs to acknowledge the president, who, the expression on many faces seemed to say, really was here, however unlikely it seemed.

Somewhere in the room there was a burst of applause that was taken up by the rest of us, "an ovation for the President and the First

Lady, and for the President of the congress and *his* first lady," one of the papers would later say.

As we all clapped and watched the presidential procession make its way between the tables towards the dais, many eyes turned towards Dr. Cook and me. Otto Sverdrup, Amundsen, Cagni—all smiled as if to say that Roosevelt was here as much to honour Dr. Cook as to honour Peary. Roosevelt, after whom Peary had named his last ship and who had intervened with Congress to help raise funds for his most recent expedition, would witness and confer his blessing on the passing of the torch to Dr. Cook. It was plain that all of them were not only happy for Dr. Cook, but far more fond of him than they were of Peary, whose farewell address they were eagerly awaiting.

Dr. Cook's colour rose as though every eye in the banquet hall was turned his way, as though he alone had just been announced by the butler and was the object of this thunderous ovation.

It felt as if the announcement had already been made and all that remained was for Peary to place upon it the final flourish of an eloquent goodbye.

Once the Roosevelts and the Pearys were seated, the president of the National Geographic Society, Willis Moore, went to the lectern and read an obviously rehearsed welcome to the newly arrived head-table guests. There was much nodding among the tables, as if everyone were saying they had known all along that Willis Moore knew what was keeping Peary, known all along that he would never allow his annual banquet to fall as flat as for a while it had seemed certain to do.

Among the head-table guests was Dr. Alexander Graham Bell, upon whom Moore called to "say a few words." Dr. Bell, he said, had been a founding member of the society and its second president, and was therefore better suited than anyone for the task he was about to perform.

Dr. Bell had been speaking for some time before I realized that the subject of his address was Dr. Cook, whose colour was even higher than before; he really was the cynosure of all eyes.

"We have with us, and are glad to welcome, Commander Peary,

explorer of the Arctic regions, but in Dr. Cook, we have one of the few Americans, if not perhaps the only American, who has explored both extremes of the world, the Arctic *and* the Antarctic regions. And now he has been to the top of the American continent and therefore, if I may presume to say so, *to the top of the world.*"

There was a marked pause. "The top of the world," Dr. Bell had said, the expression normally used to describe the North Pole.

As if, all at once, the crowd decided that this unfortunate choice of words could be erased only one way, there followed an ovation louder and more vigorous than the one that had greeted the arrival of the President.

Everyone stood, Dr. Cook included, and everyone applauded with the exception of Dr. Cook, who suddenly seemed quite composed, accepting the ovation by bowing to all corners of the room.

Then, like an actor inviting the audience to acknowledge the brilliance of his co-star, Dr. Cook extended his hands as if to say, "I give you Mr. Stead." The ovation rose in volume as I heard Amundsen and Cagni roaring, "Here, here." Amundsen, as though he was a referee and I a triumphant boxer, raised my hand in the air and turned me once about in a circle, with his free hand exhorting everyone around us to cheer louder.

As he did so, I looked up at the head table and saw Peary applauding but not looking my way, instead staring out above the crowd as though interested in something taking place at the back of the room.

When Amundsen released my hand and clapped me on the back, Dr. Bell began to speak again and the guests sat down. My pulse was racing, the blood pounding at my temples. I looked at Dr. Cook, who warmly smiled at me. It was to be be *our* night, not just his.

"I would ask Dr. Cook and Mr. Stead to speak," said Dr. Bell, "except that I have been told that a more appropriate moment for them to do so is still to come." At these words, knowing looks were universally exchanged.

When Dr. Bell finished speaking, Willis Moore called on President Roosevelt to award the Hubbard Medal to Peary.

The President, who was either extemporizing or had memorized his speech, began. "Civilized people," he said, surveying the guests with a glance that seemed to say that they were the epitome of civilized people, "live under conditions of life so easy that there is a certain tendency to atrophy of the hardier virtues. But Commander Peary is proof that, in some of the race at least, there has been no loss of the hardier virtues."

I looked at Jo Peary. How much healthier she was than when I had seen her last. I remembered the narrow, furrowed nape of her neck; her cropped hair hidden by her cap, so that it seemed she might be bald beneath it. Despite how she and her husband had parted at Etah, they had somehow reconciled and here she was, publicly supporting him. More forbearing than Mrs. Cook, it seemed.

I don't know how long I was looking at Jo Peary before I realized that she was looking back at me. She smiled, which at first I took to be an acknowledgment of what we both knew—of the announcement Peary was about to make, from which Dr. Cook and I would benefit. But then I saw that the smile meant something else. It said, How far we are, Mr. Stead, from the place where we met. How different that world is from this one, and how oblivious to that other world all these people are. It was as though we were sharing a joke. I smiled back, and after a second or two, she looked away, still smiling.

"The basis of a successful national character must rest upon the great fighting virtues," President Roosevelt said, "which can be shown quite as well in peace as in war. For months in and months out, Commander Peary, year in and year out, you have faced perils and overcome the greatest risks and difficulties while having to show, in circumstances that were surely like those of war, the moral and compassionate qualities of peace. You bore, in short, the burdens of both war and peace, and even so nearly made it to the pole, came closer to doing so than any other man who ever lived. You have, if I may say so, led your Roughriders up the San Juan Hill of exploration. I present you with this, the first Hubbard Medal, in recognition of the great deed you have done for your country, for the world and for all mankind."

There was an enthusiastic but not riotous ovation, as if that were being saved for the last note of Peary's swan song.

Peary, with assistance from his wife and Willis Moore, rose and scuffed to the podium like some slipper-shod invalid. He shook the hand of President Roosevelt and fought to keep his balance when the President embraced him.

I felt sorry for him. I could summon up no malice for him now, not because of the injury he did my hand, the words he whispered to me or his niggardly acknowledgment of the debt he owed me. Why should I hold anything against him, I asked myself, now that his day had come and gone, now that he was on the verge of saying so?

While he had been seated, he had forever stroked his moustache, but standing he could not do so because to keep his balance while not moving he had to cling to something. When the President released him, he all but lurched to the lectern, which he grabbed with both hands.

For several seconds he stood there, the lectern wobbling as though he was trying to subdue it but could not. His face, for a few moments, took on the ghastly expression it had worn while he hung from my hand between the *Erik* and the *Windward*. Now and then his right hand twitched, as though he wished he could raise it to his face to stroke his moustache.

Peary, I realized, was trying to find some way of standing that would make bearable the pain in his feet. He was wearing formal leather shoes, as round in the toe as the occasion would allow. That his weight was restored to its normal two hundred pounds bode well for the health of everything except his feet, which had to bear that weight, and which, only a few months ago, had somehow sustained him through the rigours of his farthest north. There had been rumours that he had stayed on his dog-pulled sled the entire time, while Matthew Henson, who was not in attendance at the banquet, did the driving, often pushing the sled over great obstacles of snow and ice.

Finally, he stopped shifting his weight from one foot to the other and, grimacing, began to speak. The flow, the rhythm of the words, seemed to ease or distract him from the pain. About once every fifteen seconds, between sentences, he clenched his teeth, his face as red as if he were enraged. He *spoke* as if he were enraged, as if only at a wrathful shout could his voice be trusted not to break.

He recited a retrospective of his accomplishments. It was a suspenseful moment each time he had to remove one hand from the lectern to put aside the page that he had just read. He teetered to the point that I wondered if he ought not have someone beside him to move the pages for him, or if he ought not have opted to give his speech while sitting down.

Each item in his inventory of accomplishments was met with some applause, in which, following Dr. Cook's lead, I took part. Peary mentioned the North Greenland expedition of 1892, on which the man thought by the world to be my father had disappeared. I applauded. Even for what I suspected were embellished stories about his last failed attempt to reach the pole, I applauded.

No one unfamiliar with his history could have guessed that he was only forty-eight years old. His skin was like that of a man who, just the night before, had stepped off a ship from Greenland after two years in the Arctic. He was but ten years Dr. Cook's senior, but he could have passed for his father. His face did not revert to normal between expeditions, like those of other explorers. He had got to the point where the leathering of skin that derives from long exposure to sun, wind and cold was permanent.

There was something grand, almost noble, it seemed to me again, as it had in Etah, in his physical ruination. There was about him the splendour of a monument whose installation no one could remember. I felt more magnanimous towards him, more willing to forgive his many wrongs, than I ever had before. Lear, at the end, was more to be pitied than blamed, and Prospero, through whom Shakespeare bade to the world his own farewell, bowed out with a wistful grace born of old age and experience. Such were the thoughts I was having, thoughts that seemed appropriate to the occasion.

Finally, Peary began to sound as though he were leading up to his great pronouncement. He said that between 1903 and 1905, he had, for the first two consecutive years since 1891, not been north of the Arctic Circle.

"How I missed the Arctic only those of you who have been there can understand. And yet, I felt stirring within me memories of what my life was like before I set foot in the Arctic, what it was like not only to live normally, but to have normal expectations, to not be hounded forever by the knowledge of a task not yet completed—a task many times undertaken which must be taken up again, which would not let me rest, no matter how I longed to be rid of it, to be free of it forever. Again, my fellow explorers will understand."

He paused and drew a great breath, as though to stifle the urge to weep.

"Which brings me to the present," Peary said and paused again.

There was a stir in the banquet hall. Here at last was the great pronouncement.

"Let no one doubt," Peary said, "that I believe in doing the thing that has been begun, and that it is worth doing before shifting to a new object."

There was much nodding and some applause. Then people throughout the hall began to stand. Soon everyone was standing in silent tribute and anticipation.

"The true explorer does his work," Peary said, "not for any hope of rewards or honour. The fact that such names as Abruzzi, Cagni, Nansen, Greely and Peary are indelibly inscribed upon the white disk close to the pole shows that the polar quest is the most manly example of friendly international rivalry that exists. It is a magnificent galaxy of flags that has been planted around the pole, and when eventually some one of them shall reach the pole itself, it will add to its own lustre without in any way detracting from the lustre of the others or leaving any sense of injury or humiliation in its wake."

"But tonight, Mr. President, the Stars and Stripes stand nearest to the mystery, pointing and beckoning. God willing, I hope that your administration may yet see those Stars and Stripes planted at the pole itself."

I assumed that this was the prelude to his abdication.

"This is a thing which should be done for the honour and the credit of this country." He paused, looked up from his speech and surveyed the mass of delegates before him from around the world.

"This is the thing which it is intended that *I* should do," he shouted. "It is the thing that I *must* do. It is the thing that I *will* do."

There was perfect silence in the hall. I think we believed that we had misheard him, that he would yet say something to correct himself, to sweep aside the misunderstanding he had caused.

But Peary took up the pages of his speech and began to shuffle back across the stage towards his chair, beside which Mrs. Peary was standing.

I looked at Dr. Cook, who was staring at the tablecloth, his mouth slightly open, leaning on the table on the knuckles of his two clenched fists. I looked at Amundsen and saw that his eyes were filling with tears, which he left unchecked when they began to trickle down his face. Cagni was shaking his head in disbelief, looking at Dr. Cook as if he could not understand what was keeping him from falling to the floor. I looked around and saw that many people were looking at Dr. Cook, and at me—some with astonishment, some with undisguised pity, a few smiling.

How could we have so profoundly misperceived everything? Absolutely nothing was what, mere seconds ago, it had seemed to be.

I put my hand on Dr. Cook's, and he responded by moving his hand and beginning to applaud, loudly, and at long intervals, as if he was the only person of the four hundred gathered to whom it had occurred that Peary's speech had yet to be acknowledged.

Suddenly, there was an ovation that caused the floor to shake beneath my feet. Cups rattled and spoons jumped as men pounded on the tables with their fists. The word "hurray" or something like it was shouted in many different languages. Old men stamped their feet and applauded with their hands above their heads.

After a few dumbfounded seconds, I managed to join the others in applauding. "Without leaving any sense of injury or humiliation in its wake." I was stung by the irony of Peary's words.

I wondered if the great effort I was making to control myself and conceal my disappointment was apparent to those around me. I felt as self-consciously foolish as if my every thought since arriving at the banquet had been heard by the other delegates.

It occurred to me that in his announcement, Peary had slighted, if not Dr. Cook in particular, then that group of explorers who had done what Peary said he did not believe in doing: "shifting to a new object" before finishing "the one that has been begun." Like Mt. McKinley. Like the South Pole. Peary's ambition for the pole had been unswerving and remained so. Dr. Cook had been more versatile, more catholic in his pursuits. Now it seemed to me that he was being rewarded for his versatility by being lumped in with the gadflies of exploration.

I wondered what had gone wrong, why Bridgman had spoken to Dr. Cook the way he had, what speech it was that he had shown Dr. Cook. Might the whole thing have been a hoax engineered by Bridgman? To what end?

I knew that the man Dr. Cook had examined three years ago in Greenland would not, even if he regained all the strength it was possible for him to regain, reach the North Pole. How could anyone believe that the man who had hobbled and shuffled from his place at the head table to the podium would one day reach the pole? That the Arctic club members would unknowingly be wasting their money on Peary when they might have got the ultimate return for it from Dr. Cook and me was something I wished I could have stood up and shouted. I wished I could have told them all that Peary was in denial of what to all the explorers of the world was obvious. Yet Dr. Cook and I had been made to look like fools.

While the ovation was still at its height, Dr. Cook stopped applauding and again rested his hands on the table, this time palms down, though his head was unnaturally erect, as if he were fighting the impulse of his body to assume a posture of dejection. He began to applaud again, then stopped, again leaned on his hands, perhaps resisting a wave of dizziness or nausea.

The instant Peary made his announcement, Dr. Cook's expectations, which everyone in that banquet hall had shared with him, seemed absurdly grandiose. Everyone had looked at him as if *he* had led *them* to believe that he would be taking Peary's place—as if *he* had been spreading the rumour all week that he had been chosen to replace Peary, something that otherwise would never have occurred to them.

Amundsen was now standing beside Dr. Cook, and the two of them, though not looking at each other, were speaking, Dr. Cook nodding and somehow managing to smile, to convey the impression that he and Amundsen were conferring about Peary's announcement just like everybody else.

As the ovation at last began to subside, I was able to hear what they were saying.

"I know," said Dr. Cook, "but the speech I have prepared is entirely inappropriate."

"Shall I tell them you are ill?" Amundsen said. "Shall I speak in your place?"

"No, no," Dr. Cook said. "I must speak. I must say something. Otherwise they will see, they will know. Though perhaps they have already seen."

"You are among friends, Dr. Cook," Amundsen said fervently.

The delegates sat down. Dr. Bell invited Dr. Cook to give the closing remarks. There was vigorous applause from which a few, including Amundsen and Cagni, tried to work up an ovation, but it petered out. Dr. Cook rose and made his way to the head table and the lectern.

Eyes downcast, he acknowledged the head table, starting with the President and Mrs. Roosevelt. He thanked Dr. Bell for his earlier tribute and thanked the National Geographic Society and the organizers of the congress. At last he looked up.

"What an extraordinary evening this has been," he said. "In this room are gathered or represented all the great explorers of the world. I myself have gone exploring with many of you. May I say what a privilege that has been. I shall not forget it. Nor shall I forget the camaraderie and fellowship that all of us have shared these past few days. Thank you, all of you. And until we meet again, goodbye."

This time there was polite, bemused applause that ended quickly when the unseen orchestra struck up the anthem, after which the Roosevelts and the Pearys began to make their way from the head table to the doors, though their path was soon blocked by well-wishers.

When Dr. Cook took me by the arm and led me towards the back of the room, no one seemed to take much notice. I wound my way with him and Amundsen among the tables. Suddenly, our route became a gauntlet. Hands clasped Dr. Cook's and mine, others thumped our backs. I heard myself addressed over and over but did not reply. It was all well-meant, a sympathetic tribute of some sort. But I felt as though the whole assembly was extending its condolences to us. We might have been leaving the company of these people for good. I felt that at the age of twenty-four, I was being consoled for having failed.

By the time I made it to the door, it seemed that my life depended on my getting out into the open air within the minute.

I pulled myself away from Dr. Cook and Amundsen and, wearing only my hat and tails, hurried outside, where it was snowing heavily. I walked along the sidewalk at what, to observers, might have seemed to be a briskly cheerful pace.

· CHAPTER THIRTY ·

ON THE TRAIN BACK TO BROOKLYN, WE SAT OPPOSITE EACH other in our berth. Dr. Cook might have been returning from what he knew was *his* last try at the pole, so desolate was his expression. Gone was the kind, indulgent, faintly amused look with which formerly he regarded even a landscape devoid of people.

My mind was reeling. I had for hours been trying to raise his spirits. I would have been happy just to make him angry. But he merely stared out the window, watching as a succession of snow-covered towns went by, looking as if everything we passed was to blame for what had happened. To blame, yet irreproachable, remote, indifferent, oblivious to anything he said or did.

"There is no point denying that what happened changes everything," said Dr. Cook. "They saw me fall, laid low. They saw me as no man should ever let himself be seen by other men. So vulnerable. So defenceless against scorn and pity. I was completely fooled. I have always, even when all signs pointed to success, prepared myself for failure. 'There is many a slip / 'twixt the cup and the lip.' That has been my motto. Never presume. Never celebrate too openly, lest you seem and feel all the more foolish when your hopes are dashed.

"Yet I left myself open to be jilted in public, so certain did the outcome seem this time. There is something ominous about near triumph, Devlin. It is a rule of the universe that anyone who comes this close and fails will never get a second chance. Everyone in that banquet room sensed it. In the eyes of the money-men, I am tainted with bad luck.

"Even if Peary undertakes but one more expedition and, when he fails, gives up at last, I will not be chosen to succeed him. No one who was there last night will forget the way I looked. That I was in no way to blame for what happened, that I in no way brought it upon myself, will not matter. What will matter is that they saw me brought down from the height to which *they* had raised me.

"Last night I told myself that I could bear it if someone else makes it to the pole before me or you, as long as that someone else is not Peary. Last night, in my room, I said out loud, over and over, 'Anyone but Peary.' How absurd it seems. I have been reduced to bargaining with destiny by a man whose efforts are foredoomed to failure. I know he will not reach the pole, yet I cannot help dreading that he will."

"It is not over for us," I said. "If it is not yet over for Peary, think how much remains for us to do."

He shook his head.

"Not everything is lost," I insisted, fighting back tears, as I had been doing for hours, though I had let them flow freely in my room the night before. When we met in the morning, my swollen eyes made it so plain to Dr. Cook how I had spent the night that for a moment he took me in his arms. "We may have to do things some other way than we had planned," I said. "That's all."

"I am sorry for what has happened to you because of me," he said.

"Not because of you," I said. "Because of... I don't know who to blame."

"You *should* know," he said. "Who do you think started that rumour? By whom was I misled?"

"You might not have been misled," I said. "Some people say that the rumour was well-founded, that the speech Bridgman showed you was not a forgery, but that Peary changed his mind at the last second, in part because he was urged to do so by the President."

"When do they say that Peary changed his mind? Are these the same people who started the rumour in the first place?"

"They say that he changed his mind just minutes before he arrived. That even Jo Peary, as she sat there listening, did not know what he planned to say. You heard the speech. Right up to the end, it sounded like he was saying goodbye. Perhaps all he did was change the last few words."

"I wouldn't be surprised if Peary put Bridgman up to it."

"What if Bridgman didn't know that Peary had changed his mind? What if Peary didn't know that you had seen his speech and Bridgman didn't know that Peary had changed it? It might all have been completely innocent. An accident."

"It was no accident," he said.

In my mind, I saw Peary shuffle, slump-shouldered, across the stage towards his chair, where his wife was waiting for him. He had looked as if he had done what everyone expected him to do. He had looked done in. The ovation he received was exactly as I had imagined it would be. A roaring, raucous send-off for a man who, after surviving feat after feat of exploration, had just renounced his ultimate quest, just bequeathed it to a younger man. Minutes before Peary made his intentions known, I had seen Dr. Cook smiling and applauding as if, now that Peary was no longer a rival, there was no need for reserve, no reason not to join the others in this last salute to the grand old man of exploration. How nightmarishly close it had all been to what Bridgman had led us to expect.

I couldn't help thinking how different things would be now if I had been a fraction of a second slower grabbing out for Peary when he fell. He would already be forgotten. Dr. Cook would long ago have been chosen to replace him. He—we—might have made it to the pole and back by now. Dr. Cook would have been president of the congress and guest of honour at the banquet. He, not Peary, would have won the first Hubbard Medal. He, not Peary, would have walked into the banquet room with Roosevelt.

I felt ashamed of myself for thinking such things. For Dr. Cook, I foresaw unhappiness that I felt helpless to prevent. I wondered what would become of him and me if he had to face up to the certainty of failure—what would sustain us through all the secrecy, all the pretence and collusion, if we ceased to be explorers. What would he feel for me once he put aside the hope of redeeming his betrayal of my mother?

But how unfair of me it was to doubt him now.

"What must I do, Devlin?" Dr. Cook said. "We were to have undertaken polar expeditions together. I was to have taught you, prepared you to lead expeditions of your own. I can see no way now that this can happen. Marie cannot help us. Underwriting the cost of climbing Mt. McKinley is one thing, but a series of polar expeditions, even one expedition, is beyond her means. Perhaps you should apply for a place on other expeditions. I'm sure that Amundsen would take you with him on his next try for the South Pole if we asked him to."

"I will not take part in any expeditions without you," I said. "Perhaps both of us could go with Amundsen. You would greatly increase his chances of success. And if you were part of a successful try for the South Pole, the backers here would be impressed. You would be keeping your hand in the game. And I could learn from both of you."

"I cannot go back to serving under someone else," he said. "Not even Amundsen. Besides, if I was part of a *Norwegian* expedition that made it to the pole, I would be *persona non grata* in New York. My participation in the Belgian expedition did not win me any friends here."

"Nothing has happened from which you cannot recover," I said.

"We may never get there, Devlin," he said. "In spite of what I promised you—"

"No one could be certain of keeping such a promise," I said.

"Then you doubt me, too?" he said.

"No," I said. "No, I just meant... it would not be as though you had broken your promise wilfully."

"You mean," he said, "it would not be as though I had betrayed you?"

"I was not thinking of betrayal."

"I have devoted my life to fulfilling that promise."

"Perhaps you have invested too much of yourself in me," I said. "Your wife and... and your other children—"

He shook his head and winced, as if to say, "If you only understood, you would not mention *them*."

"I am meant to be destroyed by this," he said. "As important as it is to Peary that he succeed, it is just as important to him that I fail."

"Why?" I said. Then I added, when he did not answer, "Is *his* failure as important to you as *your* success?"

"*Our* success," he said. "Yours and mine together. Never forget that. But no, I am not like him. I do not share his motives. He has done things I would never do."

Eyes closed, he was silent for a long time. I thought he had fallen asleep.

"Devlin, there is something I must tell you. Perhaps I should have done so before, but I had hoped to spare you. Perhaps there is no other way, however, of making you understand why Peary must not be allowed to reach his goal."

I felt the same dread as I had when we first met in the drawing room.

"I told you that on the North Greenland expedition, Francis Stead took me aside one morning and told me his story, including what Peary had told him: that I was the man with whom his wife betrayed him, the father of her son. But he also told me something else.

"We sat on the 'bench,' the ledge on the back of the tolt of rock some distance from Redcliffe House. As we spoke, he puffed on his cigars. It all happened just as I described to you before. He told me that when he and his wife had been married nearly two years, he had abandoned her and gone to Brooklyn."

Under a pseudonym, Francis Stead booked passage on a steamer to St. John's. He wore a disguise that he bought at an auction. The props of a play that had closed were being sold off: muttonchop whiskers, thick eyebrows, a florid moustache and heavy burnsides, and a suit of clothing of a style that had been in fashion twenty years earlier. He had no need of makeup, for his face, even then, was leathered from the time he'd spent up north.

This was in late March. There was a channel through the ice, barely enough for the steamer to make it to the Narrows, just inside of which it docked, for all the berths in the harbour were either occupied or crammed with ice. It was not far from where the ship docked to Devon Row.

Francis Stead tipped his hat to the one or two people he passed along the way to the nearest hotel. St. John's is a seaport. There are always strangers, strange-looking strangers, on the street. No one paid him much attention.

After checking in under his pseudonym, he went straight to the house. It was about one-thirty in the afternoon. He knew that the boy was of school age and would not yet be home. They had never had servants. It was likely that his wife had none now. There were no vehicles about except the cabriolet, which he recognized as hers, and that meant she was unlikely to be having visitors. Either she was alone in the house or it was empty. If someone other than her answered the door, he would pretend he had the wrong address and leave to find some other way of contacting her.

He struck the knocker several times. The door opened, and there she was. It seemed to him that she looked exactly the same as she had when he left, that she was even dressed the same. She did not recognize him, not even when he said her name. "It's me," he said. She looked at him for a long time, then walked backwards, holding the door with both hands as if to keep it between them, to shield herself with it. It seemed that for a few seconds, she did not realize he was wearing a disguise. She seemed to take his appearance as the measure of how long they had been apart.

She said nothing at first, only sat on the edge of a chair in the front room, looking at the fire. He wondered what she thought, his showing up like this on the doorstep after all this time. Done up like this.

"Devlin will soon be coming home from his aunt's house," she said.

He asked her if they might make their separate ways to Signal Hill, where they would have some privacy. "I believe you are as anxious as I am that no one know I came to visit you," he said. She said nothing. He assured her that she would not keep the boy and his aunt waiting long.

"What is it that you want to speak to me about?" she said.

He asked her if he might wait to explain himself until they met on Signal Hill.

She went upstairs, changed for the outdoors, came back down. He told her to wait for twenty minutes, then take the cabriolet to the top of the hill. He asked her to pretend, if they were approached by anyone on the hill or if someone later asked her who he was, that he was a visiting relative or an acquaintance of her husband's from New York. He took her silence for agreement.

He went outside and strode briskly up the road. A raw cutting wind was blowing from the west, but his exertions kept him warm. She passed him when he was near the top of the hill. She looked at him, but he looked straight ahead.

She had been waiting perhaps five minutes in the cab by the time he reached the crest. There was no one else about. They could not be seen from the blockhouse, though he could tell by the smoke that spewed out along the ridge that it was occupied.

He joined her in the cab.

"Even Pete does not remember you," she said. It was true. The horse, had he recognized his voice or scent, would have been tossing his head about by now, in greeting or in protest. "What do you want, Francis?" she said. "Obviously you do not mean to stay or you would not be dressed the way you are."

For a trace of a second, she smiled in a way that infuriated him. "Dressed the way you are." On the occasion of seeing him for the first time in years, she was trying not to laugh at how he looked.

They were sheltered from the wind and the noise it made by the hood of the cab. He told her about Peary, said that Peary had given him the name of the boy's father. At this she gave a start and looked at him, but then she turned away again, as if she thought he might be trying to fool her into revealing the man's identity. As he continued, she listened, her face expressionless, he thought, until he realized that she was mute with fear, realized that he was shouting, screaming at her.

He tried to calm himself.

"If you will just admit that you lied to me," he said, "if you will just admit that much, that would be enough. I will not insist on your telling me his name or how you met, or anything else. If you will admit that you lied, I will not even ask you why." If she had spoken up then . . . But it seemed to him that despite her fear, she could not bring herself to take him seriously.

"I told you the truth," she said, "and I will not speak of it again." She said it with such finality he knew that further questions would be pointless. He took her by the upper arm, put his face close to hers and tried to kiss her.

She pulled away from him and jumped from the carriage, began to run towards the road that led down to the city. He ran after her, blocked her way. She turned again and ran towards the blockhouse. Again he caught her, blocked her path, though he did not touch her.

"What are you doing?" he said.

She screamed something, but the wind carried the sound away from the hill.

Seeming to know just what she was doing, seeming to think it led to safety, she began to run down the hill towards the sea. She must have misremembered, miscalculated something, thought she knew of a path but, in her panic, was unable to find it. It was a very great distance to the bottom, but the grassy slope was so steep that he could run no faster than she could. On this, the side of the hill that in the spring faced the wind and rain, there was no snow left. When she could go no farther without plunging off the grassy ledge above the ice, she ran a little to the side, then stopped. She shouted something, seeming to have realized what a blunder she had made by running down the hill.

She turned to face him. Both of them were gasping for breath. "It crossed my mind," she said, "down at the house. Just for a second, it crossed my mind that this was your intention. But I told myself you would never do such a thing. Yet it was only that you could not bring yourself to do it in that house. Francis, please think about the boy. The boy has no one else but me."

"What do you mean?" he said. "What is it that you think I have brought you here to do?"

He had never seen such fear in a person's eyes before. Behind her, perhaps fifteen feet below her, wave after wave of slushy water shrugged itself ashore from the edge of the ice.

"If you tell me his name, I will let you go," he said.

She tried to get past him, but he caught her around the waist and dragged her to the edge. "Tell me his name," he said, "or it will be your son's turn next."

"All right," she said. "All right."

"Do not lie to me," he said. "If I find that you have lied to me, I will come back for the boy."

She spoke the name.

"Let me go," she said.

He could not believe how strong, how wild she was. She got loose from him two or three times, punching, biting, clawing at his face. A smaller man would have been no match for her. He believed that if she got by him, he could not have caught her going up that hill.

He grabbed her around the waist from behind and threw her over. She made no sound. She disappeared beneath the water and did not come up. Not once.

He climbed the slope, then descended the other side of the hill on foot. He met no one on the road. He did not really expect to get away with it. Though he had taken pains to avoid detection, he felt almost certain they would fail. He felt as though he didn't care one way or the other.

He went back to his hotel and stayed there, waiting for the knock on the door that never came. He read in the paper the next day that her empty horse and carriage had been found on Signal Hill and her body in the water at the bottom. He was startled when he saw his name, thinking that he had been found out: "Wife of the explorer Francis Stead, who for the past few years has lived in Brooklyn, New York." That was all it said about him, the words seeming to imply that, deserted by her husband, abandoned, she had died by her own hand. "Cause of death as yet unknown," it said.

He booked passage out on a ship that would make port in two days. By the time the ship arrived, the whole city was talking about "poor Mrs. Stead who drowned herself," though the official cause of death was accidental drowning. It had never occurred to him that suicide would be suspected. More than suspected—assumed. Apparently, she had long been regarded as "odd," "peculiar," something of a hermit, people said.

Her reputation was his alibi. It seemed to him that he was meant to get away undetected.

His ship made port, and he went back to Brooklyn.

"I have known of this for so long," Dr. Cook said. "I did not think it would pain me so much to speak of it."

He covered his face with his hands and sobbed. I, too, was crying, looking out the window of the train at my reflection.

"I cannot bear to think that she died that way because of me," Dr. Cook sobbed. "Alone, at the bottom of that hill, at the hands of a man driven mad by what I did. I turned away from her, Devlin. Three weeks. Three weeks I knew her, and every day I think of her and wish that I had had the courage to answer her last letter, to say yes.

"Nothing in her life was undone by the manner of her death. I tell myself that over and over."

I could speak no words of comfort to him, nor even *feel* anything for him. I had never really felt my mother's presence, her absence, until now. For the first time in my life, I felt sorrow for her, which was so much heavier, so much more gravid, than mere sadness. Had I been standing, I would have fallen to the floor beneath its weight.

I thought of that unremembered afternoon when I had sat in the house, wondering until it got dark where my mother was, why she was not there to meet me at the door as she always was.

"She told him my name, Devlin, in the hope of saving you. For all she knew, he would go straight to the house anyway when he was done with her. But there was at least a chance he would not. I'm sure it was not just in the hope of escaping that she struggled with him. She tried to throw him from the ledge or pull him over with her."

A shudder of revulsion passed through me. Francis Stead, while I sat alone in my mother's house as it grew dark, had sat in his hotel room less than a hundred yards away, also waiting, wondering when they would come for him.

Dr. Cook looked at me.

"When Francis finished his story, I asked him what he meant to do with me. 'Nothing,' he said. 'I joined this expedition with the intention of killing you. But I have changed my mind. I mean to do nothing at all.' He turned and began to walk back to Redcliffe House. Then he faced me again. 'I have told Peary everything,' he said. 'Just a few hours ago. I also told him that I would confess to you.'

"That night, he walked away from Redcliffe House and was never seen again."

He looked as drained as if he had just heard of her death for the first time.

For ten minutes, as the train jostled about on the tracks, we both looked out the window.

"Over the next few months," he said "some parts of Francis Stead's story kept coming back to me. Such as his account of how ferociously your mother struggled for her life. There should have been bruises on her body that gave evidence of such a struggle, bruises that even someone predisposed to think that she had killed herself would have noticed. Her forearms, especially her wrists, would have been bruised from where he held her to keep her from striking him. She would have had bruises on her face, especially around her mouth from having tried to bite him. Her clothing would have been in a tell tale state of dishevelment, certainly torn and probably with pieces missing. Yet her death had so quickly been ruled an accident and the rumours of suicide had been allowed to flourish.

"I was so puzzled that about a year after the expedition, I visited St. John's to conduct an investigation of my own. I discovered that there was no coroner, as such, in St. John's at the time of your mother's death. Post-mortems were conducted, at the request of the police, by whatever physicians were available. I looked up your mother's death certificate. Accidental drowning, it said. It was signed by your uncle. I am not suggesting that he was in any way involved in your mother's death. He might have guessed, however, or considered it a possibility, that Francis was responsible. Without ever having communicated with Francis, he might have done what he could to cover it up, but it does not seem very likely. I think something like this happened: The police allowed him to do the post-mortem as a favour to one of their own, so to speak, a favour to a doctor they had often worked with in the past. Given your mother's circumstances, the police would have presumed suicide, as would your uncle. A matter to be handled delicately, everyone would have agreed. Your uncle might have asked if he, a family member, could do the post-mortem just to keep gossip to a minimum. Then, to his surprise, he finds evidence of murder, which he withholds from the police not to protect Francis, but to minimize the scandal, to keep it from getting out that his brother's wife was murdered. People are almost never murdered by strangers. There had, I discovered from talking to some people when I was in St. John's, been rumours about your mother. Unfounded rumours, I have no doubt whatsoever, though your uncle might have believed them. Even if he was certain or thought it likely that the rumours were unfounded, he would have known that people would draw their own conclusions: that she was killed by one of the many men she supposedly consorted with, disreputable men. In the public mind, her having been murdered would, perversely, confirm the rumours, especially if the murder went unsolved, which he would have known was likely, given the absence of any suspects. Better to cover it up for the sake of the family name, for his and his brother's sake, and even, I supposed, not yet knowing your uncle, for Amelia's sake.

"When I wrote to him, I told him that Francis had confessed to the murder of Amelia. I did not, of course, tell him that I was your father. I made no explicit threats, no mention of the death certificate. I was fairly certain that he would co-operate. Francis spoke often about your uncle. I think he was the only man that Francis Stead understood. He understood his brother much better than he understood himself, even though the two of them were very much alike.

"If accusations that Amelia had been murdered came out—if I made public the story I was told by Francis Stead and it was revealed that your uncle had signed her death certificate, citing accidental drowning as the cause of death—he would have been suspected of having covered up the murder of his brother's wife. It would have ruined his reputation.

"So he complied with my every suggestion. I asked him to forward my letters to you unopened—that is, with the seal unbroken. I let him assume that I had instructed you to tell me when a seal was broken, and that I had devised some system whereby you would know if he had withheld a letter from you. I'm sure he never read the letters. You may think of what I did as blackmail. But I enlisted his help without harming him or extracting from him anything he valued. I felt I had to. Corresponding secretly with a grown-up is difficult enough. To do so with a child impossible without some such arrangement as I devised."

So Uncle Edward, as I had suspected, did not know that Dr. Cook was my father.

"I should have told you before how she died. But imagine my dilemma. You had for so long believed that your mother had taken her life. Should I now break your heart a second time and tell you she was murdered by her husband?"

"Why have you told me now?" I said.

"So you would know that Peary is in part to blame for your mother's death. Because he, for the pettiest of reasons, gave Francis Stead my name. Peary knows that I blame him, though we have never talked about it. He knows that he *is* to blame—he and I and Francis Stead. He despises me. How I regard *him,* he is well aware. It has never been more important to me that you understand his nature. That you understand why his failure is as important to me as our success."

· CHAPTER THIRTY-ONE ·

THE NEW YORK PAPERS DID NOT REPORT DR. COOK'S
humiliation as fully as we had feared they would. Since there had been
no mention of Dr. Cook in the stories about Peary's plan to "abdicate,"
there was also no explicit mention of the affect of Peary's change of
heart on Dr. Cook. *The New York Times* said that Peary had "unambiguously declared his intention to keep trying for the pole," that he
had expressed the fervent hope that he would succeed while
Roosevelt was in the White House, and that his announcement had
taken many by surprise, "including the evening's alternative guest of
honour, the mountain climber Dr. Frederick Cook."

Still, I wondered how we would be received by Manhattan society. I had no doubt that it was widely known that the congress of
explorers had all but thrown Dr. Cook a parade in advance of Peary's
speech, that he and I and countless others had assumed that we would
return from Peary's city to our own in triumph, Dr. Cook wearing the
mantle that Peary had discarded.

"Perhaps we should wait a while before accepting any invitations,"
Dr. Cook said. I told him that would only make things more awkward
when we did accept one.

At first, it seemed to me that we were not regarded much differently than before. No one mentioned what took place in Washington.
And therefore it seemed to be invoked by every word.

I wondered if *I* should talk about Washington, enough to give the
impression at least, however transparently untrue it might be, that no

great harm had come of what had happened, that we had merely suffered a rough knock of the sort to which, as explorers, we were well-accustomed. We had come out the worse, I might imply, but our friendly rivalry with Peary was far from settled. But I was not sure I could bring it off.

"They hardly seem to care about what happened," I said one night as we were heading home from a Christmas party.

"Of course they care," said Dr. Cook. "Everyone knows and cares. We are, if anything, even more interesting to them than before. A highly interesting chapter has just concluded, but it is still too soon, because of you, to guess how the book will end. I believe I would no longer be invited out if not for you."

I told him that this was nonsense, that it was clearly his company they valued more. He said nothing, as if I had protested so lamely that I had proved his point.

"I think I would prefer it if they simply let me be," he said. "There really is no reason why you cannot attend these functions by yourself. They believe that you are still worth watching. But they will soon see that *I* am not."

This seemed to me to be an unfair assessment of the people at whose homes we were dining every other night and attending balls and parties. Most of them seemed to me to be far more sympathetic to us than he made them out to be.

"I am like a match," he said. "They use me to start a conversation and then discard me."

I demurred, but I soon realized that there was some truth in what he said.

Not that he was avoided or ignored. If anything, he was approached, addressed, even more often than before.

One evening, a woman asked him which of the poles he thought would be discovered first.

"The South," said Dr. Cook. "In the Antarctic, there is a landmass beneath the ice and snow, so one does not have to deal with ocean currents. You see, there is no fixed North Pole *per se*, for the ice is always moving. The north polar explorer seeks after what is merely an illusion."

This was followed by many disapproving murmurs and much shakings of heads.

"But surely, Dr. Cook," said a man whose family had made its fortune in the manufacture of steel rivets, "those same ocean currents could be used to one's advantage if one knew what was one was doing. If, instead of travelling against the currents, one travelled with them, one would make up time, not lose it, would one not?" But he looked for a reply not to Dr. Cook, but to a young man who sat across from him and nodded vigorously before elaborating on the other man's suggestion. Neither of them had the faintest idea what he was talking about, but it was clear that Dr. Cook's appraisal of their ideas would not be welcomed. He could, if he wished, have been just one of many disputants at the table, but this was not in his nature. He sat there in silence.

In this way, throughout dinner, were started conversations from which, after making a few contributions, he wound up being excluded, or excluding himself. No longer consulted, no longer inclined to offer his opinion, he sat there expressionless.

It was clear that everyone felt a great deal more sympathy for me than they did for him.

It seemed to me that at our first few gatherings after the congress, the men gave my hand an extra, encouraging squeeze and everyone's tone was more solicitous than usual, as if they wanted me to know, without embarrassing me by a direct allusion to it, that they thought that what happened to me in Washington was a bit of bad luck that could have befallen anyone who happened to be seated next to Dr. Cook, and that no one thought any less of me because of it.

It seemed to have become the collective mission of Manhattan society to salvage me from the wreck of Dr. Cook. Clearly, people were concerned about my being fastened to someone whose star was falling. I even sometimes suspected that those little extra squeezes of my hand were meant to tell me something, perhaps that I should consider whether it would be best for me to strike out on my own, as Dr. Cook himself had come close to suggesting.

I saw Kristine two weeks after I came back from Washington. I began to ask her if she had heard of what happened, but, as if she hadn't heard a word I said, she wondered if it might not be time for us to start calling each other by our first names. "Or should I just be grateful," she said, "that you call me *something* instead of just looking at me when you speak as you do with Dr. Cook?" I told her that first names would be fine.

"Then I will say yours first," she said. "That way, it may take you less than five years to get around to saying mine. What do you think of that, Devlin?"

"That's fine with me," I said, and paused until she prompted me by raising her eyebrows expectantly. "That's fine with me, Kristine."

"There," she said, "that wasn't so difficult, was it? That's what names are for, you see, Devlin. They're a way of letting people know that you remember having met them before, that you aren't mistaking them for someone else or that you believe that everyone who is not you goes by the name of 'you.' They help us sort out who is talking to whom and who it is we are talking about. They help us avoid confusion such as you might have if ten people answered the same question all at once. Names make it possible to get someone's attention from a distance, rather than getting everyone's attention and then having to point and say, 'No, not you, *you*' a lot. Am I teasing you too much? The truth is, I love names. I love to say them and hear mine being said. You can tell a lot by how people say each other's names. You can't let someone know you like them without calling them by name, can you?"

"Kristine," I said. "Kristine, Kristine, Kristine."

· CHAPTER THIRTY-TWO ·

EVERY NIGHT, I HEARD HIS FOOTSTEPS IN THE HALLWAY AS HE made his way to the drawing room. He no longer turned on any lights, no longer spoke out loud or paced about. All I saw beneath the door was the faint, wavering glow from the fireplace. All I heard were the sounds of the fire.

Some mornings when I left my room, the doors of the drawing room were still closed. I believe that he would have stayed in there past the start of his office hours had I not woken him by knocking. "I'm up, I'm up," he'd shout in weary protest, and I would hurry away to spare him the embarrassment of being seen.

This went on throughout a perfunctory celebration of Christmas, including Christmas Day, when Mrs. Cook invited me for dinner and I met my half-sister, Helen, for the second time.

Mrs. Cook, now that she could attribute her husband's unhappiness to the events in Washington and now that it seemed possible that his days of exploration were over, was not so resentful of my presence in her house.

If not for the sullen silence of Dr. Cook, we might have passed the day quite pleasantly. I felt him watching as Mrs. Cook and I chatted amiably and took turns noticing what Ruth and little Helen were doing.

"A Mr. John Bradley has asked to meet with me," said Dr. Cook one day after reading the mail that I had brought him. "He wishes me to take him up north on a hunting expedition. He wants to shoot walrus and, if possible, a polar bear."

Dr. Cook was often asked to lead what he called "a slaughter charter" to the North. But he seemed unaccountably excited at having received an offer from this particular trophy hunter.

He told me that Bradley was the millionaire owner of the Beach Club gambling house in Palm Beach. "But he has an apartment in Manhattan," said Dr. Cook. "West Sixty-seventh Street. Very elegant."

"You've been there?" I said.

"No, no," said Dr. Cook. "I just meant that part of Manhattan."

When he got back, he told me nothing of his meeting with Bradley except what Bradley looked like. He had lunched alone with the flashily dressed Mr. Bradley, who had the square-shouldered, smooth-waisted look of the dandies we so often gawked at in the streets, though he was much older than they were.

His hair was parted down the middle, and except for a trim moustache, he was clean-shaven. He must have been on his way to some formal event after lunch, Dr. Cook said, for he was wearing a very high, stiff collar that made it impossible for him to lower his chin even slightly. He also wore a stiff-bosomed shirt that further restricted his movement, so that he had to all but stand to look behind him.

A few days later, as we were taking the Third Avenue el train back from Manhattan to the Brooklyn Bridge, where we would change trains for Bushwick, he made an announcement.

"I have decided to accept Mr. Bradley's offer," Dr. Cook said. "It is quite a generous one. The money I will make I can put to good use someday."

"When will we leave?" I said, trying to sound excited at the prospect of going north as the employee of a man like Bradley.

"In the spring," he said. "You will learn something, even from an expedition of this kind. But I should warn you that there is no 'hunting' to be done up north. It will just be target practice with live four-legged targets. Not even that. The muskoxen, for instance, will not even *walk* away if you approach them. There will be a bloody slaughter, a slaughter in which I will be expected to take part. But you will not."

His tone of voice was completely at odds with the words he was speaking. He sounded almost euphoric.

As we crossed the river, I was reminded of the day I crossed over from Manhattan for my first meeting with Dr. Cook, the scrolled letters in the doctor's bag, which I held on my lap with both hands, so conspicuously fearful that someone would steal it.

Dr. Cook was staring out the windows of the train as if this was *his* first crossing of the bridge to Brooklyn, gazing dreamily at the water, which on the west side was in the shade of the riverside factories and warehouses. He turned in his seat, glanced over his shoulder at the skyline of Manhattan, the palisade of buildings lit aslant by the pink cast of mid-winter twilight.

I felt a sudden rush of affection for him. If not for me, I told myself, this man—who is my father, but for whom I have no name that I can bring myself to say or that he can stand to hear—would be alone. More alone than I have ever been.

The number of people by whom we were surrounded—in the train, on that bridge between the two great boroughs of Brooklyn and Manhattan—seemed to be the measure of his loneliness. I felt an urge to link my arm in his and assure him, son to father, that even if he spent the rest of his days leading slaughter charters to the Arctic, everything would somehow be all right.

On behalf of his employer, Dr. Cook purchased a fishing schooner that he found in Gloucester, Massachusetts, and renamed the *Bradley*. It weighed 111 tons after it was overhauled. It was braced fore and aft, its bow and stern sheathed with steel plates and its sides with interlocking blocks of oak. The rigging and the sails were replaced and a fifty-five horsepower Lozier gasoline engine installed.

It was no *Roosevelt*, said Dr. Cook, but "it will get us as far as we need to go."

Cabins were built for the captain, the mate, Bradley, Dr. Cook and

me. He and I would have one each this time, unlike on the rescue
expedition. There was hammock space for five sailors and a cook. The
captain was Moses Bartlett, a relation of the Bartletts who had manned
the *Windward*.

When Dr. Cook returned from Gloucester, he left the doors of
the drawing room open almost every night. We sat for hours in front
of the fire. He was full of what I took to be false bluster, eager to talk,
to be listened to.

"They say that Peary will leave again for the North a year from
now," I said, when I had a chance to interject. "They say that he has
been pledged well over a hundred thousand dollars—"

"We, too, will be leaving for the North next year," he said. "We
will finance our expedition with the money we make from Bradley's
slaughter charter. Peary will be livid, thinking that we are trying to
steal his thunder. We will have to stay out of his way, which we can easily do since the route I plan to take is very different from his."

"Will we really be able to afford it?" I said.

"With the money from Bradley," said Dr. Cook, "with a contribution from Marie and from some other sources who have promised
they will help, we should be able to mount a solid expedition of our
own. It is not necessary to spend what Peary plans to spend to reach
the pole. I know how it should be done, Devlin. Explorers have been
going about it the wrong way for years. We will reach the pole the way
we reached the top of Mt. McKinley. Once we were past a certain
height, Bill Barrill and I climbed and kept climbing, sleeping only
when we had to. That way, you see, we did not weigh ourselves down
with equipment and supplies. Beyond a certain point, such things are
just nuisances that slow you down."

I had no idea how much wisdom there was in all of this. I had yet
to do any polar travelling, yet to spend a winter in the Arctic. I had no
idea what was possible and what was not, what recommended one
strategy over another. But I could not help being excited just at the
thought of trying next spring for the pole, however unlikely it was that
we really could afford to make a bid for it that soon.

"Please do not speak to Marie about this hunting expedition. I have told her that I am going along with Bradley to study and photograph the Eskimos. She knows of Bradley and does not approve of my association with him. Nor should she, I suppose. Even though she knows that I will be back in September, the mere fact that I am going north upsets her. She thinks I am not yet fully recovered from climbing Mt. McKinley. She keeps asking, as she has asked me before all my other expeditions, 'Well, suppose you don't come back?' What can I do except remind her that she knew what I was when she married me? And I tell her, of course, that I will come back. I tell her that we will rarely have occasion to leave the ship, and that when we do, we will always have dry land beneath our feet. You have been to the Arctic in the summer, Devlin. This trip will be even less hazardous than that one was. Like summering on Signal Hill."

BOOK FIVE

· C H A P T E R   T H I R T Y - T H R E E ·

WE SET SAIL FROM GLOUCESTER ON JULY 3, 1907, DR. COOK having said his goodbyes to Marie and the children in New York. I said goodbye to Kristine while walking with her in Prospect Park, where she had agreed to meet with me when I told her I was going north again. It was the first such meeting we had ever had. "I wish you weren't going," she said after we had walked in silence for some time and had doubled back to our el train station, where she would go one way and I the other. She kissed me so quickly on the lips there was no time to kiss her back. "There," she said. "Don't say goodbye." She ran up the stairs to her station platform.

Dr. Cook had arranged for four months' supply of food, plus another year's allowance in case of stranding or shipwreck. He ordered five thousand gallons of gasoline. He issued all the orders for equipment, overseeing everything down to the smallest detail.

We were not a week gone when I was wishing that I could go to sleep and wake up to find that two months had passed and we were headed home again, home to Kristine. I wished this was a polar expedition, *the* expedition on which he had years ago invited me to join him.

When the hunting trip was almost over, Dr. Cook gave to Bradley a letter for Mrs. Cook, which she would receive in about a month, and which, by way of breaking the news to me, he let me read.

My dearest Marie:

*I have wonderful news, though I fear that it may be some time
before you are able to fully share in my excitement. I find that I
have here a good opportunity to try for the North Pole and therefore
plan to stay here for the year.*

She would be unable to believe what she had read. I sat down and
read it again, and still could not believe it. I had thought we were
leaving for home in a week. I had been looking forward to it, but I
was anything but disappointed now. We were trying for the pole. Not
next year. This year, just as in my pipe dreams I had hoped. I hugged
Dr. Cook, who laughed and clapped me on the back with both
hands.

*I have never known the game to be more plentiful. The
Eskimos tell me it has been the best hunting season that even the
oldest of them can remember. They predict that next year will not be
nearly so good. They also predict that once the Arctic night has
passed, conditions for travelling by dogs and sled will be ideal. If we
winter here, with so much fresh meat to sustain us, I think we will
be strong enough when the sun comes back to make it to the pole.*

*I know how surprised and disappointed you must be. But the
opportunity is here, and I feel that I must take it. The conditions
may never be more favourable. I will not be alone. Devlin is with
me. It is important that you tell Bridgman as soon as possible that I
am trying for the pole before he hears it unofficially from Bradley or
one of the others. The news will cause quite a stir. I hope that whatever animus you hold against me now as you read these words will
pass, and that you will do what you can on your end to help me.
Please assure everyone that I left Gloucester with the intention of
returning to Brooklyn in September and decided to try for the pole
only because of how unforeseeably favourable to success I found all
things to be in Greenland.*

Please do not think badly of me. I know that if you think things through with an open heart, you will see that this is something I must do. Kiss Helen and Ruth for me.

> *Your loving husband,*
> *Frederick*

The young man who on the voyage had served as our cook, a German from Brooklyn named Rudolph Franke, accepted Dr. Cook's invitation to join us on the expedition.

I wrote and gave to Bradley a short letter for Aunt Daphne, telling her that our plans had changed, that we were trying for the pole and would be away for longer than the expected four months. I also gave him one for Kristine. "I think constantly of you," I wrote. "Perhaps I ought not to say so for the first time in a letter, but I love you."

A few days before the ship departed, Dr. Cook, impressing upon me the need to be discreet, admitted that he and Bradley had been preparing for a polar expedition since long before the ship left Gloucester.

"Bradley agreed to back the expedition the day we met," said Dr. Cook.

They had been partway through their lunch, Dr. Cook said, when he put down his knife and fork. "Why not try for the pole?" he asked Bradley. "It would cost only eight or ten thousand dollars more than you plan to spend."

"Not I," Bradley said. "Would you like to try for it yourself?"

Dr. Cook said he did not know which surprised him more, hearing himself blurt out the question or receiving Bradley's instant agreement to back an expedition.

"We'll fit you for the pole," Bradley told him, "but we'll say nothing to anyone about it. We don't want the papers getting at it. Peary is waiting to go. We don't want him to get to Etah first and take all the best dogs for himself. And I want to shoot on the way up, so I don't want to be in a hurry. Look at it this way. If we get to Etah and the

Eskimos are sick or there aren't enough dogs or something else is wrong, we can say it was just a hunting trip and come back home."

Dr. Cook said that Bradley wrote him out a cheque on the spot for ten thousand dollars. "This is for the pole," he said, handing it to Dr. Cook. Then he wrote out another, larger cheque. "And this is for *my* part of the expedition."

Bradley asked him about Mrs. Cook, and about me.

"I will put off telling them the truth for as long as possible," Dr. Cook said. "After all, we may not try for the pole, in which case all my wife's worry will have been unnecessary. It is a harmless lie that may spare her a few months of fretting and Devlin some disappointment."

"Get there and get back," Bradley said just as the ship left with its cargo of furs and tusks. Bradley, his hands on Dr. Cook's shoulders, winked at me.

Bradley's demeanour made Dr. Cook's bid for the pole sound like a shady business venture from which, though Dr. Cook would take the risks, Bradley hoped to profit. In this, he was not unlike any backer of a polar expedition. Something about him, however, about the way he kept looking appraisingly at both of us, unsettled me.

"You might make it. Who knows," Bradley said, laughing, as if he had bought a lottery ticket in aid of some worthwhile but amusing cause.

"How does Dr. Cook plan to make it to the pole without proper equipment or a ship?" Captain Bartlett asked me, having failed, he said, to get a satisfactory answer from Dr. Cook. I told him that I did not know what Dr. Cook's strategy was.

"Even though your life depends on him?" said Captain Bartlett.

"I'm sure he knows what he is doing," I said.

"No one starts for the pole from this far south in Greenland," Captain Bartlett said. "Your ship should take you hundreds of miles north of Etah before it turns back. Dr. Cook will have to sledge all those extra hundreds of miles. It makes no sense. It can't be done."

As to whether our base camp was too far south, I could not say, but I knew that we were not, as was commonly believed among the crew of the *Bradley*, ill-equipped, for Bradley had left us with what Dr. Cook described as everything we would need to make it to the pole and back. When Bradley and the crew went up Smith Sound to the walrus grounds one day, Dr. Cook, Franke and I had unloaded a large amount of equipment and supplies that had been secretly put on board the *Bradley* in Gloucester, including several sledges of Dr. Cook's design, as well as several compasses, a sextant, a thermometer, a pedometer that measured distance covered on foot, a chronometer, an anemometer for windspeed, an aneroid barometer for air pressure and altitude.

I stood with Franke and Dr. Cook on the beach, watching as first the ship itself and then the *Bradley*'s sails passed from sight.

I had been eager to be rid of the captain and Bradley and the others. But how strange the place seemed once they were gone. How different the beach at Etah seemed in the absence of Peary, without his tent at the far end, near the cliff. I had never seen the harbour at Etah empty of a ship before. There were not even kayaks on the shore, for the Eskimos carried them up to the hill at the end of every day.

It felt as though a ship at anchor was some natural object whose disappearance was a harbinger of winter. Already, though the ship was barely gone, I felt marooned. Before, it had seemed that all that separated me from home was time and space. But now it seemed that nothing led from here to there.

The harbour and the hills were exactly as they had been when we were here before to rescue Peary, exactly as they had been since then, in our absence. This should not have seemed odd, and yet it did. I felt as fixed here as they were. It was a curiously oppressive feeling, especially with what Dr. Cook called the "real" weather already setting in.

I looked at the tupiks and the Eskimos on the hill for reassurance. They were proof that winter in the Arctic was survivable. How unconcerned the Eskimos seemed, preparing in a cheerful frenzy for a winter that they knew would be like all the other winters they had made it through.

But I did not feel reassured. It was the long night that I dreaded most.

The Eskimos were refurbishing underground stone igloos that were decades old, but we would be spending the winter in a Redcliffe House–like dwelling. The box house, we called it.

We used the packing boxes that had carried our supplies to make walls that enclosed a thirteen-by-sixteen-foot space. We used the lids of the boxes for roof shingles and insulated everything with turf. A middle post supported the roof, and around that we built a table.

During the eight days it took to build the house, our supplies lay nearby, covered with the old sails that had been flying from the *Bradley* when Dr. Cook bought her in Gloucester. We installed a small stove, which without almost constant tending would go out.

Dr. Cook said he could think of no reason why, if all went well, we would not be back in Brooklyn by the end of next summer. We would be gone fifteen months at the most, he said, assuring me that we would not hang on pointlessly for years on end like Peary. We would try once, and if we did not reach the pole, we would go back home. And when we were ready, we would try again. There was no point attempting to convalesce up north.

My first night in the box house, I lay awake in my sleeping bag, trying to imagine the coming months. As a child, I had read every account of Arctic travel that I could get my hands on. But almost all were written in a flat, laconic style, as if to vividly depict either beauty or hardship would somehow contravene the explorer's code.

What the chances of success were of this suddenly hatched plan to try for the pole I had no way of knowing. I had only the vaguest notion of what Dr. Cook meant when he spoke of the "unforeseeably favourable conditions."

It was our good fortune, he told me, that these "conditions," really did exist, though it was not, as he had led his wife to believe, because of them that we had stayed behind, which I was glad of, for I could not help thinking that a hunting trip that by sheer fluke had become a polar expedition could only have failed.

· CHAPTER THIRTY-FOUR ·

BY THE MIDDLE OF SEPTEMBER, SNOW CAME AND COVERED THE dories that Bradley had left for us, a half-dozen of them buried upside down on the beach.

The snow set in for good long before the harbour froze. Everything was white but the water, which was grey. The incongruity of it seemed to mesmerize Dr. Cook. He would stand at the water's edge at dusk, staring at the waves that washed ashore as if there was some implication for him in the sight of the snow-surrounded water that he could not puzzle out.

One morning, when we awoke, the harbour had disappeared. It had frozen and snow had fallen on the ice, so that what the day before had been open water was now a flat white field.

As secondary layers of ice began to form on the harbour, they were pushed up onto the beach, where they were left at low tide, a never-melting, meandering high-water mark of ice that, by the time the harbour was fully frozen, had risen to a kind of seawall, a break-water that looked like our first line of defence against invasion. The Eskimo women would stand behind this wall at sunset and stare out across the harbour and the larger sound beyond it, as spellbound as Dr. Cook had been by the water, all of them silent and strung out at even intervals along the wall, all with tears streaming down their faces. It was a custom that Dr. Cook had witnessed before but whose meaning he could not discover, so reluctant were any of the Eskimos to talk about it.

We did not have to hunt. We merely traded with the Eskimos for meat and clothing, thereby saving the energy that Dr. Cook predicted we would badly need to get us through the months-long polar night. We traded tobacco, rifles and cartridges, biscuits and soap (with which, for some reason, the Eskimo women washed themselves from the feet up).

In exchange, the Eskimos made coats and stockings from the furs of foxes and hares. From the fur and hide of reindeer that the men had killed, the women made us sleeping bags that they sewed together with sinew, painstakingly working the thread, which they clenched between their teeth and manipulated with both their fingers and their toes. From seal hide, they made us sealskin boots and coils of lashing for the sleds.

Dr. Cook spent much of his time making sledges out of the hickory wood, which came from trees he had cut on his brother's farm. He made runners for the sleds by first heating and then straightening the staves of barrels. He made seven sledges and lashed them upright to the outside of the box house so they would not be crushed by snow. He made hickory snowshoes, the toes of which he turned up because, he said, this would make for better walking over the ice and snow of the polar seas.

Finally, he made one large sled that would pull the tent he had made in Brooklyn, in which we would shelter whenever it was not possible to build a proper igloo.

Our fuel, during our winter stay in the box house, would be coal. Bradley had left us a heap of hard coal, which was preferable to the soft kind because it did not leave grimy black dust on everything or clog up the stovepipe.

The already short days grew swiftly shorter. Ever since the box house was finished, the Eskimos had been coming down from the hill to visit us for cups of tea. Starting from the middle of the afternoon, they had been coming in groups of two and three. But as winter set in, they came in larger groups and stayed longer, so that their visits overlapped and the box house was often crowded.

The Eskimos, as if, off-puttingly, they dreaded the coming polar night as much as we did, hated to leave and became morose when told it was time for them to go back to their igloos on the hill.

Eventually, a "day" consisted of an hour-long twilight, the sun barely clearing the almost-flat horizon to the east before it began to set again.

We could not keep our minds from reacting as they normally would to the light conditions, could not help feeling that this was the dusk of a day in which the sun had run its course across the sky and now was setting. We did what people do at dusk: gave in to reflectiveness, to thoughts of the past and what the coming days would bring.

We could not, for a few hours every day, resist regarding the night as a welcome break between the days. And then we would brood on the fact, which always seemed to dawn on us like some disheartening surprise, that there *were* no days, only these recurrent dusks, with long stretches of darkness in between.

It was as if that distant line of light was all that remained of the past, of all things recorded or remembered, as if history and memory were fading and soon nothing would be left of them but darkness. This notion was not unique to me. "The light of other days," Dr. Cook said once, quoting what he said was the first line of a poem in Palgrave's treasury of English verse. He said he had first called the ebbing light that on the Redcliffe expedition.

One day the sun failed to clear the horizon, showing all but a fraction of itself, then sinking slowly. As the days went by, less and less of it showed: nine-tenths, three-quarters, a half, a third. It became a great red dome, then was crescent-shaped, then like a sickle, until soon all we saw when we dropped everything and watched was the barest skullcap-like rise of red, after the disappearance of which, on October 25, we had a few weeks of pale, zodiacal light until even that shrunk in from the sides and faded to a faintly luminous, amorphous glow, a faint candle encased in frosted glass, which we still referred to as the sun.

Long after that was gone, we kept a daily vigil for the sun, staring at the place where we had seen it last, waiting as if we believed that it would somehow rise out of season.

What would the Arctic night be like? The question nagged at me more and more as each day the twilight grew shorter. Nothing like Etah had been. That much was clear already.

Dr. Cook noticed my apprehension. "You will do fine, Devlin," he said. "We will not be cold or hungry. There is only the darkness to contend with. We have our work to do, our books to read, a great adventure after Christmas to look forward to."

Every day, he spoke some such words of encouragement to me. "You are by nature well-suited to the Arctic night," he said. "You are patient, even-tempered. You are not unused to loneliness."

Dr Cook assured me that we would not be cold inside the box house, or even outside it, though it would be some time before I knew from experience that this was true. Peary himself, as he gripped my hand, had assured me that I knew nothing of the Arctic from having spent one summer on a beach in southern Greenland. With a bed on the well-stocked *Erik* to sleep in every night, I had found Etah *easier* than summering on Signal Hill.

I thought of the ice trench—the grave that had been dug by the crew of the *Belgica* for the body of Lieutenant Danco, the only casualty of the South Pole expedition—dug to a depth of six feet, as though the ice, like earth, would stay forever fixed in that one place. It was not the cold that had killed Danco but the darkness.

I had never really tried to imagine myself as a member of a real polar expedition. Ice igloos. Makeshift huts like Redcliffe House, through every crack of which the wind would shriek, the wind that the members of the North Greenland expedition had wound up speaking to, screaming at, begging for mercy. I doubted that I would make it through months of darkness and confinement, that I would ever become what people thought I was, an Arctic explorer.

I thought of the state to which the Arctic had reduced a man as large and strong-minded as Peary. I remembered the colour of his face as he hung from my hand in the gap between the *Windward* and the *Erik*. How presumptuous I had been to think that I could endure what a man like Peary had barely endured.

I tried to resist these thoughts, but they weighed more and more on my mind. There was not much of a purposeful nature to do once the most severe cold set in, though Dr. Cook devised all sorts of outdoor games for us: stone-throwing contests; a version of marbles played with pebbles; three-legged races, in which we competed in pairs with the Eskimos, who found inactivity unbearable.

I told Dr. Cook of Captain Bartlett's misgivings about starting a polar bid from so far south. A southern start would ensure us fresh supplies of meat through the winter, Dr. Cook said, as well as fresh dogs. It was true that our route would be four hundred miles longer than Peary's, but it would take us through country where game was plentiful.

I made no attempt to disguise my scepticism.

"Try to imagine how you will feel when you see the sun again," said Dr. Cook. "You can make yourself feel better simply by pretending to feel better. Remember how hot and bright it was the day we met, the day you stood outside my house for hours in the sun? Remember how good that glass of orange juice I gave you tasted?" I tried what he suggested, but remembering sunlit days only made me pine for them that much more.

There came upon me a reluctance to speak, the urge to horde up words, as if by speaking I would lose something, as if, like everything else, language was in short supply and I had no intention of sharing my allotment of it with the others.

Dr. Cook devised a strict schedule to which he said Franke and I would have to adhere if we wished to avoid becoming ill. We rose at six, had breakfast at six-thirty, read or wrote until ten, when we had coffee, then went outside to perform exercises, a regimen of calisthenics that Dr. Cook had first prescribed for the ship-bound crew of the *Belgica* expedition. When the sky was cloudy, the darkness was absolute. If not for the lanterns we kept burning on either side of the box-house door, we could not have seen our footprints in the snow.

We had dinner at noon, after which came everyone's favourite part of the day, when there was no work to do and the Eskimos came to visit in great numbers. They brought with them drums made from animal skins, which they played while they chanted and danced about the house. Thick smoke from the tallow candles, and from cigars and cigarettes, made the air of the box house almost unbreathable. The Eskimo dancers, women included, stripped to their waists and cavorted about until their torsos gleamed with sweat. Everyone drank tea and ate dried auk's eggs, of which the Eskimos seemed to have an unending supply. The more loath we became to venture out into the cold, the more eager were the Eskimos to visit us.

There was sometimes a great deal of work done on these afternoons, when, as Dr. Cook put it, the box house became a "factory" for polar equipment and supplies. The Eskimos made pemmican for us with dried walrus meat. They cut it into six-inch strips, and hung it on hooks for three days, during which time all the moisture and the oil dripped from it into pans that littered the floor of the box house. When it was dried, we packed it in tins whose lids we tied in place with wire. Then the Eskimos hung another "crop." In all, they made fifteen hundred pounds of it. For weeks, it hung on the walls of the box house like some aromatic form of decoration. When the last crop was taken down, the walls and hooks looked so conspicuously bare that we hung on them everything that was not nailed down.

And the Eskimos continued to bring fresh meat, hunting and trapping in the darkness as best they could. We would give them three biscuits for each eider duck they brought us. They hunted hare by moonlight with rifles they borrowed from us, then came back to the box house and gave us half of what they had killed.

Dr. Cook fashioned in the box house a little darkroom in which he developed his photographs, chinking all the cracks in the room with flour paste that when it dried was like cement. The Eskimos would line up to take their turn one by one in the darkroom with Dr. Cook, to see the red light and the magical emergence of the pictures on the submerged squares of paper. "*Noweeo*," each of them said. "*Noweeo*," we heard time and time again from inside the room.

They referred to Dr. Cook as Tatsesoah, the big medicine man.

They remembered him from previous expeditions, including the North Greenland expedition. They recalled in far greater detail than he could what had happened on these expeditions, especially the illnesses of which he had cured them, for which they were no less grateful now than they had been fifteen years ago.

Because they regarded the past as almost coterminous with the present, they could not get past the idea that I had come to Greenland in search of my father, Francis Stead. My increasingly morose manner only reinforced this notion, and they were always disappointed to see how little consolation I seemed to derive from their company.

Each day, when we met, they would pantomime a search, looking about them as if they had mislaid some precious object, then sadly shake their heads. They were assuring me that years ago, when Francis Stead went missing, they did everything they could to find him.

I found myself resenting Dr. Cook for having conferred upon Rudolph Franke, a cook who had no experience in Arctic travel and whom he had known but a few weeks, the same honour it had taken me years to earn.

Franke was taller, more robust than I was. As his English was poor and he was by nature taciturn, we hardly ever spoke. He and Dr. Cook spoke German to each other, or rather, Dr. Cook issued orders in his broken German and Franke, mumbling a few words in reply, did what he thought he had been told.

I wondered if it was because he doubted me that Dr. Cook had invited Franke to stay behind. It seemed possible that from the moment we met, he had been disappointed with me but had kept this hidden to spare my feelings. He might merely have been going through the motions of making me an explorer because he did not want to break his promise to me. I felt as if Franke had usurped my place. Perhaps Franke had known about the polar bid before the ship left Gloucester. He was, like Dr. Cook, a German from Brooklyn. Dr. Cook might have known him for quite some time. I could not resist such absurd speculation.

Fighting my darkness-induced doubts, I went for weeks without speaking to poor Franke, if not for whom, it seemed—for such was my state of mind—Dr. Cook would not have doubted *me*.

I knew it was not unusual for explorers to send their subordinates back at some early stage of an expedition, beyond which, they believed, they would no longer have need of their assistance. Dr. Cook was perhaps planning to send me back and thereby save my life. I vowed that I would refuse to leave him, refuse to go back unless he went back.

At last, the winter storms that made it impossible for the Eskimos to venture even as far from their igloos as the box house set in. We no longer had visitors, were no longer able to go outside to do our exercises in the darkness.

Lying there in my warm sleeping bag, I felt ridiculously unsuited for a polar expedition, deserving of being left behind. Dr. Cook, I was convinced, had detected in me some fundamental weakness, some crucial flaw, some remnant of the Stead boy, all traces of whom I thought I had shed long ago.

All day and all night long, there was no sound from outside but the roaring of the wind and, occasionally, that of the Eskimo dogs, which, having picked up the scent of the pemmican, came down from the hill, climbed up onto the roof and tried relentlessly to claw their way through the turf, pummelling in silence, as if they believed that if they did not bark we would not notice them. When Dr. Cook threw what meat he thought we could spare outside, they went away for a while. Soon, it was simply to make him throw out some meat that they clawed at the roof, making a few perfunctory scratches at the turf, then jumping down to wait outside the door for their reward.

I felt a constant weariness, a chronic urge to sleep that I saw no reason to resist, it being warm and safe inside my sleeping bag, which I left less and less often, despite the urging of Dr. Cook. Other days, after sleepless nights, I could neither get to sleep nor summon up the will to leave my sleeping bag. I lay in my bunk with my eyes closed, my mind racing as if energy was being diverted to it from my body. Sometimes, with Franke's help, Dr. Cook would stand me up, so that the sleeping bag fell about my feet. Then they would walk me around the box house until I was fully awake and Dr. Cook would assign me some task, like planing the runners of the sled he was making or keeping the stove supplied with coal.

But the length of our confinement took its toll on Dr. Cook and Franke as well, and soon they were making only token efforts to keep me from sleeping all the time.

In early December, when there was a lull in the weather, Dr. Cook decided to take a journey in the darkness to test the sledges and snowshoes he had made. He told us he would be back in two weeks. Several days after he left, I fell into a fever from which I did not fully emerge until long after he returned.

I dreamed that I was back in the Dakota; that Dr. Cook had not taken me with him on this expedition; that I was waiting for him to come back from the Arctic, waiting to hear if he was still alive, waiting for a letter from him. I felt as I had years ago, when, because he was on some expedition, it had been months since his last letter and there was no telling when or if the next one would arrive.

I dreamed that he had written to me from Etah just as he had written to Mrs. Cook, explaining why it had been necessary to mislead me. Here I was, once again, being written to by this man with no way to write him back, no way to ask him what the real meaning of his words might be. I had no doubt that when I next heard from him, it would be by letter.

I awoke momentarily from the fever to find Dr. Cook taking my pulse, his hand holding my wrist. "When did you get back?" I said. He smiled at me but either did not speak or said things I could not hear. The next time I came to, I was sitting up. Franke had his hands on my shoulders, holding me in place, while Dr. Cook moved his stethoscope about my bare back.

I returned to lucidity for good on Boxing Day. "The midnight of winter passed two days ago, Devlin," said Dr. Cook. "The sun is on its way back."

The worst of the storms had passed. We were able to go outside again. I knew we would leave for the pole in February, which meant that I had a little more than a month to recover from my illness.

I tried so hard to make myself a model expeditonary, performing more than my share of tasks, continuing my calisthenics long after Franke and Dr. Cook had finished theirs, that Dr. Cook warned me I was risking a relapse.

We saw, for a few minutes each morning in the east, a Milky Way–like cloud of light that Dr. Cook said was the first sign of the sun.

"There will not be sufficient food for three of us," Dr. Cook said. I had been expecting him to say some such thing for weeks. I felt fully recovered from my illness, but I knew that having seen me reduced to such a state so early in the expedition, Dr. Cook had to have grave doubts about my ability to survive a bid for the pole. At the very best, he had to think I would impede his progress and ensure the failure of the expedition.

He smiled at me—smiled, I thought, as if to say that he knew what a disappointment it would be for me to be left behind, but he hoped I would understand why it was necessary that he and Franke proceed without me, and he believed that I would receive the bad news grace-fully, such was my nature. I prepared myself.

"Franke will not be going with us to the pole," he said.

I threw my arms around him and hugged him and danced about in imitation of the Eskimos.

Dr. Cook told me that he had known from the moment he invited him to stay behind with us at Etah that he would send Rudolph Franke back long before we had reached our goal or turned back ourselves.

"We needed his help to build the box house, and I knew we would be grateful for the company of an extra man, a man from Brooklyn, during the Arctic night. That might sound ruthless, but I told him from the start that at some point, I might send him back."

Dr. Cook told Franke of his decision after the sun returned. They spoke to each other in German, Franke gesticulating at me, clearly saying that it was unfair of Dr. Cook to send him back and take instead the illness-prone man both of them had been tending to all winter.

After arguing for days with Dr. Cook—who never raised his voice but simply told him that someone needed to stay behind to guard the box house and its contents—Franke finally relented.

CHAPTER THIRTY-FIVE

WE LOADED THE ELEVEN SLEDGES, PILING THEM WITH GUNS, ammunition, pemmican, furs, three alcohol field stoves, spare snow-shoes and the tent.

Dr. Cook chose, from the many volunteers, twelve Eskimos to go with us. Only two of them, he said,—and which two, he had not yet decided—would go with us to the pole. The Eskimos who were not chosen offered Dr. Cook some of their dogs. We had 103 of them by the day we left, enough so that we could alternate dogs, letting groups of them take their turn running unharnessed beside the others.

The sun was rising halfway, both preceded and followed by long intervals of twilight, by the time the caravan of sleds and dogs and men left Etah. Those who were staying behind merely raised their hands to us, for the Eskimos, Dr. Cook said, seemed to have no word for good-bye. Franke, though he had politely bade us both goodbye that morning, stayed in the box house. I felt sorry for him, and sorry for the thoughts I had harboured against him throughout the polar night.

We set out with our Eskimo guides across Ellesmere Land. Despite its arduousness, sledge travel was much easier to endure than the monotonous gloom of the Arctic night. For the first time in my life, I had a beard, though as there were no mirrors, I could only feel it with my hands.

My illness had been more psychological than physical, so I was not as debilitated as I had feared. Every now and then, during the first week or so, I became so fatigued that I had to sit on one of the sledges for a while and let myself be pulled along, a useless passenger, a burden to the dogs, mere dead weight to the expedition.

But I was soon able to match the pace of the others, soon learned from them the knack of half running on my snowshoes and taking my turn behind a sled on the smooth terrains. Dr. Cook unloaded the fourth and smallest of the sleds from the largest one, of which he was the driver, piled some of his equipment and supplies on it and entrusted it to me. I swiftly learned the knack of "driving" it, the main secret of which was to trust the dogs to know where they were going. Dr. Cook gave me a pair of amber-tinted goggles like those he wore to prevent snow-blindness. The sight of me goggled like Dr. Cook so amused the Eskimos that they could not look at me without bursting into grins.

Once we were clear of the ice blocks on the shore, the ice was fairly smooth. But we soon began to encounter the usual polar obstacles. Pressure ridges that took days to cross, open water, leads that forced us to detour from our route. If no way could be found around pressure ridges, we chopped our way through them with our ice axes, which we could not have done had there not been so many of us—fourteen men hacking away at the ice like miners at a vein of ore, our purpose being not to chop a passage straight through the ridge, but only to fashion a kind of road on which the sledges could be dragged or pushed uphill.

One day, encountering nothing but flat ice, we travelled twenty-nine miles in fourteen hours. Another day, we made no forward progress at all, only chopped our way through a ridge that we did not cross until the next day.

At Bay Fjord, the temperature was −83°F. We found muskoxen there, enough to provide us with supplies for the polar bid and for caches that we laid out at intervals for our return journey.

Upon our arrival at prominently marked locations on his map, Dr. Cook announced their names. Eureka Sound, Nansen Sound, Svartevoeg—the last aptly named, for the cliffs there were jet black. Then the utmost north of Axel Heiberg Land, from which both Dr. Cook and I saw the polar sea for the first time.

There we left all but the barest essentials, sending back six of the

Eskimos. When we were just short of losing sight of land, Dr. Cook sent back four more Eskimos. Dr. Cook chose to accompany us to the pole two men named Etukishuk and Ahwelah. He chose them, he said, not because they were the best or strongest guides, but because they were young, impressionable and credulous. They would do what he told them to. They would not defy him.

Each day left everyone so exhausted that it was hard to believe we had ever found it difficult to fall asleep. I slept as I had never slept in my life, straight through the night, without dreams, without moving, waking up in the same posture I had assumed upon crawling into my sleeping bag. I lay down my head and, the next instant, felt Dr. Cook's hand on my shoulder and heard him say, "Morning." He always sounded as if he had come in from outside to wake me. He never seemed to sleep. He said it was the dogs, which, at the first sign of the sun began to bark, that woke him, but no amount of barking would have woken me. Sometimes I woke up to see him scribbling in his notebooks as if he had had been doing so all night.

We would be under way for barely half an hour when the dogs would stop barking, so caught up were they in the rhythm of the march. There was no need to urge them on, no need for us to speak to one another. Dr. Cook consulted his compass in mid-stride, and all the other sleds simply followed his. Only when a sextant reading was required did we stop, and even then we did not speak. The only sound heard while Dr. Cook consulted his instruments was that of the laboured breathing of the men and the dogs. I realized that we always breathed this way, but that the sound of it was drowned out by the stamp and shuffle of our feet, the jostling tumult of the dog teams in their traces, the rasping screech of the wooden runners on the snow.

We otherwise stopped only to light an alcohol stove, to melt snow in a teapot, to stare at that little miracle of flame, to huddle round it to keep it from being blown out by the wind. It seemed that all that remained in the world of the element of fire was that blue flame.

Our two pleasures were hot tea and sleep. We ate the pemmican without relish, for it was nothing more than fuel, as brittle as taffy.

Soon, we were travelling where the Eskimos had never been. They had even less knowledge of the use of the compass and the sextant than I did. We were out of sight of all land, all landmarks. There was nothing by which the rest of us could gauge our progress, nothing in the distance to which Dr. Cook could point and tell us how long it would take us to reach it, for everything ahead of us, behind us and around us was moving, imperceptibly in flux. If we were to take exactly the same route back, nautically speaking, Dr. Cook said, we would come across nothing that looked familiar. We would find no trace of the igloos in which we slept. Had we laid down a trail of paint behind us, we would look in vain for it when we returned, even if, in the interval, not a flake of snow had fallen. The ice of which our "route" was composed would long have been dispersed, for its location and shape were changing constantly.

This was something on which it was best not to dwell, for it gave rise to the sense that, more than moving, we were *being moved*, all but floating, helplessly and aimlessly caught up in some illusion on this seemingly fixed and solid surface. We could not look behind us at the start of every day and see where we had come from, for what lay behind us looked nothing like it had when we stopped the night before. For that matter, what lay *ahead* of us looked nothing like it had when we stopped the night before.

Through all of this our only guide was Dr. Cook. He alone knew where we were, was charting our progress on his maps. He would point to a place on a map, and we had no choice but to take his word for it that we were there, though we did not understand how he had calculated our position.

With his instruments, he kept track of the weather and the ice conditions, calculated the ocean currents, kept a daylight log, noted the lengths of our shadows at different times of the day. I envied him his ability to read those instruments and apply the data that he gathered from them to the maps, to locate himself in this non-coordinated sea of white.

The Eskimos, who had never been out of sight of land before, were terrified. They were unused to trusting someone else to navigate. Unable to understand even the concept of a map on which no land appeared, they probably suspected that we were lost, that Dr. Cook mistakenly believed he knew the way and that none of us would ever see our homes or families again.

The two showed no animosity towards Dr. Cook, but once the day's march was done, they whispered between themselves, shaking their heads sadly as if our fates had already been decided.

Occasionally, Dr. Cook took photographs and tried to develop them inside the tent, but we could not make it quite dark enough and nothing appeared on the paper but a faint spot of light.

Man-wide cracks formed in the ice during the calm that followed every storm, cracks caused by the sudden drop in temperature. One night, as we slept in our tent, a fault-line opened right beneath us. When we awoke, the tent was slipping into it from both sides. We barely scrambled out in time to avoid dropping straight into the water, or being caught in the trench and crushed when the fault-line closed again.

The polar sea was unlike the sea between South America and Antarctica, Dr. Cook said. The ice, though it moved ceaselessly, was older, denser, thicker, more compressed. To reach the South Pole, which lay at the heart of a continent, one would have to cross more land than sea. And just knowing that beneath the ice, beneath one's feet, lay land made the place seem less alien. As you walked on the polar sea, you could not feel the movement of the ice beneath your feet. I sometimes fancied that there was no water under it, that the ice went on forever, as though a million years ago, it was thrust up like white lava from the centre of the earth.

But then we would come upon a steaming lead of open water that seemed like an apparition. The ice had so recently parted that the water had just begun to freeze. And at fifty, sixty, seventy below, we could *see* it freeze. First, crystals formed and proliferated like flowers until a veined scale of ice extended from side to side. Through this new but porous ice, vapours rose like steam, only to freeze instantly to a kind of dust-like frost that fell back to the ice and gathered there until the ice became opaque. Dr. Cook took algae samples, though often there was not even algae, only sterile water.

To escape a storm coming from the west we were forced to cross one such lead, sleds and all, before it had finished freezing. The ice gave and sagged and cracked beneath our feet like half-shattered glass. Dr. Cook told us to spread our snowshoes as wide as possible to disperse our weight. Somehow we made it across.

Sometimes we thought the dogs that we released had scented game, only to find, upon catching up with them, that all of them were sniffing the long-abandoned blowhole of a seal or a polar bear. Eventually, we were so far from land that there was not even the possibility that we would encounter other forms of life.

The days grew longer, until the time of least light was a prolonged dusk and then a near sunset, a midnight sun. The ice looked like a field of fire—orange, blue, purple—an unfuelled fire that, without consuming anything, would burn forever. During the time of the midnight sun, we travelled at night, when the sun was lowest, to escape the blinding glare from which not even our goggles could protect us. We slept by day, though it seemed a foolish waste to do so, to simulate night inside the igloos or the tent while outside there was so much light. What we had longed for during the polar night, we now had more of than we could use.

We woke up sometimes to find the igloos buried in snow, snow driven by winds that, as we lay inside our sleeping bags at night, we pretended not to hear. We knew that day had come only because light came very faintly through the walls.

What an effort it took, every morning, to leave the warmth of my sleeping bag. How tempted we all were to remain inside our bags, to never leave them, for they lent us such an illusion of safety, tempting us to forget that all that warmed us was the heat of our own bodies. We kicked each other awake, each hoping one of the other three would be the first to rise, the first to venture out and disinter the dogs, of which all that showed on such mornings was their rime-encrusted snouts.

In the sleeping bag, I marvelled in the warmth of my own skin. I would withdraw one hand and wait till it was cold, then bring it back inside and touch my face with it. How warm it made me feel, that singular shock of cold.

There came a time when the polar sea always had the same twilight tint of blue about it, as if we were caught in a late-winter afternoon, a day that was forever ending yet never ended, as though time had stalled at this melancholy hour of reflection that back home had always seemed so fleeting, so precious.

Soon, too tired, at the end of a day's march, to build igloos, we all slept in the small silk tent, falling asleep on the floor of it the instant we stopped moving, four of us so exhausted we did not notice the cramped quarters. We slept in our furs, hoods, snowboots and mitts, no longer bothering to light the little stoves.

My hair, and Dr. Cook's, was as long as the Eskimos'. When we did remove our hoods, the hair hung down to our shoulders, fell forward in front of our faces when we inclined our heads. It was best not to cut it, Dr. Cook said, for it was keeping us warm, as were our beards, protecting our faces from frostbite. It was our one natural advantage over the Eskimos, who had no facial hair.

What kept the natives going I could not understand. We had our purpose to sustain us, our reasons for being where we were, but they had none except their loyalty to us, which they gave because we asked them for it, not in exchange for their "pay" (which was nothing next to what they could have earned had they remained at home and hunted). Sometimes they were so tired they could barely raise their arms to crack their whips or their voices to urge the dogs to move.

One day, Ahwelah chanted over and over: "*Unne Sinig pa—so ah tonie I o doria*" (We should not fear death when to go on living is unbearable). From then on, Dr. Cook no longer took his turn riding on the sleds but walked in front of them, for he knew that the Eskimos would take his walking as a challenge to them and would be more determined not to let him down.

I was myself determined not to let either of them come to harm, determined that they would not die while helping two white men make it to the pole. We killed the weakest of the dogs and fed them to the others, keeping some for ourselves. Eventually, we had to feed the dogs our spare sleeping bags, on the reindeer hides of which they chewed for hours.

"We are 160 miles from the pole," Dr. Cook told me when he came into our tent from outside one night. "If we are at all delayed in getting there, we may not have sufficient supplies to make it back. I do not know what to do. If this was the Antarctic, I would conserve supplies by leaving the three of you behind and travelling the last stage by myself. But if we were to separate on this drifting ice, I would never find you. When the risks are so great, I cannot expect men to obey my orders. The three of you will vote as to what we should do. I will abstain."

All three of us voted to continue.

Often the wind blew straight against us, forcing us to walk bent over, staring at the ice, unheedful of what lay even immediately ahead of us, Dr. Cook steering his sled by nothing but his compass, each dog team following the boots of the driver of the team in front of it.

It occurred to me that only we would ever know if we made it to the pole, for we would never make it back alive and our bodies, if they were found, would be nowhere near the pole, having drifted with the ice.

Unlike during the polar night, I did not dream, not while walking or while lying down, though I slept while walking. My mind slept while my body kept on moving through sheer habit. I would wake up to the sound of my own footsteps. I thought often of Kristine, wondered what she had thought when she read the letter in which I told her that I loved her. I thought of Aunt Daphne. Remembering how I had waited to hear of Dr. Cook when he was overdue on the South Pole expedition, I knew all too well what both of them were going through.

"Morning." With that word from Dr. Cook, each day began. Not until the next morning, when he woke me with that word again, would I hear his voice. The rest of us no longer spoke at all.

On April 19, 1908, Dr. Cook told us that we were two days from the pole.

"We are almost there," said Dr. Cook, smiling, as if his most recent observations and instrument readings had pleasantly surprised him, as if he had thought we were far from the pole but, having noticed and corrected some miscalculation, suddenly realized that we were "almost there."

He had used this phrase before to keep us from growing too despondent, only to repeat it or qualify it days later, telling us that by "almost there," he had meant we were "at most a week away."

"We are two days away, possibly less," he said when he noticed my scepticism. He told the Eskimos, and soon they were talking excitedly.

"We will get there late today," he casually said the next morning.

As we set out, our three sleds behind his, I searched the terrain ahead of us, expecting it to change abruptly, expecting to enter some sort of polar zone, some clearly demarcated area at the heart of which would lie what was unmistakably "the pole." I drew my sled up beside his.

"We are at the 89th parallel," said Dr. Cook, as if to provide me with the sense of distinctiveness I was looking for.

We did not get there that day, or the next.

"Today for certain," said Dr. Cook. "For certain, Devlin."

The dogs, who sensed our excitement, began to bark and, without urging from us, ran faster than they ever had before. I could not help regarding the pole as the end and not the halfway point of our journey, as if there would be fixed shelters there and food in great abundance.

We crossed an unusually flat stretch of ice, and thinking this might be the pole, I looked expectantly at Dr. Cook. He smiled and shook his head.

We had proceeded at this frantic pace for perhaps three hours when Dr. Cook reined in his dogs, dug out his compass and his sextant and, staring at the compass, began to walk in long strides.

Now he walked more slowly, still staring at the compass. There was no sound but the crunching of the ice beneath his snowshoes. He stopped, pocketed his compass and looked up at the sky.

He pointed as though at something in the distance, though all things, to my eyes, looked the same.

"Devlin, I want you to walk in a straight line," he said, "and stop when I tell you to."

I walked, barely able to resist the urge to fall to my knees, to lie down on my side and go to sleep. I walked for what seemed like a very long time, suspecting that I was no longer in earshot of the others, and that, if I turned around, I would not see them.

"STOP," I faintly heard Dr. Cook shout. I stopped, turned and looked back to see him a hundred yards away, staring at his compass. He looked up at me. Even at that distance, I could see that he was smiling.

"YOU ARE THERE," he shouted.

I looked about me, searching for some clue as to what he meant.

"YOU ARE AT THE POLE," he shouted. "YOU ARE THE FIRST."

The meaning of his words had only begun to register on me when he started to run towards me. Ahwelah and Etukishuk urged their dogs forward, while the other dogs, with their unmanned sleds, followed close behind.

Dr. Cook jumped up and down, windmilling his arms, spinning in a circle.

It was April 22, 1908, a clear, cold day.

I could not believe that Dr. Cook had bestowed upon me the honour of preceding him and the others to the pole.

"The pole, Devlin. The pole, the pole," he shouted as he ran towards me. I felt that I should run to meet him, but I could not bring myself to leave the spot.

Dr. Cook and the sleds reached me all at once. The dogs tipped back their heads and, almost in unison, began to howl. Dr. Cook threw his arms around my waist and somehow found the strength to lift me in the air. "THE POLE," he screamed. "THE POLE AT LAST.

WE'RE HERE, DEVLIN. WE'RE HERE, BOYS. WE'RE HERE."

I hugged him, then joined him in his celebratory dance. Etukishuk and Ahwelah did the same.

We had reached the pole on our first try—the pole for which Peary and all the others had tried so many times without success.

It was like standing at the origin of ice.

There was no time in this place where all meridians met. I fancied it would be possible to cross from one side of the globe to the other with one step, to forever alternate between midnight and midday.

Here, at the pole, each year would have but one day and one night. South lay in every direction. There was no north.

"Ours at last," Dr. Cook said as he looked around at this place that I realized we would never see again. "I cannot bring myself to realize it. The prize of three centuries, yet it all seems so simple, so common-place."

"Ours at last," I said.

"Congratulations, Devlin," Dr. Cook said, looking at me from beneath the fur fringe of his hood.

"Congratulations, sir," I said.

It was the first time I had ever addressed him as anything. Many sons called their fathers "sir." I was surprised I had not thought of it before.

"She would be so proud of you," he said.

"Of both of us, sir," I said. After a long pause, during which the smile faded from his face, he nodded, then turned away. He fell to his knees and covered his face with his mitts, remaining in that position for so long that our two guides fell to *their* knees beside him.

I knelt beside Dr. Cook. He put one arm around my shoulders, the other around Etukishuk, who put his arm around Ahwelah. There we knelt, the four of us, as though we were posing for a photograph in that place of perpetual twilight where no other living thing had ever been.

We pointlessly planted a flag and buried by it in the snow a tin containing a piece of paper on which Dr. Cook had written our names and the date of our arrival, "claiming" the spot as if the next person to make it to the pole would see that we had been there first. It would have made as much sense to mark a spot in the middle of the open sea with that tin and flag. Yet it seemed necessary.

· CHAPTER THIRTY-SIX ·

WE TURNED BACK.

We were for so long trapped in our tent by storms that without realizing it, we had drifted far west, far into the Crown Prince Gustav Sea. There was open water everywhere, no route to Axel Heiberg Island, where we had buried the nearest of our caches of food. We had no choice but to go south with the ice. Dr. Cook hoped that we might reach Lancaster Sound and catch a Scottish whaling ship at Port Leopold, to which we were closer than we were to Greenland. But by September, we were near the shore of Baffin Bay, without food, fuel or ammunition.

Every so often, I became convinced that one of the others was missing, only to look around to find that there were still three of them, ahead, beside, behind me. At other times, I was certain that if I looked up from the ice, I would find myself alone, having strayed from or been abandoned by the others while I slept.

Strangest of all was the feeling I sometimes had that a fifth man was walking with us. Once, I was sure I saw him, trudging side by side with Dr. Cook. Sometimes he walked with Ahwelah or Etukishuk, head bowed as their heads were, though his hood was smooth and pointed, cowl-like. I wondered if the others saw him, too, but was afraid to ask, afraid to hear that they saw him at *my* side.

Death it must be, I thought, a hallucination that, to the others, would be a sign that, for me, the end was near. Yet it was them he was walking with, not me. To confirm this, I looked, when I could not see him, to the left and right, and glanced behind me, relieved that as yet he had not chosen me as his companion.

But I awoke once from my walking sleep to see the other three in front of me, and at my side, visible at what might have been a deferential distance, a form at which I dared not look, keeping time with me inaudibly, the only one of us without a sled. As it seemed the others had done, I ignored him, hoping he would vanish. I dozed, but when I awoke again, this unknown fifth presence was still there, having stayed longer with me, it seemed, than he had with any of the others, as if death had appraised the four of us and chosen me, the youngest and the weakest.

When it seemed certain that he would not leave me, I decided to face him down, address him, convince him that my time had not yet come. The instant I raised my head, he raised his, each of us turning to face the other.

What had been a cowl was now a shawl framing the face of a woman who, though younger than me and looking nothing like "Amelia, the wicked one," I knew to be my mother. Hers was not the face of an expeditionary. It was not ravaged by the elements or by privation. It was pale, almost translucent, and the eyes were blue. It was otherwise featureless.

She smiled. "You have nothing to fear from me," she said.

I must have dozed again, though I remember only waking up to find that she was gone. I was too exhausted to dwell on this vision. I kept walking, and from then on saw her only in my mind, her face in its all-but-featureless perfection, smiling at me. I remembered her voice, which had seemed so close it might have been my own, assuring me that I had no need to be afraid.

We went westward to Cape Sparbo, where we decided to spend the polar night in a kind of cave. A centuries-old hubblestone house in the recess of a massive rise of rock, it had a sod-and-whalebone roof. Ahwelah said that his ancestors had built it. We found a ship's hatch cover and a number of planks, and from these we made harpoons with which we hunted. We lined the house with the skins of muskox and polar bears. Luckily, game was easy to come by. Even when one of their number had just been killed in their midst, the rest of the muskoxen had to be shooed away from the den.

Dr. Cook convinced me to join him in the habit that he had first taken up on the *Belgica* expedition. We lay outside on the ground at night when the wind was calm. I looked up at the sky through the blowhole in my sleeping bag, from which the vapour of my breath spouted at intervals. Once, I saw Etukishuk and Ahwelah peering out at us from the doorway of the house, clearly wondering if we had lost our minds. All I did as I lay there wide awake was watch the stars.

Sometimes, when the moon was full and especially bright, we went out walking with no practical purpose in mind, which also unnerved the Eskimos, who would scrutinize us all over when we returned, assuming that we had about our persons something we had gone out to retrieve.

I soon stopped thinking of the pole, finding it difficult to think of anything. Even in my dreams, my frostbitten fingers burned. In dreams, heaven was warm and balmy and the other place was cold.

The weather became so bad that we could not go outdoors. If it had come during the polar day, such a storm would have caused a white-out. But at night, we could not even see the snow.

Because the house faced south and the wind blew from the east, no snow came inside when the door was open. Able only to hear the frenzied sifting of the snow, I reached out my hand and drew it back, soaking wet, red with cold. At times, it sounded like the whole house was submerged. The world outside existed only as sound.

For weeks, there was little to do but sleep and, for Dr. Cook and me, read and write. The few books we had with us I read over and over. The wind, because it drowned out all other sounds, became a kind of silence, a roaring monotone that made conversation impossible. We communicated with our hands, pointing, making gestures, drawing pictures in the air.

Eventually, I could neither read nor write, nor even find the energy to eat.

One day when I awoke, it seemed as though the wind had begun to drop. I listened closely. The sound was muffled, as though my hands were covering my ears. I watched as Dr. Cook went to the "porch," which was really just a crawlspace between the ground and an overhang of hubblestone. He pulled away the frame of fur-draped whalebone that served as our door, and I saw that the opening was blocked by hard-packed snow. He punched it and made but a tiny dent. Etukishuk crawled out of his sleeping bag and gave him his harpoon. Dr. Cook pushed it as far into the snow as he could, but he could not make an airhole.

The remote, muffled sound of the wind was the measure of just how deeply buried we were. Too deep to dig out. Dr. Cook was exhausted by his few minutes of exertion. Like me, Ahwelah had remained in his sleeping bag, watching their frenetic struggle with disinterest. There was nothing for us to do, Dr. Cook said, but get back in our bags and conserve our small supply of air by moving no more than we absolutely had to.

A day later, we were still conscious, so I knew that some air was getting in through the snow, though there was no telling how much longer it would last. I wondered if the whalebone roof would hold. I used my watch, which I feared would not resume its ticking each time I rewound it, to keep track of the days.

The sound of the wind grew ever more faint, until I began to wonder if it was doing so because the snow in which we were entombed was getting deeper or because I was becoming less and less able to attend to sound.

The four of us lived in a perpetual state of drowsiness, unable to resist the urge to sleep, to close our eyes, always waking up with a start, wondering if we were still alive or if we now inhabited some other world.

I assumed that the end would come when I could no longer hear the wind, so I strained to hear it, as if the sound was air, a precious trickle of it seeping in—as if as long as we could hear it, we could breathe.

Then, one day when I woke up, the sound was gone. Dr. Cook, who was lying beside me, took my hand. "Don't be afraid, Devlin," he said, his voice a hoarse whisper. "Don't be afraid, my son. Go back to sleep."

It seemed that the moment the wind came back, we all woke up at once. We shouted as though to someone passing overhead who did not know that we were lost—someone who, if we could only make ourselves heard to him, would dig us out.

The sound began to climb the scale again, growing louder every minute, as if the wind, though blowing with the same force as before, had changed direction and the snow was being swept away. We were never so glad to hear the rising of the wind. We greeted the return of sound as we so often had the return of light.

In less than an hour, the snow within which we had lived for weeks was gone.

The surfeit of fresh air was as unbreathable as water for a while. But even as we coughed and gagged, we smiled at each other like boys who, because of their own recklessness, had got into trouble and survived by the sheer luck for which they were famous.

When the wind subsided, we made our way out. Except for what had made its way inside the crawlspace, there was no loose snow, only frozen crust from before the storm. The dogs, the discontinuation of whose barking I had not noted, were gone. Whether they survived, were claimed as wild by someone else, we never did find out.

We somehow managed to walk from Cape Sparbo to Etah, where we arrived in mid-April and found a hunter named Harry Whitney staying in our box house, having been left by Peary, who the previous summer had set out for the pole.

The box house. Etah. The Eskimos in their tupiks on the hill. How could all this still be here? It was like returning in old age to one's childhood home to find it just the same as when you left.

Dr. Cook chatted with Whitney, who spoke disparagingly of Peary, said that Peary had mistreated him and that he had not got his money's worth on this hunting trip.

Dr. Cook had kept a record of our journey in a mass of notebooks, which he said contained scientific proof that we had reached the pole. The covers of the notebooks had disintegrated. The ragged and filth-ridden pages were held together with paste and reindeer lashings. There was no question of our waiting with Whitney for Peary and his ship, since Peary would never allow us on board. The nearest shipping port was Upernavik, to which we would have to walk on foot, which would take about four months. Dr. Cook said he was certain that if he travelled this distance on foot with the notebooks, they would fall to pieces.

"I must leave these notebooks with you, Mr. Whitney," he said. "May I trust you to bring them back safely with you to New York and leave them with my wife? Otherwise, they will soon be of no use to anyone."

Whitney assured Dr. Cook that he would take good care of the notebooks and would say nothing of them to Peary.

Dr. Cook told me we had to get to Upernavik as quickly as we could, there being no telling when Peary would return from up north or how far he would claim to have gone.

At Upernavik, we parted with Etukishuk and Ahwelah. They were bewildered at the fuss we made over them, hugging them and trying not to cry. When we were through, they smiled sheepishly, then turned and headed back towards Etah.

A Danish ship called the *Hans Egede* took us on board. It was bound for Copenhagen but detoured to Lerwick, the most northern city of Scotland, the capital of the Shetland Islands and the nearest port with a wireless. The Danes told us that going straight to Copenhagen would give Peary a better chance to stake his claim first. They favoured us over Peary, if only because to them would go the honour of transporting us, not only back to civilization, but to their own country, which would be the first to celebrate us and our accomplishment.

From Lerwick, Dr. Cook telegraphed to the Lecointe Observatory in Brussels the news that we had reached the pole on

April 22, 1908. He sent the telegram September 1, 1909. We had spent the past sixteen months making our way back.

I sent a telegram to Kristine: "I am safe and will soon be home." I wondered if after all this time, my safety still mattered to her. Dr. Cook sent one telegram to his wife and another, two thousand words in length, to the *New York Herald*. The latter was a sketchy account of our attainment of the pole that the *Herald* ran on its front page on September 2.

"I felt an intense loneliness, despite the presence of Mr. Stead and the Eskimos," wrote Dr. Cook. "What a cheerless spot to have aroused the ambition of man for so many ages. An endless field of purple snows. No life. No land. Nothing to relieve the monotony of frost. We were the only pulsating creatures in this world of ice."

We travelled to Copenhagen.

What an unlikely way this was for a man to make his first journey to the Old World from the New. I had all but walked to Europe from the pole. To Denmark, by whose tribes those of England were defeated. From whose people those of England were descended. Old Denmark. Old Copenhagen. Dr. Cook, the Eskimos and I had journeyed like a tribe of four against the course of time. We had gone back to the Stone Age at Cape Sparbo. Lived in a cave, hunted animals with weapons that we made from bones.

As the *Hans Egede* steamed into the harbour at Copenhagen, I was reminded again of my first sight of Manhattan. The harbour was a brilliant blue, reflecting the sky that had cleared from a storm the night before. It was cluttered with small boats, many of them flying the Stars and Stripes. A chorus of ship's whistles and sirens went up. Bands we could not see began to play, each blaring forth a different song, the only one I recognized "See the Conquering Hero Comes."

Life seemed to have become a series of discoveries set in motion by our having made it to the pole. Cape Sparbo, Upernavik and Copenhagen might all have been unknown to the outside world until we found them, so foreign did everything seem to me. Dr. Cook said it was twenty-seven months since we had set out by train for

Gloucester from Manhattan. The number thirty, the idea of a month, meant nothing to me. To measure time in numbers or in distance seemed absurd. I wondered for how long this feeling would last.

· CHAPTER THIRTY-SEVEN ·

WE MADE PORT AT COPENHAGEN, SUDDENLY AWARE OF WHAT A sight we were. Dr. Cook and I were wearing the ragged skins of seven different kinds of animals. At quayside, the crown prince of Denmark shook our hands and doffed his hat to us. They had cleaned us up some on the ship. The day before, I had had hair down to my shoulders, as had Dr. Cook. I had been filthy for so long that no amount of soap and water could restore my complexion to normal. But no one seemed to mind.

Thousands of people had come out to get a look at us. No one knew just what sort of tribute was appropriate. Some sang the Danish anthem, some the American. We were introduced to clergymen who seemed as mystified as we were as to why their presence had been called for. By the end of the day, our hands had become so raw from being shaken that to shake them was forbidden, to remind people of which we wore gloves indoors and out.

How anomalous, how tenuous Copenhagen seemed in comparison with the vast emptiness we had travelled through to get there. It seemed to me that everyone in Copenhagen lived in denial or ignorance of the great darkness that contained them as surely as the sea contains a sunken ship. Buildings, bridges, horse-drawn cabs and motor cars, electric lights—all seemed inconsequential.

Though much was made of Dr. Cook's having ushered me ahead of him at the last moment so that I could be the first to reach the pole, it was seen as a purely symbolic gesture. The expedition had been his. As one of the Copenhagen papers put it: "Dr. Cook generously allowed his fledgling protégé to walk the last few feet to the precious spot. So although we say hurray for Mr. Stead, it is Dr. Cook whom we honour as the first man to reach the pole."

For a while, Dr. Cook revelled in how eager people would be from then on to take advantage of us, in how much money we had already been offered. From *Hampton's* magazine, Dr. Cook accepted an offer of thirty thousand dollars for exclusive story rights, despite the objections of those who assured him he could get ten times that. From Frederic Thompson, the lecture-circuit promoter, $250,000 for 250 lectures. Harper and Brothers would soon make a bid for book rights.

We spent three weeks in Copenhagen at the Hotel Phoenix, where crowds gathered all night in the rain beneath the windows of our rooms, exhorting us to show ourselves, which we did from time to time to much cheering and applause. We stayed in adjoining suites and took turns going to the windows, going together only once or twice, which brought the loudest cheers from the crowds. "Cook and Stead, Cook and Stead" they chanted.

After we were installed in our hotel by government officials, who assured us that all our expenses would be taken care of, my first thought was of food. I all but fainted just reading the room-service menu and would have gorged myself had Dr. Cook not warned me against it, explaining that I would be sick if I ate any amount of anything, so shrunken was my stomach, and especially sick if I ate rich food, to which my body would react as if it were poison.

Everywhere we walked in Copenhagen, beautiful young women followed us. Once, as we disembarked from a cab, a group of them showered us with flowers, then began to hug and kiss us. They ran after the vehicles in which we travelled through the streets, shouting, "Ve looff you, Dr. Cook and Mr. Stead."

At first, we were repulsed by all the luxury after so many months of deprivation (to which we had become so accustomed that we could not get to sleep except by stretching out on the floor beside our beds). It took me two weeks to wean myself from the floor and fall asleep atop a mattress.

We visited Bernstoff Castle, where we had tea with Princess Marie of Denmark and the visiting Princess George of Greece. Both the princesses spoke fluent, if heavily accented, English, as did most of the people in whose houses we were guests.

How strange it seemed, after two and a half years away from civilization, to return to it and find that everyone's first language was one I did not understand, as if this were the measure of how long we had been away. The language of the Eskimos had not made me feel as incongruous as the language of the Danes did.

I was surprised that although from a distance they looked just like the ones back home, I could not read a word of the newspapers. Everything seemed familiar but skewed, slightly off, as if my ordeal had altered my perceptions, as if in time the gibberish written and spoken everywhere in Copenhagen would resolve back into English, the streets and buildings would resume their former shapes, and people would once again wear what they had worn and look as they had looked when I saw them last.

I went about the city in a daze with Dr. Cook, walked with him and our hosts through narrow cobblestone streets. Everyone in our coterie spoke English, but all around us was this unintelligible hubbub of voices. There were times when, almost overcome by residual fatigue, so dizzy I could barely stand, I believed that I was still following behind the sled, that I had just awoken from a dream in which we had made it to the pole and back again, only to find ourselves in a world that in our absence had somehow been transformed, a world in which, though we were treated well, we would never feel that we belonged, but would always, for some reason inscrutably related to our having been to the pole, be looked upon as strangers.

Dr. Cook seemed to be in all ways unfazed, merely patting me reassuringly on the back when I tried to explain to him the strange sense of displacement I felt.

"It will pass," he said, speaking, I presumed, as one from whom such feelings had passed after previous expeditions.

Dining with the royal family of Denmark (the names of whom I hadn't known until we were introduced), including an eight-year-old prince and a ten-year-old princess, did nothing to dispel my sense of other-worldliness.

All of them put aside their unimaginable lives for the duration of our visit, as if our adventure was more remarkable to them than an account of one day of their lives would have been to us. As surreal as a fairytale, it was. Two explorers from New York come back from the North Pole, emerge from the Arctic on foot to have dinner with the king and queen of Denmark. We seemed to have travelled as far in time as we had in space, back to a former century in which there were castles, kings and queens, crown princes and royal astronomers. Of the castles and mansions we visited, I retained almost no impression. I remember only antiques contained by structures that were themselves antiques.

Dr. Cook, because he had been the leader of the expedition, had many honours conferred upon him by the Danes. The Danish Royal Geographical Society's gold medal was presented to him by King Frederick at the Palais Concert Hall. I was standing beside him, and no sooner had the medal been placed around his neck than he took it off and placed it around mine, to a thunderous ovation from the audience.

· CHAPTER THIRTY-EIGHT ·

THERE WAS A CERTAIN AMOUNT OF SCEPTICISM IN EDITORIALS IN newspapers around the world about Dr. Cook's claim of having reached the pole, editorials that were reprinted in the Danish papers.

The New York editorials, aside from those of the *Herald*, were reservedly, noncommittally congratulatory. The British papers said they would reserve judgment on Dr. Cook's claim until his "proofs," about the very existence of which there was some question, had been examined.

But the explorers of the world quickly came to Dr. Cook's defence—explorers such as Ernest Shackleton, just back from a far-thest south in the Antarctic, and Gen. Adolphus W. Greely, of the infamous Greely expedition.

"The word of a gentleman explorer has always been sufficient 'proof,'" said Roald Amundsen. "I can see no reason why this should not be the case with Dr. Cook." Ernest Sverdrup professed to having not the slightest doubt that Dr. Cook and I had reached the pole.

But only Amundsen continued to speak publicly in support of Dr. Cook after what was called "the revelation at the Tivoli."

A reception was held for Dr. Cook and me at the ballroom of the Tivoli Casino, the gilded walls of which were hung with wreaths of roses in our honour.

During the celebration, a man tiptoed from the back of the room to the head table and handed Dr. Cook a piece of paper as if he was officially serving him with some legal document. Dr. Cook glanced at it, then handed it to me. The paper read: "Peary Says Stars and Stripes

Nailed to the Pole. Claims the Pole as His." Someone snatched it from my hands.

Dr. Cook's expression was suddenly so at odds with everything else—the garland of flowers that he wore around his neck, the white tablecloth spread with glasses of sherry and champagne, the merry-making Danes with their glasses held aloft. A melting ice sculpture, someone's version of the North Pole, lay in front of him.

The man who delivered the piece of paper said that Peary had, that very day, laid claim to the pole, and had said he could prove, as he was sure Dr. Cook could not, that he had been there. Peary and the members of the Peary Arctic Club were hinting that in claiming to have reached the pole, Dr. Cook was more than just "mistaken," and that the world would soon know what they meant. The Danes on either side of Dr. Cook all looked grimly resolved, as if they had just heard that a long-predicted war had broken out at last.

Dr. Cook recovered his composure. He smiled and, holding aloft a glass of champagne, proclaimed to my astonishment that in the discovery of the pole, there was such glory that he would not mind sharing some of it with Peary.

In the wake of the revelation at the Tivoli Casino, there were new revelations every day. A controversy began that we were told was crowding all else from the front pages of the New York papers.

We learned that while we were returning from the pole, in the summer of 1908, Peary left Washington for Cape Sheridan on the *Roosevelt*. Shortly after his arrival, as the papers reported in mid-August, he encountered an emaciated, scurvy-ridden Rudolph Franke. The papers said that Dr. Cook had told the at first disappointed and resentful Franke that if he kept on going north, he would either die or "wreck" the expedition. Dr. Cook assured me he had said no such thing.

By the time Peary found him, the papers said, Franke was glad that Dr. Cook had sent him back, so unnerved was he by the prospect of another winter in the Arctic. Franke said that when he last saw him, Dr. Cook was well and proceeding north with Mr. Stead, a group of

Eskimos and a team of dogs, his intention being to leave everyone else behind once he believed he was close enough to the pole to attempt the last leg on snowshoes. But Dr. Cook had not returned to Etah as expected in the summer of 1908. By the fall of that year, the where-abouts of both the Cook and Peary expeditions had been unknown.

It was reported in the *Herald* that Peary, a year later, on his way back from the pole in August, had encountered Harry Whitney at Etah. He was said to have caught Whitney in possession of some note-books that Dr. Cook had asked him to take back to New York and give to Mrs. Cook. Peary said that he would strand Whitney in the Arctic if he tried to take on board anything of Dr. Cook's. It was said that at Peary's instructions, Whitney and Robert Bartlett, Peary's first mate, buried Dr. Cook's notebooks at Etah, though exactly where, no one, not even Whitney and Bartlett, seemed to know.

"Perhaps it was unwise of me to have left things of such value with an associate of Peary's," Dr. Cook told the Danish press, "or indeed to have let them out of my sight, but I dared not take them with me on my journey by foot over Greenland lest they fall to pieces."

I confirmed Dr. Cook's account of how decomposed the note-books had been and said that Whitney had been the only hope of preserving what was left of them.

"Until I have those notebooks, nothing but another expedition to the pole using the very same route as I used could prove with *absolute* certainty that I was at the pole," Dr. Cook told reporters. "Polar explorers, through the ages, have always been taken at their word. Why have I not been extended this courtesy, while Peary, who has no more proof than I do, has been taken at *his* word—by the press at least, if not by the people of America."

Associates of Peary's countered these accusations with a host of their own, saying that Dr. Cook's account of reaching the pole was so vague and simplistic that it might have been written by a child and was therefore impossible to verify.

It was said that Dr. Cook's account of his attainment of the pole differed every time he told it. His compass and sextant readings, inasmuch as he had reported them at all, were inconsistent. His description of the land he crossed and saw on his way to the pole seemed to contradict those of other explorers, whose reports were far more detailed and scientifically composed. The only thing he said consistently was that he knew he was at the North Pole because his compass needle pointed ninety degrees dead south—but it had long been known that at the North Pole, a compass would read ninety degrees south.

It was said that astronomers took exception to Dr. Cook's descriptions of shadows at the pole. He had kept no record, or at least had none in his possession, of the variations in the earth's magnetic field, which would have registered on his compass as he neared the pole. Had he kept such a record, these variations, the numerical value of which could not be predicted by scientists, could have been confirmed by a future expedition. Peary had not kept a record of these variations either, though he claimed he could prove that he had made allowances for them in his navigations.

Peary's supporters said that in what few calculations Dr. Cook had divulged, he had failed to take into account the curvature of the earth, instead talking as if he believed the world was flat. They said that his two Eskimo guides, who at first confirmed that they had gone with him to the pole, had retracted their stories. They were said to have laughed when asked if they and Dr. Cook and Mr. Stead had made it to the Big Nail, asserting that at no point on their journey had they ventured out onto the polar sea far enough to lose sight of land.

Dr. Cook's supporters: Peary, too, had no records, had made statements that were contradicted by the works of earlier explorers. As for the Eskimos, it was well known that in their eagerness to please white men, they would agree with *any* statement that was made and were therefore bound to contradict themselves.

Peary's descriptions of the effect on the ice of the ocean currents and of the weather conditions were almost identical to those of Dr. Cook, who had published his report first. But Peary's went unquestioned, while every detail of Dr. Cook's was scrutinized.

Dr. Cook pointed out that Peary had sent back the only member of his expedition who had sufficient knowledge of the compass and the sextant to verify that he was at the pole. This man was Capt. Bob Bartlett, whom Peary said he sent back because he did not think that Bartlett had earned the right to share in the glory of reaching the pole, never having made a bid for it before. Matthew Henson and some Eskimos had, according to Peary, gone with him to the pole. To them, as they were not white but belonged to what Peary called the "inferior races," went none of the glory.

Peary's supporters replied that Dr. Cook, too, had sent back the only member of his expedition who could have verified his claims, Rudolph Franke.

Franke, Dr. Cook's supporters pointed out, was a cook who was making his first trip to the Arctic and had no knowledge of navigation, unlike the experienced explorer and ship's captain Bob Bartlett. They added that "Dr. Cook did not send back his long-time assistant, Devlin Stead," but Peary's supporters dismissed the idea that Mr. Stead could settle the controversy, declaring that he had no navigational knowledge and adding that, in any case, he would back up anything Dr. Cook said, so blindly was he devoted to him.

The controversy became so nightmarishly complicated that I wondered how laymen could possibly be convinced that Dr. Cook had beaten Peary to the pole.

"I wish I understood the science of it all," I said. "If I did, I would be spending all my time defending you with proofs, with arguments, instead of just vouching for your honesty. You must not lose any time. You must defend yourself. Show what you remember of your records to experts who can verify your claims."

"There are no experts who can verify my claims," said Dr. Cook. "Nor any who can verify Peary's. As for understanding the science of it all, no one does. Science is, as yet, too primitive. There is an expert in every subject, and not even the experts understand each other. As I told the press, my claim can be proved only by someone who retraced my footsteps as I remember them. And who is going to undertake an expedition to the pole just to prove that someone else got there before him?"

He waved his hand as if to dismiss the whole idea of defending himself against Peary and the members of his Arctic club. I decided to drop the matter temporarily, but to return to it before we left for home.

In the middle of all the controversy, the celebrations continued.

Dr. Cook met in the chancery of the University of Copenhagen with the rector magnificus, Professor Torp, and the royal astronomer, Professor Stromgren, whose technical questions Dr. Cook answered so satisfactorily that it was decided the university should confer upon him an honorary degree. This was done at the Great Hall, where he told the audience members—who had heard that, elsewhere, his claim was being met with scepticism and, in Peary's case, outright accusations of fraud—that the two Eskimos who went with us to the pole would confirm his story, as would his records of observations, which, though not now in his possession, soon would be.

He stood in an elevated, canopied pulpit, leaning out over the rail of it towards his audience like the figurehead on the prow of a ship.

"I can say no more. I can do no more," said Dr. Cook, extending his arms. "I show you my hands. I show you my hands. They are clean." A great ovation followed.

That night, he received a telegram from Admiral de Richelieu: "Green-eyed envy and jealousy are doing their envenomed work, Dr. Cook, but we believe in you."

We heard that the Danish poet Dr. Norman Hansen challenged to a duel a member of the press who had dared to call Dr. Cook's claim of reaching the pole "a fairytale."

Again, we had dinner with the Danish royal family at the Charlottenlund Palace, where we sat at the right hand of King Frederick.

Mountains of telegrams of congratulation were sent up to our hotel rooms, along with telegrams inviting us to dine, to speak, to simply "appear." We no longer mentioned Peary, not even to one another.

· CHAPTER THIRTY-NINE ·

IT WAS ARRANGED THAT WE WOULD SAIL HOME ON THE *Oscar II*, the flagship of the Danish-American Steamship Company. Among those seeing us off were officials from the university and various geographical societies.

All I could think as we stood at the rail of the ship and waved to the thousands who on the shore were bidding us goodbye was that our odyssey had only stalled in Copenhagen and now had begun again.

I knew that our course would take us southwest through the North Atlantic to America, but this knowledge did not impress me as much as the fact that soon we would once again be out of sight of land.

Not that there was much solitude to be had on this crossing of the *Oscar II*.

It was as if the population of a small city had been appointed our official escorts from the Old World to the New. The discovery of the pole was the sole theme of the voyage.

In the dining room, in the ballroom, on the promenade deck, we were applauded. I sometimes felt like we had discovered the pole ten years earlier and had been hired for the entertainment of the passengers, paid celebrities of the Danish-American Steamship Company.

Parties were thrown in our honour. The whole voyage was a party. Honeymooning couples, retired travellers, professors of everything on their way to give lectures in New York—all said that they believed in us. I hoped the voyage would never end.

"I hardly know how I came to be caught up in all of this," Dr. Cook said one night, throwing up his arms and looking about him as if his cabin was packed with celebrants.

"You did what you set out to do," I said. "All of this is no more than you deserve."

"The Danes are a wonderful people," he said. "They all but adopted us as two of their own. If we were Danes, our own countrymen would not turn against us."

"No one will turn against us," I said.

He shook his head slightly.

"It is too much," he said. "Don't you think so? All this adulation, all this worship for just two men. I am overwhelmed. The accomplishment of two men should not mean so much to others."

"We beat Peary to the pole," I said. "You once wrote me that it was your intention to make sure that no man who did not deserve it won the prize. You have done exactly that."

"The North Pole now seems to me to lie behind a veil," he said. "There was so little there to perceive that my memory of the place is all but blank. What I remember best is the agony of getting there and the agony of getting back. I feel as though I have been celebrated enough already. The Danes did more for me than any man deserves. I wish I could simply put a stop to it now. Just say, 'No more,' and for the rest of my life be left alone. History will record our accomplishment. That is all I have ever really wanted: that you and I be remembered for what we did together."

"You are tired," I said. "You should have been resting these past few weeks."

"There will soon be time to rest, I hope," he said. "I am done with expeditions. I will be a father and a husband and a doctor from now on."

To whom, I wondered, would he be a father if he was done with expeditions? What part, from now on, would I play in his life?

"The other pole," he said, "the unscaled peaks of other continents, all the yet-to-be-accomplished feats of exploration and discovery seem pointless to me now. I have fulfilled my life's dream, though it seems an *ignis fatuus*. I suppose there remains only for me to collect on my achievement, which I must do, for I owe it to those who, because of my absence, have endured so much. Prizes, book contracts, a year, at most two, lecturing around the world, and then it will be back to Brooklyn for us for good. I can hardly stand to think of spending that much time among so many people after so much time up north.

"I will never forget it, Devlin, living with you in that cave. One hundred nights we spent in that wretched dwelling at Cape Sparbo.

"It is hard to explain to you, Devlin, what I am feeling and why. I have a strange, foreign feeling of being native to nowhere, of being, no matter where I go, exotic."

"I feel the same," I said.

"We have been to the white/dark desert of the Arctic. It is as devoid of features as the sea. Yet it exerts on the soul a greater pull than all the marvels, all the wonders of New York.

"One day, as I lay there in that cave by myself, waiting for you and the Eskimos to come back from checking the traps, I felt the presence of your mother."

"I felt it, too," I said.

He seemed not to have heard me. "And I was suddenly, and for the first time ever, certain that we would not make it back alive. I was certain that we would die. I felt that I had betrayed her yet again. Betrayed you. How can I step back into the world without your help, Devlin?"

"You will have my help," I said.

"It seems as though something has happened in the world since we stopped attending to it. Even Copenhagen seemed always to be on the brink of some—it is hard to say just what—some culmination. Something in Copenhagen was stirring that I fear is roaring in New York. How long has it been since we were there?"

I began to wonder if he was having some sort of breakdown. "Twenty-eight months," I said. "We left in the summer of 1907."

"The summer of 1907," he said. "And now it is the fall of 1909. So long."

BOOK SIX

· CHAPTER FORTY ·

ON SEPTEMBER 20, AT THREE IN THE AFTERNOON, THE *Oscar II* dropped anchor off Fire Island in Upper New York Bay. The American Arctic Club which, unlike the Peary Arctic Club, had accepted Dr. Cook's claim to have reached the pole, had asked that the ship not proceed up the East River until the next morning so that plans for Dr. Cook's reception could be finalized. The ship had already, at the club's request, spent the previous night anchored off Sandy Hook, off Boston Harbour, for the same reason. Mrs. Cook had sent word that because she was not feeling well, she would wait until the morning to see her husband.

Ships that had assembled from all over the world for a naval review were moored on the Manhattan side of the river, the shape of each ship traced out in coloured lights, but the Brooklyn docks were as desolate and silent as they always were after dark, in contrast to the ceaseless clamour that rose up from them by day.

Several celebrations were converging on the city all at once. It was three hundred years since Henry Hudson had "discovered" the river that ever since had borne his name. It was the one-hundredth anniversary of the invention of the steamboat by Robert Fulton. Millions of electric lights had been strung throughout the streets of the boroughs of New York, most of them in Brooklyn and Manhattan. It was said that Wilbur Wright was going to fly his new machine from Governor's Island to the Statue of Liberty and back again. It was predicted that, over the next couple of weeks, millions of visitors would come to

New York. And into the middle of all of this, Dr. Cook and I were soon to sail on the *Oscar II*.

Dr. Cook sent for me. I was shown by a ship's officer to his cabin. Somewhere inside the ship, an orchestra was playing, and passengers bearing champagne-filled glasses strolled about the decks.

The officer, a Dane not much older than me who spoke fluent but heavily accented English, rapped twice, loudly, on the door of Dr. Cook's cabin.

"You may go in, sir," he said, "but you are to close the door behind you." He then tipped his hat to me and strode away as if he were following very specific orders.

I opened the door and thought at first that the cabin was empty. It was quite spacious and unlit except for two oil lamps that flanked a row of porthole windows.

I could dimly make out the lavish furnishings: six plush chairs around what might have been a card table, two sofas at right angles, a revolvable mirror in a wooden frame. I saw that a door on my left led to another large room. I slowly made for it and was about to say Dr. Cook's name when he said mine.

He was seated on an armless chair that was positioned in a direct line from the door, his legs stretched out so that the chair was resting on its back legs, his hands clasped behind his head, which he leaned against the wall. He said my name as though he were wearily relieved that I had come. His reflective, stock-taking posture, and the gloom of the cabin gave me the momentary sense that I had been taken to visit a well-accommodated prisoner whose guard was standing just outside the door. Slowly, deliberately, he let the chair fall forward, unclasped his hands, rose to his feet and sighed in the manner of someone who, though glad to see me, wished we were meeting under other circumstances. His face was thinner than when we left Copenhagen, every hollow and shadow, every feature, more pronounced. He had, several days before, admitted to me that he was so in dread of our arrival in New York that he could not bear to eat.

His posture and his expression affected me in some way for which

I would not find the words until after I had left the cabin. It was as though he had at last become the man I imagined him to be before we met. His were the eyes of a man humbly and indulgently resigned to the loneliness of greatness, a man who, though he knew he would never meet his equal, had a gentle, all-forgiving view of humankind. But at the same time, there was that barely perceptible look of amused disdain, a universal dismissiveness, an inclination to regard all things, himself included, as ultimately inconsequential.

He stood up, put his hands on my shoulders and held me at arm's length as if to gauge how much I had changed since we left New York more than two years earlier. I never felt more urgently the need to address him by some name, call him *something*, but I could not, especially not now, bring myself to call him Dr. Cook. Father. The word was in my mind. On my tongue. Perhaps he sensed this, for he turned me about and, with a hand on the small of my back, led me to one of the sofas.

Suddenly, even allowing for physical weariness and his usually reserved manner in private, he seemed quite sombre. Perhaps, I thought, this is how you feel in the wake of some great accomplishment to which you have dedicated your entire life. Once the day you have so long looked forward to has come, what then? What next?

I wondered if my being there was affecting his mood, if he was inhibited by the presence beside him of an impostor, of someone about whom he had fooled the world just as, some were saying, he was trying to fool it now with his claim of having reached the pole. How completely discredited his claim would be if it became known how we two were related.

"I fear the coming months will be unbearable," he said, "unless someone I can trust is at my side."

"Someone you can trust *is* at your side," I said. "You must not doubt it for a moment."

He nodded but said nothing.

"You mustn't worry," I said. "On the ship, they say that almost everyone in New York believes you. Almost everyone in America. Far more than believe Peary. It is only those who backed Peary who have their doubts about you. Or claim to. They know that you were at the pole a year before Peary got there, if he ever did. They know it."

He nodded and smiled. "Unless I am very mistaken," he said, "you suspect there are still some things that I have kept from you."

I began to protest, but he raised his hand.

"Listen to me. There *is* something."

I did not feel the sort of dread I had felt on previous occasions when he had made this admission. I was his son. Together we had made it to the pole. The possibility of catastrophe had passed.

"At Etah, Devlin, shortly before we arrived on the rescue expedition, Henson told Peary that he was saying some things during his bouts of delirium that he would not want others to hear. Peary told Henson to keep everyone away from him until he was well again. But Henson was so concerned that, without medical assistance, Peary would die.

"The first thing Peary said to me was that he knew I could be trusted to keep to myself anything he said while I examined him. This is how Peary asks for something, by telling you that he knows you will give it to him. I told him I would be discreet. And I have been, all these years."

"What did Peary say?" I said.

"He said, 'It can be done, Dr. Cook. I have thought it through, and I am sure it can be done.'"

"The North Pole," I said.

Dr. Cook nodded. "That's what I thought he meant. That he was sure he could make it. And that therefore I should take his wife and child back home but leave him behind. But there were times, over the next few days, when he seemed to be saying just the opposite. 'I see now that it can't be done, Dr. Cook,' he said. 'It simply cannot be done.' I thought he was uncertain, wavering. So whenever he said, 'I see now that it can't be done,' I told him he was right. When he said that he had thought it through and was sure it *could* be done, I disagreed with him and urged him to leave with us and thereby save himself.

"This went on for days, until one afternoon, when he was seemingly lucid but really more delirious than ever, I realized that I had been mistaken all along. I had misunderstood him. When he had said, 'I see now that it can't be done,' he meant that he had come to the conclusion that to reach the North Pole under any circumstances was impossible. 'The pole will not be reached,' he said. 'Not by me. And therefore not by anyone.'

"When he had said, 'I have thought it through, and I am sure it can be done,' he meant that it was possible to fool people into thinking you had reached the pole. 'A man who knew what he was doing could get away with it,' he said. 'It is just the sickness, Dr. Cook,' Henson said. I nodded and said no more about it.

"But I was sure that Peary, when he was lucid, really had thought things through and come to those conclusions. How long ago, I had no way of telling. Nor did I know if he would ever bring himself to act upon them. There would be so much risk involved."

"But on this last expedition . . . I said. "You think he—"

"I am certain of it," said Dr. Cook. "Just as I am sure that he remembers, has remembered all along, what he told me in that tent. If not, then Henson told him. But I think that when he was lucid, he remembered what he said when he was not. Perhaps he merely saw it in my eyes, saw that I *knew*. I saw fear in *his* eyes. Fear of me, fear of the consequences of what he had let slip in his delirium."

"You have always seemed so certain that he would not reach the pole," I said. "You have always seemed so unconcerned about it. How could you stand it, knowing it was possible that before you could get to the pole yourself, he would pretend—"

"I believed that if he faked the pole, I could *prove* he had faked it. I believed that he would not dare to fake it knowing how closely I, who had heard him say it could be done, would scrutinize his records, his proofs, his account of his great deed."

"So you will prove it now," I said. "And then everyone will know that you alone have made it to the pole."

He smiled, almost sadly, and shook his head. But then he nodded.

"Exactly," he said. "When the time is right, that is exactly what I will do."

"When—"

"It is late," he said. "You must be going."

I sensed that there was more, but that he had lost the nerve to make a full disclosure.

"The organizers of my reception are soon to board the ship," he said. "I have agreed to meet with them. In a few hours, I will make my first public appearance in America since returning from the pole. Already, thousands have gathered to witness my arrival. I dread it, Devlin. I fear a repetition of the scenes in Copenhagen. I will smile gratefully and wave at people who think of me as some sort of persecuted saint. Well, I will do what I have to do. We will both do what must be done. Try to get some sleep."

At nine o'clock, when there was still a thin mist on the water and we were just off Bedloe's Island, we were transferred by tugboat from the *Oscar II* to the *Grand Republic*, a side-wheeler that had been chartered by the American Arctic Club and was all decked out in flags from bow to stern, American and Danish flags. In some cases, pairs of them had been intertwined to form one hybrid flag, one-half composed of the Stars and Stripes, the other of the white cross on a field of red. On the foredeck was a large banner bearing Dr. Cook's name and some other words that, in the morning mist, I could not make out.

Dr. Cook was reunited on the *Grand Republic* with his wife and children. Upon seeing me beside her husband, Mrs. Cook scowled and looked as if, were we not surrounded by strangers, she would have accused me of something.

Hundreds of passengers from New York who had paid for the privilege of seeing us first came up from below deck as a band on the upper deck began to play "The Star-Spangled Banner" and the sirens of the *Grand Republic* blared out across the water.

Several men hoisted Dr. Cook on their shoulders and carried him around the deck. His protests that far too much fuss was being made of him were mistaken for modesty, further inciting the crowd.

The *Grand Republic* was hemmed in on all sides by press boats in which stood reporters busily taking notes. What an odd sight they made, that cluster of bobbing sentinels around the *Grand Republic*. In some boats there were men wielding cameras, whose clicking began all at once, as if an order had been issued to open fire.

A young woman holding a wreath of white tea roses began to make a speech in honour of Dr. Cook but was ignored, so she chased after the men who still had him on their shoulders and tossed the wreath of roses round his neck.

As Dr. Cook was carried to the top deck, he called out my name. I went aloft, following behind Mrs. Cook and her two little girls.

"Welcome, Dr. Cook," said a tall, top-hat-wearing, red-faced man who grandly introduced himself as Bird Coler, the president of Brooklyn. The borough president, he meant. He confided to Dr. Cook that the mayor of New York had declined an invitation to head up the reception committee.

By this time, many ships in the harbour were blasting their whistles, so that the words of the next speaker, the president of the American Arctic Club, Admiral Schley, went unheard, as did those that Dr. Cook made in reply, except for his opening remark that the Danes "have guaranteed to all other nations our conquest of the pole."

As the *Grand Republic* passed beneath the Brooklyn Bridge, thousands threw confetti down upon us from the walkway and all traffic on the bridge stood still—horse cars, motor cars, el trains. Drivers and passengers gaped from their vehicles at the overloaded, festooned ship.

Dr. Cook waved and blew kisses.

We continued up the East River. We passed under the Manhattan Bridge and then the uncompleted Williamsburg, from which workers waved and shouted while hanging from the cables. I looked up as though into the rigging of a ship so large it had to be constructed in mid-air.

The *Grand Republic*, after several turns up and down the river, docked at last at the wharves at the foot of South Fifth Street in Williamsburg, just below the sugar refineries in whose shadows Dr. Cook had spent his childhood.

Tens of thousands of people lined the shore, cheering, screaming, having by this time seen the *Grand Republic* go by them without stopping half a dozen times. The warships gathered in the harbour for the naval parade began to blow their whistles. Soon the whistles of the refineries were blowing, too. Men leaned out the refinery windows waving with both hands.

We walked down the gangway, Dr. Cook with Helen on his shoulders and hand in hand with Marie and Ruth, who stood on either side of him. I followed close behind like some obscure but inexcludable relation.

The police, about a hundred of them, formed a cordon around us, escorted us to a convertible motorcar, where I sat beside the driver while the Cooks, with Dr. Cook in the middle with Helen on his lap, sat in the back.

A parade of two hundred motor cars streamed out behind us. Directly behind us, on a large flatbed truck, there was a brass band that began to play even as the drivers of the cars began to blow their horns. The combined sounds of all the ship whistles and sirens, the refinery whistles, the blaring and honking car horns, the brass band and the cheering crowds was deafening, raucously discordant in the early morning. When I turned around to look at Dr. Cook, I saw that Mrs. Cook and her daughters were sitting with their eyes closed and their hands covering their ears. Dr. Cook was standing in the tonneau, waving with both hands, rising to the occasion with more enthusiasm than I had expected.

Along the five-mile parade route, a crowd later said to number one hundred thousand waved and cheered. The crowd was so large and the parade so long that the trolley tracks were blocked. Dr. Cook, still wearing his wreath of roses, doffed his derby and bowed like an orchestra conductor, at which the crowd laughed as though he was well known for such antics.

On Bedford Avenue, an American flag flew from every house. We passed the milk depot where Dr. Cook had worked with his brothers to put himself through school. On the roof of it was a massive wooden bottle, painted white and bearing the company name, Cook Bros. Milk wagons were parked end to end along the curb.

As we came into view of the intersection of Myrtle and Willoughby, not far from 670 Bushwick, we saw a huge triumphal arch spanning the intersection like a train bridge, higher than the el-train viaduct beside it, made of canvas and wood. It was hung with laurel wreaths and garlands and bore a giant globe, from the North Pole of which flew an American flag. It was a garish spectacle, painted with Arctic scenes and hung with imitation icicles, a child's vision of the North, all of it bordered with electric bulbs that in the sunlight shone to no effect. At the centre of the arch was a giant cameo-shaped portrait of Dr. Cook, and above it a banner that proclaimed, in letters six feet high, "WE BELIEVE IN YOU." As we passed beneath the arch, a number of white pigeons were released.

CHAPTER FORTY-ONE

I WAS WALKING IN MANHATTAN. DR. COOK WAS LECTURING IN
Boston. I had decided not to go with him, feeling that I could use a
break from all the public appearances we had been making since the
day of our parade. Also, it gave me a chance to spend time with
Kristine. When we met in Central Park for the first time in almost
thirty months, we hugged and kissed, unheedful of the disapproving
stares of strangers. "I thought I would never see you again," she said.
She showed me the letter in which I had told her that I loved her. "I
read it every day," she said, "wishing I could write you back and tell
you that I loved you, too." I told her that regardless of what her mother
thought of Dr. Cook, I would have to meet her soon.

Everywhere, newsies were hawking papers, on the front pages of
which were photographs of Dr. Cook or Peary, or both of them side by
side, as if they had been linked in some unravelling conspiracy. My own
photograph was appearing in the papers, though not often on the front
pages. Still, I was recognized from time to time, addressed as Mr. Stead
by strangers who told me they were pulling for me and Dr. Cook.

With no purpose or destination in mind, I strolled along
Broadway until I came to the edge of Union Square, where I sat down
on a bench to rest. Horse-drawn vehicles of many kinds shared the
street with motor cars, all teeming ceaselessly past.

I was not on the bench a minute when I heard my name spoken
by someone who had sat beside me. I turned to see a man who looked
like he had once been prosperous but doubted he would ever be again.

He raised his derby as if to let me see his silver hair, as if it was proof that he was not a crank of some kind. He introduced himself as "George Dunkle, insurance man."

He said that an old friend of Roald Amundsen's, a Norwegian sea captain named August Loose, was staying in his house during a brief visit to New York. Mr. Dunkle said that he and Captain Loose believed Dr. Cook's claim to have reached the pole was "not only true, but ver-ifiable." Dr. Cook's claim, Mr. Dunkle said, was deficient only in "navigational vocabulary," something Captain Loose could help him with. Dunkle said he had planned to telephone me to invite me to his house to see Captain Loose, but he had happened to spot me on the bench. Would I like to go with him to his house now?

Although I was sceptical, I thought I ought to at least give this friend of a friend, this Captain Loose, a hearing, so I went by car with Dunkle to a brownstone house in Gramercy Park. Dunkle showed me to the front parlour and excused himself, saying he would soon be back with Captain Loose. He closed the parlour doors behind him. Looking around the room, I realized that to whomever this elegant house belonged, it was not Mr. Dunkle.

The doors slid open and standing there was not Capt. August Loose but Comm. Robert Peary. There was no sign of Mr. Dunkle.

"I was tricked into coming here," I said. "I'll be leaving now."

"I need only a few minutes of your time," Peary said.

"Whose house is this?" I said.

"It is, as a matter of public record, the house of Herbert Bridgman," Peary said. I had never been in the house before, having always met Bridgman at his office.

Peary was clearly staying as a guest, for he was wearing a pullover sweater and woollen trousers. It was the sort of outfit he might have worn in his quarters on a ship, or at home when he was convalescing from an expedition and not accepting visitors. Despite his recent polar expedition, he looked more like he had in Washington than he had in Etah, robust but roundly so, less muscular, less angular than when I saw him last.

He scuffed across the floor as he had along the beach at Etah and to the podium in Washington. With an effort so great that it almost inspired in me the effrontery to offer him assistance, he slowly lowered himself into the chair across from mine, wincing and grunting until, in one motion, he dropped the last few inches, causing the chair to momentarily tip back slightly on two legs.

He looked at me. His eyes had a wistful, almost forlorn look about them, as if he had just heard of some great disappointment. I would soon realize that this was his permanent expression, and that it was not so much one of disappointment as it was the look of a man who knew that he could have no life beyond exploration, that he had to sacrifice everything to it, that even were he to succeed, he was past the point of being able to derive any benefit or satisfaction from it. He was resigned to the absoluteness of his obsession. All else had been forsaken. He might have been alone on the polar sea, staring out across the ice, his mind made up that he would never make it home.

"You saved my life once, Mr. Stead," he said. It was a simple statement, a declaration of fact, an admission, the closest thing to gratitude that he could muster, I supposed.

"It may not be too late to save yourself," he said.

"What do you mean?" I said.

"You have been duped by Dr. Cook," he said. "As of now, you are guilty of nothing more than gullibility. But things may change."

"I have not been duped," I said. "There is no doubt in my mind that I was at the pole with Dr. Cook."

You who can barely cross this room, who could barely have crossed it *before* your expedition, would have the world believe that you have just been to the pole, I restrained myself from saying. There was no point arguing the merits of his claim, repeating criticisms of it already made a hundred times by his detractors.

Peary looked as if he had long known that such a meeting would take place between us. Then suddenly he laughed in a way that was so familiar I thought I had seen him laugh before until I realized that I was remembering Dr. Cook's description of it. There was no mirth in it, but nor was there derision or malice. His mouth came open, a laugh-like sound came out, his mouth closed again, his back teeth clicking loudly as if some mechanical part had clamped back into place.

"It is not for me to make Dr. Cook's case," I said. "Especially not under these circumstances."

"I knew your mother, Mr. Stead," he said.

"I know," I said.

"I met her once. Briefly. At a party for some doctors in Manhattan. That is where she met Dr. Cook. That is where we all met."

He paused as if to see what effect this revelation would have on me.

"I know, as you do, that Dr. Cook is your father. But there are things about Dr. Cook that you do *not* know, Mr. Stead. Tell Cook that if he does not tell you what I mean by this, I will."

"You are only trying to make me doubt him," I said. "I will tell him nothing."

"I suspected as much. He has not had the courage to tell you everything. He has almost convinced himself—But I will say no more about it. Confront him. Confront your father. He will tell you. I will not recount his story, having played no part in it worth mentioning. No doubt he will twist things. Let him. I would rather you heard his sordid story from his lips. Confront him. Tell him what I said. If you are not satisfied with his response, come back to me. And perhaps when you know the truth, you will be a gentleman and admit that you were fooled, and that the honour that you thought was yours and his belongs to me."

I could not think, let alone speak.

"Cook will tell you," Peary said, "so it is unlikely that you and I will ever meet again."

He shifted slightly in his chair. I thought he was about to extend his hand for me to shake. I was not sure what I would have done if he had. How strange it would have been to hold that hand again. His eyes were no longer blue. They were black and shining like water at the bottom of a well. They brimmed over, and two uninterrupted streams of tears ran down his face.

"I will not have it taken from me," he shouted, though his expression did not change. "I will not share it with a cur like Cook. I will not let him make them doubt me. There must be no doubts. If there are doubts, then it will all be spoiled. I must be remembered for what I did, not for what I might have done. There must be no controversy. It must be settled, absolutely settled, or else Cook will be remembered, too."

Peary was well into this tirade before I realized that he was no longer speaking to me, looking not at me but at someone in the doorway.

I turned and saw Jo Peary. Peary stopped shouting, stopped pounding the arms of his chair with his hands.

I had not seen Mrs. Peary since Washington. I thought I detected in her a change that corresponded to the one I saw in Peary. There would be no life for them after exploration, the look in her eyes seemed to say. I think that she had always assumed there would be, that he would accomplish or renounce his goal when he was still a young man and then their real life would begin. But he had spent the better part of his life trying to reach the pole, and he would spend the balance of it trying to prove that he had done so.

Mrs. Peary looked at me.

"Perhaps you ought to leave, Mr. Stead," she said. She smiled slightly at me, a smile of goodbye in which I could find no malice or unkindness. Yet surely she knew what her husband knew: that Dr. Cook was my father. She looked and sounded so detached. I saw that she would hold a part of herself in reserve from him for the rest of their life together. She would not, any longer, let him have all of her. Her happiness would not depend on his. It would no longer be her purpose to make him happy, for that could not be done. She would stay with him, support him, commiserate with him, but she would have this other inner life that she would keep apart from his.

CHAPTER FORTY-TWO

You have been duped... That is where we all met... There are things about Dr. Cook that you do not know... Tell Cook that if he does not tell you what I mean, I will.

Those words, which I kept telling myself were just the ravings of a broken man, kept running through my mind as I rode the el train back across the bridge to Brooklyn. Peary had had me followed just so he could say those words to me and tell me to repeat them to Dr. Cook.

A few nights later, after Dr. Cook had returned from Boston, he and I sat in the drawing room of the Dakota, staring at the fire. He had shaken so many hands in Boston that, just as in Copenhagen, his right hand was a swollen mass for which he had fashioned a bandage and a sling. He sat there, his bandaged hand removed from the sling and resting palm up on the arm of the sofa.

He had been so exhausted upon arriving home that I had not expected him to visit the drawing room. But I had listened for him anyway and thought it was just my imagination when I heard the sound of creaking floorboards. Upon getting up and peering out into the hallway, I saw that the doors of the drawing room were open.

I found him slumped on the sofa, his eyes closed, looking almost as haggard as he had just after his emergence from the Arctic. He opened his eyes when he heard me, asked me to close both sets of doors, which I did before joining him on the sofa.

"I am told that support for me over Peary is thirty-five to one among the public," he said.

"That's wonderful," I said.

He shrugged. "I am leading because I staked my claim first, and because I made it back to New York ahead of Peary. I was the first to be celebrated. That, at least, is something that cannot be changed. It is unlikely now that Peary will even have a parade. He will certainly not have one in New York. It would seem absurd—"

"I met with Peary," I said, unable to wait any longer.

"Why on earth would you do that?" he said.

"I should say that he tricked me into meeting with him." I told him of meeting Dunkle on the bench in Union Square. "Peary said that he knows you're my father. When he saw that I was not surprised, he told me there were things about you that I did not know. He said that if you did not tell me what he meant by this, he would."

Dr. Cook sat forward as suddenly as if he had had a seizure. He stood up and grabbed the back of his neck with his left hand while allowing the bandaged one to drop as if he had forgotten it was injured.

"I was certain it would never come to this," he said.

"What do you mean?" I said.

"How desperate he must be. Devlin . . . Oh, Christ, I was certain it would never come to this."

"Certain what would never come to this? I don't understand."

"Do you remember, just a few nights ago, you said that no one would turn against me?"

I nodded.

"You are wrong," he said. "Many people will. Some who are very close to me will turn against me. You have promised to believe in me no matter what, but even you may turn against me."

"I would never do so," I said. "Never. No matter what."

"No matter what?"

"No, but—"

"Then you must let me tell you everything. And this time, it will be everything. There will be no secrets between us any more. What a great relief that will be. If you will just hear me out, Devlin. It may be that once you have heard the whole story, you will understand."

He sounded so unconvinced that I felt a dread greater than any I had felt at any time on our expedition to the pole. *There are things about Dr. Cook that you do not know.* I felt as I had long ago, when I thought he was about to tell me that he had deceived me, that he was not really my father.

"Before I tell you what Peary meant, I must tell you something else. It turns out that I was wrong about something. I was wrong and Peary was right."

"I don't know what you mean—" I said. He put up his hand.

"I have known it for some time," he said, "long before I went to meet with Bradley about the slaughter charter. It was only when I met with Bradley that I made up my mind."

"About what?"

"We were never there, Devlin. We never made it to the pole."

"No,—" I said.

I pulled away from him as he reached his hand towards me. He drew up to full height again.

"I decided that, to quote Peary, I was a man who knew what he was doing. Remember, in the tent at Etah? 'A man who knew what he was doing could get away with it.' I think you know what I am saying."

"But I was with you," I said. "*We* were with you. The four of us. We did it together. We risked everything, and we did what no one else has ever done. You asked us if we wanted to turn back, and we said no. I know you. You would never do what Peary did."

"Devlin," he said, "it was Peary who did what I did. McKinley was a kind of test case. You see, Devlin, I never reached the top of Mt. McKinley. I pretended to in such a way that if it was discovered that I had not reached the top, it would seem that I had made an honest mistake, that I honestly thought I had made it and had not set out to wilfully commit a hoax. But it was not discovered. My claim to have climbed McKinley was accepted. And it was then that I began to wonder if Peary might be right about the pole. I thought about it for a long time, especially after Washington. I tried to work out in my head if it could be done. Right here in this drawing room, night after night. If

441

only we had been able to get back to civilization sooner than we did."

"You risked the lives of three other people," I said, "to accomplish what you knew to be a hoax?" I stood and gave in to the urge to cry, turning my back to him.

"I did not mean to risk anyone's life. According to all my planning, there ought not to have been any great risk. But the ocean currents were not what I had had every reason to expect. Dozens of other explorers all reported the same currents on the route we took. It seems impossible that so many men could have misread them in the same way. And yet they did."

"Why did you ever write to me?" I said. "What did you want from me?"

"I told you that if you heard me out, you might understand. Will you wait until the end to pass judgment on me?"

I could not speak.

"You must not think that what I have done rests lightly on my mind. If there was any other way, I would not have chosen this one. I could not let a man like Peary prevail.

"What a torment these past few weeks have been, I could never make you understand. Every time an honour was bestowed upon me, every time I was embraced, every time someone shook my hand or professed his faith in me, it seemed that the magnitude of my betrayal grew. That it was necessary to my real purpose that I betray the trust of so many people did not make it any easier for me to do it. And the worst still lies ahead for me. Some of the people who at first supported me have already turned against me. Peary has far more money and power behind him. Every attempt will be made to discredit me. But it will be enough for me if this controversy is never settled. Like me, Peary will always have his detractors, people who will do all they can to prove that he was never at the pole."

He was speaking at a frenzied pace, in the manner and tone of someone declaiming in solitude as he had so often done in this room while I lay in bed across the hall. I clung to the perverse hope that he was mad, that every word he was saying was the product of exhaustion.

"Peary says he must have fame. Well, I have followed my own imperatives. One has been that you must have happiness. Another that Peary must *not* have fame. Just why this last imperative is so important, you do not fully understand yet. It is not only because Peary gave my name to Francis Stead."

"Why have you done this?" I said. I was still crying. "You did not need to do this. You are not that sort of man. You are a kind, honest man to whom others are drawn, whom others admire. You are a doctor to whom people come for help when they are sick. Everyone who knows you, who really knows you, would vouch for you absolutely. You treated the Eskimos no differently than you do the patients who come to see you here in Brooklyn. You have done so much for me. More than I have told you. I don't understand it. I don't believe it. What you are saying can't be true."

"Devlin, listen to me. You think that I have betrayed you as I betrayed your mother. But the very opposite is true. I left your mother's last words to me unanswered. But I have not turned away from you. All that I have done, I have done *for* you and *for* your mother."

Dr. Cook crouched down in front of me, as if I was a child to whom he was about to reveal something that he doubted he could make me understand.

"On the afternoon of the day Francis Stead confessed to Peary and, later, to me . . ."

Peary asked Dr. Cook to join him in a search for a star stone about which he said the Eskimos had told him. They set out from Redcliffe House on snowshoes, walking in silence for several miles up the coast from McCormick Bay.

Quite abruptly, Peary stopped and looked out across the ice.

"Stead spoke to you," he said.

"Yes," Dr. Cook said.

"When Stead returns to New York," Peary said, "he will tell others that he killed his wife, and why. You and I will both be ruined. No backer will ever again have anything to do with us. And that is not an exaggeration. My chief backer, Morris Jesup, is known as a pillar of society. He is a member of the New York City Mission and Travel Society, vice-president of the American Sunday School Union, one of the leaders of the Crusade for the Suppression of Vice and Obscenity. Can you imagine how a man like that would regard me if Stead repeated to the authorities what he said to us? Stead convinced me that he can prove he killed his wife. He can tell the police what she was wearing when she died, give them the pseudonym he used to book passage to Newfoundland and register in his hotel. Things that can be verified, and that no one else could know. Also, there are certain letters. I live in Philadelphia. Stead and I sometimes correspond. If, in the context of his murder of his wife, my letters to him were made public... 'You will never have a moment's peace until you confront her with the truth,' I once wrote to him. He is such an amusing fool that it never occurred to me he would do anything. Besides, I took precautions. I never mentioned names in my letters. You, for instance, I referred to only as "the doctor" or "the father of the boy." I destroyed his letters after I finished reading them. But Francis, without my knowledge, made carbon copies of his letters, in which your name and others were often mentioned. And since my letters are obviously replies to his, the whole thing, under the circumstances, leaves me somewhat compromised."

"You speak as if her death is nothing but an inconvenience to you," said Dr. Cook.

"I did not know the woman as well as you did," Peary said. "I am guilty of nothing but misjudging Stead."

Dr. Cook began to walk away.

"Is the boy's safety of any concern to you?" Peary shouted. Dr. Cook came back.

"What did Stead say about the boy?"

"He told me that he planned to pay him a visit," Peary said. "He told me some other things, too."

Peary and Cook spoke for some time.

Later, at Redcliffe House, the members of the expedition had their customary after-dinner brandy and cigars.

Francis Stead slept beside Dr. Cook on the floor of Redcliffe House that night, as he had on every other night of the expedition. It was as if their conversation of that morning had never taken place.

In the middle of the night, Dr. Cook woke up from a fitful sleep and saw that Francis Stead's sleeping bag was empty. Certain that Stead was standing over him, he rolled over onto his back and crossed his arms in front of his face, expecting to see the muzzle of a rifle pointed at him or an axe upraised to strike him. He almost cried out for help. But there was no one standing over him, no sound in the house but that of the breathing of the others, who seemed to be deeply asleep.

He looked towards the other "room" and saw Peary, paraffin pot in hand, standing fully clothed at one end of the curtain, his torso and face lit up by the tiny blue flame that flickered from the pot. He opened his mouth to speak, but Peary put his finger to his lips. Peary did not go back inside, did not draw the curtain. He looked at Francis Stead's empty sleeping bag, then at Dr. Cook. He nodded ever so slightly, almost imperceptibly. Then he looked away and withdrew behind the curtain.

As quietly as he could, Dr. Cook got up, put on his moccasins, took his parka from the wall. The door was unbolted. As he was about to open it, he heard a rustling of the curtain that divided the crew's quarters from those of the Pearys.

Taking a lantern, Dr. Cook opened the door as silently as he could. No draught swept in, as the night was calm. But he saw when he lit his lantern that it was snowing heavily, the flakes falling straight down. He went outside and closed the door. As they had to have done when Francis Stead went out, the dogs sprang up, but when they saw that he had no food for them, they lay down again.

There was no sign of Francis Stead's footprints, and when he looked behind him, he saw that his own were fast filling in with snow. So much the better, he thought. The snow will cover everything.

He made his way towards the tolt of rock and soon saw Francis Stead, saw him far away, sitting on the "bench", his form lit by a lantern that was on the bench beside him.

Dr. Cook quickly extinguished his lantern.

He was not yet close enough to Francis Stead to see the falling snow except as a blurring of the light, such as might have been the effect of fog or mist. All he could make out of Francis Stead was an amorphous form in the light of the lantern.

He walked towards that lone light through a darkness so absolute he was able only to hear and feel the falling snow, which, though his hood was up, gently brushed against and melted on his face, so cold it made his forehead ache, the water running down his cheeks into his mouth and onto his beard, where it turned to ice again.

Soon Dr. Cook was able to make him out more clearly. He was sitting on the bench, his hands clasped about his drawn-up knees. Nothing else was visible but that nimbus, that gloriole of light that seemed to be emanating from that hunched figure at the heart of it. As if the snow was falling nowhere else but on that tolt of rock.

It was so dark, so silent, that it was hard to believe that Redcliffe House still existed, let alone such things as towns and cities.

He stopped perhaps fifty feet away from Francis Stead, directly in his line of sight. Francis Stead had been sitting there almost motionless for so long that snow lay inches deep on his hood and shoulders and on his legs. The snow combined with the furs he was wearing to round his form, enlarge it and obscure his face, so that it might have been some massive-browed, white-haired ape that was hunched there on that rock.

He circled around, keeping his distance from him until he was almost directly behind him.

He recalled the last part of the conversation he and Peary had had before they returned to Redcliffe House that afternoon.

"I want Cook to kill me," Francis Stead had told Peary. He had set out to Peary exactly when and how it should be done, and what would happen if they did not go along with his demands. "I will do to the boy what I did to his mother," said Francis Stead. "And when I get back to New York, I will ruin you both."

All the after-dinner drinks, except his own, Dr. Cook's and

Peary's, Francis Stead had mixed with laudanum. Dr. Cook was to have stayed awake until after Francis Stead had gone outside, but he had somehow nodded off and Peary had had to wake him.

Now he moved closer to Francis Stead, so close that he could smell the smoke from his cigar. Between exhalations of blue smoke, Francis Stead rapidly breathed out white plumes of frost. Though motionless for so long, he was out of breath, chest and shoulders heaving rapidly.

Dr. Cook was close enough to touch him. His hand trembling, Francis Stead raised and lowered his cigar, the tip of it glowing momentarily. There was a faint sigh as he exhaled.

He knows that I am here, right behind him, thought Dr. Cook. He knows what is about to happen.

The snow was falling so heavily now that it made a multitude of hissing, sifting sounds, a faint sibilance, as if all the flakes were melting as they landed. How beautiful, how serene it was; how rare a night at such a latitude.

Dr. Cook doubted that, if not for the ether, which was Francis Stead's idea, he could have brought himself to do it. The ether was used to subdue animals so that their hides could be brought back unblemished. He had two vials in the pockets of his coat.

He took one out and poured the ether onto a piece of cloth, all but gagging from the fumes. Francis Stead shifted, slightly but abruptly, as though about to turn around, but then he faced forward again, his breath now rasping in his heaving chest.

"Get it over with," he said. "For God's sake, get it over with."

Dr. Cook waited for him to lower his cigar, which he feared would ignite the ether. When he rested his cigar hand on his knee, Dr. Cook put one hand behind his head, on his hood, and pushed it forward to meet the piece of cloth. Though Francis Stead was overcome instantly, falling limp against the rock, he kept the cloth in place.

He lit his lantern and walked what he guessed was halfway to the nearest crevasse in the glacier, placing the lantern on the ground, then made his way back to the tolt. He took Francis Stead under the arms and dragged him off towards the glacier, his heels making a pair of furrows in the snow.

Using the lamp-lit tolt of rock as his pilot point, he made his way towards the other lantern. When he reached it, he used *it* as his pilot point and continued dragging Francis towards the glacier until he felt the ice begin to slope beneath his feet. He lay Francis flat on his back and used his knife for traction, digging it into the ice with his left hand while he pushed Francis with his right, gripping the front of his coat.

When he felt a sharp increase in the slope of the ice, he stopped and removed from his pocket the vials of ether and the cloth and stuffed them into one of his moccasins. He could barely make out Francis Stead, just enough to see that his face and body were covered with snow.

He pushed Francis a few feet more, until the body slid slowly away from him. He could go no farther. He prayed the body would not bring up short of the crevasse. Then he saw it suddenly somersault.

Francis Stead neither spoke nor screamed. Dr. Cook heard a series of muffled thumps. The sounds, as if the crevasse was bottomless, did not so much stop as trail off into silence.

Again using his knife, he inched back up the slope, his gaze fixed on his lantern in the distance and, beyond it, the uplit tolt of rock. Soon he was able to stand safely.

As he set out towards the lantern, his body shook, his teeth chattering as if he had just stepped straight out of the warmth into the cold. Was it only for the boy? He asked himself.

He gathered up his lantern, extinguished it, then made his way to the tolt of rock, where he lit the lantern once again and extinguished Francis Stead's. The other man's cigar still smouldered in the snow. He ground it out with his foot. The tolt and the ground around it reeked of ether, but he doubted that, with the snow falling so heavily, this would be the case come daylight.

Putting the cigar butt in his pocket, he proceeded across the scree of snow-covered rocks to the igloos, where he woke some Eskimos, who said they had not seen Dr. Stead since that afternoon. Then he went back to Redcliffe House to announce Francis Stead's disappearance.

The others were up and having breakfast. He asked if any of them had seen Dr. Stead.

"Then you have not found him?" said Peary.

He shook his head. "I've been looking for him since you sent me out," he said. "I'm not sure what time that was. About four-fifteen, I think."

"It was more like four-forty-five," said Peary. "Where can that fool have gone?"

Four-forty-five. Barely an hour ago. Not time enough to do what Cook had done. Not long enough ago to make anyone wonder why he had waited so long to come back to the house.

"Well, he seems to be missing," said Dr. Cook, at which Peary became enraged, reminding them all that one of the rules of the expedition was that no one venture out from Redcliffe by himself, except at his instructions. When the others assured him that Stead would return when he felt like it, Peary roared and stormed about.

Francis Stead's plan had been a good one. It would not have made sense for both Peary and Dr. Cook to follow him outside. If, in spite of the laudanum, one or more of the others had happened to wake up and find all three of them gone, they might have gone out looking for them.

"These were all I found," said Dr. Cook. "Out by the tolt of rock. His lantern. And"—he dug in his pocket—"this." He showed them the cigar butt. "It was cold when I found it," he said. "He must have left it there hours ago."

The search lasted three days and turned up nothing. The Eskimos corroborated Peary's statement about what time it was when Dr. Cook went outdoors.

In Redcliffe House, Dr. Cook found the rucksack in which Francis Stead had kept his journals, but it was empty. What Francis had written in them, he had no idea. He prayed that he or Peary would find them first. But like him, they were never found. Perhaps Peary had disposed of them. Perhaps Francis Stead had.

"We shall speak to each other again only when it is absolutely necessary," Peary said when one day during the return voyage he called Dr. Cook to his cabin. "It will be best if we keep our distance from each other from now on."

He believes, Dr. Cook thought, that I have sullied myself, debased myself in a way that he has not; that he has carried himself with as much dignity as possible considering the circumstances.

"It has been almost intolerable to me," Dr. Cook said. "All these years, knowing that I conspired with a man like that—that we were, and always would be, partners in the death of Francis Stead, joined for life by something as unspeakable as murder. As for Peary, who knows what memories return to him in dreams?

"During those strange afternoons we spent together in that tupik on the beach at Etah, we spoke of her when Henson wasn't there. And of you and Francis Stead. He said that I had killed Francis Stead for the same reason he wanted him dead: to save my reputation, to preserve my good name and secure my future. 'Why don't you admit it? You did not even kill him for revenge,' Peary said. 'You cared nothing for the woman *he* killed. If you had, you would not have turned your back on her. As for the boy, you did not even know him. You had never met him or even seen him when you murdered Francis Stead. Did you even know his name?' 'When *we* killed him,' I kept saying, but Peary would shake his head. He seemed to have almost convinced himself that he had had nothing to do with it, that it had merely been his good fortune that Francis Stead had died before he had a chance to do him harm.

"Peary sent you to me in the hope that, once you had heard everything, you would turn against me, renounce me, perhaps even admit that we never reached the pole. And it seems that he has won. He has driven us apart. I can see it in your eyes."

"You're wrong," I said. "You did what you did for me."

"If only I was certain that was true," he said. "I betrayed myself long ago, Devlin. I lose nothing by this hoax I have concocted. But you, if you stay with me, will lose everything. I will not let you be destroyed, by my enemies or by yourself."

He put his face in his hands and shook his head.

"I never dreamed, when I first wrote to you...I cannot bear to think that I have lost you. And yet it seems certain that I have."

"You have not lost me," I said. "I am your son. You are my father. That will never change."

With tears running down his face, he hugged me.

I felt an exhaustion of spirit that I was sure would last forever. "I must go," I said, but before I could get up, he slowly left the room.

How strange it was to find out, so many years after it happened, that my life had been saved, let alone how and by whom. And that for years, I had figured in the lives of people I had never met or even heard of.

In a place far removed from where I lived, at a time when I had no reason to think that Francis Stead was not my father, or that my mother's death was not a suicide, a man I had never met or even heard of saved my life. And that man *was* my father.

CHAPTER FORTY-THREE

DR. COOK WAS AGAIN ABSENT FROM HOME FOR SEVERAL DAYS. I dared not glance at a newspaper, knowing it would be full of news about the polar controversy, about him and Peary and what each was doing to undermine the other's claim. I slept late every morning, then went to the Dakota, instructing the servants that I was not to be disturbed. I tried to think, and unable to do so, I tried to read, only to find myself stalled for hours in mid-sentence.

It seemed a deliverance when I received an invitation from Kristine's mother, Lily, to meet with her in her apartment. There would be no other guests, she said. She was a widow and Kristine was visiting relatives in Philadelphia. If the date mentioned was not convenient, I could suggest another.

Kristine lived with Lily in an apartment that they had bought following the death of Mr. Sumner some years before. I could see that they were well provided for. An elevator opened directly onto the entrance hall, whose floor was made of lozenges of black marble over which an Oriental rug was laid. Reflected in the marble was an overhanging silver lantern in which burned brightly a single large electric bulb. In the dining room and drawing room, the walls were wainscoted, the panelling made of oak. There was a look of plain elegance about the place. There were no gilded walls, no ostentatious reproductions of Greek and Roman sculpture. Most of the paintings and photographs were of New York—the half-completed Brooklyn Bridge, workmen sitting astride the girders of some building. A painting of Manhattan as it might have looked in 1650. Artifacts of the New World.

"Kristine speaks often of you," she said. "She had all but stopped accepting invitations out by the time she met you. She did not much like the sort of young men and women she was meeting, she said, which did not surprise me, since I knew just who she meant. I know their parents, anyway, and the apple does not fall far from the tree. My late husband came from an old, established family, the kind whose name endures long after its money has run out. Which is why I can decline invitations and let people think I do so out of snobbishness. They think I come by it honestly. But Kristine has become a social gadfly since she met you. She is out of sorts for days if you do not turn up at one of those awful events. She was so unhappy while you were away."

I felt myself blushing. "I missed her very much," I said.

It was clearly from her that Kristine had inherited her appealing, forthright manner. There was no hint of self-consciousness about her or of any concern about what sort of impression she was making. I could not imagine her spending one moment of her widow's solitude in brooding self-absorption.

"I'm very pleased to meet you, Mrs. Sumner," I said.

"I want you to call me Lily," she said.

A woman as old as my mother would be now.

I was relieved. I could not even think of her as Mrs. Dover, since I had for so long thought of her, and heard her referred to by Dr. Cook, as Lily. Her eyes darted about as she examined my face.

"You have your mother's eyes," she said. "You have your mother's kindness in your eyes. Unmistakably."

"Thank you," I said.

I looked into *her* eyes to see if I could tell how much she knew of me and Dr. Cook. She smiled slightly, as if to say she knew precisely what I was looking for.

"Your mother and I began writing to each other when we were schoolgirls," she said. "Me telling her about Manhattan, her telling me about St. John's." I thought of how it must have been for my mother when she was about to make her own first visit to New York, to meet at last her own long-time correspondent.

"Devlin, I know that Francis Stead was not your father," she said. "And I believe that you know about your mother and Dr. Cook. I assume he told you."

I nodded.

"I thought so," she said. "I could think of no other explanation for your coming to New York. You are not only his son—you are all that remains of Amelia for Dr. Cook."

"Yes," I said. "He has often said so."

"I should not have taken her to so many parties when she came to visit me. She had never had a drink before she visited Manhattan. But she was so rarely out of my sight. I have always felt responsible, you see. I think about it often: what might have been if I had been more care-ful, taken better care of her. How overwhelmed by New York she was."

"You are not to blame for anything," I said.

"Your mother wrote to me frequently after she went back to St. John's," she said, "just as she did before she came to New York. We had an epistolary friendship for years before we met. I loved her letters. She told me that she loved mine. We were already well-acquainted by the time we met. Already best friends."

"You don't like Dr. Cook, do you?" I said.

"I loved your mother," Lily said. "How, knowing what he did to her, could I go on liking him? Because yes, I did like him once. Perhaps only because Amelia loved him. I'm not sure."

"He was really just a boy back then," I said. "He's different now. He regrets not answering my mother's letter to him. He calls it the great mistake of his life."

I saw Lily's face fill with emotion, which at first I thought was anger. Her eyes welled up with tears that might not have spilled out had she not smiled.

"They were *so* much in love," she said. "Perhaps that's why I can't forgive him for what he did. I have never been in love like that. It was so strange being with them. Wonderful, in a way. It was as if they spoke different languages and needed me to translate for them. But sometimes they went for hours without speaking, to each other or to me. I did almost all the talking. I talked about people we saw in the park, about my parents, about how fast New York was changing. Small talk. But it was as though I was speaking in code. Telling her what he felt. Telling him what she felt. Helping them conspire. Make plans. He was very soft-spoken. Your mother was shy, with Dr. Cook at least. Perhaps it was guilt more than shyness. We often spoke about her fiancé. As for me . . . well, I was said to be vivacious. A polite term for a chatterbox, perhaps.

"I was so drained by the end of every day. Exhausted. The instant he left us, your mother would want to talk. About him. About Francis Stead. Should she break off her engagement with him if Dr. Cook asked her to? Did I think he *would* ask? All I could bear to do was listen. For three weeks, this went on. I don't know how he got away from work so often. He said he sold milk. Delivered messages. Worked as a clerk in an office—real estate, I think it was. He seemed to be holding down half a dozen jobs at once. Yet somehow he made time for her. For us. Perhaps, if it had been possible for them to spend some time alone each day, they would have felt, by the end of your mother's visit, that they were committed to each other, that no . . . no physical pledge was necessary."

Physical pledge. She had all but gestured to me when she said these words. She winced when she saw my reaction.

"I did not mean to speak with such regret," she said. "I can assure you that where you were concerned, your mother had none."

"What were my mother's letters like?" I said. "The ones she wrote to you after she was married. After I was born."

"They were always about you," she said. "She wrote very little about Francis. I was not surprised when she told me that he had found some excuse to live away from home and still remain married to her. I never met him. Even before she came to New York, she did not often mention him. I could tell, from what little she did say, that she didn't love him. But that wasn't unusual. Women often marry men they do not love. And vice versa, I suppose. Though Francis loved her. At first, at least.

"But as I was saying, she often wrote of you. How fast you were growing. How the colour of your eyes was changing. You made her happy. She wrote almost every day. I felt guilty for writing her only every other day. She sometimes mentioned Dr. Cook in passing, often by way of comparing you to him. It was sadder than if she had written ten pages telling me how much she missed him.

"I had to be so careful with her letters. I never spoke of him in mine. But there, in hers, from time to time, would be his name. It was the first thing I noticed when I opened her letters, even before I read them. I would scan each page, looking for that name. Frederick. It stood out like it was written in different-coloured ink than the words around it.

"She was the sort of person who would not give in to sorrow. That's why I have never believed the rumours about her death. She would never have done that. I know that is often said of suicides, but I have not the slightest doubt. When your uncle Edward wrote to me to say that Amelia had drowned accidentally, the other possibility never occurred to me.

"But my mother somehow heard the rumours. I overheard her speaking to my father about Amelia. I rushed into the parlour and asked them how they could repeat such things, believe such things about Amelia. I have *never* believed it.

"But I worried about how the rumours might one day affect you. I didn't want you to think, you see . . . to feel guilty about what happened to her. I was worried you might someday think she took her life because of you.

"No one who loved her child as she loved you could have lost hope so completely. She did not think of herself or the man she loved in tragic terms. She planned to go on with her life, as she assumed he would. She still loved him, and she hoped he would be happy. If the thought of him finding happiness without her tormented her, she showed no sign of it.

"She was a woman of great resilience. One of her few flaws was that she believed others were just as resilient. She had to have thought that Francis was. I doubt that when she decided to break off her engagement with him, she realized how badly, how permanently, that would have wounded him. And when, after she did not hear from Dr. Cook, she changed her mind, she had to have thought that Francis could bear to raise as his own a child his wife had conceived with another man. He could bear it, she believed, because she knew that she could if she had to.

"I thought of writing to you and assuring you that the rumours were untrue, or of writing to your uncle and asking him to tell you what I said, but then I thought how strange it would be for a child to receive such a letter. A letter denying awful rumours about your mother that you might not even have heard. And I could not bring myself to reassure you about your mother while at the same time withholding so much from you."

"I received stranger letters as a child," I said. "Letters from Dr. Cook in which he told me he was my father."

"Your aunt and uncle knew about those letters?"

I shook my head.

"I can't imagine Dr. Cook taking such a risk, writing such letters to a boy. If people had found out that although she was engaged, he asked her to marry him—"

"You're right about my mother," I said.

"I'm so glad you think so, Devlin."

"I have something to tell you, Lily, and it will come as quite a shock to you. My mother, as you say, did not take her life. She was murdered."

Lily put her hand on her throat as if I had told her that my mother had been choked to death.

"Oh no," she said. "The poor, sweet thing. I hoped that some-how . . . You see, Devlin, I have often thought it likely that someone did her harm. Because of the circumstances, I mean. I have long thought it could not have been by accident that she wound up in that water so far from where she left her horse and cart, so far down that hill."

"Francis Stead killed her," I said.

Lily covered her face with her hands, covered everything except her eyes, with which she looked at me as if *I* was Francis Stead and had just confessed.

"How do you know this?" she said.

"Francis Stead confessed to Dr. Cook," I said. "On the North Greenland expedition. Francis said he would let her go if she told him who my father was. He said that if she lied to him, made up some name, he would come back and kill not only her but me as well."

"Oh, my God," Lily said. "How could anyone do such a thing? Oh, my poor Amelia. My poor dear friend. I have thought for so long that someone might have killed her, but I never suspected it was Francis— in part because he lived in Brooklyn then, and in part because I pictured him as being so, I don't know, so inconsequential. And if he had suddenly turned up in St. John's, people would have noticed, remembered having seen him when they heard that she was dead. Oh, my God, Devlin, I feel like I did when I first heard that she was gone."

"I'm sorry," I said. "Perhaps I should not have told you."

She got up and came around the table to me, reaching out her hands. I rose and took her in my arms, thinking she had come to me for comfort until I realized something that she had already seen in my eyes: that it was I who needed comforting.

Hearing Lily talk about my mother as no one else ever had, not even Dr. Cook, had brought her to life for me at last. I had just told Lily of the death of my mother, not of the death of Dr. Cook's Amelia or Francis Stead's Amelia, not even of the death of Lily's cousin. For something in the way Lily spoke about her made me feel that I remembered her, made her seem familiar, as though I had recognized something of myself in the woman she described, the part of her in me surfacing at last.

I cried. Lily cried.

"Don't tell Kristine," I said. "I would like to tell her myself."

I told Kristine when she came back to Manhattan. I was worried that my strange story, the story of the letters from Dr. Cook and the murder of my mother, would put her off. I told her *everything*, just as I had told Lily everything. I related the death of Francis Stead at Dr Cook's hand and Dr. Cook's admission that we had never reached the pole. I spoke of Peary. I did not ask either Kristine or Lily to be discreet. I knew they would be. I was determined that, between us, there would be no secrets. Kristine hugged me so fervently when I finished speaking that it was some time before I realized that, in between sobs that she struggled to suppress, she was whispering my name.

I told her about "the Stead boy," about Aunt Daphne. I told her about the night I spent in the blockhouse on Signal Hill. My foolish falling-out with Aunt Daphne, whom I believed no longer had faith in me, but had, like everyone else, come to regard me as the Stead boy. My flight from St. John's, my journey to New York to meet Dr. Cook. I told her of my life in the Dakota, half of that sad house in Brooklyn. The furniture shrouded in dust covers. Dr. Cook and I talking by the fire in the drawing room at night. Etah. Peary. Washington. Copenhagen. Dr. Cook's confessions.

I went to the Sumners' frequently. I tried not to think of Dr. Cook. We almost never spoke of him.

Once while I was having dinner with them, Lily kept making up excuses to go upstairs, to leave us alone. She would be gone for minutes at a time, then she would descend and offer no explanation of her absence.

When Lily was upstairs for perhaps the fifth time, Kristine moved her chair closer to mine so that our thighs were touching. With her hands in her lap, she looked at me.

"How often are you going to let my mother climb those stairs before you ask me to marry you?" she said.

CHAPTER FORTY-FOUR

Dear Father:

At last it is me who is writing to you. This, though I am leaving, is not a letter of goodbye. A time comes when every son must leave his father's house.

I know that even though I will not be far away, they will use my leaving against you. They will say, no matter what I say, that I am leaving because I no longer believe that you and I made it to the pole. Whatever they say, no matter what happens, I shall not abandon you. I think you are right that Peary did not reach the pole, though it seems absurd to say so. Like saying that I think you are more entitled to faking that accomplishment than he is.

I shall never speak again to anyone but you about the pole, though I must tell you that I have told Lily and Kristine everything. You have nothing to fear from them.

It is not because of Peary that I will keep your secret. I have decided simply to turn away from Peary. Whether, in your circumstances, I could do so is something I will never know. It would therefore be presumptuous of me to judge you, or even to offer you advice.

All I can offer you is love and gratitude. You gave me life. Before we met, before you knew that we would ever meet, before I had even heard of you, you saved my life.

I will have more, much more, to say when we meet again,
which will be very soon.

Love,
Devlin

He and Mrs. Cook departed the day after I left the letter for him on his desk. I got up and went to his study, intending to say goodbye, to tell him I would be leaving the house that day, but he was not there. The doors of the drawing room were open, the fireplace cold, the sofa empty. There was a letter from him on my desk.

I hoped that he was still in the Cooks'. I went to their half of the house and found only empty rooms until I came upon a maid throwing dust covers on the furniture in the front parlour.

"They have gone away," she said when she saw me. "No one knows where. No one knows how long. He left some money for you." She handed me a thick sealed envelope.

They had left very early in the morning, dismissing all the servants on the spot, giving each of them an envelope like mine, which contained their pay.

"He asked us not to wake you," she said. "He told me to wait for you so that the house would not be empty when you woke up. I am sorry, Mr. Stead." She covered another chair. Soon the whole house would be like the Dakota.

It would later be discovered that, with their two children, Dr. Cook and Marie had sailed for South America, where they travelled under the pseudonyms of Dr. and Mrs. Craig.

CHAPTER FORTY-FIVE

IT IS BEST THAT THE EPILOGUE OF THIS STORY PRECEDE THE ENDING.

By the time the Cooks returned to New York, several months later, the Danish Konsistorium had met in Copenhagen to reconsider Dr. Cook's claim to have reached the pole. Their verdict was that it was "unproven."

"So is Peary's claim unproven," Dr. Cook told reporters, and he pointed out that the Danes had revoked none of the honours they had bestowed upon him. His supporters noted the "world of difference" between "unproven" and "false," while Peary's said the two words were synonymous and claimed victory.

Bill Barrill, with whom Dr. Cook claimed to have climbed McKinley, came forward and said that Dr. Cook had faked the climb with "clever photographs." Other climbers set out for McKinley to see if this was true. They presented their case that Dr. Cook *had* faked the climbing of McKinley in magazine articles that were themselves attacked by the Bradley-led supporters of Dr. Cook.

Although the U.S. Navy, in 1911, verified Peary's claim to have reached the pole, there were many who remained unconvinced, so many that Peary's supporters found it necessary to continue their attempts to discredit Dr. Cook.

The many years of controversy that followed are well documented. Even if you read everything that has been written, you will only rarely come across my name.

I never granted another interview after I moved out of 670

Bushwick. I was besieged by reporters for a while, as were Lily and Kristine after Kristine and I announced our engagement. But they soon left us alone, the last public word on me being, as I had predicted, that I had left Dr. Cook because I knew his claim to be a hoax, that I had been "hoodwinked" and had no more idea than Etukishuk and Ahwelah where Dr. Cook had really taken us.

Not long after the Danes declared his claim to be "unproven," I attempted one evening to visit Dr. Cook at his new house. The butler who answered the door went inside, and Mrs. Cook came out and told me that her husband did not wish to meet with me again. "Not ever," she said and slammed the door.

I was certain we would, sooner or later, meet by chance. Until then, I would write to him. Perhaps we would write to each other. Live two miles apart and never communicate except by letter. Cross-river correspondents.

But my letters to him went unanswered, and we did not meet by chance. A few years after returning from South America, he left Brooklyn for good.

I wrote hundreds of letters to Dr. Cook, but he did not write back. It was as though I were reversing the order of the one-way correspondence by which he had drawn me to him, to New York from Newfoundland.

I wrote the letters as if I knew that he was reading them. I told him what was new since I had written last. I related my life to him— the life from which he had exiled himself.

I imagined him eagerly looking forward to the letters in the manner of a prisoner who can have no visitors. The meaning of my letters was that I forgave him. But perhaps believing that he did not deserve it, he would not accept forgiveness from me.

I kept writing to him after he left New York and went out west to explore for oil. I thought he might write back to me when Peary died in 1920, but he did not.

Peary had spent his last years at his Cape Cod refuge on Eagle

Island, off the coast of Maine, worn out, so the story went, from his efforts to prove his polar claim beyond all doubt. It was said that, knowing he would soon die, he had lain for days on a couch that was covered in muskox furs, looking out in silence across the bay.

I might have been content to wonder forever if Dr. Cook was reading my letters if not for a misfortune that befell him not long after Peary's death.

He wound up an inmate of Leavenworth Prison in Kansas, having been sentenced to fourteen years in jail for oil-stock fraud in Wyoming. The polar controversy was still unresolved, and many felt that Dr. Cook was the victim of a malicious, or at least overly zealous, prosecution in which Peary's supporters had had a hand.

By this time, 1923, Marie Cook had divorced her husband and he had not remarried. The thought of him alone in Leavenworth was more than I could bear, so I made a surprise journey to the prison in an attempt to see him. I was told that when he was informed that he had a visitor named Mr. Stead, he merely shook his head.

I returned to New York and began, in my letters, to implore him to reply, saying that I was greatly concerned about his health and state of mind.

He neither answered nor sent back my letters. Unable to stand it any longer, I wrote to the warden at Leavenworth, asking, as it had not occurred to me to do before, that someone ask Dr. Cook if he was reading my letters and if he wished me to go on writing to him.

I expected a reply from some prison official. Instead, six weeks after I wrote to the warden, I received an envelope that bore only my name and address, printed in pencil, the upper-left corner conspicuously blank. Inside the envelope was a single sheet of paper, blank but for one pencil-printed word in the middle of the page: YES.

This is the sole letter from Dr. Cook to me that still survives. It is pinned to the wall above my desk, a yellowed, fading affirmative, inscrutable to others.

Not long after Dr. Cook's death in August 1940, I received, from Dr. Cook's daughter, Helen, a letter telling me that he had died and thanking me "for being such a faithful correspondent all these years."

It was clear that she thought he had been answering my letters, all of which he had saved and were now in her possession. They were full, she said, of "vague and cryptic references to unnamed persons and unspecified events" that she hoped I would one day explain to her. She still believed that he had reached the pole and presumed that I still thought so, too. She said she further hoped that despite my expressed intention never again to speak in public about the expedition—a reticence that she said she found mystifying—I would, as a co-expeditionary of Dr. Cook's and the first man to set foot at the pole, join in her campaign to prove her father's claim, a campaign that had been ongoing for years, but that she expected would gain "new life now from the recent developments of which you may have heard."

I had. "DISGRACED EXPLORER RECEIVES DEATHBED PARDON FROM FDR," read the headline of a story that had recently run on the front page of The *New York Times*. I had seen the story before I heard from Helen, and my first thought was that the president had pardoned Dr. Cook for pretending to have reached the pole. I had momentarily forgotten that Dr. Cook had admitted this pretence to no one but me. The pardon was for his stock-fraud conviction, however, which was by that time widely regarded to have been unjust. The story was a brief one, contained no mention of me and credited Dr. Cook with having perpetrated the most infamous hoax in the history of exploration. It concluded with the observation that this hoax, even though quickly discovered, had prevented the true discoverer of the North Pole, Comm. Robert Peary, from being accorded the full measure of credit and fame that he deserved. Other papers said the polar controversy was "still unresolved" or "unlikely to ever be resolved."

Only the *New York Herald Tribune* maintained unequivocally that Dr. Cook and I had been the first to reach the pole, and the paper chided Peary and the Peary Arctic Club for their lifelong campaign to discredit Dr. Cook.

I replied to Helen that while I wished her luck in her efforts to prove her father's claim to have been the leader of an expedition that had reached the pole, I planned, for personal reasons, to maintain my silence on the matter. She returned to me, unopened, my last two letters to Dr. Cook, which had arrived too late for him to read. I never heard from her again.

· CHAPTER FORTY-SIX ·

OF MY MOTHER, DR. COOK SAID, "NOTHING IN HER LIFE WAS undone by the manner of her death."

Nor by the fact of it. Life is not undone by death—nor a single moment by all the moments that come after it.

I have no reason, then, even knowing what happened in "the end," not to finish the story years before the end, not to write the ending as if I really do not know what happens next.

Later on the same day that my hosts and their children left Brooklyn under assumed names for parts unknown, I let myself out the door by which Dr. Cook had first admitted me to his house, a door I had not used since then.

For the first time, I descended the steps that I had climbed that day ten years before. It made me feel as though I had not left the house since the day that door seemed to open by itself and I stepped inside.

I looked at the spot on the other side of Bushwick where I had waited in the shade of nothing but my hat on that hot day in August 1901, dressed for the summer of the colder country from which I had come to Manhattan, to America, the day before. I would not have been surprised to see my successor standing there, a boy as terrified, as apprehensive, as I had been, conspicuously waiting, gripping with both hands and holding in front of him a valise that appeared to be a doctor's bag.

My valise, bearing Francis Stead's initials, I had left behind after feeding the scrolls of letters one by one into the fire in the drawing room.

I had fallen asleep fully dressed the night before, lying on the sofa in the drawing room. I was surprised that I had been able to sleep, and that I had had no dreams.

I decided, after leaving the house, that I would walk to Manhattan. I walked along the Myrtle line to the Brooklyn Bridge, in the shadow of the el tracks, weaving in and out among the beams, looking up when the train rumbled overhead.

At Myrtle and Willoughby, the triumphal arch bearing Dr. Cook's likeness had been taken down, though the wooden scaffolding remained, as if repairs to the viaduct were soon to start.

People, most of whom I had never met, waved to me and said, "Good morning, Mr. Stead," and asked me to pass on their good wishes to Dr. Cook.

I passed the winding wooden stairs to all the waiting rooms, the stairwells from which friendly strangers pointed at me. Some, noticing the commotion, looked furtively at me as if they thought they recognized me but could not remember why I was famous.

There were throngs of people on the boardwalk of the bridge—sightseers, most of them, who looked as if they were either making their first trip to New York or were New Yorkers who had never walked the bridge before. There was a deafening tumult of traffic below me. The el train, motor cars, the clopping hoofs of horses.

I thought of the day when I first rode the el train to Brooklyn from Manhattan and the passengers on both sides let their windows down when we reached the crest, so a fresh breeze blew through the car. I had smelled the ocean then as I did now.

Soon the wind was blowing so hard I could hear nothing else. Two young women, mouths open in soundless laughter, clung girlishly to one another and with their free hands held onto their hats.

When the ship from which my mother got her first look at New York came up the river, the two halves of the bridge had not yet met. The ship sailed between them as if a massive canal bridge had been raised to let it through.

I thought of Cape Sparbo, where it had seemed the wind would roll the roof back like a rug, roll back the sod until nothing lay between us and the storm but sticks and bones.

A subway train now ran between the two boroughs, beneath the riverbed, just as the newspaper I had read on my first morning in Manhattan had predicted. It was said that on calmer days, as the subway train crossed beneath the river, its vibrations made a kind of path of agitation on the surface, so that you could see not only the progress of the train from side to side, but also its shape, as though it was casting a shadow upward on the water.

If anything, that newspaper, which had seemed to me so extravagant and naïve in its predictions, had been short-sighted and conservative. There were more things in New York in 1909 than had been dreamed of by anyone eight years before.

At the height of the walkway, I stopped and stood at the rail, looking up the river. My clothing flapped loudly in the wind, as if I was some flag marking the midway point of the Brooklyn Bridge.

I thought about the expedition. There were parts of it that, despite the hoax, remained unspoiled for me. Most of it. I knew I would never see or do such things again. The time I spent recovering from fever in the box house. I lay there, languishing longer than I had to in my sleeping bag, revelling in aches and pains that I knew would not get worse, and that somehow added a coziness to my recovery. I had not been to the pole, but I had walked on the ever-moving surface of the polar sea. I had been farther north than where the Old Ice came from, the ice that flowed past Newfoundland each spring. I had risked death.

There had been moments on the polar sea when I'm sure that even Dr. Cook forgot our purpose for being there—forgot that it was all a grand deception—so diverted was he by some sight like the parting of the ice, the crust ripping slowly to reveal, at the bottom of a jagged trench, the steaming apparition of green water.

I knew that Dr. Cook would come back to Brooklyn, that this sudden flight from his house to parts unknown was just the prologue of a story that would peter out—a story in which it was possible for him to start again, to reinvent himself somewhere else where no one had ever heard of him. There was no such place, but neither, if there was, would he have stayed there.

He would come back and live in Brooklyn in some house from which he could see Manhattan.

Perhaps, from now on, Manhattan would remind him of me, for I had decided that I would live in the city where my parents met and where I was conceived. I was certain he would not insist that we remain apart forever.

I would never again speak in public about the expedition.

But I would not run from Peary and the members of his Arctic club. I would neither help nor hinder their ambitions. If they had me followed, if they came to visit me, if they insisted that I meet again with Peary or someone else, then so be it. I knew the whole truth now, and they would soon see that to pester me was pointless.

I could go to some university or college. I had had enough of exploring, though I knew my reputation would help me find a job. I could all but see an item in the papers or a sign in a window naming as the new addition to some firm the young man who was a partner with Dr. Cook on his disputed expedition, and who years ago had saved the life of his enemy and rival, Robert Peary. It would not matter that I had ended my professional association with Dr. Cook, or that I preferred not to speak of my adventures. I could stand to be "the enigmatic Mr. Stead" for as long as people chose to think of me that way.

I would prove myself, and though my part in all of it might never be forgotten altogether, it would fade and I would be allowed to make my way as Devlin Stead, who had had something to do with "that Cook and Peary business." It was something to hope for anyway. It was not as if I had a choice. The fame and infamy would follow me no matter where I went.

But for now, for today, I had no plans. I would wander through the streets of the Lower East Side, and among people who had never heard of me, who could not read the papers, who had seen Manhattan from a distance only once and had never crossed the Brooklyn Bridge and never would, I would think about my future for a while. My life with Kristine.

I would go down to the Hudson Pier, perhaps, and watch the immigrants come ashore from the Ellis Island ferries. Or I might take the el train to its northern limit and see if any trace remained of the shanty towns.

Most of what I knew about my mother happened here. I knew the story of those three weeks better than I knew the story of her life. She had known only happiness here.

My mother as Lily remembered her.

My mother as, in his first two letters, Dr. Cook remembered her.

· CHAPTER FORTY-SEVEN ·

I KEPT MY PROMISE TO AUNT DAPHNE THAT I WOULD RETURN TO her someday. Lily and Kristine went with me. I wanted Lily, who was to have gone there thirty years earlier for my mother's wedding, to see St. John's at last. I wanted Kristine to see many things, but especially the sea from Signal Hill.

For a while, our ship, which made port at Boston and Halifax, followed the coast, so that we stayed in sight of land. But from Halifax, we went northeast until we were in what Dr. Cook called the "true open sea." Kristine, who had been to all the great seaboard cities of America and had gone west by train to San Francisco, had never been so far from the continent as to lose sight of it. Watching her stare landward from the deck long after land had disappeared—on her face that look of fear and wonder I had seen on the faces of so many others who were sea-surrounded for the first time—I felt a sudden surge of love for her well up in my throat. Nothing so reminds you like the sea that the enemy of life is not death but loneliness. I put my arm around her waist and drew her close to me. She rested her head against my cheek, her hair wet from a mist so fine I could neither see nor feel it in the air.

My mother had gone back to St. John's from New York on a ship like this. She must have thought her life was just beginning. And she was, without even knowing it, pregnant with me. How strange that seemed. That I had made that journey with her. That she had come to Manhattan alone and borne me back to Newfoundland.

What might have been the clouds of a distant storm were the headlands of the southeast coast of Newfoundland.

"There it is," I said, and Kristine and Lily squinted dubiously, as if there lay out there nothing that remotely looked like land. Then Lily smiled and both of them pointed almost at once.

The three of us stood at the rail of the foredeck as the ship approached the Narrows. "Signal Hill," I said, pointing up and to the right. The stone tower on top of it, which had been under construction when I left, was now complete, dwarfing the blockhouse, from which several flags were flying, one of them signalling to the city that our ship was soon to dock.

Kristine and Lily looked up momentarily, but they were drawn, as I was, to look at the base of the cliff where the waves were breaking. I guessed that they were looking for the ledge from which Francis Stead had thrown my mother to her death, but from this perspective, the face of the cliff seemed flat. The sky was cloudless, the water outside the Narrows the deep blue that I remembered from cold but sunny days. Though the seaward side of the hill was in the shade, it did not look like the setting of Francis Stead's crime.

We were too far from shore to hear the waves—the alternating surge and retreat of the sea through the fissures in the rock—a sound that had always made me think the hill was hollow, a great shell through whose unseen channels the sea ran like a river. Seagulls, likewise inaudible, swarmed the hilltop, hoping for scraps of food from people who were waving at the ship. I guessed that it was about a month since the last of the ice had drifted by.

As we were docking, I saw Aunt Daphne before she saw me; she was surrounded by a multitude of people who were there to meet the ship but unmistakably alone. She was searching the rails of the ship for me. Her eyes passed over me several times without the slightest pause. Not even after I removed my hat and began to wave and shout her name did she recognize me. I realized how much I must have changed since she had seen me last. She had changed, too, but not so much because of age as because of the years of waiting, when not only was I up north, but my whereabouts were often unknown and she was not even sure if I was still alive. She had said, in her one letter to me, after Etah and my first encounter with Peary, that the people of St. John's were now talking as if my sole imperfection was shyness. I wondered if they had come to regard her differently as well, or if she was still, had been for ten years, looked upon as the odd aunt of an odd nephew, in part to blame for my oddness and a bane to her husband, one of the two Stead doctors who were brought down by their wives.

How concerned, how anxious she looked as her eyes darted about. It was as if in spite of the telegram I had sent her telling her that we were coming, she was all but certain that some mishap or misunderstanding would prevent it.

Only now did I realize that many on shore were shouting my name, that more people than Aunt Daphne had turned out to meet me. Cards that bore the word "Press" protruded from hatbands. Photographers began to take my picture. There were small explosions of light and smoke along the dock. It was just such a homecoming as I had dreamed of when I lived here, almost surreally so, with signs and banners everywhere proclaiming my accomplishments and my countrymen chanting my name. "We believe in you, Devlin," I heard them say. I momentarily forgot that it was for my part in the polar expedition that I was being celebrated. It was as if the people of the city had turned out en masse to admit that they had been wrong about me, to make amends for having regarded me as "the Stead boy." I was tempted to give in, to acknowledge their adulation as if I was deserving of it, to act as Dr. Cook had done on his return to Brooklyn. I had no doubt that it was common knowledge here that I was adamant in my refusal to comment on the expedition. Perhaps the people were hoping, by this show of support, to change my mind—hoping that I would settle forever the question of whether one of their own had won the race for the pole. How strange it felt to be back among these people for whom Francis Stead would forever be my father, his death forever a mysterious suicide. For whom my mother would forever be the woman whose grief over his leaving her was such that she took her life.

Aunt Daphne turned to a man beside her, who immediately pointed straight at me. For a moment, as our eyes met, she put her hand to her mouth, as if she didn't want me to see how shocked she was by my appearance, for I looked ten years older than I was. I saw in her face that in spite of my having abandoned her, in spite of my having been so foolish as to think she doubted me, she had loved me unreservedly when I had no one else, and had loved me no less in my long absence from her life.

She saw me. She dropped her hand and, smiling, began blowing kisses, even as she fought her way through the crowd towards the gangplank, which was just now being fixed in place. By the time, with Lily and Kristine behind me, I met her on the dock, tears were running freely down her face. As if she saw in *my* eyes that I was about to tell her I was sorry, she faintly shook her head. We hugged, broke apart, hugged again without a word, until at last, as if it was all she could manage, she exhaled my name.

We were both crying when I introduced her to Lily and Kristine.

"Devlin thinks so much of you," Kristine said. "He's been talking about you ever since we met."

"Hello, my dear," Lily said, linking arms with Aunt Daphne.

She and Uncle Edward, though he had refused to grant her a divorce, had been living apart for several years, ever since she had left him and become a tutor to the children of those few parents who had pledged her their support. Uncle Edward, calling her a "scandalous embarrassment," had been offering her ever-increasing sums of money, trying to bribe her into leaving Newfoundland for good.

"You'll come back to New York with us, Daphne," Lily said one evening at dinner. "We'll all be so much happier that way." Aunt Daphne looked about at the three of us as if she would not let herself believe that she had found happiness after having lived for so long without it.

"New York would be such a change for me," she said. "But yes, if you really want me to, I'll go with you."

But she would not take a cent from Uncle Edward.

Much of my week in St. John's was spent dodging or merely ignoring reporters who followed me about, hoping for my exclusive account of the Bradley expedition, some saying they would pay me if I would just answer yes or no to the question "Did you reach the pole?"

I was often recognized in the street, and although I'm sure that the polar controversy and my complete refusal to speak about it made people wonder if I had really changed as much as they had imagined, many of them shook my hand and congratulated me on having been the first to set foot at the pole, at which, always, I nodded noncommittally and smiled.

We put flowers on my mother's grave, arranged for fresh ones to be put there once a month and for the upkeep of the plot, which I was not sure that I would ever see again.

Kristine and I drove up Signal Hill in Aunt Daphne's cabriolet, the one in which my mother had passed Francis Stead as he made his way on foot towards the top the day she died.

I wanted to show Kristine everything—the sea, the blockhouse where I was forced to spend the night, the place in the woods where I went to read Dr. Cook's first letter.

As we drove up Devon Row, I thought of dropping in to see Uncle Edward. No doubt he knew that I was in St. John's. I wished that I could have surprised him as he came up the stairs one morning. "Hello, Uncle Edward," I imagined myself saying as I looked up from the book on my lap. But we went on past his house and past his surgery. I glanced at the window of the room where I used to read and copy the letters while he waited, the still-unoccupied, unlit surgery of Francis Stead. In Uncle Edward's rooms, the lights were on, but I could not see him.

A couple of other vehicles, one of them a convertible motor car, faced seaward on the hilltop, their occupants at once wind-blown and spellbound by the view. Remembering the visit I had made here with Aunt Daphne as a child, I pointed out to Kristine the directions in which lay New York, London, Labrador and Greenland.

As I was speaking, she removed her hat and stowed it behind the seat, then she began to pull out the pins that held up her hair, which was soon streaming out behind her, horizontal in the onshore gale. Before I could move to help her, she got down from the carriage and, hiking her dress, ran to one of the paths that led down to the sea. I sat and watched her, thinking she just wanted to get a better view. But she did not stop, just went running down the path until I lost sight of her. By the time I got down from the carriage and reached the path, she was well on her way down the hill.

"Kristine," I shouted as I ran to catch her. The slope was so steep that I could descend no faster than she could, and so could gain no ground on her. I thought I might catch her on the upslope of the second, lower hill, but she was already on the far side of it and out of sight again by the time I reached it.

"Watch out for the ledge," I shouted.

When I topped the second hill, I saw that she had stopped and was looking about as if trying to decide which direction she should take now that the path had petered out. Soon she was off again, lost behind the last ridge. "Kristine," I shouted, wondering if she would still be there when I cleared that ridge myself.

I saw her standing directly below me, saw the top of her head, her shoulders, her chest heaving as, with her back to the cliff, she tried to catch her breath. I climbed down and stood beside her, still gasping for air when her breathing had returned to normal.

"This is the ledge?" she said.

I nodded.

"I knew you would come here," she said. "And I wanted to make sure you didn't come here by yourself. You could not have gone back to New York without coming here again. In the daylight. Knowing what you didn't know when you were here before." I hadn't set aside a time to come here, hadn't really thought about this pilgrimage, but I knew she was right. I would have come here by myself and might never have told her about it.

It was later in the year than when my mother and Francis Stead had struggled here. Bright green, treacherously slick grass grew on the ledge, which angled slightly downward. The water was not so much crashing in waves below us as rising and falling, flooding the ledge a little more each time it rose. Here it had happened, on this ledge, which bore no trace of that event or any other, which was as it had been for a thousand years and as it would be for a thousand more.

The chase down the hill had seemed, eerily, like a re-enactment of Francis Stead's story, Kristine preceding me down the hill, fleeing from me while I called her name as Francis Stead must have called my mother's. "Amelia," I had half expected to hear. Half expected to see my mother, her husband in pursuit, on one of the other paths that led down to the water.

"The tide is coming in," I said.

"So close to shore," Kristine said, though she spoke as if an infinite gap lay between us and the water. We were ten feet above the sea one second and almost awash in it the next, well within reach of a rogue wave, for any sign of which I scanned the water farther out. Froth lopped onto the ledge, and the wind, as the water peaked, blew the spray against us, lightly spattering our clothes and faces. I tasted salt, the brine of the sea, which always took me by surprise, for I found it hard to think of water that looked like that as being anything but wet and cold. In just such water by which I was being drenched and whose taste was in my mouth, my mother drowned. An unambiguous death. His crime as unambiguously motivated as her sacrifice. With my face already dripping with salt water, I began to cry.

Kristine knelt gingerly, then lay down on her stomach, her head just out over the ledge. When she patted the ground, I lay down beside her on her right.

We looked at the sea. It was as though it was the ledge that was rising and falling. Each time the water rose, I felt certain that we would be submerged. But the rising black water turned white when it struck the rocks, spouting up to our faces like some roaring fountain, so cold it left us gasping. Kristine's hair hung down in long, dark, dripping strands, water streaming from her brow, her nose and chin as it had to have been from mine. She unbuttoned the left sleeve of her dress and rolled it up. She dipped the tips of her fingers in the water, then her whole hand, at which she gasped so loudly that I reached out for her arm. But she pushed me away with her free one.

"My God," she said, "I never knew water could be so cold."

She lowered her arm farther, to the elbow, as the water crested. She closed her eyes for a while, then suddenly withdrew her arm as if she could not have kept it immersed for a fraction of a second longer, as if her whole body was surfacing for air. She stood up, cradling her arm in her left hand as if it was broken.

"We are older now than she ever was," she said.

We kissed. Like mine, her lips were chattering. Our mouths were salty from the sea.

"We will have long lives, Devlin," she said. "And we will never be apart."

Kristine removed from around her neck a large locket that had been a gift from me, and that at one time had contained our photographs, miniature cameos as though on opposing pages of a book.

Now it contained something else.

"We'll hold it together," she said.

We each held one side of the chain and lowered it as close to the water as we could. At first, the locket swayed from side to side.

"Wait for the wave to go out," she said. We were again engulfed by water. All I could see was white. My forehead ached as if a block of ice was being held against it. Then the white water fell back into the sea and the wave, as it withdrew, went black.

"NOW," Kristine said.

We let the locket fall. It dropped, chain extended as though someone was still holding it. The locket entered the water first, and then, link by link, the chain.

We watched it sink, the golden gleam of it fading as it descended, until, for a while, I thought we would still be able to see it as it rested on the bottom. But then, abruptly, it was gone, falling for who knows how much longer.

In the locket, folded tightly to make it fit, was Dr. Cook's last letter to me, the one that was on the desk of his study the morning I woke up to find him gone.

My dearest Devlin:

I have been thinking about your mother's letter. "You have only to say yes or no..." My choice was no, but I could not bring myself to say it. I suppose it seemed less shameful to say nothing. "If I do not hear from you, I will not write to you again." I used to think that she offered me that third choice because she knew I would take it whether she offered it or not.

I once described her letter as "forgiveness in advance." But I was wrong. If she had known what my answer would be, she would never have told me about the child. She would have told me she that had changed her mind, chosen her fiancé instead of me.

I think she dreaded not hearing back from me even more than she did my saying no. I think she mentioned that third choice to warn me away from it, because she foresaw what its effect on me would be. Perhaps, when I did not write back, she regretted having presented me with a choice I could not stand to make, let alone live with.

But I doubt it. Your mother did not believe, as I have come to believe, that the odds are always in favour of unhappiness. She thought it most likely that my answer would be yes, that I would see, as she had, that we would be happier together than apart, no matter what the circumstances.

I might have saved your life, but it was not only to protect you that I murdered Francis Stead. As I walked through the snow towards him, I had an intolerable thought.

My renunciation of her, her marriage to Francis Stead, his

*abandonment of her, her struggle with him on that ledge, her final
moments, when she knew beyond all hope that she would die—
what if even she could not withstand such things? What if there had
come a moment when she felt forsaken, tempted beyond even her
powers of resistance by despair? Could a nature such as hers be in
its very essence overthrown, transformed so entirely that even of its
past existence, no evidence remained?*

*I have said that nothing in her life was undone by the manner
of her death, but I did not believe it the night I murdered Francis
Stead. And there have been many times since when I did not
believe it.*

*I think it would be best for you if we do not meet again and
that this be our last communication. Even if I was able to follow
your example and turn away from Peary and the pole, it would be
best for you to have nothing more to do with me. I would not have
you be my partner in disgrace.*

*But at any rate, I cannot turn away from Peary and the pole.
What I have begun with Peary must be played out to the end, but
not at the cost of your happiness. I fear that, were we to continue
our association, you would change for the worse in ways that nothing could repair.*

*You have it in you to be happy. You have inherited my blood,
but not my history. I believe that I am unhappy neither by nature
nor by circumstance. What I have done, I have done of my own free
will. In you runs a half-measure of your mother's blood and a half-
measure of that of the man with whom she fell in love.*

*It seems hard to believe that I was ever such a man, but I must
have been. It has been nearly thirty years since I last saw her face. I
have no photographs of her. Nothing of hers but that one brief letter,
a single yellowed square of paper that I have not read since I
showed it to you for fear that, with one more unfolding, it would fall
to pieces.*

*Of course, I know it by heart. There are times when the whole
letter runs through my mind like a prayer learned in childhood.*

Sentences, phrases from it, crop up in my daily train of thought, non sequiturs that recur like punctuation marks.

"You have nothing to fear from me." Sometimes, when I wake up, it seems as though she has just stopped speaking those words, as though I hear them while coming up from sleep, as though the last one, when I surface, is still ringing in the air. "Me." I am for a few seconds certain that she is in the room, has asked me a question whose last word was me. "Do you love me?"

Were she still alive, I might pass her in the street and not recognize her face. Who did Francis Stead prevent her from becoming? What would she look like, my Amelia, who would be fifty now? I knew her for just three weeks. Guilt, regret, shame, none of these afflicts me as much as simple sorrow does.

The day before we met, I watched you disembark from the ship. Even had your uncle not sent me a photograph, I would have known that it was you. I followed you to your hotel and hours later slipped that note beneath your door. It seemed right that I not meet you in Manhattan, where I met your mother.

The next day, I watched you from one of the upstairs windows while you waited on the other side of Bushwick in the heat. I would have called you in, but there were still servants who had yet to leave. There you stood, on the brink of entering my life, like somone conjured up by the letters I had written.

How unreal it all seemed at first, you standing there so motionless, staring straight ahead, incongruous in those heavy clothes. But then, for a few seconds, you removed your hat, and there you were. I saw your hair, your face, at which you dabbed with your handkerchief.

"My son," I said, as if it had not occurred to me that the young man I had seen the day before and had been watching for the past few minutes was my son. You became my son while I was looking at you, passed from strange to familiar in an instant. And now it seemed that I had always known you. The stranger in you was beyond recall.

"Devlin," I said. And you, as if my saying your name had prompted you, looked at your watch, dropped it back in your pocket, then made your way across the street.

"My son," I said again as you passed from view beneath the window and I hurried down the stairs to let you in.

I have never told you of my last moments with your mother.

After emerging separately from our hotel, we met again at a preappointed place just up the street, a tearoom where, for a while, we sat and talked, lingering, not wanting the afternoon to end.

When we left, it was getting dark. I had to make my way by ferry back to Brooklyn, while she was already long overdue at Lily's house and would soon have to hail a northbound horse and cab.

She said that she wished the bridge was finished so that she could walk with me to the midpoint and turn back. I told her that years from now, we would walk across it with our children on Sunday afternoons.

She took a foolish chance and, right there on the sidewalk, while the lamps were being lit, kissed me on the lips.

I have often imagined myself as she must last have seen me from the cab, as I made my way on foot towards the river, my hand on my hat lest I lose it in the wind that funnelled up between the buildings from the water.

We were young. We did not doubt that we would meet again. Remember, Devlin.

In the language of the people who live where you and I have lived, there is no word for goodbye.

Love,
Your father

Brooklyn
October 26, 1909

This is a work of fiction. At times, it places real people in imaginary space and time. At others, imaginary people in real space and time. While it draws from the historical record, its purpose is not to answer historical questions or settle historical controversies.

· A C K N O W L E D G M E N T S ·

Many thanks to Gerry Howard, peerless editor and friend, at Doubleday/Random House. Also to Ben Bruton, my indefatigable publicist.

Printed in the United States
by Baker & Taylor Publisher Services